# A JAVANESE LOVE AFFAIR

## N. WATSON

**MINERVA PRESS**
MONTREUX LONDON WASHINGTON

**A JAVANESE LOVE AFFAIR**
Copyright N. Watson 1996

All Rights Reserved

No part of this book may be reproduced in any form
by photocopying or by any electronic or mechanical means,
including information storage or retrieval systems,
without permission in writing from both the copyright
owner and the publisher of this book.

ISBN 1 85863 765 1

First published 1996 by
MINERVA PRESS
195 Knightsbridge
London SW7 1RE

Printed in Great Britain by
Antony Rowe Ltd, Chippenham, Wiltshire

# A JAVANESE LOVE AFFAIR

# CONTENTS

| | | |
|---|---|---|
| Chapter 1 | A First Encounter | 7 |
| Chapter 2 | A Journey | 15 |
| Chapter 3 | A Job Begun | 24 |
| Chapter 4 | An Evening's Entertainment | 36 |
| Chapter 5 | A Wrong Word | 52 |
| Chapter 6 | Parting | 67 |
| Chapter 7 | Coming Home | 79 |
| Chapter 8 | Return | 87 |
| Chapter 9 | A Visit Upcountry | 95 |
| Chapter 10 | A Jakarta Weekend | 105 |
| Chapter 11 | Gin and Tonic | 119 |
| Chapter 12 | Breakfast, Lunch and Dinner | 129 |
| Chapter 13 | Surabaya and Back | 144 |
| Chapter 14 | Reunion | 153 |
| Chapter 15 | Confessions | 163 |
| Chapter 16 | Saturday Lunch | 173 |
| Chapter 17 | Sunday and Departure | 186 |
| Chapter 18 | A Barbecue | 194 |

| Chapter 19 | A Game of Cricket | 204 |
| Chapter 20 | Going Back | 224 |
| Chapter 21 | Mr Chan Again | 240 |
| Chapter 22 | My Stomach Ache | 250 |
| Chapter 23 | Boroubudur | 264 |
| Chapter 24 | Return to Jakarta | 274 |
| Chapter 25 | Departure or Not | 286 |
| Chapter 26 | Mr Chan's Reward | 295 |
| Chapter 27 | Fate is Sealed | 306 |
| Chapter 28 | Catherine's Revenge | 316 |
| Chapter 29 | Saturday Morning | 338 |
| Chapter 30 | Monday | 356 |
| Chapter 31 | "I Knew You'd Come Back" | 378 |
| Chapter 32 | A Javanese Sales Tour | 393 |
| Chapter 33 | Stuart's Relief? | 406 |
| Chapter 34 | Anwar's Help | 418 |
| Chapter 35 | Bali | 435 |

# CHAPTER 1

# A FIRST ENCOUNTER

Stuart Morgan looked down at the neat piles of clothes laid out in orderly ranks on the double bed before him. He was a man who liked a certain amount of order in his life, although he could never be described as a creature of habit. His wife had often described him as a man who had a tidy mind but he only allowed this to show on the outside in little bits. He had, over the fourteen years or so that he had been travelling with his job, arrived at a routine which usually ensured that he had everything he needed. If the start of a trip was accompanied by the feeling that something had been forgotten, then everything was usually in order. On those journeys which had started with a feeling of confidence something had invariably been forgotten. From forgetting things as simple as a toothbrush, through leaving all his underpants, to forgetting his passport, travellers cheques and, on one occasion, all the documents for his work, that feeling of confidence now filled him with nervous anxiety; this was despite the fact that there were no ill effects from previous forgetful episodes, even the forgotten passport.

He was a little unsure of exactly what to pack. The trip was his first to South-East Asia. All of his previous journeys outside Europe had been west and south, to the USA, Canada and South America. The East, and South-East Asia in particular, were a closed book to him. He had no more idea of the region, the countries and peoples than contrived television images from travel programmes, documentaries and the news. He knew that it would be hot, but he had been very hot in America; and perhaps wet and humid, but he had been wet and humid in South America; so, using these as a guide, he had laid out a number of short-sleeved cotton shirts, polo tee-shirts, light trousers and his one lightweight summer suit. As always, the biggest problem was what to wear on the way to the airport. It was early February and it was a very cold winter. He settled on a cotton jersey and decided on no overcoat or raincoat and hoped that he wouldn't be exposed to the cold for too long.

He surveyed the piles one final time, going through a silent mental check list one last time. He opened a small suitcase, battered by countless encounters with airport baggage handlers, and identified by a number of hotel and airline stickers. It was his favourite suitcase, his companion on many trips, and he awaited its appearance on the luggage carousels as if waiting for a missing child to return. He checked the small elasticised pocket at the back. It contained a number of hotel sewing kits, scissors, nail clippers and other useful items. Tucked away in the left-hand corner he noticed a small cardboard packet. He smiled to himself as he remembered how the pack of condoms had come to be left there. They had been away for a weekend, just him and his wife; the children had been left with their grandmother. The condoms were a leftover from that unusually happy weekend last autumn. He picked them up and stared at them for a minute. Turning, he made as if to put them with the rest in the small box on the bedside table. He stopped in mid-motion, looked at them hard, waving them back and forth rhythmically, before, for no real reason, depositing them in the same left-hand corner of the suitcase pocket from where they had come.

As he finished packing the suitcase and was lifting it from the bed, Catherine, his wife, appeared at the bedroom door. She leaned against the door frame, arms folded, with her right leg crossed over the left, resting on its toes.

"Finished?" she said quietly.

He nodded once.

She unfolded her arms and pushed her hair back with her right hand, leaning her head back at the same time. It was a movement that he had always found almost irresistible. She was four years his junior and they had met at university. He was a year late starting and his course was a year longer than most. They had loved for a year and separated when he had left to find a job. He had been her first lover, and after two years of other men, she had found none better. She found him, still missing her, by accident when she got a job in the same town. They were married less than a year later, had two children and had been, and still were, happy. She had always been regarded as very attractive in an unusual way: not pretty, but undeniably desirable. Her hair was the first thing which he had noticed, a reddish brown mound of thick and wavy hair that fell below her shoulders like a mane. Her face was square with a small delicate mouth. Her nose was large and slightly hooked. Her eyes were a piercing green colour set against her pale English complexion.

He admired her as she stood in the doorway, backlit by the stairway light. The hair was somewhat shorter now. Like most English women, he reflected with sadness, the older they got the more frequent the visits to the hair salon became, the shorter the hair became the more it was coloured, permed and generally messed about with. He kept trying to persuade her to leave it as it was, to let it grow, but there was some status symbol in the number and expense of the visits to the salon. This was part of her middle-class, provincial upbringing. His mother-in-law was a typical example of these petty pretensions. He had never voiced these feelings to anyone, especially not Catherine, but he kept them nonetheless.

She pushed herself lightly off the door frame and stood straight up facing him. She had a typical English figure, large hips and bottom, with a small bust. At university and in her twenties, she had been able to disguise it well by being fit and slim and very sensual in her movements, but the two children and a comfortable life had had their effects. She was still a graceful mover; her hips and legs moved easily in swinging curves. Her posterior, although a bit enlarged, still retained some of the shape he had first found so irresistible fifteen years ago. She knew, and always had known, how to dress to accentuate her best features. She walked towards him in a way that made his stomach a little tight and his breath a little short.

"How long will you be away?" she breathed quietly when she stood only a few inches from him. She was almost as tall as he and, with him in bare feet and her in shoes, she could look him straight in the eyes.

"Ten, maybe twelve days," he replied, his voice just a tiny bit dry.

"Mmm..." She looked him in the eye, her eyes seemed to mist as she brought her mouth closer to his, then they closed as the two sets of lips met and they kissed. Half an hour or so later, he lay back on the bed, propped up on pillows watching the nude figure of his wife walking out of the bedroom to the bathroom. Her naked bottom retained some of the grace he had first discovered in the cold attic room of his university flat. He revelled in the private show before him. It had been an enjoyable and reasonably passionate encounter, although she had not had an orgasm while they were making love; that had followed after with a little help. Despite this, he guessed he was lucky: they still retained a good sexual relationship and in earlier years they had sometimes climaxed together during love-making. The frequency was less now than before, but that was to be expected, he supposed. Many of his friends, and most people if you believed what was written in so many books and magazines, had never had an orgasm together. He often found that the best times were just before he went away or when he came back. The prospect of a separation coming or one ending seemed to heighten her sexual responsiveness. He always believed that it had something to do with the constant separations and reunions which had characterised the early part of their relationship at university.

He heard her washing herself in the bathroom. As she finished, he got up and sloped into the bathroom. He looked at himself in the full-length bathroom mirror. Like his wife, he was a little fatter now, maybe one or one and a half stones heavier than his rugby playing weight at university. But he too enjoyed a comfortable life with good food and wine so he supposed that he could not be critical of his wife's rounding shape. He brushed his hair. It was still full – he had lost none since he left college. He guessed that he was still quite handsome, but no woman had come near him, nor had he invited attention, since he had been married. Later they lay closely and harmoniously entwined and then fell asleep. He was undoubtedly happy with his lot.

He stared vacantly out of the train window in the late afternoon of the following day. The train sped along through the dank Cheshire countryside, the grey posts which held the electric wires aloft flashing by with hypnotic regularity. The train was relatively quiet and smooth, and slowly he was lulled into a half trance-like state. He remembered the evening before. How he hated to travel over the weekend. Now it was Saturday afternoon: he should be shopping with the family or watching their eldest child, Ralph, play rugby at his school. Instead he was sitting in a crowded second-class railway carriage surrounded by families and noisy children. His slightly hypnotised mental state helped him to block out the chaos which flowed along the carriage in waves.

As he sat in his partially comatose state, he had the usual, but nevertheless frightening sensation that he had forgotten something. He jerked quickly into a fully awake state. Apologising to the woman on his right, he retrieved his small piece of hand luggage from the overhead rack. He checked again for the presence of his passport, travellers cheques, tickets and credit cards. Satisfied, he took out his diary by way of an excuse, and then replaced the bag on the rack, apologising once again to the woman, who eyed him with ill-disguised disgust.

Then suddenly, despite the checking, he felt a sense of dread, a feeling of hopeless blackness, fear of the unknown, a terrible longing to be at home with his wife and the children overwhelmed him. Was it fear of flying, he wondered, or the fear of not returning? No, it was not such a tangible reason, more a blind primeval fear which knew no reason. He gripped his diary with his hands, and, looking out of the window at the late winter Cheshire landscape, tried to rationalise the feelings. He had had such feelings on other occasions at the start of trips and they had, on balance, boded neither ill nor good. Despite his attempts to rationalise his fears, it was not until the train approached London that the tension began to release.

He left the train at Euston, carrying the small suitcase and shoulder bag. He used the tube; it was not too busy and it saved about twenty-five pounds on a taxi fare. He enjoyed the section of the ride on the Piccadilly Line beyond Hammersmith. Here the tube, the Underground, ran above ground, above the level of the streets and houses, affording an unusual view of the London suburbs. The feelings of desperation had all but subsided in the rising excitement of the now unfolding adventure of travelling to a new country. The sky was beginning to darken as they rattled through the final few stations, Boston Manor, Osterley, Hounslow East, Central and West before the tube became the underground again, diving beneath the approaches to Heathrow.

Even after so many years of travelling, he still felt a surge of excitement when he came close to Heathrow. This time it was a stronger feeling than usual: the new countries to be visited, a whole new world of experiences, and, curiously enough, the earlier dread gave the trip some added spice.

Terminal Three, as the starting point for most long-haul flights out of the UK, was always crowded in the early evening. So many people travelling and three times their number were seeing them off. He moved with purposeful directness through the massed ranks to the check-in desk, some three hours before the scheduled departure. The check-in was quick, he was so early, and he got his favourite non-smoking window seat. The crowd became thicker the closer he got to the entrance to the departure gate, as the hordes of people seeing off those travelling clamoured to have the last kiss, the last handshake, the last view of their departing families. Those that were left still stood looking after them, some crying, others resigned, all blocking the way. He pushed his way through this multicoloured mass and queued silently to show his boarding pass. Beyond lay the relative peace of the passenger only departure lounge.

He wandered around the departure lounge. It was under reconstruction and much was cordoned off with wooden boards. 'We apologise for the inconvenience' signs were everywhere, but the buffet and a small bar were still open. He had a few pints of beer and a sandwich, not because he was hungry or thirsty, but out of boredom and habit. He bought a book and two magazines and checked out the duty free but didn't buy.

He spoke to no one other than to buy beer. He rarely spoke to anyone once a journey had commenced. His worst nightmare was having to sit next to the chatty person on the plane. He remembered the old ladies on their first trips, the flying experts, and, worst of all, the enthusiastic Americans who wanted to introduce themselves, shake hands and become your lifetime friend on the one hour flight from London to Paris. He had obtained his favourite seat location, a window seat, so he could only be attacked from one side. He kept a close watch on the television monitors for the boarding information. The flight was opened forty-five minutes before the departure. With half an hour to go he walked slowly to the gate.

He had chosen Singapore Airlines, mainly because they were the only airline to fly non-stop London to Singapore, but partly because of the reputation of the service. As he entered the gate they were already calling the back seat rows forward to board. As an employee of an economy class company, he was located well to the back. He liked to board early and settle before the masses came on, pushing, shoving and fighting over the locker space. This usually meant, however, that he had read the interesting parts of the in-flight magazine long before departure and had the prospect of fourteen hours with only articles on haggis-making or the life and times of Japanese fishermen for company. It was almost, but not quite, enough to make you talk to the enthusiastic American in the next seat.

He didn't stop to sit down at the gate: the flight was boarding and he continued straight through to board. Nothing in his life had quite prepared him for the experience he was about to undergo – not the visit to the paradise beaches of Brazil, the years of sordid sexual marathons at university, the cool blue fair delights of Scandinavia, or the friendly, enveloping warmth of the all-American girl – no, none of that was a preparation for this. He walked along the pier towards the open door of the Jumbo Bigtop 747, still unaware that his life was on the brink of a drastic revision. In the entrance stood the slim, willowy figure of the most beautiful woman, he was sure, that he had ever seen. She was bending slightly forward, her hands clasped in front of her, her head tilted upwards smiling at him. The jet-black, straight hair was cut to her shoulders, with a perfect fringe. Her round face, with its smooth nutmeg-coloured skin and brown almond-shaped eyes, displayed not a blemish. Her lips parted in a full ceremonial smile and the perfect white teeth shone out from behind the delicate lips.

He felt his mouth drop in surprise. He wanted to ask her to marry him there and then. He had never been confronted with such a vision of loveliness before. He was so stunned that he stuttered to a halt and stopped short, causing the man behind to crash into him. He felt nothing.

"Can I see your boarding pass please?" she asked with a larger smile, this time of amusement at the collision and Stuart's apparent disregard of it.

'My God,' he thought, 'she can speak as well. She is real!'

"Mm, yes, here it is." He fumbled inelegantly for his piece of card.

"Forty-five J." She smiled again as she looked carefully at the card. "Across the aisle, turn right – it's a window seat," she continued.

Her eyes met his for a brief moment, then she turned her head and gestured with her left hand towards the inside of the plane.

"Thank you very much," he mumbled and stumbled forward into the plane.

He had had his first close encounter with South-East Asia.

## CHAPTER 2

## A JOURNEY

As he settled into his seat, Stuart, still slightly numbed by the vision he had just beheld, watched with trepidation to see who would be sitting next to him for the next thirteen hours. A number of unsuitable-looking candidates stopped and checked their cards before being directed to their correct seats by the ever-attentive staff. Each time he breathed a sigh of relief. Finally, a youngish woman, of obvious Asian origin, with a small daughter of maybe seven or eight years, occupied the two seats between him and the aisle. The mother sat by the aisle with the small daughter next to him. She was much larger and more heavily built than the stewardess – what Stuart would have called a 'hockey player' at university. She had a big, broad, although not unpleasant, face. The woman smiled at him and he smiled back. He was reasonably happy with his flight companions, although the small daughter gave him some cause for concern.

Stuart had travelled in jumbos many times, but this was his first time in the new Bigtop 747-300 model. The interior was clean and neat – the whole operation exuded efficiency. After fifteen minutes of taxiing and waiting in the usual Heathrow manner, which failed to exude any efficiency at all, they were ready and positioned at the end of the runway. It seemed to take a long time to wind the engines up to speed. He guessed that the pilot was reaching full power before releasing the brakes. When the plane finally lumbered forward, it gathered speed more slowly than Stuart remembered from previous flights. Eventually the fuselage rotated and the plane lifted off. The twinkling lights of Heathrow and London were soon left far below. The climb to cruising altitude was long and slow. It was almost forty minutes before the 'fasten seatbelt' sign went off. The length of the flight at thirteen hours, and the heavy load of fuel required, was undoubtedly the cause, Stuart reasoned to himself, rather than any problem. His mind flashed back to his blind panic on the train and he wondered if this was the flight to provide a reason for that panic, but the stewardess began to serve drinks and the memory dimmed with the first sip of gin and tonic.

Stuart looked for the air hostess that he had seen at the door. To his great delight she was serving in his section. He had an opportunity to study her at his leisure. Her body was of a slim, willowy build, very curvaceous without being luscious: an Englishwoman as slim as she was would lack the curvaceousness and have an almost bony appearance. She moved with graceful ease, guiding the trolley around in a way no British Airways hostess ever could. And what surprised him more was the presence of more air hostesses of almost equal beauty, each as stunning in their own way. He could not take his eyes off them: they were better than the adverts and descriptions of his friends.

He ate his meal, drank his drinks, listened to music, watched a film and then slowly drifted off into a half sleep. He had lifted the arm rest and the woman's daughter stretched out, her head in her mother's lap, her feet on his. Her mother apologised at first but he assured her it was no problem and the little girl slept. Eventually his half sleep turned into a full sleep. He awoke a number of times and ordered orange juice from the hostess who floated past at intervals. His sleep was not deep and punctuated by jolts as his head moved or his neck became stiff.

He woke up finally with more than four hours still to go. He cracked open the window shutter and glanced out. It was very bright, so he quickly closed the shutter to avoid disturbing others. He read fitfully, listened to the music and waited for the flight to end. The last hours were always the worst.

He watched the increasing activity in the galley in front: breakfast was near. The little girl and her mother were awake, so he excused himself and went to the toilet. Once breakfast was served the time passed more quickly and soon they were on the final approach. He looked out of the window into the gathering darkness of the tropical evening for his first view of Singapore.

He waited until the rush to leave was over, said goodbye to his travelling companions and made his way off the plane. At the door he said goodbye to his air hostess. He must have looked terrible, he knew, after his thirteen hour flight, but she looked exactly as she had thirteen hours ago in Heathrow.

Even though the pier was air-conditioned, he felt the blast of hot, damp, tropical air coming through an open doorway adjacent to the control panel of the pier. He walked quickly into the terminal building, grateful to be out of even that short taste of the tropics. Once inside it was cool, almost to the point of being chilly. The gate was quite close to the central spine of the H layout of Singapore's Changi Airport, and Stuart did not have far to walk to reach the transfer desk to confirm his onward flight to Jakarta. The airport was busy without being crowded. He was amazed at the sheer variety of people who moved around, some purposefully, some aimlessly. Every colour of skin, every creed, every type of human being seemed to be here. 'Where are they all going?' he asked himself. 'The crossroads of the world.' He continued in his train of rather stereotyped travel brochure thought. It was, however, in this case equal to the hype.

He found a seat in the small lounge bar with a Chinese man playing a baby grand piano in one corner. Stuart ordered a local Tiger beer from a small Chinese girl. Her long black hair hung almost to her waist. She was clad in a tight cream dress which reached to her ankles. It clung to the curvaceous shape of her little behind, with the sides split to mid-thigh, revealing her legs as she walked. He was still stunned, even shocked, by the beauty of the women he had seen so far. The shape of their bodies seemed to be different from that of English women or even the large, luscious beauties that he had seen in South America – the small neatness, much more proportionate between hip and breast, a willowy smoothness of shape, an effortless grace of movement, a firmness of figure and a silky appearance of skin were the characteristics and features that Stuart noticed all at once and then one at a time. He was, without a doubt, entranced by them all.

The short flight to Jakarta was not full. A European woman sat one seat away from him. He filled in his landing card and customs paper with care. She remained silent while he did so, holding her papers in front of her. When he had finished she leaned across.

"May I borrow your pen please?" she asked, her accent revealing her to be English.

"Of course," he smiled and handed her his biro.

Once finished she handed it back. "Have you been to Jakarta before?" she asked.

"No – my first time to Indonesia, or anywhere in Asia for that matter," Stuart replied, thankful that it was only a short flight as he was obviously sitting next to a 'talker'.

"Well, it's not like England," she replied rather superfluously in a rather superior tone. "Be careful. So many people suffer from culture shock on their first visit here," she added.

Stuart paused before answering, "Yes, I guess some might, but I've spent a long time in South America and I've seen a few things there that would give anyone culture shock."

She was slightly rebuffed: her status as the most experienced traveller advising the novice was dented.

"Mmmm... But here there is a certain smell you'll find," she continued, attempting to re-establish her position.

"Yes, the drains smell in all Third World countries," he interrupted, guessing her game.

"No, not those," she replied quickly. "Although they do smell somewhat," she continued in a condescending tone. "No, it's a different smell but very distinctive – you'll soon see what I mean." Her position as the most experienced traveller in this region at least had been reasserted. "Business or pleasure?" she continued, having gained the upper hand.

"Business," he replied, "and maybe a little pleasure."

She glanced rather severely at him.

"I like to spend at least one day on a trip looking at the sights," he added hastily to counter the accusing look. Most Western men, he knew, thought a 'little pleasure' meant only one thing. "Can you recommend some places to go?"

"Yes, of course. There are a number of museums and Taman Mini Indonesia, that's Indonesia in miniature, and outside the city there are botanical gardens in Bogor and tea plantations in Puncak – many things. I'm sure your hotel will be able to recommend something. If you're serious." She couldn't resist the final dig at him and through him all the other European men who thought that pleasure meant only one thing in South-East Asia.

She had assumed, wrongly, that he was just like most of the other businessmen on a trip wanting something to tell the boys back home about. But Stuart had never been unfaithful to his wife, not really even close to it, although on a number of occasions on other business trips, especially in South America, he had been in the company of colleagues in many a seedy dive where unfaithfulness was expected, or almost even demanded, but to date he had resisted all temptations. They chatted aimlessly about her husband's job – he was a civil engineer working on the new toll motorways in Jakarta – and about Stuart's business, a sales engineer for textile machinery. The short flight passed quickly and in the end Stuart was quite glad of her company.

Sukarno Hatta International Airport was unlike any other airport he had ever visited. Whereas Singapore's Changi was all marble, glass, air-conditioning and efficiency and Heathrow was a great British compromise struggling to work, this one was different. It was constructed from huge, brown, steel tubes in the manner of a mammoth, square bamboo hut. These 'huts' where grouped in little clusters, linked by bamboo-like walkways. These clusters formed three different terminal buildings, which were, Stuart discovered later, in turn, linked by a curved main building. The pier and walkway from the plane were not air-conditioned as in Singapore. Instead, the corridors were shielded by what looked like large, fixed, metal venetian blinds. The heat and humidity wafted in, making his clothes feel clammy after the short walk to the terminal building. Even inside the terminal the relief of air-conditioning was short-lived. The corridor below the departure lounge into which they descended, which was reserved exclusively for arriving passengers, had large windows devoid of glass. The tropical night was all around. The small, delightful gardens between the corridors were illuminated with various lamps, around which flies and moths flitted around in their suicidal mating dance. Inside the building, groups of men and women in light blue overalls stood around the toilets or absently pushed brushes around. Where Changi had been all bustle and business, Sukarno Hatta was laid-back and relaxed almost to the point of sleep.

He cleared immigration and collected his favourite suitcase when it appeared like a faithful friend on the carousel. He changed a hundred pounds into local currency and was amazed at the amount of money that resulted, both in the number of *rupiah*, over three hundred thousand, and the number of notes – the largest denomination appeared to be ten thousand. The girl gave him two hundred thousand of his money in five thousand rupiah notes, making a wedge far too thick to fit in his small wallet. After considering the problem, he put one hundred thousand in the wallet and stuffed the rest into his hand luggage. He handed his customs paper over to the guard who just waved him through with a smile.

He prepared to face Jakarta for the first time.

Beyond the glass doors, immediately after customs, he was faced with a fence of black iron posts some five feet high. The whole area was roofed to protect it from the rain, but it was open on all sides except the back whence he had just emerged. Over and around the fence a thousand faces stared towards him and the other emerging travellers. A sea of humanity, all brown faces, brown eyes and black hair; they watched intently. The air was hot and damp and it hung like a wet sheet over him now that he stood out in it for the first time with no prospect of air-conditioned relief. The smell came to his nostrils. He didn't need to be told it was the smell – he knew. The noise surprised him; people shouting, the shrill of a whistle being blown repeatedly, car engines and, above all, car horns, everywhere, continuously tooting and honking. He stood transfixed by the scene, like a rabbit in a car's headlights, unable to move left or right, forward or back. Finally someone struggling with a large suitcase pushed him from behind and he was forced to move. Most people turned left, so he followed suit. As he came to the opening in the fence, a number of men approached him.

"Taxi, sir?"

"Taxi, mister? Hello mister."

'Like taxi touts all over the world,' he mused. He shook his head.

Some gave up but some persisted.

"Taxi, sir? What your hotel, mister?"

He looked around for an official taxi rank or hotel courtesy bus. He could see none. Then he saw a small man with a white plastic board. The word 'Kedutaan' was written crookedly in blue felt tip. The man wore a dark pink jacket and a little round hat. Stuart pushed his way towards him. When the taxi touts saw this, they realised the game was up.

"Mr Morgan," Stuart said. "Mr S. Morgan. From England."

"Oh, ya, ya, is here," the little man said. "You want limo or taxi, Mr Morgan?"

"Limo," Stuart answered without hesitation. The idea of a taxi filled him with fear.

"OK, you waiting just minute, sir." He disappeared, leaving Stuart standing by himself. A few minutes later the man returned.

"Your car, please sir, is here." He led Stuart to a white Toyota something.

"Fifteen US dollar. OK, sir?"

"OK, fine." Stuart was just glad to have a car.

"You pay at hotel," the little man instructed.

Stuart tipped the hotel man a thousand rupiah, for which he looked very grateful. Stuart guessed it was probably twice what was necessary.

The drive from the airport started reasonably well. The first part of the journey was along a fast dual carriageway with little traffic. He tried to see what was around but he could make out little in the darkness. The road had a few large illuminated signs advertising various products, golf courses and the usual Japanese cars. At the end of the dual carriageway, the driver paid a toll, and a short distance beyond Jakarta traffic proper started.

Stuart sat back in his seat, amazed at the driving skills being demonstrated, the artistic use of the horn, indicators and lights as the cars, buses, mini buses, lorries, bikes, scooters, push bikes and pedestrians vied for the very limited road space. They skilfully avoided the numerous pot holes, weaving around the slow-moving obstructions of hand-pulled carts laden with water containers, animal fodder or rubbish. Occasionally a curious contraption mounted on two bicycle wheels side by side and pushed by a man appeared in the outside lane of the road, usually going against the traffic. Stuart froze in terror on a number of occasions, but the driver thought nothing of it as he wove around them without so much as a check in the rear-view mirror.

At traffic lights, each driver manoeuvred and shunted forward in an effort to gain some tiny microsecond or millimetre advantage over his neighbour. And then there were the horns: all the time they blew, a constant barrage of tooting and honking; even before the lights turned green the horns were on. And then, because the last of the oncoming traffic always went through on red and blocked the junction, the next set, having seen part of their green taken by the backlog of the other, invariably crossed on red to make up. The result was that on green most cars were stationary, whilst on red most moved. Progress towards the city proper was slow. Road building work was everywhere. He half expected to see and recognise the Englishwoman's husband with his hard hat on, working away under the floodlights. But the sites were filled with a multitude of little men going about their business.

Eventually the roadworks and crawling pace gave way to a wide thoroughfare. In each direction were two separate roads, one of two lanes and one of three. Trees were planted between the roads, and some were illuminated with a myriad of tiny white lights.

High office blocks towered on either side, and Stuart noticed a few hotels. The driver noticed Stuart's interest. "Jalan Jeneral Sudirmam," he said.

Stuart nodded. At the end of this road was a spectacular fountain in the centre of a large roundabout. A statue of a man and a woman stood on top of a steel pillar in the middle. From the top of this ran strings of white lights to the edge of the roundabout, with the fountains playing in the centre. A number of large hotels lay around the outside of the roundabout. Stuart stared in wonder: it didn't look much like a Third World country, but then the capitals usually were deceptive. Beyond the statues and fountains, the road continued towards a large illuminated tower which stood in the centre of a large park. "National Monument," the driver said with obvious pride. They crossed a railway line and then arrived in front of a largish square of grass and garden.

The Hotel Kedutaan was on the left as they approached, facing the square. It was a fairly anonymous building in grey painted concrete. At first sight it appeared to have palm trees growing right through the first three floors. The front was floodlit and the tropical gardens were attractively arranged. The car stopped and a man dressed in the same costume as the one at the airport greeted him and opened the door. "Check in, sir?"

"Yes, thank you."

The man handed Stuart a white card in exchange for his baggage.

"Please sir, follow me." The driver beckoned Stuart forward towards the steps which led to the reception.

A tiny girl, no more than four foot six high and dressed in the uniform of a bell boy, held the door open for them and smiled. The driver led Stuart to the reception desk.

"Please, you sign for me," he asked, after a brief unintelligible conversation with the girl behind the desk.

Stuart looked at the paper. It was a receipt for the journey. He took out his wallet.

"No money sir, from hotel," the driver explained.

Stuart gave the man a tip.

"Thank you sir, thank you," he said and then he smiled and disappeared.

"Check in, sir?" A small woman in glasses smiled at him from behind the reception desk. It was a roguish, cheeky smile, given with her head slightly tilted. She handed him two small lemon-smelling towels, presented with a small orchid on a glass plate. He towelled his sweaty face.

Once the formalities were complete, he retired to his room. It was ten-thirty local time, three-thirty in the UK, and he was tired. Once his case arrived he showered and slept.

# CHAPTER 3

# A JOB BEGUN

Stuart was rudely awakened by the insistent ring of the telephone in his right ear. He struggled to a sitting position in the half light of the room. The light came through a gap in the curtains, indicating daylight beyond. He glanced at his watch. It was eight o'clock. He had slept very well despite the seven hour time change. He picked up the phone, struggling to shake off the nine hours' sleep and the jet-lag.

"Good morning," he said as politely as he could.

"Mr Morgan?" the voice said

"Yes."

"Ah... Good morning, this is Mr Anwar. I hope you have slept well," the voice continued.

"Yes, fine thanks, I've just woken up," Stuart replied. He remembered Mr Anwar from the briefing he had had before he left the UK. This was the agent, the Mr Fix It, the type of man without whom doing business in Indonesia would be quite impossible. Stuart tried to clear his head again.

"OK, I call you late this morning because I know it's your first day!" Mr Anwar said, with a laugh.

'If this is late what the hell is early?' Stuart thought to himself.

"That's very kind of you," he said, hoping that the sarcasm in his voice didn't show.

"My driver will be at your hotel at nine o'clock to bring you to our offices. I will see you then if that is OK for you," Mr Anwar continued.

"OK, that's fine, see you then, 'bye."

"Goodbye Mr Morgan."

Stuart got up, showered and dressed in his lightweight suit. He breakfasted on tropical fruits, cereal and coffee to wake him up. At nine o'clock his phone rang again.

"Mr Morgan, this is reception. A driver is here for you."

Stuart left the room and headed downstairs. Another small girl held the front door for him.

'They must have a special order for small girls,' he thought as she smiled up at him.

The weather was not yet hot, maybe only twenty-eight or twenty-nine degrees, and it did not feel too humid. The sun was shining but there was a haze in the air, even at this early hour, which dimmed its brightness somewhat.

The car was a large white Toyota Crown. The seats were fitted with white tailored seat covers and the air-conditioning was very effective. It seemed to glide through the traffic with ease. In the daylight the city took on a different appearance from the previous evening. It looked shabby and overworked. The roads and pavements were crumbling under the sheer number of people and cars. The large office blocks and hotels apart, the rest of the small shops and houses looked rough and uncared for. Air-conditioning units hung on the outside of many buildings in seemingly precarious positions, while electricity and telephone cables festooned posts and buildings at random.

At some sets of traffic lights, young boys ran between the lines of traffic, selling newspapers, drinks, cigarettes and snacks. At some, crippled beggars sat holding their hands up in a kind of prayer, heads bowed. Stuart was not unduly shocked: he had seen worse in some parts of South America. In the Southern states of the United States of America there were some examples of extreme poverty, and now, even in England too, he reflected, as they continued on their way.

After half an hour of driving, during which they had probably gone no more than two miles, they arrived at a medium-sized office block. The driver told him where to go and Stuart left the car. Inside it was cool and clean. He ascended to the fourth floor and entered the offices of P.T. Gurya Cipta.

"Hello sir, can I help you?" a girl asked him from behind a reception desk.

"Yes, I've come to see Mr Anwar," Stuart replied to the small bespectacled lady.

"Do you have appointment, sir?"

Stuart smiled and nodded. He put his bag down in front of the counter. She picked up the telephone and had a quick conversation in what Stuart assumed was Indonesian.

"OK, please you sitting over there. Thank you." She indicated a group of easy chairs tucked away behind the door.

Stuart sat for almost fifteen minutes before Mr Anwar appeared. Stuart was beginning to feel a little angry at the delay, but he knew that he had to suppress the anger. He had been briefed about some of the Indonesian etiquette and showing anger at the first meeting would result in a very short meeting.

"Hello Mr Morgan, I am Anwar." A shortish Indonesian man stood close to Stuart, extending his hand. Stuart stood up immediately and returned the hand, shaking it firmly.

"Stuart Morgan of Ormistons, in Manchester."

"I know, I know," Anwar replied, laughing heartily. "Your boss, Mr Jackson, said he would send his best man, and that must be you."

Stuart was embarrassed.

"Well, I don't know if that's true but I am here and I'll do my best."

"Do your best like all good boy scouts." Anwar laughed again at his joke.

Stuart laughed as well. Anwar's English was very good, and he even had a sense of humour in English. Stuart's boss had not told him much about Anwar and certainly nothing about his character.

"Come," Anwar said, turning towards the reception desk. "Come to my office, we'll be more comfortable there."

Anwar was a few inches shorter than Stuart and of medium build for a European, which meant quite substantial for an Indonesian. His hair was, of course, jet-black and straight. He had a small moustache and a wide smile of straight white teeth. His skin was somewhat lighter than most of the people that Stuart had seen since he had arrived, and his facial features showed some hint of Chinese. Stuart guessed he was of mixed blood.

In his office Stuart sat on a hard chair in front of the desk. Anwar sat in a high-backed swivel chair in black leather. The office was furnished in very good taste. The furnishings were plain and simple but of the very best quality. A number of small ornaments and pictures adorned the shelves and walls.

"So." Anwar broke the silence after Stuart had taken in the room. "So," he repeated, "your little company in Manchester wants to do some business in Indonesia."

He smiled as he said the word 'little'. Ormistons was one of the world's three largest suppliers of textile-making machinery. They had supplied to just about every country, but, curiously enough, never to the Far East, one of the world's largest producers of textile products. So far India represented the furthest east that they had progressed. The realisation that there was only one other company operating in the region had led to Stuart's presence in Jakarta after the initial visits by his boss. Stuart confined his response to a smile.

"You see," Anwar continued, "doing business in Indonesia for a foreign company is very very difficult." He rocked back in his chair, linking his fingers together in front of him. "Very difficult indeed." He paused. "You have to know the rules, Mr Morgan – the rules are important." Suddenly he lunged forward in his chair, pushing his hands forward, palms down on the desk, bringing him much closer to Stuart. He looked at Stuart straight in the eye. "Do you know the rules, Mr Morgan? Do you know the rules of my country?" he asked, his voice fierce and strong.

If Stuart was taken aback, he did not show it. Instead he looked Anwar in the eye, smiled and composed his reply.

"Do you know the rules in my country?" he asked with a smile. Anwar laughed loudly, and before he could say anything else Stuart continued, "When I started this job fourteen years ago I didn't know anything about anywhere, not even my own country." He paused for effect. "Since then I've worked in America, north and south, and most parts of Europe, and I've had to learn the rules in all of these countries." He paused again to see if Anwar would interrupt, but he didn't. Stuart continued, "So now we want to try in Indonesia. So we start to learn the rules of a new country. To learn those rules we must have a good guide and teacher, someone who knows who is who, what is what, someone who can advise us." He looked at Anwar seriously. "We are very serious about this country so we have chosen the best teacher and guide." He didn't want to say

Anwar's name but he knew that Anwar had taken the message. Stuart knew that everyone has an ego. The higher the position, the more important the man, the bigger the ego. It never did any harm to massage an ego.

Anwar was quiet for a while. He looked hard at Stuart, trying to weigh him up. Then he smiled. For the first time Stuart saw a different type of smile. Not the smile of Indonesian formality but the smile of respect. Eventually Anwar spoke.

"Truly, Mr Jackson has sent his best man." He paused. "I think we can do some work together, Mr Morgan. You understand. I can tell. What do you think we should do?"

"Well, isn't that for you to tell me?" Stuart asked, enjoying his meeting very much.

"Of course, but I want to know your ideas," Anwar responded with another smile. Stuart was now convinced that the smiles and attitudes of Mr Anwar were favourable.

"I would like to meet the people from the three companies that Mr Jackson identified as soon as possible. But I know my boss." Stuart continued, "He is good and solid in the markets he knows, but I would like to take a look myself to see if there are any others and, if we can arrange it, to meet them as well."

"I have already arranged meetings tomorrow with the companies that Mr Jackson mentioned. But, like you, I feel that Mr Jackson did not consider enough of the others. After tomorrow we can go exploring." He paused. "Together," he added finally.

The meeting continued for another two hours in the office. They identified a number of target companies, small ones, but vigorous expanding ones. Stuart's boss had stuck largely to the major internationally known names and government organisations. At twelve o'clock Mr Anwar suggested lunch.

"What sort of food do you like?" he asked Stuart.

"I will usually eat anything. I don't like to stick to European food. I usually try to eat the food of the country that I'm in so Indonesian will suit me fine."

"Have you ever tried Indonesian food before?" Anwar asked.

"No, but then there's a first time for everything," Stuart replied, a twinkle in his eye. Anwar caught it and laughed extravagantly.

"OK, I take you to a really traditional restaurant – Javanese food."

They dined on boiled rice, charcoal-grilled freshwater fish, caught before their eyes, blanched vegetables and beer.

"To enjoy this food properly you should use your fingers," Anwar said, rinsing his right hand in a small bowl of water with a piece of lime floating in it.

Stuart followed suit and watched Anwar for clues and hints. The food was quite delicious, the fish so fresh and simply cooked, and it was not hot at all. Stuart had heard about the fierce spiciness of the food in Indonesia.

Then Anwar showed him the little stone dish of red sauce. "Sambal," he said. "This is very very hot."

Stuart tried a little with his fish, but even though he was the master of the chicken vindaloo in his local curry house, admittedly usually after eight pints of beer, a little of the sambal was all he tried.

As they sat full and satisfied, Stuart finally plucked up the courage to ask Anwar a question which had been worrying him since they had started lunch.

"You drink beer, Mr Anwar?"

Anwar looked at him with his head on one side. "But of course. Why not?"

"Well, my guidebook says that Indonesia is a predominantly Muslim country."

Anwar laughed. "Don't believe all you read in those silly books. I am a sort of Muslim, well, I am a Muslim." He continued, "My father is part Chinese and Catholic and my mother is a pure Javanese Muslim and quite strict. My father changed his religion when they got married and he's even been on the *Haj*."

"The *Haj*?" Stuart asked, puzzled.

"Mmm, the pilgrimage to Mecca that every good Muslim is supposed to make once in his life," Anwar responded. "Anyway," he continued, "my father and mother wanted a good education for me. My mother wanted a religious education in Saudi Arabia, my father wanted Sydney, Australia." He raised his glass with a wicked smile. "Guess who won?"

They both laughed

"So you see I know all that the Australians know about beer and its drinking. I'm a Muslim with exceptions. You will find a lot of Muslims with exceptions in this country as well as some fanatics, but most people are relaxed but devout."

After lunch, Anwar set about arranging meetings with the other companies. Stuart felt very tired in the middle of the afternoon. He left and returned to the hotel with Anwar's driver.

Stuart lay down on the bed to watch the television. Before he realised it, he was asleep. He slept for two hours. When Stuart awoke, it was after five-thirty. He felt terrible: his mouth was sticky and stale, his head felt heavy and his shoulders were stiff from sleeping in a peculiar position. He lay around for a further hour, half watching the television and half drifting in and out of sleep. Finally he made an effort to wake himself up. He knew from experience that the worst thing he could do was to continue to sleep. He would wake up some time in the middle of the night and keep his sleep patterns disturbed for days to come. The only cure was to get active.

He showered for the second time that day, to try to revive himself. Once dressed in a short-sleeved cotton shirt and jeans, he went down to the lobby to see what he could see.

He sat down in a sofa in the lobby lounge and ordered a beer from a golden-skinned, black-haired waitress who wove her way amongst the tables and chairs with graceful ease. After two beers and an hour of observing the people coming and going, Stuart felt the need for some food. The lunch had been quite substantial but he felt the pangs of hunger in his stomach. He crossed to the coffee shop. After the exotic lunch, he wanted something light and normal and he settled for what turned out to be an enormous club sandwich and another beer. Even when he had finished the club sandwich and his beer, it was still only eight-thirty. He looked around for something else to do. He was not feeling particularly adventurous and did not want to leave the confines of the hotel. The receptionist who had checked him in the previous evening was working again. She smiled at him as he wandered aimlessly past the reception.

"Good evening Mr Morgan," she said brightly. He was surprised that she had remembered his name. "How are you?"

"Oh, I'm fine, just walking around," he replied.

"Where are you going this evening, Mr Morgan?" she asked with an eyebrow raised in a flirtatious manner.

"I was hoping that you could tell me where I should go," he replied, equally flirtatiously.

"Have you tried The Inne?" she asked.

"No, is it far? And is it a good place?"

"Oh, of course it's a good place, it's in the hotel, it's the 'in place to go'," she said loudly with an air of mock anger. "Just go out of the main door and turn right. The Inne is down the stairs."

"Thanks." He left the reception and followed her directions. Stuart had read about The Inne in the hotel literature. It was described as a part English pub and part German beer cellar. It was not a combination that Stuart considered would work. He smiled at the man on the door. "Please sir, you resident?" he asked.

Stuart nodded.

"OK sir, please." The man waved his hand towards the entrance.

Once inside Stuart's eyes slowly became accustomed to the semi-darkness. A central, square bar was the main focus of the room. A number of tables and chairs lay on either side of the bar, whilst directly in front were a number of barrels converted into standing-height tables. A small stage was set up beyond these. It was equipped with instruments and microphones but no performers. Stuart saw a spare swivel stool on the corner of the bar. He sat down and ordered another beer.

Before he was halfway through it, a number of girls came from the opposite side of the bar. Five of them, all dressed the same. Stuart guessed that they were the band. Two men accompanied them. They climbed on the small stage and distributed themselves around the instruments. Both of the men and two of the girls took up instruments. The three most attractive ones remained in front of the microphones. All five girls were dressed in white jackets with a black tee-shirt underneath and tight shiny black leggings finished off with black high-heeled shoes. Their hair was long and curly and worn hanging down. They were all light-skinned but obviously South-East Asian. Stuart wondered if they were Indonesian or not.

"Hello everybody and welcome to the second set of the Manila Seven all the way from Manila in the Philippines."

His question was answered. They went on to say hello to a number of the guests and read a few requests. Then they started to sing. Stuart decided after a few songs that they were decidedly good. They sang a whole selection of old sixties and seventies songs, songs that Stuart knew, the Beatles, ABBA, the Rolling Stones, Rod Steward, Tina Turner and other songs he recognised but didn't know who the artists were. He hardly noticed the time passing, so good was the entertainment, and in a very short time, it seemed to Stuart, it was the end of their second set.

Stuart turned to face the bar.

"Beer please," he asked the nearest waiter.

"A goddamn Limey," he heard someone say.

Looking round for the source of the voice, Stuart thought to himself, 'Everywhere I go there is always some big loud-mouthed Yank.'

He saw two men sitting almost next to him on the corner of the bar. They both raised their glasses to him. Despite his initial thought, neither were particularly large and had they not spoken Stuart would not have known that they were Americans.

"Everywhere I go in this bloody world," Stuart said with a half smile, "there's always some noisy Yank spoiling things."

The two Americans looked a little taken aback. "And do you know the worst place for bloody Americans?" Stuart continued. They both shook their heads. "The USA," Stuart said in deadly seriousness.

The two Americans laughed loudly. "Orr, shit man, I thought you were being serious for a minute then," the closest one said, extending his hand. "Rick, Rick Johnson. We're here on a power station project, building boilers. And this here is my pal Hank F. Gordon."

Stuart shook hands with Rick and then Hank. "Stuart Morgan from England. I'm here trying to selling machinery for textile mills and the like."

"I haven't seen you in here before," Rick continued. "Can I buy you another beer?"

"No, I've just got one. And yes, it's my first time in here, in fact my first time in Jakarta," Stuart answered.

"Well, you've found the best place in the town. We've been around, haven't we, Hank?"

Hank F. Gordon nodded in silent agreement.

"And this is the best – best group, best atmosphere, best everything."

"Have you been here long, in Jakarta I mean?" Stuart asked.

"Only five months. We have stayed here for all that time. It's a good place."

They chatted for ten minutes more. Stuart discreetly attracted the attention of a waiter and ordered three more beers. When they arrived the two Americans thanked him with genuine surprise. Then the Manila Seven were back.

Some time before the end of the third and final set, Rick and Hank excused themselves and left. Stuart stayed and watched the band. He had learned to identify the differences between the three singers despite the fact that they changed places for different songs, and looked very similar in the costumes. They were even of very similar height and build. One of the three caught Stuart's eye more than the rest. She moved with more conviction and rhythm than the others, she looked as if she was enjoying the pleasure of entertaining and singing. He kept his eyes more or less exclusively on her. And then she looked at him, straight at him, in the eye, or did she? Was he only dreaming or imagining things? And then there was the look again, straight at him, straight in the eye. But then she and the other two looked at all the people in the bar. Yet the other two never looked at him; maybe they had a code and chose which people to look at, perhaps it was part of the show.

The songs continued until twelve-thirty. And when they were over, Stuart was still sitting in the same place at the end of the bar. As the songs finished, the group packed away their instruments and came down into the bar. Stuart swivelled his stool round to face the bar and ordered another beer. As he did so he became aware that a singer, he couldn't tell which one, was close to him on his left side. After taking his beer, he swivelled his stool again to the front. She, the one who had looked at him from the stage, was sitting on the next stool facing him. It was difficult to turn the stool without his knees touching hers. He tried but just brushed her knees. She was dabbing a paper napkin against her sweaty brow. As their knees made contact, she looked at him and smiled. She had a wide mouth and a sort of cheeky, pouty, very expressive face. He smiled shyly, nervously back at her and cast his gaze to the stage again.

She exhaled loudly and fanned herself with another napkin. He turned to face her again. Sweat ran down her slim muscular neck, a testament to her enthusiasm on the stage.

"It's hot work," she said.

"Mmm. I guess it must be," Stuart replied rather lamely. He was always nervous when faced by a woman he found attractive.

"What's your name?" she asked, putting the napkin fan on the bar.

"Stuart."

"What?" she asked again, screwing up her face and putting her head on one side.

"Stuart," he said louder, and then with a single quick move he pulled a card from his shirt pocket. "Stuart," he repeated, handing her the card.

She took it and examined it closely.

"Oh, St... u... a... r... t," she said, drawing the word out. "Well, I am pleased to meet you, Mr Stuart Morgan from England." She held out a small hand. He held it and shook it gently, surprised by the strength of the grip of the small hand. She smiled at him.

"I have to go now, time for my sleep." She pushed the card in the pocket of her jacket. "Will you be here again?" she asked.

"Yes, I think so."

She turned the stool round, getting ready to go.

"What's yours?" he called after her. "Your name, I mean."

"Frances, call me Fran," she said back, smiling again. She stood up. She was not very tall down here on the floor, maybe five foot four, but on the stage she had looked so tall and in control. She started to walk away.

"It was good," he called after her. "Your group, your singing, very good."

She turned her head again and smiled and then continued on her way without saying anything more.

He felt confused and flustered: feelings ran through him which he hadn't felt for many a long year. He shuddered and shook himself. He glanced across to the other side of the bar, hoping to catch another glimpse of her, but she was gone.

## CHAPTER 4

## AN EVENING'S ENTERTAINMENT

At half past five the following afternoon, just as the sky was beginning to darken for the tropical night, Stuart sat in the right rear passenger seat of Anwar's white Toyota Crown. He sat slumped, his head leaning back on the top of the rear seat. From this position Stuart could see vertically out of the car's rear window. He was totally shattered and exhausted from a number of causes: jet-lag, a seven o'clock start that morning, and a day of frustration Indonesian style. Mr Anwar had arranged three meetings for the day. None of the meetings had lasted more than an hour but it had taken something over ten hours to get round them. Half the extra time had been spent in the car in the Jakarta traffic and the other half waiting for the meetings to start. Stuart had realised that Anwar was quite a rich, important man, yet he had sat with Stuart outside one office for something over one and a half hours without complaint. "The Indonesian system," he had said to Stuart, when Stuart had become restless. Patience, it seemed, was not only a national characteristic, but a necessity. 'But then', Stuart thought, 'how could a nation of people so patient in everyday life and business become impatient, horn-blaring, madmen when in control of any vehicle from a push bike to a bus?' Stuart considered it one of the mysteries of the East.

Despite the eventual convening of all three meetings, and the friendly smiles during all three, Stuart felt depressed about the prospects. All the companies had long-standing relationships with the main supplier in the region, a German company. Stuart got the feeling that they were not about to change. Anwar and Stuart were received very well in all three offices but the message was definitely negative. Sitting next to Stuart as the car progressed at a snail's pace through the early evening Jakarta traffic, Anwar was aware of Stuart's gloomy depression. He reached over and touched Stuart on the arm.

"Don't worry. It is just the beginning. It can take years to build the good relationships that will lead to an order. Here we have something called '*laganan lama*', the long-standing customer. It applies as much to you selling textile machinery as to the woman buying a chicken in the market."

Stuart lifted his head off the seat back and sat upright.

"I suppose you are right. I didn't have much hope for any of those, but I still feel deflated."

"Tonight," Anwar started to say, "tonight my car will come for you at eight o'clock to the hotel," he continued.

"That's if we ever get home," Stuart answered as the car halted again.

Anwar laughed. "That's if we ever get home," he repeated, "and then we will go out and have some dinner together. Yesterday we had Indonesian and today nothing much at lunchtime so tonight we must try something else."

"What about your wife and family?" Stuart asked, trying to be polite.

"Not your problem. My wife is very understanding about my business." Anwar waved his right hand in a dismissive gesture. "The most important thing is the choice of food."

Stuart thought hard but could come to no real feeling about what he wanted. "What do you have in Jakarta?" he asked.

"Anything you want. Indonesian of course, Chinese, Italian, Korean, French, Japanese, whatever you want."

"I've never tried Japanese."

"Japanese it is," Anwar said directly, almost before Stuart had finished speaking. "A good choice," he continued. "Eight o'clock and we will go to a little place I know not so far from your hotel."

They rounded a corner and were in sight of the hotel. The car halted and the doorman held the door for Stuart.

"Eight o'clock?" he asked.

Anwar smiled back. "Eight o'clock," he repeated.

Stuart climbed the steps and watched the car leave. He called for his key.

"Hello Mr Morgan." The same girl with glasses was on duty. "I'll just check for messages," she said as she handed him the key. She tapped on the computer terminal hidden below the counter level. "No. No messages for you," she said, scanning the screen.

At eight o'clock sharp Stuart was collected by Anwar. Stuart had slept for an hour, and he felt much refreshed, especially after a shower. The traffic flowed much more freely at this hour and they arrived at the restaurant, unimaginatively named Tokyo, in no more than fifteen minutes. The street in which the restaurant stood was lined with a number of small stalls and open-air eating places. They were lit with hurricane lamps or gas lights and shielded with thin canvas advertising cloths hanging vertically from the roofs. Rows of benches were laid out. The people cooked, served and washed up in tiny kitchens mounted on the curious contraptions similar to those that Stuart had noticed being pushed along the road on his first journey into Jakarta from the airport. He looked closely at them as they passed.

"*Kaki Lima*," Anwar explained, noticing Stuart's interest. "Five feet," he translated.

"Five feet?" Stuart asked puzzled.

"Yes. Two wheels, a stand to rest on and the man's two feet: five feet," he laughed. "Some say that the best food in the country comes from these places. We can try one day if you are feeling brave."

Stuart nodded in polite, but unsure agreement, "Yes, I'd love to try but I worry about my stomach."

"No problem. I will choose the best for you." Anwar patted him on the shoulder.

They wove in and out of the stalls and entered the restaurant through a small door. Inside, the restaurant was in total and complete contrast to the scene outside. Air-conditioned and cool, clean, neat and beautifully arranged in the classical Japanese tradition; it was another world from the street outside. The waitresses, whilst they were all Indonesian, were dressed in Japanese traditional costumes. Anwar spoke to one girl and they were shown to a strange looking table. The centre of the table was a large, flat, stainless steel surface. Around the edge was an area laid with place mats and chop sticks.

"*Tepanyaki*," Anwar said. "I am sure that you will like it."

A hatted chef appeared and began to lay out a variety of foods on and around the stainless steel plate. Stuart was enthralled. The cook plied his trade with considerable panache, waving the knives around and holstering them at his side with a spin of which John Wayne would have been proud. The food was delicious, a mixture of tastes and textures.

They drank hot sake. It was a new drink to Stuart, but one he liked instantly. They talked and laughed their way through the meal, becoming more friendly as the evening wore on. Stuart was impressed by Anwar's business activities. He owned factories and import licences and moved in very high political circles. 'Why', Stuart wondered, 'should he be spending time on a seemingly improbable venture with Ormistons?' Still Stuart was glad that he was and was glad of his presence.

After the meal, for which Anwar paid, Stuart was dropped at his hotel. Anwar declined the offer of a further drink as it was already almost eleven o'clock. Stuart watched him leave from the steps of the hotel. He looked at the entrance to The Inne on his right. He turned and began to ascend the steps, then, as if drawn by a magnet, he stopped and turned towards The Inne's entrance. He descended the stairs. 'Just one drink,' he thought to himself. Just one drink, the world-famous start to many a night of drunken debauchery.

The Manila Seven band were on stage when he entered. As he walked in, the girl on the end of the stage closest to him turned and smiled while she sang. She raised her left hand a little in a half wave to him. He looked and recognised the girl, Frances, who had talked to him the previous evening. He smiled back.

He stood at the corner of the bar and ordered a beer. He felt very full after the Japanese meal and sake. He did not feel drunk but drinking the beer made him feel even more full and congested. He noticed the two Americans, Hank and Rick, on the other side of the bar. They acknowledged him by raising their glasses together. Stuart made his way over to them.

"How you doin' there, Stuart?" Rick asked with an extended hand.

Stuart shook hands with Hank and Rick before he answered.

"Not so good, not so bad," he replied vaguely.

"This country's like this. You'll get used to it. Just remember that they need stuff from the West to help them. Without us they 'ain't got no development. So you just hang in there, give it a few months and then see where you are," Hank said. It was the first time that he had spoken. Up to this point he had been a silent partner in the Hank and Rick double act.

Stuart guessed that what he was saying was good advice. Time was the important thing. He had, and his company too, to be patient, to play the system and follow Mr Anwar's rules. Stuart tried to put the problems of work and the day's events out of his mind. The dancing ladies before him provided ample distraction.

The Manila Seven band finished singing after one more song, promising to return after forty-five minutes. Frances and the rest of the group had disappeared behind the bar as soon as they had finished. Stuart had looked around to see if he could see her, but they were nowhere to be seen. He felt a pang of disappointment. They were replaced almost immediately by an all-male Indonesian band who sang Beatles and Beach Boys numbers and one heavy metal track by Deep Purple. They were good but lacked the life and flair and feminine charms of the Filipino band. Stuart talked with the two Americans for most of the time the Indonesian band played. As they played their last song, Hank and Rick left.

Stuart remained, hoping to talk to Frances again. The Filipino band returned about an hour after they had left. The three singers mounted the stage quickly without pausing amongst the audience. The first up on the stage introduced the band. In turn the three girls offered welcome to the guests that they knew. Frances, the last to speak, looked at Stuart during her introduction time. "And hello to Mr Stuart from England," she said, smiling and looking directly at him.

He smiled back. He was on cloud nine after that: he felt as if his feet were not touching the floor and that if he moved away from the barrel table against which he was leaning he would fall to the floor. Feelings ran through him which he had not experienced since he was a young man. The feelings associated with the first glance from the older girl at school on whom he had had had a crush, the time the girl at university, who had been voted the sexiest during the first week of term, had walked up to him and led him on to the dance floor during the slow bit. 'It is stupid', he told himself, 'for a man of my age, married with two children, to feel like this about a woman – no, a girl, a small woman, a childish ungrown-up singer, whom I have seen no more than three times and whom I have talked to for three minutes.'

He had always had very strong emotions, had been very quick to become infatuated and to fall in love. He had never had the succession of one night stands that so many of his friend had had at university. He had always 'fallen in love', or so his friends told him. Now, in Jakarta, he was doing it again: the same old feelings were rushing back for this slim, delicate Filipina.

They sang and he watched. The time passed quickly. She looked at him and smiled a number of times, but then, he told himself, she looked at many people and smiled. And yet he felt that there was something else. He was convinced that she looked at him more often than anyone else. Or was his mid-thirties male ego playing tricks on him?

At the end of the final set of songs, he watched hopefully for her, hoping that she would come and talk to him. He was far too shy to go and talk to her. She stood with half of the group at a barrel table about ten feet away. She talked and laughed with her group and a number of guests. She pouted and frowned in that cheeky girlish manner which he was beginning to find irresistible. She was, he decided, an extremely attractive ungrown-up woman, all woman in fact: there was nothing ungrown-up about her body. She and the rest of the group turned to leave and Stuart felt a quick burst of panic that she was about to leave without his having the chance to say something stupidly inane as he usually did. She had started to walk away and he felt as though his worst fears were being realised, and then she turned towards Stuart. His sinking heart leapt as she did so. She let the rest of the group go and walked towards him. His heart rode up into his mouth, his throat went tight and dry and the butterflies took off in his stomach.

She smiled at him as she approached. "Hello Mr Stuart from England," she said cockily.

"Hello Fran," he replied rather lamely.

"You only come late," she continued, dropping her head forward and looking up at him with her big brown eyes.

"I had to go out to dinner with my business colleague. Are you on tomorrow? Singing, I mean," he asked.

"Yes, of course. Only Thursday is holiday. So now I must sleep or maybe I go to disco," she said playfully, her head on one side. "No, I will sleep. See you tomorrow. You have any request for tomorrow?" She turned to leave. "You think and tell me tomorrow and I will play for you." With a big smile and a squeeze of his arm she finally walked away, leaving a thirty-seven year old schoolboy enraptured in her wake.

Stuart's feet did not touch the ground all the way back to his room and his sleep was filled with a hundred crazy dreams.

Stuart woke early, unsure if he had dreamed the previous evening or not. He was still not sure when he arrived at the offices of Mr Anwar an hour or so later. He saw Anwar briefly before Anwar left for another business appointment. Stuart had no appointments or commitments so he spent the day preparing a presentation for the following day's meetings. Anwar had left his secretary at Stuart's disposal and he was able to prepare a written and overhead slide presentation. He already had a number of slides and some text from the UK. With the secretary's help, he tailored the standard company spiel into something more suitable for the smaller companies he was to visit.

The day passed agonisingly slowly. He could only think about the prospects for the evening, when he should go to The Inne, what he should wear, how he should behave. He rehearsed countless dialogues over and over in his mind, trying to find a way to take his budding friendship with the singer further. In the end he became more and more confused. His final conclusion was to just wait and see what happened.

Anwar returned late in the afternoon and they had a brief discussion about the following day's programme. Stuart prayed to himself that Anwar would not ask him out for dinner again. He didn't and, as he dropped Stuart off at the hotel, Stuart breathed a big sigh of relief. It was now six-thirty and Stuart went directly to his room to prepare.

One hour later he entered The Inne again. A rather poor group was on the small stage singing country and western songs with little enthusiasm. Stuart saw the two Americans sitting at a long table. He walked over to join them. There was no sign of Frances or her group. The table was screened from the stage by a glass and wood partition that ran along the edge of the bar.

Between it and the bar were a number of swivel stools and places to stand. The long table was close to the doorway at the end of the bar whence all the food and the group usually emerged. Stuart sat with his back to the stage, facing this door.

"Hi. How you doin', Stuart?" asked Rick as Stuart sat down.

"Great. Mind if I join you?"

"Sure, no problem."

A waiter arrived with two menus. "Two stone steaks for me and Hank, tenderloin if you please, my man." He paused and glanced at Stuart. "And for you, Stuart?"

"What the hell's a 'stone steak'?" Stuart asked, bemused.

"You bin here more than one night and you ain't never had a stone steak?" Hank asked with an incredulous expression on his face.

Stuart shook his head.

"OK, that's three tenderloin stone steaks on my bill."

"Hey no, on my bill," Stuart interrupted.

"I spoke first," growled Hank in mock anger.

Stuart raised his hands.

"OK," he said in equally mock fear. "Put the beer on my bill. Three beers please."

"OK, fair trade," Hank laughed.

They talked about the traffic, the weather, the hotel, the Indonesian system; it was the usual stuff of bar conversations between people newly met. A salad arrived for each of them, Stuart wanted to save it for his steak but Hank and Rick tucked in so Stuart followed suit. Copying people's habits abroad had been one of Stuart's ways of ensuring social acceptability. Unlike a number of his colleagues, he had always deferred to the manners and customs of the countries he visited. He had found it a way of getting very quickly close to people; he was usually well-liked, a good social performer at any level.

A waitress appeared and fixed small aprons around the three of them. Then the stone steaks appeared one after the other. A piece of raw steak sat atop a small slab of grey stone. The steak was sizzling, indicating that the stone was very hot. The two Americans began to cut the steak up and cook small pieces on the hot stone. Little pots of mustard, chilli sauce and tomato ketchup were provided to dip the cooked pieces of meat in. It was an unusual and tasty way to eat steak. Stuart thoroughly enjoyed the food and the three beers that accompanied it.

"The steak was good," Stuart said.

"The best from the USA, of course," Hank replied, waving his fork around with a piece of beef still attached.

When they had finished and the table had been cleared, they ordered a further beer. The country and western band had stopped playing and Stuart became aware of movement behind the door he was facing. His breath shortened a little and his stomach tightened: the schoolboy was back. The Filipino group began to emerge from the door and made their way towards the stage down the passageway between the bar and partition. Stuart saw Frances.

She did not appear to see him and continued with the rest past the bar.

He turned and disappointedly watched her go, with a sinking heart. He turned back to face the Americans. Then he became strongly aware of a presence behind his right shoulder. A small hand rested lightly on his shoulder. He turned to see Frances beaming down at him. Her long, wavy hair was taken up in a tight bun on the top of her head, and the clean, beautiful lines of her face were revealed in an entirely different way. She smiled again.

"Hello Mr Stuart from England," she said after a moment.

"Hello Fran from Manila," he repeated back with a smile. He was acutely aware of the small hand on his shoulder, her presence, the smell of her perfume so close to him.

A waiter struggling with a tray full of glasses passed behind her and her right hip pressed into his side. It was like an electric shock for him. He was quite unprepared for the feelings. Even after the waiter had passed, the pressure from her thigh remained.

"You come early tonight just to see me," she said in an irresistibly pouty way. "And my group, of course!" she added with a laugh.

"But mainly you," he said in a low voice.

She smiled down at him. Then she noticed the two Americans and smiled a silent greeting at them before returning to Stuart.

"What do you want me to sing?" she asked.

"How about *We Don't Need Another Hero*?" he asked. "The one by Bonnie Tyler. You know it?"

"Yes, I know that one. It's OK, in the second set. Now I must go and sing." A big smile beamed down at him and she was gone.

"Well, what do you know?" said Hank. "I've been watching those girls sing for nigh on four months and I've never talked to one or said hello and here's this goddamn' Limey guy after a few days talking very intimate with the best of them. What your aftershave?" Hank laughed.

Stuart made an embarrassed shrug of his shoulders. "I don't know. She just came to talk to me the other night and I've done nothing."

The two Americans laughed and gave him knowing looks.

"Honestly," Stuart protested.

The group began to introduce themselves and to say hello to the various guests. Stuart turned his head and could just see Frances on the end of the stage closest to him. She saw him looking at her.

"And a special hello to Mr Stuart from England," she said with a big smile in his direction. If Stuart had been walking off the ground last night, now he was flying.

He turned to the two Americans. They looked at him and shook their heads.

They left the long table and went to the front of the bar to stand by one of the barrel tables. From here Stuart got a good view of the clothes that the three singers were wearing. All three had their hair in tight buns. Their costume was a black one-piece suit made from shiny material. The suits were very baggy, but gathered tightly at the ankles, waist and wrists. At the neck they finished in a tight, high collar. Despite the bagginess of the clothes, the tight waistband and the shiny, slightly clingy nature of the cloth followed the curves of waist and bottom exquisitely. The sleeves were split from the wristband to the elbow and then from there to the shoulder. The legs of their outfits were also split from the ankle to above mid-thigh. As they moved around the stage, the audience was treated to tantalising glances of leg. Stuart found the whole costume, coupled with the movements made as they sang and danced, far more sexy than had they been cavorting around naked.

The singing was as good as before. He did not get bored with hearing some of the same songs as previous evenings, for they were such good entertainment. Frances kept looking at him while she sang and big smiles came his way all the way through. At the end of the first set, the group disappeared straightaway with no pause for the crowd.

Then after twenty minutes they returned to the bar and began to mix with the audience. Frances didn't come to talk to him. Instead she stood with one other member of the group and four men who stood beside the barrel table next to Stuart's. She talked and laughed with them in her expressive, extrovert way. Stuart felt jealousy coming, something he hadn't felt since his early days at university: the schoolboy was here again. But all the while she talked, she kept glancing at Stuart, furtive little glances with expressive eyes. His feelings of jealousy lessened with every glance from her big brown eyes. She moved around the group of men until she was very close to Stuart, facing away from him. He stood, half facing the stage, with his right elbow resting on the barrel table. Her back faced him and she was leaning against the adjacent barrel table. He could see the shape of her waist and bottom outlined against the black shiny material. Her figure was very slim. As she moved he caught a glimpse of well-muscled thigh through the slit. Then, quite deliberately, she moved her bottom in his direction. He stood perfectly still, looking at the stage, waiting for the moment of contact. It seemed an age of tantalising delay before she had moved enough, but her left thigh made contact with his very gently, very slowly, but completely deliberately. She didn't push or rub, but just held a slight contact. It seemed to go on for ever, but suddenly the other group finished singing and it was time for the Manila Seven band once again. Frances stood straight up, ending the contact. His thigh felt hot and his heart was pounding in his chest. She looked at him and smiled and gave a half wink. Then she was on the stage again. He was sure that the whole bar was looking at them, but his two American friends were watching the stage intently. He ordered another beer for them all.

Halfway though the second set of songs, Frances took the microphone in the centre of the stage, her two colleagues took the outside ones.

"Now time for a request," she said. "Especially for Mr Stuart from England, we will sing *We Don't Need Another Hero*." And she sang.

The other two girls kept her company, dancing and singing part of the accompaniment. Then, when they had finished, Frances took the microphone again as the other two left the stage. "And now a Tina Turner song, *Private Dancer*." Frances sang the song by herself with more passion and feeling than the original singer, Tina Turner, if that was possible. Despite the small, slim size of her body, her voice was deep and rich and the sound so similar to that of Tina Turner's that Stuart was sure that if you had closed your eyes it would have been difficult to tell the difference. But with Frances moving around the stage dressed in that manner, he was not closing his eyes to find out. When she finished, the guests clapped and cheered. She stood and bowed, sweat glistening on her, a testament to her effort and emotion.

The other two girls took the stage for the next song, leaving Frances at the back, who looked emotionally and physically drained.

At the end of the second set, she disappeared straightaway towards the toilets. When she returned she stood next to Stuart at the table with his two American friends. She looked up into his eyes.

"Good songs. You sing them better than Tina Turner and Bonnie Tyler," he said.

She smiled. "Do you mean that?"

"Mmmm, of course, you're just so good," he said, really meaning it.

"Who are your friends?" she asked

"Hank and Rick," Stuart said.

The two Americans raised their glasses as an acknowledgement of their formal introduction. Apart from this, they let Frances and Stuart talk undisturbed.

"Do you want a drink or something?" Stuart asked.

"Aqua," she said

"Aqua?" Stuart asked, puzzled.

"Yes, just plain bottled water."

Stuart ordered the water and some more beer.

"Are you married?" she asked him suddenly.

He was taken aback. How to answer? Lie and say no and risk her finding out some other way, or be honest and admit and risk her walking away and ignoring him. He decided to be honest – he was a lousy liar anyway.

"Married, with two children," he said without making it sound like an admission of guilt.

She looked at him without a change of expression.

"I think your children very pretty for the girl and very handsome for the boy." She laughed. "Because the father very handsome and I know the wife too very pretty. All pretty from England, yes?"

He was surprised at her response.

She could see his surprise.

"Most of the Europe men who come in here have a wife," she said with a cheeky smile, "but they do not usually say they have a wife, but I can tell if they do." She looked at him hard, "You are honest man. I like if you true and not lie." She smiled and laughed. The interrogation, the test of his character over, she returned to her original self. The drink arrived and she sank the whole bottle in one gulp.

"You work hard," Stuart said

She laughed. "Not as hard as you!"

"I know," he said. "I work ten hours every day. You only three and you enjoy it."

She pouted and put her head down like a scolded child. "No I don't, I hate it."

"I suppose you want to work in a factory making shirts," he said. "I see many girls in the factories making shirts."

"Where?" she asked.

"In many places, I sell the machines for making cloth," he continued, trying to make his job sound interesting.

"Can you make me some new clothes?" She pushed herself into a mockery of a model's pose, hips pushed left, right hand on her hip and her left hand on her head. He looked at her in silence and raised one eyebrow. She looked at the single eyebrow, suddenly relaxing the model's pose. "Do that again."

He repeated the trick and she stared at him. It took him a second to realise that she had made her big, beautiful, brown eyes completely cross-eyed. They both laughed at their private, intimate joke, a joke that no one else in the bar had shared.

Then it was time to play again. He ordered some more beer. The two Americans were getting quite drunk.

Hank put his arm on Stuart's shoulder. "Hey, my Limey friend, give me some of your aftershave, I need some help!" The three of them descended into a silly alcoholic conversation with little or no meaning. The third and final set ended very quickly, or so it seemed to Stuart. The girls disappeared to the toilet again straightaway. When they returned the two Americans were shaping up to leave. They were both well gone.

"Hey, we gotta pay for the beer, man," said Rick.

"Naw, the Limey's payin' for the beer," replied the other.

"OK, we go."

Stuart had the sudden strange notion that the two of them were gay, but maybe he was just drunk.

Frances and the rest of the group returned and spread out amongst the remainder of the audience. The other group played and Stuart stood alone. After a quarter of an hour the Manila Seven band were leaving one by one until only Frances and one other singer were left. They stood talking to a group of men at the other side of the bar. Stuart decided that he had had enough beer and called for his bill. He signed it and turned to leave. As he did so, he caught Frances's eye and smiled. Quickly she made her excuses to the other men and went after the departing Stuart. Stuart had already turned away and begun to walk unsteadily towards the exit and Frances's approach was unnoticed by him. She caught him up in a few strides.

"Are you leaving now?" she said with a disappointed look in her eyes.

"Yes, I have some work tomorrow and it's important."

Her hand rested on his right arm. He looked at her. Her eyes looked back in a strange way. There was, for a second, an expression of something that Stuart dare not consider.

"Well, good night and sleep well," she said. Then quickly, before Stuart knew what was happening, she put her right hand high up on his arm and gently pulled him forward while she stretched upward towards him. She pouted her lips and in an instant kissed him, not on the cheek, but fully on the lips. It lasted no more a fraction of a second but no kiss in his life to that day had had more of an effect on him. He just stared at her, this slim, muscular Filipina dressed in black, shiny clothes whom he hardly knew, yet there she was looking up at him with, well with what? He could not even think it, he dare not even think it – all he could do was to look at the emotion in those big, brown eyes.

"Sleep well," she said again, squeezing his arm.

He made no attempt to touch her, hold her or repeat the kiss.

She turned away and went back to the bar. She didn't look back.

When she had left through the door by the bar, he turned and walked slowly to his room.

In his room, he mechanically picked up the phone and asked for a morning call at seven, in little more than five hours' time. Then he lay down to sleep. Sleep did not come; instead the room began to spin, and this time it was not to do with the light-headed feeling of the kiss. He was faced with the awful realisation that, like Hank and Rick, he had had more than sufficient beer to drink and now he was paying the price. He jumped out of bed as a particularly rotating motion came to the room and rushed into the bathroom. He sat on the toilet and cradled his head in his hands. After a good five minutes, during which he evacuated his bowels, he returned to bed. Ten minutes later the room performed another double-back somersault in the pike position, and Stuart realised that his battle with beer was almost at an end. Again he rushed to the bathroom but this time instead of sitting he crouched in front of the white toilet bowl, resting his head on the rim.

"I'm on the rim of the bowl looking down in the water," he sang tunelessly to himself in a poor imitation of the Carpenters' hit. "I'm on the top of the world, and the only explanation I can find is the fourteen pints of lager that I've supped. It's the nearest thing to purgatory that I've seen," he continued. And then his stomach heaved and the stone steak and beer came back for a second visit.

Five minutes later he fished the last bit of food out from behind his teeth and spat into the toilet bowl. He flushed the toilet for the fourth time and then staggered uneasily to bed. This time he slept. He had barely four hours to his morning call. His mind was blank and there was not one crazy dream to disturb his alcohol-enriched – or should it be alcohol-denuded – mind.

## CHAPTER 5

## A WRONG WORD

Right on time, at seven o'clock, the telephone on the bedside table, a mere three inches from Stuart's inert head, rang out. Groping uncertainly into consciousness, his left hand reached out and took the receiver.

"Hello yes," he mumbled.

"Good morning Mr Morgan, your morning call at seven o'clock," a chirpy little voice said at the other end of the phone.

"Thanks, I'm awake," he said, not completely convinced. 'How the hell can anybody be so cheerful at this time in the morning when I feel like this?' he pondered, as he slowly raised himself into a sitting position. He hadn't felt as rough as this for many years. He remembered throwing up in the bathroom and sighed loudly. He cradled his head in his hands as he sat on the edge of the bed. Finally he stood up and walked over to the window. As he moved, he became very aware of the pain in his head. He drew the curtains and looked at the bustling Jakarta traffic below. The sun hurt his eyes a little.

For the second time in as many minutes, Stuart decided that he felt bad. He moved to the bathroom. His eyes were red and the bags beneath well-defined. He put out his tongue and looked at it critically before putting it away. He looked down at the toilet where bits of dried vomit were stuck around the rim of the bowl. He was embarrassed about his behaviour and got down on his knees to clean it up before the chambermaid came in. He had a shower and washed his hair, after which he felt well enough to go downstairs for a light breakfast.

By the time Anwar's car arrived for him at eight o'clock he was feeling about five per cent reasonable as opposed to the zero per cent he had felt at seven o'clock. Two paracetamol had had an effect on his headache and the only lasting effect was a stiff neck which must have been from sleeping in a strange position.

Anwar was waiting for him at the office. They shook hands.

"Are you OK, Stuart?" Anwar asked, looking at Stuart with a concerned expression. "You look washed out. Is it some stomach trouble?"

"Yes, it was stomach trouble last night," Stuart admitted gravely.

"Oh, I'm sorry, do you want me to cancel the appointment today?" Anwar said in genuine concern.

Stuart smiled. "The only trouble with my stomach was self-induced, overloaded with liquid refreshment."

Anwar's worried face broadened into a smile. He clapped Stuart heartily on the back. "I understand. Tonight I will invite you to my house and keep control of you," he laughed.

The first meeting was scheduled for ten o'clock. They arrived in good time and were not kept waiting long. Stuart's presentation lasted almost forty-five minutes. Eight people attended. They looked impressed and received the handouts with gratitude. Stuart asked for questions.

"Mr Morgan," began one small bespectacled man.

"Yes?" said Stuart as helpfully as he could.

"I already know your company name. You are very big company, you sell very big machines. Why do you want to see a small company like me?" he asked.

Stuart considered his reply carefully. "Well," he began, "we may be very big but we think that we have a wide range of equipment. We can find something for everyone so you should not worry about dealing with us. You are a small company but I think you are a very ambitious company and want to get bigger. With our range we can help you to expand and increase your capacity in small steps. And we can finance supplying equipment."

The ears of the audience pricked up at this statement.

"Do you mean you will fund investment?" the same man asked.

"No, not ourselves, but we can arrange finance or investment from development agencies or private places. We are very experienced in exporting," Stuart replied.

Now that he had them interested the questions kept coming. The final result was that Stuart agreed to come and look at the factory on a future trip and work out a joint financing arrangement for some equipment.

"You don't often get so many questions like that," Anwar said as they left the meeting and headed for the car. "You were very good this morning. That was a good meeting. We got further than I hoped." He smiled at Stuart. "I said we could do business together and I was right."

They had a good lunch and a second meeting in the afternoon almost as good as the first. Stuart returned to his hotel in time for a quick swim before the darkness and the mosquitoes closed in. He had two hours before Anwar was due to collect him in order to 'keep him under control'. In the quiet of his room, relaxed after a long hot shower, Stuart at last began to think and remember the events of the night before. Was he drunk and dreaming or had she really kissed him? And if she had, why had she done that?

She knew he was married, she knew he was only in Jakarta for a few days. Maybe she was very clever at trapping men and getting things from them, maybe... maybe. His head swam with the possibilities. Then he remembered that the day was Thursday, another twenty-four hours to wait before he could see her again as this was the Manila Seven band's one day off. It seemed an eternity. He was glad that Anwar had offered to look after him in the evening. The idea of spending the evening alone did not appeal at all.

Downstairs in the lobby, he waited quietly for Anwar's car to pick him up. It arrived on time. Anwar's house was a large, ostentatious, two-storied, detached house with huge pillars by the entrance and a staircase fit for Ginger and Fred. It was located in an area of Jakarta called Kemang. It was an area of large houses, expensive flats and many bars, restaurants and import shops. Anwar explained that it was one of the main expatriate living areas.

Anwar introduced Stuart to his wife, a diminutive lady with glasses and a big smile. She was very quick-witted and spoke superb English. He also met their three children, two girls aged twelve and ten and a boy of five. The eldest girl was growing into an attractive young lady. Stuart remarked that she would break many boys' hearts in the years to come. Her father nodded sagely and her mother just laughed.

An excellent dinner of Indonesian specialities was eaten. By the end Stuart was full and sleepy. At ten-thirty, Anwar called his driver and bid Stuart farewell for the evening. Stuart got back to the hotel by eleven o'clock and by eleven-fifteen he was sound asleep.

Friday was much like Thursday had been, except that Stuart was not hungover. The meetings proceeded well and one of the two companies visited wanted to know more, and future meetings were agreed. They sat in the lounge of the hotel after the final meeting had been concluded. Anwar looked pleased.

"That was two days of good work, do you agree?"

"Yes, I think so, I think it will be very important to follow up quickly," Stuart replied.

"Mmmm, yes, I think so. But I have some, how shall I say, background work to do with these people. I know that your company will be helping them to finance and provide equipment, but as individuals they will expect something from your company for themselves for placing an order with you. This I must negotiate with them in private. It may take a few visits to sort it out. You should be patient with the Indonesian system. I think you should come back in one month or maybe six weeks."

"I am in your hands, Mr Anwar, you are the expert." Stuart massaged the ego a little.

Anwar smiled and shook his head in a dismissive gesture, "You are too kind." He paused.

Stuart guessed that he was about to talk about the sensitive subject of his commission and agency fee. Anwar slowly and deliberately sipped his tea. He held the cup with both hands above the table.

"Now that we seem to be making some progress, I think that we should discuss the..." He paused and sipped his tea again deliberately slowly. "...the arrangements," he continued. He put the cup down. "You see, for my company to represent yours and make representations for you takes time and effort." He looked at Stuart.

"But, of course, Mr Anwar. I realise that, and we are quite prepared to discuss arrangements with you." Stuart stopped and left the silence for effect.

"I think that our best prospects are with those small companies that we saw today and yesterday. What will a typical order value be?" Anwar asked, probing for information.

"Difficult to say, but in the region of one hundred to two hundred thousand pounds sterling, I suppose," Stuart replied with a shrug of his shoulders.

"Well, for such small orders I must put in as much work as I would for a big order so..." Anwar shook his head with an expression of defeat and difficulty on his face.

It was a game Stuart knew and Anwar knew, but Stuart too knew a few tricks. "Of course, Mr Anwar, we both know that we are just starting out in this venture. If we make some small sales with these small companies and they begin to grow then maybe the bigger ones will take an interest. So both of us must be prepared to work hard for little return today but maybe a big return tomorrow."

"Ahh, the classic English 'jam tomorrow' theory." Anwar laughed.

Stuart smiled. "Yes, I know, but we are prepared to make no profit and make a commitment to this market for, say, four or five years."

Anwar looked genuinely surprised. "As long as that? Most companies want to give up if they don't get overnight success." He took another drink of tea. "I think that for these small early contracts we must think about ten per cent of the price to arrange the deal."

Stuart was happy that Anwar had finally come out with a figure. To a certain extent Stuart had the upper hand as Anwar had given the first figure. The question of long-term commitment was open for discussion and Stuart knew that he would have to convince his managers when he got home of the suitability of the market. Stuart had expected a commission for Anwar in double figures and he was prepared to accept it up to ten per cent. Anwar's opening gambit was ten per cent. The decision was Stuart's.

"Mmmm," he said looking unhappily at Anwar.

Anwar's face looked a little upset when he saw Stuart's expression.

"That's rather high, especially for the first ones, to gain the foothold in the market," Stuart said doubtfully.

"But you must understand that I must work harder for the first order than for the rest, so my costs will be higher for this first one," Anwar said, raising his hands.

"I understand. So are our costs, but if we are both serious then we can make an arrangement now to cover the first one or two and then develop it later."

"Will you be dealing with this country?" he asked Stuart, regarding him closely.

"I hope so," Stuart replied.

"What is this 'hope so'?" Anwar asked, raising his voice ever so slightly. "I know you a little, I know I can trust you, you are a man I understand. If you don't want to work here then I don't know what the future is. Will the next man understand what we have discussed today or not? Will he know about it?"

Stuart was taken aback by Anwar's forcefulness. Stuart knew that Indonesia was a face to face society and that personal contact was extremely important in business. He also understood the point that Anwar was making: any verbal agreement between them would have no meaning for anyone else. Stuart's carrot for the low initial commissions was the possibility of higher commissions on later easier sales.

"Mr Morgan," he began formally, "I will make a strong plea to you for you to keep working here. Please try to make sure that this happens. If it is so then I can make a lower fee for the first one or two. Then we, you and I," he emphasised, "you and I will discuss further the future."

Stuart wanted seven and a half per cent. "OK, I think that five per cent for the first two orders would be the right figure."

Anwar looked at him seriously; he shrugged his shoulders, "I think we should split the difference, seven and a half." Anwar said this decisively, reaching for Stuart's hand. They shook hands immediately. "I will make a small paper, one copy for you, one copy for me. Tomorrow we will sign and we have an understanding for the future." Anwar pointed at Stuart. "You and I, Mr Morgan, you and I."

With the business finished, Anwar looked around towards the afternoon tea buffet laid out in the entrance to the lounge.

"Shall we take afternoon tea? It's frightfully English, you know," Stuart said in a posh accent.

"OK, why not?" replied Anwar, trying to emulate Stuart's voice. They both relaxed now that the business was done and the scene set: all they needed now was an order. After the tea and cakes, Anwar left Stuart. They agreed to meet on Saturday to tidy up the details of the agreement.

Stuart went up to the room and lay down on his bed for a rest. During his half sleeping, half daydreaming rest, he remembered Wednesday night and the kiss. The forty-eight hours, the two days, had passed relatively quickly despite his earlier longing for the time to pass. Now it was Friday night. He was looking forward to seeing Frances again – longing to see her. They would meet, talk, maybe kiss, maybe go to a disco, maybe, maybe...

His mind wandered around the possibilities for the evening: where would he end up with Frances? how would things develop? He allowed himself to dream a little too far, a little too much, to dream in forbidden territory. To dream of such things was to prevent them from ever happening, but still he dreamed.

Stuart did not want to go down to The Inne too early. He planned to eat down there, but he didn't want to sit around waiting, drinking and getting too drunk. He pottered around his room, bathing, washing his hair, choosing, at great and unusual length, his clothes, even down to his underpants. He managed to use up a couple of hours and set off just before eight o'clock.

The same dull group were singing as on Wednesday. He saw the two Americans sitting at a table adjacent to the one they had eaten at on the Wednesday. He moved over to join them.

"You sobered up yet?" Hank asked Stuart with a grin.

"Just about. I didn't come down here last night. I was somewhat tired and emotional on Wednesday," Stuart replied.

"Me neither. I had one hell of a headache on Thursday morning," Hank said.

"I was fine," said Rick, smiling in a superior manner.

"Well, I guess you missed out on a few beers then 'cause you are usually the first to go." Hank punched him gently.

They had already ordered food. Stuart settled for a bowl of soup and some bread rolls accompanied by the inevitable beer. They decided to keep the bills separate this evening.

Frances and the rest of the group entered just after the food had arrived. She either didn't see him or chose to ignore him at first. She continued past the bar, on the far side of the screen to Stuart. He returned to his food.

Hank nudged him under the table. "Here she comes," he whispered.

Stuart looked round to see Frances at the top of the two stairs that led down from the seating area around the bar to the bar itself. She was looking around. Stuart wondered whether or not to wave, but before he could come to a decision she saw him and smiled. She made her way gracefully through the collection of tables and chairs towards him. She, and the rest of the girls in the group, were dressed in red, skin-tight, slightly shiny leggings which came down to mid-calf level. On the top they wore white baggy shirts with long tails which hung down below a wide black belt, like a small skirt. Their hair was just left long and flowing. On the way over to Stuart she said hello to a number of guests. Finally she reached Stuart's table. She smiled and said hello to the two Americans. Then she rested her right hand on Stuart's shoulder.

"Hello Mr Stuart. You always eating in here?" she said, moving her hand off his shoulder and replacing it with her elbow, bringing herself closer to him. She leaned forward and picked up a small piece of bread. Playfully she dipped it in the soup and fed Stuart with it.

"I have to eat," he said with mock childishness as he chewed.

"You are already too fat," she said, pointing at his stomach and pouting at him.

"That's because I come down here to watch you and I must drink beer all night."

She laughed. Then, standing up, she squeezed his shoulder. "I must go now, see you later." She turned and moved towards the stage.

"Well, I do declare our Stuart's gone and got himself in love." Hank grinned broadly at Stuart when Frances was out of earshot.

Stuart shrugged his shoulders. "I don't know why. This isn't usual for me – it's never happened before like this." He shook his head in disbelief at his own situation. Maybe the dreams were reality after all. Again he allowed himself the luxury of that thought.

They finished their food in silence. Another round of beer arrived and then they left the table for the smoky alcoves set into the screen around the bar. From there they could see the group. Stuart got his usual introduction from Frances and she even said hello to Hank and Rick. The singing and playing was up to its usual high standard. The whole bar was buzzing with excitement and enjoyment. Stuart couldn't remember the last time he had been in a bar with such a good atmosphere. Even the normally disgusting smell of smoke seemed to be an integral and necessary part of the complete scene. Stuart was enjoying himself and the beer was flowing. Wednesday night's little 'accident' was forgotten. At the first break another band came on that Stuart had not seen before. They too were very good, specialising in Eric Clapton and Blues Brothers' songs.

Frances and the rest of the girls had disappeared immediately they finished singing, and it was some fifteen minutes before they reappeared. They split up and went to talk to different groups of people. Frances talked to some people seated at a table on the other side of the bar. After a few minutes she left them and made her way over towards Stuart and the Americans.

"You sing pretty good," Hank said.

"Thank you very much," Frances replied with a polite smile.

Stuart noticed the difference in her smile when she turned to smile at him. To him she was warm and genuine, to others she was warm and friendly but there was a definite distance, a definite message to keep back just a little: with Stuart there was no such message. She took the bottle of water Stuart had got for her and drank half of it in a single gulp.

"Thirsty work," he said, trying to think of good witty conversation. He was a little tongue-tied in her presence, afraid of her beauty and aura, afraid that the dream before his eyes would vanish.

"You have a work tomorrow?" she asked, eyeing him with her head on one side.

"Yeah a little. I've got to make a deal with my Indonesian friend here. It should only take a few hours. Why?"

"Nothing," she said, tossing her head back and finishing the rest of the bottle. "Can you get me some brandy as well as water for the next break please?"

"Yes, of course." He was a little shocked at her request.

"It makes me sing good," she laughed, noticing Stuart's only partially disguised surprise.

"You don't need any help, your singing is great. I like it when you sing Tina Turner the best. Do you know..." He paused and glanced at Hank and Rick. They were engrossed in a conversation. "Do you know..." he repeated. He brought his head lower towards hers to indicate the slightly confidential nature of what he was about to say. She turned and looked at him so their faces were no more than a few inches apart. Her brown eyes looked straight into his, another of those moments. "I think", he said, without taking his eyes off her, "that my two American friends are gay."

She looked confused. "Gay?"

"Yeah, you know – queer, homo."

She burst out into a huge laugh which she quickly stifled with her left hand. "Yeah? You think so?" she said quietly, returning to her previous position a few inches from his face. She looked at him; as she did so her eyes seemed to mist a little. Then she stood up and looked at the two Americans more closely. After a few moments of concentration, she pulled his shirt, wanting him to come lower so that she could whisper in his ear. In a serious voice she said, "Which one is husband and which one", she stifled a laugh, "is the wife?"

Stuart shrugged his shoulders and shook his head. He turned to whisper in her ear. "The one with the dress on," he whispered.

She laughed again. As he pulled slowly away from her ear she quickly turned her face towards his and stole a very quick kiss from his right cheek.

"Got to sing now," she said. "Don't forget, brandy."

He nodded in a daze. She mounted the stage and took the microphone for the next session.

The two Americans were still engrossed in their conversation so Stuart took the opportunity to look around the bar. It was very full. The guests were mainly either European men or Indonesian women. He guessed that some of the girls were call-girls. As he looked around, some of them tried to catch his eye or wink at him. They hung around with the various groups of men, talking, smoking, laughing and drinking. Some of the girls touched and held the men, while some of the men attempted to touch and fondle the girls. The obvious call-girls offered only token resistance to these advances, but some of the men tried it on with the waitress or even members of the group, to their evident disgust. The girls twisted out of the way of the groping arms of these men. Stuart was a little disgusted with the behaviour of the men. It was the sort of behaviour that would result in a mouthful of abuse or a slap if they had tried it in their own country. 'So they come here to behave like absolute arseholes,' thought Stuart.

Some of the girls and call-girls were very attractive. One in particular sat on a bar stool surrounded by men. Her hair was shoulder-length and well-styled. Her skin was darker than most of the girls in the bar, the colour that every white-skinned European woman wanted to be. Her eyes smouldered at anyone who looked her way. She made smoking a cigarette into an erotic act. She wore a very short dress revealing slim, shapely legs. As Stuart looked over, she blew smoke in his direction and gave him a smouldering stare. He looked away shyly. He was beginning to feel a little tired and slightly drunk. Watching the performance going on around him made him feel morose and depressed. He tried to snap out of it before the group stopped singing, but only partially succeeded.

As the group finished its second set of songs, Stuart ordered the water and brandy as instructed. Hank regarded him curiously.

"Mixing your drinks now, Stu?" he asked.

"No, it's a special order from Fran, I mean from the singer." Stuart gestured in her direction.

"Fran is it now? On first name terms are we?" Hank laughed.

The group, as usual, disappeared for a while. Frances returned first and eagerly came to the barrel table were Stuart and the Americans were now standing. She took the brandy and sank it in a single gulp. She smacked her lips together when she had finished.

"That was good," she said to Stuart. "Thank you very much." She now tackled the bottle of water. "Sometimes I need the brandy to make me feel good." She paused. "I get nervous when I sing sometimes."

"You do?" Stuart asked, surprised.

"Mmmm," she nodded.

"I find it hard to believe," Stuart said. "You all look so confident and in control up there." He pointed at the stage.

A group of European men accompanied by an equal number of Indonesian girls, including Miss Smoulder-Eyes, stood and made preparations to leave. Stuart watched them, feeling as upset as he had earlier on.

"Look at that," he said to Frances.

"What?" she asked, swivelling her head round.

"Those European men and the local girls: they're all businessmen or tourists and they just have to have a bit of South-East Asian girl. It's not nice – I don't like to see. They don't give the girls any respect," he continued in a morose tone.

"What do you mean?" she asked, her lovely face wearing an expression of confusion at his line of conversation.

"You know what those girls..." He paused. "Well, you know."

She looked at him, her expression changing slowly from confusion to anger.

"What makes you different from them?" she asked, her voice showing signs of irritation. "You are talking to me. Is that what you think I am, like those girls?" Her voice, expression and manner were now all anger where not one minute ago there had been pleasure and happiness. Stuart realised now what she was thinking, but it was too late to take back the words, too late to stop her, impossible to put the clock back those sixty short seconds. He floundered in panic, his stomach tightening, and felt as if his lower bowel was about to lose control.

"No, no!" he said, his eyes wild with panic. The dream before his eyes was disappearing in a sea of mist and nightmare.

"Of course not, I'm sorry, I didn't mean to upset you! I'm sorry, so sorry! I wouldn't upset you."

"But you think all us girls from Asia like that?"

"No, I don't."

"I swear," she began with moistening eyes, "I swear I just like to sing and go out. I am a good girl – on my heart I swear it." She crossed herself in the manner of a Roman Catholic. "I have one more time to sing then I go to my room to cry," she said, her eyes filling with tears. She turned and walked quickly away to the toilets.

"What the hell happened, Stuart?" Hank's voice broke into Stuart's nightmare. "She was bein' real friendly to you. In all my time comin' here she ain't never been as friendly as that to another guy, you know."

This made Stuart feel even worse: the idea that he had been different from the other guests and the difference was such that other people could see it.

Hank continued, "Someone even asked me if she was your girlfriend the other day. What the hell you say to her to make her run off like that?"

Stuart shrugged his shoulders helplessly. "Oh, I don't know, I guess I just said the wrong thing. She'll be OK," he said unconvincingly. Inside he was burning up with pain. He found it difficult to drink and his stomach was tight and twisted. He felt simultaneously sick and faint.

He looked around for Frances. She was nowhere to be seen. The rest of the group and the guests carried on the talk and laughter all around him. Their voices and laughter had faded in Stuart's consciousness and all he could hear was his own heart pounding in his ears. Then she appeared and joined a group of people on the other side of the bar. She laughed and joked with them, avoiding Stuart's eyes. Then she did look at him and, despite the laughter on her face, her eyes were sad and moist. She had been crying.

They mounted the stage and started singing again. Frances said hello to Stuart from the stage, her eyes looking at him sadly as she did so. The third and final set was sheer hell for Stuart. All the songs, especially those sung by Frances, seemed to tear him apart with emotion. At the end of the session the girls quickly disappeared as usual. When they returned, Frances stood with them within earshot of Stuart. They were talking with a group of European men.

"Come on, Fran," one of the other singers said. "You always want to dance on a Friday night, so why not tonight?"

"No, I want to sleep, I'm tired," she replied.

"You said you wanted to go earlier on," the other girl persisted.

Frances glanced unhappily at Stuart. "Yes I did then, but not now. I've got no one to go with." She flashed another glance at Stuart. "Not now," she added.

He realised that she had been hinting at him accompanying her later on to a disco. He felt the knife twist inside him again.

"You can go with me," a tall, youngish Australian said, grinning at her.

She gave him a disdainful look that made the poor man feel only inches tall.

"I said someone I wanted to go with. I don't want to go with you."

"Fran, it's OK, calm down." Her friend patted her arm gently.

"I'm going," Frances said quickly and turned towards the bar side exit. She didn't look at Stuart.

Stuart stared sadly into his beer. He finished it in a gulp then turned to make his way out. As he did so he noticed that Frances hadn't left: she was sitting by herself on a bar stool by the exit, sipping a bottle of water slowly through a straw. Up to this point in the relationship, Frances had always come to him, now he was going to her. The rules of the game between them had changed. He sat down beside her.

She sensed his presence but didn't look up. She let out a big sigh.

"I wanted to dance tonight," she said in a weak, little girl voice. "But you made me too sad." She turned to face him. "Why?"

"Oh God, Fran, I'm sorry! I didn't want to upset you or make you sad." He paused. "What can I say to make it right?"

"I don't know," she said, "but don't stop trying." She looked at him with hurt affection in her eyes. "I want to go and sleep now." She put her right hand on his left arm and squeezed it gently. "You're a good man, Mr Stuart," she said, "but I'm so sensitive about some things."

He put his right hand across on to her small hand. It was the first positive physical gesture that he had made towards her; unfortunately for him, it was probably going to be the last.

"Good night," she said finally and stood up. She smiled a sad smile then turned away.

"Bye and sorry, Fran," he called after her.

Then she was gone.

## CHAPTER 6

## PARTING

When Stuart awoke on Saturday morning, he felt in as much disharmony with himself as he had on Thursday morning. The reason was, however, very different. Thursday morning was excessive alcohol, Saturday morning was... was what? Love-sickness? No, Stuart decided, infatuation maybe, but whatever it was he did not feel good. It was early, a few minutes before seven, and he didn't have to meet Anwar until after ten. He lay in bed contemplating his situation. The stumble in the course of this relationship with Frances gave Stuart an easy way out of a decision that he had worried about not more than twelve hours before in the very same bed. During his dreams, the dreams he should not have dreamed, he had worried about the moment when his dream would come true. The moment with Frances when he would have to make the choice: to make love with her and be unfaithful to his wife for the first time or to turn Frances away. He was not sure about his willpower faced with a woman of her physical attractiveness and character. Now that decision, delicious as it would have been to have had to make, would not have to be made. He was, in a sort of a way, relieved about that. But even so, the decision, whichever way he would have made it, would have been a real moment in his life. To have succumbed would have meant a great deal of pleasure and some guilt; to have resisted would have given him the inner strength of having faced the ultimate temptation and resisted. It would probably have given him the undying respect of Frances and gained him a lifelong friend.

He got up after half an hour of such thoughts and washed and dressed without enthusiasm. He could not face breakfast. His stomach was still a twisted knot of tension and his head ached with a dull all-over throb. He took a couple of Paracetamol tablets to still the pain. He picked up the paper that had been pushed under his door and went downstairs to the coffee shop and ordered only tea. He drank slowly, reading the short four page newspaper which went under the name of *The Jakarta Post*. It contained a number of sections on city, local, regional and world news. He was surprised to find that the sports section contained a review of the day's prospects in the English and Scottish football leagues. Reading slowly, reading each article in detail whether or not he was interested in it, passed another hour or so. He had a quick wash and brush-up in his room and left early for his appointment with Anwar.

Most offices in Indonesia, it seemed, opened for all or part of Saturday. The atmosphere was a little more relaxed than during the week: some of the staff wore jeans or had no tie on. A few of them had children with them.

Anwar was undoubtedly more relaxed. He beamed at Stuart when he saw him enter the office.

"Sorry I'm early," said Stuart

"No problem. Let's go straight to my office and sort the business."

They entered Anwar's office. Despite the casualness of the day, the business at hand was deadly serious. Anwar handed Stuart a piece of paper without speaking. Stuart sat down and read it carefully. After he had read it a second time, he let his hand fall slowly to rest on his knee with the paper clutched firmly in it. Anwar had been watching him intently from his vantage point leaning against his desk.

"It is based on you, Stuart," Anwar said after a pause, "on our understanding, between the two of us. I hope that you can explain this to your superiors. I want to keep dealing with you until we have some orders and an organised set-up. After that I will deal with someone else, but before..." He stopped, it was not necessary to complete the sentence.

Stuart nodded in agreement. "I will make sure of it."

"Can we sign?" Anwar asked

"Yes, we can."

"Now, the next step," said Stuart when they had finished and secreted their respective copies, Stuart's in the briefcase, Anwar's in his desk.

"The next step. Well, you have created an opening and for now that is all you need to do. Now I must do some investigating and some talking, some arranging with those people."

"OK, I would like to come back some time in the near future to spend a number of days at each of the factories to try and assess their needs and put together a package for each of them. I will investigate the financial side and see what my company is prepared to do."

"Don't expect an order, any order, in less than..." Anwar shrugged his shoulders as he paused. "Say one year, if you're lucky, or two if you're average."

"It's my job to persuade the company to stick it for that long," Stuart said

"Yes, because the market is there. I want to break the hold of the Germany company in the field," Anwar replied excitedly.

"Why are you so keen to break the hold of this other company?" Stuart asked. "Do you have any special reason?"

"Well yes, I suppose so. Their agent is a great rival of mine and he's been taking work from me in recent years. This is a good way of returning the compliment."

"I hope that your commitment will be a long-term one," Stuart said slowly and seriously to emphasise the point.

"Of course. If we are successful then who knows." He waved his hand around in a wide circle. "When will you leave, Stuart?" Anwar asked, changing the subject and lightening the mood.

"Tomorrow, Sunday afternoon, I think, unless you have any reason to ask me to stay longer," Stuart replied.

"No, I don't think so. We can keep in touch. I will call you when I have arranged something. Give a few weeks, a month at the most."

"Fine," said Stuart

"What will you do for the rest of the day?" Anwar asked him as he stood to leave.

"Well, I must change my ticket at Singapore Airlines' office and then I would like to buy some presents for my family. Where's the best place?"

"Oh there are so many. You can try Ratu Plaza or, if you feel brave, Blok M. There's a big store there called Pasar Raya. You can buy most things inside, and outside you can buy a two dollar gold Rolex, or a Cartier or Gucci," he laughed.

"That sounds good – I'll go there. See you again next time."

"Yes, until we meet again. Goodbye Stuart and take care."
"Bye."

They shook hands and parted.

Stuart left the office and took a taxi to the Singapore Airlines' office. It was barely eleven in the morning. He changed the ticket, shopped, drank tea and ate a light lunch. The activity and bustle of Jakarta had made him forget the events of the previous evening. Now that he was in the hotel they came flooding back with clarity. He felt upset and hurt again: his stomach twisted up and his throat dried at the remembrance of those events. He had a swim in the pool to try to dispel the feelings and revive himself. It partially worked. After a shower he felt well enough to partake of afternoon tea in the ambassador lounge of the hotel. It was a lavish afternoon tea, with enough food to satisfy him completely for the rest of the evening.

By eight o'clock, after a two hour sleep, he was feeling better. So much so that a beer and some entertainment seemed like a good prospect. He wandered slowly downstairs. As he entered the bar, he began to feel that sick feeling in his stomach as it twisted up. His thirst disappeared and he began to wish that he hadn't eaten so much of the afternoon tea. He couldn't face a beer. He ordered a gin and tonic instead. On the corner of the bar, propped up against their usual barrel table, were Rick and Hank, the two Americans. He went over to join them.

"Howdy Stu," said Hank, patting him on the back.

Stuart was more convinced than ever that these two were gay. It didn't bother him at all; they were good company and didn't cause any problems. They talked about work, the world and the weather, the usual stuff of bar conversations. As the music of the first, inferior, group finished, Stuart's stomach tightened and his heart began to race. He could see the Filipino group beginning to emerge from the far side of the bar. He caught a glimpse of Frances.

Rick noticed Stuart looking. "Looking for your girlfriend?" he said, winking at Stuart.

Stuart shook his head, "She's not my girlfriend, never was. I've only ever talked with her a few times."

Rick looked at Stuart carefully. "Aw come on, you could see the way she was lookin' at you. You know it was more than usual."

Stuart shook his head lamely. "Maybe, maybe not."

The group took to the stage. Frances did not come to say hello to Stuart individually, but she did say hello to him during the introductions. They sang with the usual vigour, and all too soon the first session was over. Another group came on and began to play.

Frances and the rest of the group had disappeared at the end of the session as usual. They began to drift back into the bar about fifteen minutes later. Frances was the last to reappear. She looked nervous to Stuart, glancing around as if looking for someone. She went to talk to another group of men on the far side of the bar.

Rick noticed Stuart's disappointment, "I think you're out of favour tonight, buddy," he said, stating the obvious.

"We'll see," Stuart replied, trying to be confident. The gin and tonic was beginning to have an effect and he was feeling less tense. He switched to beer.

As the new group finished its session, the Manila Seven Band began to make its way back to the stage. Frances came quite close to Stuart although she did not need to. As she passed, she gave him a little smile. As they began to play their second session, the bar was filling up nicely. Stuart and the two Americans had their spot and were not going to move. The crush and atmosphere built as the group wound its way energetically through the routine. Again, almost before Stuart realised, the second session was over.

The band disappeared once again. Stuart decided to pay a visit to the toilet. It was crowded but very clean in the toilet. A smiling janitor bustled round tidying and wiping the washroom. Stuart queued for a few moments. Once finished, he tipped the janitor who smiled ever larger and held the door for Stuart. In the short corridor outside, the door to the ladies opened and Frances stepped out. She froze momentarily when she saw Stuart.

"Hello Mr Stuart from England," she said seconds later, having recovered her composure.

"Hello Fran. You OK?" Stuart asked, with as much tenderness in his voice as he could muster. He felt sure that his heart would burst from his chest as he stood looking at her. They moved away from the corridor together.

She looked up at him as they walked. "Yes, I'm fine, I'm happy now."

She smiled but her eyes did not, at least not in the same way as they had done earlier in the week. The rapport between them had all but vanished.

"Can I buy you a drink?" he said.

"OK, water."

"And a brandy?" he asked.

"No, later."

She followed him to the bar but started talking to another group of men on the far side. He took the bottle over to her.

"Thank you," she said. "This is my friend Stuart from England," she announced to the group of men.

They acknowledged him with slightly embarrassed smiles and nods. She drank the water and then excused herself and went to talk to the other members of the band.

"Your girlfriend?" one of the men asked.

Stuart was surprised: this was the second person who had said that. Stuart was unsure of how to reply, so eventually he smiled enigmatically. "What do you think?" he asked.

They fell silent.

Stuart left and rejoined the Americans at the barrel table by the bar. The Manila Seven Band started again and the beer flowed freely. Stuart talked and joked with the two Americans until midway through the set of songs. They had played and sung the lambada, a South American song associated with a particular style of dancing. Stuart, with his long experience in South America, knew the dance and music well. The music died away to a low background noise, and one of the girls began to address the audience. She was recruiting three couples to dance the lambada on stage. Stuart paid little heed to the proceedings and continued to talk with the Americans. The band managed to get three girls to volunteer and two men. The appeals became louder. Stuart raised his head from his conversation at exactly the wrong moment. Frances looked straight at him and he looked back.

"Stuart!" she shouted. "Mr Stuart from England, come on, dance the lambada for us."

Stuart groaned and shook his head, but it was too late. One of the other singers grabbed his arm and led him to the small stage.

"Your partner," Frances said to Stuart. "Your name?" she said to the girl.

"Lisa."

"And where you from?"

"From Australia."

"And finally Mr Stuart from England," Frances continued.

Fortunately for Stuart, they were going to be the last couple to dance. In the intervening time, Stuart watched the meaningless gyrations of the first couple. Their dances bore about as much similarity to the lambada as the Gay Gordons. He regarded his partner. She was as tall as he and well-built, although not fat, and she looked as if she regularly exercised.

Stuart nudged her gently and put his mouth close to her ear. "Ever dance the lambada before?" he asked.

"No, but I've seen it a few times," she replied with a noticeable Australian twang.

"OK, I've spent some time in South America and learned to do it a bit. Do you trust me?" he asked her.

She looked at him strangely, shrugged her shoulders. "How do I know?"

"No, I mean for the dance."

"Yeah, no worries."

"OK, you stand with your legs about this far apart," he indicated the distance with his hands, "and put your right leg between mine. I'll put my right leg between yours. Then my hand goes at the base of your back, here." He put his hand on her back just above her bottom. She didn't bat an eyelid. "And then we pull close together and you put your left hand on my shoulder and we join hands in the front like this." He held her right hand with his left.

She nodded as she understood.

"And then we go round with the hips like this." He moved his hips in a circular motion, going quite low and bending his knees.

The second couple began their dance. It was of a similar standard to the first couple. They didn't even join hands, but did some sort of disco dance a yard apart.

"And now our last couple," Frances shouted into her microphone, "Mr Stuart from England and Lisa from Australia."

They took the stage.

"Now dance the lambada!" she shouted.

Stuart and his partner faced each other and she stood as Stuart had directed. He put his right hand on her back just above her bottom and pulled her close. She started at the closeness and her eyes looked surprised.

"Trust me," whispered Stuart.

She relaxed and put her left hand on Stuart's right shoulder. They joined hands in the front and put their respective right leg between each other's, with slightly bent knees.

The music started. For two people who had never met before, let alone danced, Stuart and Lisa made a remarkably good attempt at the lambada. Their hips moved in synchrony as if glued together. Stuart realised that Lisa was quite a strong, fit woman. She had no trouble in keeping up with him. Judging by the cheers from the crowd in the bar, the performance was quite something. Stuart was beginning to flag a little and recognised the end of the music coming up. He looked at Frances, who was clapping wildly. She smiled back and then waved her right hand around in a circular motion and mouthed something at the band.

The music didn't stop but continued for a second time. The crowd continued to shout and cheer as they danced. As the music came to the end again, Frances repeated the signal and the music went round again. Stuart was definitely falling behind his Australian partner and he had to take a deep breath and hang on. After the third round of the music it finally stopped. They bowed to the cheering audience.

"Our winners tonight!" Frances shouted.

Almost immediately the other two couples mounted the stage and a tray with three large jugs of beer and three normal glasses was brought out. Stuart realised that the next part of the game was a beer race. Drinking pints of warm, flat, English beer in one was not a problem, but drinking a jug of this cold, fizzy stuff was a different matter. The other couples received their drinks, the men taking the jugs, the women the glasses. As the waiter approached Stuart and Lisa, she reached over and grabbed the jug, leaving Stuart with only the glass. She winked at him.

"OK, now drink!" shouted Frances.

The music started again. Lisa downed the jug in one, beating the other men with ease. Stuart just managed to consume his glass without a pause.

Lisa held her jug up in triumph and the crowd clapped and hooted wildly.

As they left the stage Lisa nudged Stuart. "Well, one good turn deserves another," she said. "You did the dance, I drank the beer."

"Thanks, it was good."

"Yeah, we weren't half bad," she said.

Stuart was perspiring as he returned to his barrel table with the two Americans.

"Well, that was quite a show. Let me shake your hand, buddy," said Hank, laughing.

"Yep, I haven't seen anyone else do that dance in here quite like that. It almost looked like you knew what you was doin'," added Rick with a smile.

"I did. I learned the dance in South America," Stuart said, slightly offended.

"Here's another beer," Rick handed Stuart a glass.

"Boy, that woman sure could drink beer," Hank said, shaking his head slowly. "I've never seen anyone, woman or man, do that before."

"Oh yes there was," Rick said. "There was that big fat guy from Australia who did last month."

"Naw, he left some, I'm sure."

They argued inconclusively about the subject for a few minutes more.

Suddenly it seemed that everyone in the bar was Stuart's friend. People walked up to him and shook his hand, patted him on the back and generally congratulated him. Lisa, on the other side of the bar, was receiving similar adulation. In a break from the handshaking and congratulations, Stuart watched the band playing on. The bar was packed and the group responded to the crowd. As he watched Stuart became aware of someone standing close by. He looked around and saw an Indonesian girl standing by him. She did not appear to be with any group of people, she just stood in between Stuart's table and the next one. He returned his gaze to the stage.

At the end of the song, he looked again and the small girl was still there. She seemed small, a little over five foot four, Stuart guessed. At first he thought that she was one of the bell girls from the hotel but he realised that her hair was too long: the bell girls all had shortish hair to fit under the round caps they wore. This girl's hair was a little over shoulder-length cut with a fringe. It was thick, shiny black and wavy. She extended her hand to Stuart.

"Hello Mr Stuart," she said. "You dance very well. I think it was very funny."

"My name is just Stuart," he replied, taking the small delicate hand and giving it a shake. He was a little wary. After he had dismissed the idea that she was a bell girl, he entertained the idea that she could be a call-girl; the forwardness of her approach had given him the idea. But then as he looked there was little else about her to suggest that she was a prostitute. She wasn't smoking as all the others seemed to do habitually, nor was her face made-up to any great extent. Her clothes too suggested that she was not, for they were plain, simple denim jeans and an orange tee-shirt that looked too big for her – the shoulders were halfway down her arms. She just didn't have the look of a call-girl: too innocent.

"What's your name?" Stuart asked by way of conversation.

"Ita," she replied, "Ita Maria."

"The second one doesn't sound very Indonesian."

"No it's not. My parents wanted a European name as well as an Indonesian one."

Stuart turned away and watched the band playing. Finally they announced and sang the last song. They stepped down from the stage. Frances came over to Stuart.

"You danced very good," she laughed.

"Did you have to go through the song three times?" he asked.

"Of course, you were enjoying yourself."

She made to leave.

"I'm going tomorrow, back to England."

She stopped. "Really?" A flicker of disappointment ran across her face. "Will you come back?"

"Yes, I think so, in six or eight weeks. Will you still be here?"

"Maybe. We have a contract for another two months, so maybe." She looked a little sad.

Stuart was surprised at her disappointment.

"I hope you come back soon and to see us all again."

"I will," said Stuart.

"I must go now." She made to leave again. "With my friends," she added almost apologetically. She held out her hand. Stuart took it and shook it gently.

"Bye Fran."

"Bye Mr Stuart." She smiled at him, turned and left.

He watched her go. He began to think of what might have been. She was a fantasy for him and the trouble with fantasies was that they were never as good when they came true as when they remained only fantasies. But this had been a fantasy which had been so nearly true, one that was so real that other people had noticed too. He stared ruefully into his beer. Finally he drained the glass and turned to see Frances disappearing.

He noticed that Ita was still standing next to him. She was looking at him. He smiled at her. She smiled back, a big smile revealing a row of perfect white teeth.

"You like a drink?" he asked her.

"Yes please, I'd like a glass of beer."

Stuart gave her a surprised look. "Beer?"

"Yes."

"But you cannot drink beer. It's against your religion, isn't it?"

She laughed, "I'm not Islam, I'm a Catholic."

"That explains the Maria," Stuart said. "Two beers," he said to the waiter who hovered at his elbow.

"I can only drink one," she laughed, "otherwise I get very drunk and fall over."

"Your English is very good. What's your job?"

"I'm a secretary for an American company; they train me to speak English."

The second band started playing again. The bar was beginning to empty and the music had dropped down in tempo. The area around the bar where Stuart and the Americans were standing was still full.

Stuart looked at Ita as she stood beside him watching the band. Like many Indonesian girls, her skin was a lovely shade of light brown and without blemish. Her eyebrows would have been considered thick by European standards but this did not distract from the overall impression.

Her nose was a curious mixture of flatness at the top with a gentle concave shape to the end. Depending on the angle of viewing, it could look European or Oriental. Her jeans were quite baggy, but fitted in a way which revealed that beneath the jeans lay a curvaceous figure. The baggy tee-shirt top effectively hid the rest of her shape from him.

They drank and listened to the music. Stuart offered her his seat and, as she sat down, she rested her hand ever so lightly on his arm for a brief second.

"You want to go to a disco when the music here finishes?"

"Whereabouts?"

"In Blok M," she replied.

Stuart looked at the two Americans. "What's Blok M like? I mean for a disco."

They looked a little uncertain. "OK, but you have to be careful."

"Do you want to go?" Stuart asked them.

"No, not really. It's already almost two and we'll be wrecked for the rest of the day tomorrow."

Stuart turned to Ita. "No, I don't think so, maybe another time."

"But you're going home tomorrow, aren't you?"

"Yes I am, but I'll be back some time."

The band finished playing and they all left together. She called a taxi and he watched her go. He doubted if he would ever see her again. What was more of a worry to him was if he would ever see Frances again.

## CHAPTER 7

## COMING HOME

At a little after six-thirty in the morning on the following Monday, Stuart stood unsteadily, collected his things from the overhead locker and filed past the assembled ranks of Singapore Airlines' cabin crew.

"Thank you, sir."

They were all so happy and pleasant. Stuart felt like death. Airline breakfasts always had a strange effect on him. He had eaten about an hour and a half before, a big, yellow, turd-like object that all airlines have the cheek to call an omelette. He wished he had tried the lamb thing but that would have left him burping lamb kebab all the way home. That was probably marginally more offensive than the prospect of the yellow turd sitting in his stomach. His mouth felt dry and sticky. He guessed that his breath smelt like rancid cheese. He sniffed his armpits – they definitely smelt like rancid cheese despite the use of much deodorant at the last visit to the toilet. Returning to the UK was always worse than going out. On the way out there was so much to look forward to. Coming back it was a return to the grind of daily life.

One thing for which Stuart was grateful was the UK passport queue. In many countries, their own nationals had to queue with the foreigners, but not in Britain. The Brits had their own special channel. Most likely it would be manned by a turbaned Sikh – something Stuart always found unnerving, being allowed back into your country by someone who looked like an official of the country you had just left. But today it was a fat Englishwoman. She gave his passport a cursory glance and waved him through. The queues for the foreign passports were enormous. Early in the morning is the worst time to arrive in Heathrow. With flights arriving from all over the world, it was a mass of people. To Stuart, who had spent the last week in the teeming city of Jakarta, it seemed quite calm.

His trusty case arrived quickly and he pondered the alternatives ways of getting to Manchester.

He quickly gave up the prospect of the tube and train. Instead he chose the super shuttle. He sat amongst the early bird businessmen in their smart suits and ties, him with his rancid armpits and foul breath, uncombed hair and a day's growth on his chin. Another airline breakfast arrived. He prodded it unhappily with his fork, eating little and drinking only the orange juice.

He was in his office only half an hour later than his usual time when coming from home.

Stuart didn't mind coming back to the office after a trip too much. There were, of course, the people – usually those who had never been away on a trip – who would always ask, "Had a nice holiday?"

These were the sort who could only ever associate foreign travel with holidays and enjoyment. Sometimes business travel was enjoyable and Stuart would always admit to that, but there were the other times when it was not. Like the time he had spent Christmas Day in a departure lounge in São Paulo waiting for a defective jumbo to have its engine fixed, or arriving at midnight in some godforsaken, small, middle-of-nowhere airport and having to find the one crazy taxi driver to the town's only hotel. But those people never could see that side, could never, or simply refused to, accept that such trips were anything but jolly.

The rest of the people, the other travellers, all knew and were interested only in the business and the delights of the country visited and not in making silly remarks. As only the second person in the company to visit the Far East on business, Stuart knew that he was in for a lot of questions. The first job, however, was to have a shower and freshen up in the office shower room. He changed into some casual clothes which he would never normally wear to the office, but he did not shave. He wanted to preserve some of the attributes of his trip. The second job was sorting out the expenses, followed by a visit to his boss. Then a meander around the office to talk to people. This was the bit he liked best. Even though he had been away for only a little over a week, there was always gossip and news to catch up on. Then there was lunch, a more or less obligatory part of returning home.

By four o'clock in the afternoon, the combined effects of the trip, a seven hour time change and the alcoholic lunch left him feeling somewhat jaded. He excused himself and called Catherine, his wife. She was a teacher and finished at about four. She was already home.

"Hi, it's me. I'm at the office and I want to come home – can you collect me? Like now?"

"Hi Stuart, how are you?"

"Fine, tired but fine. Can you collect me?"

"Of course. The traffic's bad at this time but I should be there in half an hour."

"If it's going to take you that long I can get a lift in less time." His voice whined a little.

"OK then. See you when you get here." She sounded a little annoyed.

In his early days of travelling, the return home was usually the signal for a terrific row. He often felt strange and remote. It was difficult to adjust to being back home again.

His wife expected him to be full of the trip, wanting to talk, but he had been to the office and expended his talk there. All he wanted at home was quiet, a rest, a drink and some sleep. In recent years he and his wife had discussed the problem and come to an understanding. The strange feeling had also reduced as the number of trips had grown. He had become more experienced in handling it. This time he felt as strange and remote as ever he had done in the early days. He was not looking forward to meeting his wife, especially now that she was annoyed.

He got a lift within ten minutes of the phone call to his wife. He arrived home at a quarter past five or so. He let himself in and dropped his suitcase, holdall and briefcase in the hall. He walked into the kitchen. His wife was standing over the work surface preparing vegetables.

"Hello," he said simply.

She turned to face him, vegetable knife in her rubber-gloved hand.

"Hi Stuart, darling. How are you?"

"Not too bad – tired, the usual crap," he said non-comically.

She turned back to her vegetables.

"So how was it?"

"Hot," was his monosyllabic reply, which by its tone indicated that no further questions should be forthcoming.

"OK," she said quickly, raising her hands in a gesture of surrender, "sorry."

She went back to her vegetables.

After a pause of several minutes he spoke. "Where are the kids?"

"Ralph is off with some of his friends and Colleen is upstairs."

Colleen was their daughter, seven years old and definitely her Daddy's favourite.

He went to the foot of the stairs.

"Col!" he shouted up the stairs.

"Daddy?" she shouted back. "Daddy!"

The noise of her jumping off her bed and rushing to her bedroom door followed. She flew downstairs and jumped off the last few steps straight into his outstretched arms.

"One day", he said, "you will be too big to do that and you'll break your daddy's back." He kissed her on the cheek.

"What have you brought me?" she asked without hesitation. She knew her daddy always brought something home.

He carried her into the hallway where he had dropped his bags. He put her down and opened his holdall. He took out a carved wooden box and handed it to his daughter.

"What's this?" she said rather contemptuously.

"Open it," he said.

She opened the box. Inside was a selection of small trinkets and souvenirs for her large collection.

"Oh thanks, Daddy!" She kissed him and ran to show her mother.

"Where is my present?" his wife asked.

"There's a bottle of gin in my bag for you."

"Very funny," she said a touch angrily. "You're not in one of your 'come home' moods, are you?"

"I'm going to my room," Colleen said, sensing the disharmony in the conversation.

"I guess a little."

"Why? After all this time?"

"I don't know. Maybe the new place, new things to see."

She signed loudly.

"All I needed – a moronic husband for a week. Go and have a bath or something, open some wine and get unwound."

He left the room without saying a word.

He had a bath, changed into the second set of fresh clothes that day, unpacked his bags and finally came downstairs. His wife was still in the kitchen. He didn't talk; instead he selected a bottle of red wine and opened it. He poured a glass for his wife and set it beside the cooker. She didn't say anything. He left her and slumped in front of the television.

By the time she called him in for his tea, Stuart had emptied the bottle with the exception of that still remaining in his glass. He moved unsteadily into the dining room, where both children were sitting quietly.

"Hello Dad," said Ralph.

"Hi kid!" Stuart said, waving his arm in his general direction.

"Dad's drunk," Colleen whispered to her brother.

"Quiet!" snapped her mother. "Your father" – she always called her husband 'your father' when she was trying to explain his errant behaviour – "has just spent twenty-four hours travelling and a day in the office. He's a little tired." She paused and smiled.

'Tired and emotional' was a standard polite euphemism for pissed as a fart. "And emotional," she continued. "Don't say that he's drunk, Colleen, when you don't know what it means."

"Yes I do," she protested.

"Quiet!"

Stuart ate and very soon after slept. He woke early at around five, jet-lag again, and was at his desk by seven-thirty.

By the end of the week, normality had been restored to the Morgan household. At work Stuart worked hard, not out of dedication to duty, but because he wanted to make sure that he would be back in Jakarta within two months, to make sure that he could see Frances again.

The first news came in from Jakarta some three weeks after he had arrived home. It was a ten page fax from Anwar. In it he detailed the equipment and situations at the two smaller factories of the three that Anwar and Stuart had selected. On the basis of this data Stuart began to prepare his proposals. Anwar promised the information from the biggest factory within a week. Once he had prepared the initial proposals Stuart sent them to his boss, Frank James. It was Frank who had made the initial visit to Jakarta and made contact with Anwar.

Frank, for all of his thirty-five years in the business, was a conservative man with little enthusiasm for adventure. He had been very reluctant to go to South-East Asia in the first place. Breaking into new markets was not his idea of a quiet life. He was backing further and further away from the small orders, preferring the large ones with established customers and profits to match. Stuart was one of the younger ones who pointed out that it was only a matter of time before more predatory competitors began to eat away at that business.

A day after Stuart submitted the reports he was called into Frank's office. He sat opposite Frank. Frank was in his early fifties with a balding head, steel-rimmed glasses and a spreading waist. He was a good sort who had built his reputation during the sixties and seventies with a number of long-term deals with various countries. The system had amounted to almost a cartel of the main producers, but that was beginning to break up. Stuart and a number of the other younger people thought that Frank could not, or did not want, to come to terms with this. It was against this background that Frank had been sent by the managing director to establish the new market area in the Far East. Others were poaching in their markets so it was time to feed them their own medicine, the managing director had argued. Frank had been unconvinced but Stuart had been enthusiastic.

"What's this?" Frank asked, pushing Stuart's proposals across the desk towards him as Stuart sat down. Frank rocked back in his chair. "It's small potatoes all this. There's not two hundred thousand in the whole lot. Hardly worth your trip," he paused.

Stuart had been prepared for this. When he judged the pause had continued long enough he made to speak, but Frank had not finished.

"Didn't you visit the people from those large factories? The ones I recommended."

"Yes, I did, Frank," Stuart answered with a sigh. "I did, but they are all heavily involved with our friends in Germany, as you know." Stuart gave Frank a telling glance.

Indonesia had been given to the German company by Frank when they had agreed to keep out of India and Pakistan. Recently they had been chipping away at Ormistons' dominance in India. The loose gentleman's agreement was becoming less gentlemanly.

"Anwar told me that they will not leave their supplier for a new one until they see the new one has a presence in the country."

"They won't buy until we have a presence and we can't have a presence until they buy," said Frank, scratching his chin absently.

"That's why we need to go for the small companies. Both of these", he gestured towards the report on Frank's desk, "are trying to expand and want to modernise. Most of their gear is old and worn out. They can't expand because of the machinery limitations and they can't buy new because they don't have the money."

He looked at Frank who was leaning back in his chair looking at the ceiling with his hands behind his head.

"So that's why we offer them a complete package with finance as well."

Frank took his glasses off and massaged the bridge of his nose.

"We are engineers and manufacturers not bloody bankers," he said with contempt.

"I know that but we have to offer them something, otherwise they cannot buy."

"OK. You know, I think we should be out of the small machine side of the business," Frank said, putting his glasses back on with a tired gesture.

"I know that," said Stuart. "We've a reasonable order book in that section and this lot would fill it up for another year."

"When do you expect an order to result from all this?" Frank asked.

"Anwar said a year." Stuart paused, "If we were lucky."

"Okay, okay," said Frank. "Against my better judgement, carry on. Is there anything that you need from me?"

"Only your signature on my expenses," Stuart said.

Frank laughed. "No problem."

Stuart took his report and left Frank alone. He had expected Frank's resistance and ultimate surrender. Frank knew more than most the changing nature of their business, but he was still reluctant to change his successful past for an uncertain future.

The final batch of information from Anwar arrived some two weeks after the first.

By working hard, Stuart managed to get everything finished so that he could leave for Jakarta almost exactly two months after he had returned home. He hoped that she would still be there.

When the date was fixed, Stuart broke the subject with Catherine.

"I'm going away again," he said one evening after the kids were in bed.

"Where to?" she asked.

"Back to Indonesia, maybe for a month or more."

Her face fell a little. "Why so long?"

"I've got to visit three factories with these proposals and do some negotiating with all of them. I'm sorry, but it's a new market and the company are looking to me to develop it. I think it's a good opportunity for me. Maybe I can make a bit more of a name on the back of this, instead of following Frank's cartel."

She nodded unhappily. She knew the nature of his job and that Stuart was hoping to be in the running for Frank's job in a few years. Trips and jobs like this were an integral part of climbing the slippery pole. Still she felt uneasy about the trip. Stuart's behaviour when he had first returned stayed in her memory and she could not rationalise it or her feelings now.

## CHAPTER 8

## RETURN

On a Saturday evening, nine weeks after he had been in exactly the same position for the first time, Stuart sat strapped in his favourite window seat of a 747 Bigtop of Singapore Airlines. He listened to the four gas turbines winding up to their full output as they sat at the end of the runway at Heathrow. He was on his way again. The plane was a little less full and there was a vacant seat between him and his neighbour, a dour-looking Englishwoman, with whom he had not spoken or exchanged so much as a glance since he had sat down almost half an hour ago. Stuart hoped that this would continue for the whole trip as it was something which would suit Stuart and seemed to suit her. The plane began to roll down the runway, lumbering up to its take-off speed. The thirteen hour flight had begun.

Stuart was filled with apprehension about the forthcoming trip. He had hardly slept the night before and was worried that Frances would no longer be there when he arrived. Stuart's sleepless night the previous evening, a couple of drinks in the airport and two glasses of white wine on the plane contributed to a sleep of a little over nine hours on the plane. Not even the sight of the still radiant and beautiful air hostesses could keep him awake. His sleep was so deep that even when he left the plane in Singapore he was still groggy and sleepy. Despite his previous experience with the usual airline breakfasts, he had again opted for the disgusting, yellow, turd-like impression of an omelette. Now, as he left the plane and walked up the ramp towards the main airport building, the thing lay in his stomach like a lump of soggy dough.

He was in the marble and glass splendour which is Changi Airport. He meandered around in a semi-sleepy state for the two hours of his transfer time. He paused only once, to buy a bottle of aftershave. Buying aftershave was not something Stuart normally did. His wife bought the odd bottle at Christmas or on his birthday, but he rarely used it. However, on this occasion, he bought a bottle without really knowing why.

Almost before he knew it, he was on a plane again. The one and a half hour flight passed quickly. He ate the meal, hoping to reduce the bad feeling in his stomach. The result was the opposite – it made him feel worse. Then he was arriving in the bamboo-inspired, ethnic ambiguity of Jakarta's Sukarno Hatta. He greeted it like an old friend. He felt at home in the slow lazy atmosphere, with the smell of clove cigarettes hanging in the air giving the air the unmistakable tang that the Englishwoman had described on his first trip. Like an old hand, he piloted his way through immigration, the baggage area and customs without problems. Outside the main building, in the open-sided, cavernous hall that was the taxi and meeting area, he aimed straight for the pink-hatted man from the Kedutaan Hotel standing waiting with his little board. It was this area that Stuart had found so oppressive and overwhelming on his first visit. Now he knew what to expect, it was not so fearsome; in fact Stuart actually smiled to himself as he walked through the throng, shaking his head to the repeated requests of the taxi touts. He felt happy to be back.

In the quiet of the air-conditioned car ordered by the pink-capped Kedutaan man, he regarded the mass of humanity at the roadside, the strange architecture of the buildings, the slums and the traffic with a sort of self-satisfied superiority of one who had been there before. After his long sleep on the plane and the zombie-like transit in Singapore, Stuart was beginning to wake up. By the time the car arrived at the hotel, he was fully awake and prepared for action. The reason for his wakefulness was only partly explained by the sleep he had had. The proximity of the hotel and the possibility of meeting Frances again contributed more. He was in a state of nervous excitement, the sort of condition which he had last experienced, before he had met Frances two months ago, some fifteen years previously during his time in university. The woman who had generated those feelings had later become his wife.

As he walked into the central reception area, Stuart noticed the girl behind the reception desk. She was the cheeky one with the big smile. He recognised her, of course, but he was astonished when she held out her hand to him.

"Hello Mr Morgan," she said brightly as if Stuart was her long-lost friend. "It's so nice to have you back again."

'How could she possibly remember me of all the guests that had passed through the hotel in the last two months?' He had, after all, only stayed a week. He was glad at this happy welcome. He raced upstairs to his room once the formalities were completed. Once in his room he wanted to complete the three Ss, as he called them – 'shit, shower and shave' – as fast as he could. But, until the bell boy brought his bags up, he couldn't start. He paced the room impatiently; it seemed an age until the doorbell rang.

"Hello... Bellboy," the weak voice came through the thick door.

Stuart swung the door open rapidly and handed him a tip almost before he had put the bags down.

"Thank you, sir," he said, smiling and retreating backwards out of the room.

Stuart flipped the catch on and then rapidly removed his clothes to begin the first of the Ss. As he stood facing the mirror to complete the third and final of the three Ss, he picked up and opened the small bottle of aftershave and splashed it on to his newly-shaven face. It stung mightily. He was not a regular user so the shock was a surprise. He pulled a face in the mirror at himself. He dressed with care and then sat for a minute to collect his thoughts, trying to slow his madly beating heart and lose the red flush on his face.

He left his room and descended in the lift to the reception area. He left the main building and took the familiar turn to the right, down the marble-treaded stairs that led to The Inne. As he made the one hundred and eighty degree turn at the bottom, he entered the covered corridor which led to the main door. As he moved along the corridor, the noise of the band grew steadily. Was it the Manila Seven Band or not? He agonised in the short walk. He opened the door and the noise grew louder, it was almost recognisable but he wasn't sure. He walked straight past the two men who sat behind the desk at the entrance and they smiled at him. Along the corridor, past the plants and wall ornaments, he was sure that he could see Frances. His heart beat faster the closer he got to the bar.

In his usual way, he turned left and walked behind the bar, ordering a beer as he passed along the gap between the bar and the glass partition which separated it from the rest. On a Sunday night it was not too full. He found a seat at a barrel table at the front. Frances was dancing and singing at the same end of the stage. He looked up at her. She appeared to look even more beautiful, desirable and downright sexy than he remembered. Usually the opposite occurred. His mind, when remembering happy events or girls, normally embellished the memory with nice but non-existent details or unwarranted increases in attractiveness which inevitably resulted in disappointment when a reunion took place. Frances was different. She had maintained her attractiveness to the point that she looked better to Stuart than before.

He looked at her, waiting for her to see him. When she did, her eyes lit up and her singing mouth broke into a wide grin. She waved her right hand in a little wave. After half an hour or so they stopped singing. She came straight to him, not following the usual routine of going to the bathroom to freshen up first. She stood in front of him, sweating. The sweat ran down her neck and the side of her face. She wiped herself with a small towel. She was wearing the same black shiny one-piece suit he had seen her wearing one time before, the time she had stood close to him and pressed her thigh against his.

She held out her hand.

"Hello Mr Stuart from England."

He took her small hand and shook it gently.

"Hi Fran. I'm so glad you're still here."

"We shouldn't be. Actually we wanted to go home last Saturday, yesterday, but the new group are late."

"How long will you stay now?"

"Until Wednesday, then we go back to Manila."

Stuart's heart, at first happy that she was still here, now fell at being told just how short a time she had left in Jakarta.

"How are your wife and children?" she asked.

"Fine, all of them are very well. How are you?" He paused. "And the rest of the group?"

"We are all good, but we want to go home. We've been here for more than six months and we miss our home."

"And your family?" Stuart said. He was half probing to see if she had a boyfriend or anything.

"Yes, I want to see my mother and sisters."

"What about your father?"

"Oh, he died ten years ago. This why I sing, then I can send the money to my mother and sisters."

"Oh, I'm sorry. You have no brothers?"

She shook her head.

"No, no brothers. I am the oldest so I must work for my family." She looked away with a sad expression on her face.

Stuart didn't know what to do next.

She broke the silence first.

"Just a minute, I want to see my friend." She left him alone.

They sang one more set and then left. He waved at her as she left and she gave him a sad smile. Somehow he had managed to make her sad again. Stuart left the bar and went to his room with a heavy heart.

The next three days passed quickly, work in the day and then long nights in The Inne. And then on the Wednesday evening at about one o'clock she said goodbye to him for the last time and was gone.

Stuart spent the next few days in a daze. His work went well but he could think of nothing else except the Filipina singer who had come into his life and aroused feelings he had not had for so many years and then disappeared so abruptly.

It was Saturday evening before he ventured back into The Inne. Sunday was to be the start of his first trip upcountry to visit one of the factories. Stuart and Anwar were due to leave in the late morning, so Stuart felt like a good night out. He went down at just after nine in the evening. The bar was full, every table was occupied and the area around the bar in front of the stage was heaving with people. Smoke wafted up from numerous cigarettes and stone steaks. The smell of frying food and clove cigarettes was, at first, quite overpowering and made Stuart's nose twitch and his eyes water. He almost turned to leave, but checked himself and continued down the three steps in front of the stage. He managed to work his way through to the bar and attracted the attention of a barman. Stuart stood leaning his back on the wall at the corner of the bar. The local band was performing in their usual style. Stuart watched and sipped his beer.

The evening wore on. Stuart was bored with the local band and the new Filipino band, which had only two girls, neither of whom could sing or looked as good as Frances and the Manila Seven Band.

The crowd thinned as the time passed midnight. Stuart found a seat by the bar and sat sadly with his back to the band. He looked around the square-shaped bar at the people still remaining. He thought that he recognised a face on the far side of the bar. He smiled, but the face showed no sign of recognition so he looked away. He thought that it was the girl he had talked to the night he danced the lambada but he wasn't one hundred per cent sure. After a few minutes he looked again at the face on the other side of the bar. This time when he looked at the girl, she looked back, not just a glance, but a long look, as if some spark of recognition had ignited in her. He struggled to remember her name – it was something Indonesian and something else.

She looked at him again and then looked away without a smile.

Stuart decided, rather uncharacteristically, to take the matter into his own hands as he was now convinced that it was the girl to whom he had talked that night. Picking up his glass, he made his way through the thinning crowd to the side of the bar where she stood.

As he made his way carefully around the bar, he became more and more sure of her identity, although her name still eluded him. She looked nervously at him as he approached. She did not smile, but there was some recognition, albeit confused.

"Hello," he said brightly.

She smiled back.

"You don't remember me?" he asked.

"Mmm.. I think so," she said, not really remembering.

"Lambada," he said.

A sudden dawning of light flashed across her face and she became much more animated.

"Yes!" she exclaimed. "Mr Stuart from England, of course." She held out her hand towards him.

He took the small delicate hand in his and shook it once, gently. Her name returned to his mind.

"Hello Ita. Can I get you a drink?"

She shook her head. "One glass of beer is enough."

She looked up at him with a slightly hurt expression on her face. "Your girlfriend's gone home?" she said.

Stuart was taken aback by this. He assumed she meant Lisa, the Australian girl who he had danced with.

"Who do you mean?" he asked as innocently as he could.

"Frances, of course. You remember the Filipina singer?"

There was something unusual in her voice. Stuart tried to place it and came to the conclusion that it was a little bit of jealousy.

"Frances was never my girlfriend," he said, trying to sound convincing. "Sure, I liked her and talked to her but," he paused and looked into his beer before returning his gaze to Ita, "but," he repeated, "she was never my girlfriend."

He paused again and looked directly at her. "After all, I'm married as well and I'm not like most of the men you meet here. I don't take extra girlfriends." He looked rather severely at her.

"No, maybe you were not her boyfriend but I think you could have been. She liked you very much."

This news was quite a shock to Stuart. How did she know about Frances and her feelings?

"Why do you say that?" he asked.

"She told me. She told me that she liked you very much and it didn't matter about your wife. She is not like some of the singers who will go with any man for..." She paused as if embarrassed to say it. "...money," she whispered. "No, she will only go out with a man if she like him."

"But I upset her," Stuart protested, feeling confused and mortified.

"She would have got over that if you had been here long enough."

Stuart was silent for a long time. He finished his beer and made to leave.

"Are you going?" Ita asked him with disappointment in her voice.

"I was going to," he replied. He looked at her and then waved at the barman for another beer. "But I guess I'll stay a bit longer." He smiled at her and she gave him a big smile back.

They stood and talked for half an hour, about England, the weather in England, his job, her job, the usual stuff of getting to know someone new. At the end of the evening, as the band wound up its performance, Stuart asked for his bill and turned to leave.

Ita smiled at him. "Are you going this time?"

He nodded as he handed back the signed bill.

"No disco?" she asked a little imploringly.

He shook his head. "Not tonight, I've got to leave early tomorrow."

She looked alarmed. "Are you going back to England tomorrow?"

"No," he smiled, "only to some place called Semarang or something. I'll be back on Thursday."

"Give me a ring when you come back." She hastily scribbled a number on a song request slip.

"Home or office?" he asked.

"Home," she replied.

"OK Ita, maybe I'll ring you next week."

She looked at him with her head on one side.

"No maybe," she said, patting his right arm as it rested on the bar.

"OK," he laughed, "no maybe."

"Bye." She held out her hand again.

He took the small offered hand and shook it again, this time for a number of shakes. She gripped his hand quite hard this time, surprising him. He left the bar and went to bed.

## CHAPTER 9

## A VISIT UPCOUNTRY

At nine o'clock the following Sunday morning, Stuart checked out of the hotel and met Anwar in the reception.

"Ready?" he asked Stuart.

"Of course," Stuart replied shaking Anwar's outstretched hand firmly.

"This way," Anwar said, leading Stuart out to his waiting car. The driver put the cases in the boot.

"I don't need the big one for a short trip like this," Stuart said.

"No problem, my driver will look after it."

They got in the car and had an untroubled ride to the airport. At the airport they stood and queued in the heat of the open-sided, barn-like reception area.

"You have to queue every time you want a ticket," Anwar explained in the early morning heat. "It's a shuttle service with no advanced booking," he continued.

As they approached the booking window, a jet of cold air blew deliciously from the hole in the booking window. Anwar bought the tickets and led the way into the relative coolness of the check-in area. The domestic terminal was built in the same style as the international one. However, beyond the check-in area it was open-sided and hot. They ate a simple meal in the small restaurant.

"You'll have to get used to this type of food. They don't sell anything else upcountry," Anwar laughed.

Stuart smiled back. "I don't mind, I'll try anything once."

They waited for half an hour in the restaurant until an announcement triggered Anwar into life. They walked across the open-sided section of the building and into the air-conditioned departure lounge. From there, they descended steps and walked across the warming concrete towards the small Fokker F28 jet parked close by. Stuart took his seat next to the window and began to realise how hot and humid it was on board the small cramped plane. The air-conditioning was not switched on and a number of people fanned themselves with the safety cards to alleviate the unpleasant conditions. Stuart followed suit, but despite this he could feel the sweat trickling down his back. His shirt was dappled with damp sweat patches on his chest. He pushed his free hand back though his hair. It was damp with sweat. Anwar sat unconcerned in the heat.

It seemed an age until the two air hostesses pulled the stairs up and secured the door. The engines started and Stuart fiddled with the overhead air vent, trying to persuade some cooling air to come forth. Slowly a little air did come but it had little effect on Stuart's sweating. Relief for Stuart only came when the plane took off and the air-conditioning got fully into its stride. The jets of air had traces of white mist in their stream, such was the heat and humidity inside the plane. Condensation formed on the overhead panels and dripped down on the passengers. Stuart wondered for a second what such condensation did to the air frame but put the thought quickly out of his mind.

They landed forty-five minutes later at the small airport of Jenderal Yamin, Semarang. The weather was even hotter than in Jakarta, the concrete of the apron reflecting the unrelenting fury of the sun making Stuart sweat on the short walk to the rudimentary terminal building. He could smell the sea in the light breeze that blew across the airport. It was a hot, sticky breeze.

Once inside the terminal building, the heat did not leave Stuart. It was an open-sided building, packed with a throng of people: passengers, welcoming families, airport staff and porters. Stuart felt the same overwhelming oppression in the crush of people and the heat. He prayed for a quick delivery of the bags.

The luggage collection was haphazard: a barrow loaded with baggage was pulled into the terminal building. The porters picked items off the barrow and pushed them across a counter in response to the demands of the passengers. Stuart didn't have a case but Anwar shouted louder than the rest for his and was quickly served.

They left the building and stood in the heat in front of the terminal. Anwar appeared to be looking for someone. A small man shuffled forward and a few words were exchanged. A little later a car appeared and the cases were stowed. Stuart was glad of the cool air-conditioning and quiet inside the car. He slumped back in his seat and paid only cursory attention to the passing scene outside the window.

Stuart half dozed for almost an hour while the car moved comparatively smoothly from the airport, through the city and out into the countryside. He was only fully woken when the car pulled up in front of a small roadside restaurant.

Anwar nudged Stuart gently.

"Come on. Time for some lunch."

Stuart pulled himself into a non-slumped sitting position.

"Where are we?"

"About an hour from Semarang, maybe another three to go. So it's definitely time for some food."

They left the car and Stuart stretched himself awake. Anwar ordered a meal of Indonesian food. Stuart overcame his initial trepidation and enjoyed the food and the glass of hot milkless tea that went with it.

After he had finished, Stuart wandered out to the toilet. The toilet was at the back of the restaurant, down an open passageway which led past the kitchen. Beyond the back of the restaurant lay nothing but rice fields. Stuart had never seen a rice paddy before. He stepped beyond the limits of the restaurant and into the fields. He walked a few yards along the edge of a paddy field. Each of the numerous small fields was set at a slightly different level from the next. A wall of earth formed the boundary between the fields and it was on top of one of these walls that Stuart stood surveying the panorama before him.

To his left was the one paddy field with a water level a few centimetres below the level of the earth wall on which he was standing. To his right, a second paddy field was approximately thirty centimetres below the level of the first. Each was a shimmering shallow pond of brown water, with fragile-looking bright green shoots poking out of the water at regular intervals. The level in the upper field was maintained by a small notch cut in the earth wall. Stuart squatted down to examine the trickle of water flowing over the lip and into the lower field.

He stood again and looked around. Below the lower field, the rice paddies stretched off into the distance, each a little lower than the last one in a carefully arranged pattern which ensured a complete and full flow of water to each and every field.

He marvelled at the skill and ingenuity in the creation of this intricate system of cultivation. In the middle distance, about a hundred metres away, one of the fields was full of people, bent double in water which came up to their knees. He wasn't sure what they were doing, but guessed that they were planting the individual rice plants in neat, regimented rows. Beyond them he looked towards the rows of palm and banana trees which fringed the far edge of the rice paddies. In the far distance a classical volcanic mountain shimmered through the heat haze. It was a scene which, if painted, would have been dismissed as over-stylised and unrealistic.

He stood for a number of minutes, trying to take in the whole scene. The heat did not seem too oppressive here, unlike that in Jakarta. There were no concrete pavements reflecting the sun mercilessly and no rows of cars generating pulses of intense heat as they passed. A gentle breeze blew in his face and the only sound was the gentle trickle of water by his feet as it flowed between the two fields. He didn't know how long he stood looking, but his concentration was only disturbed by a distant voice.

"Hey Stuart!"

Stuart looked around towards the source of the voice. Anwar was standing by the toilet, waving his hand in Stuart's direction. Stuart hadn't realised how far he had walked from the restaurant. Anwar was shouting, but his voice was almost lost in the distance. Stuart waved back and began to trace his way back carefully along the earth wall towards the restaurant.

"Sorry," he said to Anwar when he was back within reasonable earshot. "I guess I just wandered off for a look."

"Why?" Anwar looked surprised. "It's only a paddy."

"Well, we don't have them in England," said Stuart, reaching out for Anwar's outstretched hand to climb the last step up from the field."

"No, I don't suppose you do," Anwar laughed. "What do you think of them?"

"Fascinating, and very clever."

Anwar shrugged his shoulders in the manner of someone who is surprised at a sophisticated foreigner finding something so simple and basic so clever and interesting.

"Come on, we have a schedule to keep," he said, guiding Stuart away from the rice fields and back towards the car.

It was only when Stuart got back in the air-conditioned car that he realised how hot it was outside and how much he was sweating. He hoped that the hotel had a nice cool shower and full air-conditioning. He settled down in the cool comfort of the car and watched the passing landscape with renewed interest.

The road was comparatively wide – most parts were wide enough for two lanes in each direction. The traffic was heavy, very heavy in some places, and Stuart watched the unusual procession of vehicles. There were cars of course, of every age from brand-new to downright decrepit. Wobbling tyres and rusty panels creaked along the road in a manner which frightened Stuart just to look at. There were lorries and small trucks, some dangerously overloaded, crawling along with screaming engines.

Each had three men crammed in the small cab. Stuart could not imagine the heat in such a small cab sat directly on top of the engine. In the towns and villages the cars and lorries of the open road were supplemented by horse-drawn carriages, bicycles, motorbikes and three-wheeled, peddle-powered, rickshaw-type vehicles which had two passengers perched rather precariously, in Stuart's view, on the front. They appeared to obey no traffic rules and moved in any direction totally independent of any other vehicles.

And then, back on the open road, there were the buses or coaches. Chronically overloaded with standing passengers, they were all driven by maniacs who habitually drove in the right-hand lane as fast as they could before swerving to the left across the lanes and braking furiously to pick up passengers. The buses barely stopped before launching themselves back into the traffic with a blast of the horn, a fog of black diesel exhaust and without so much as a glance at the other cars on the road. Most of the buses had darkened windows and fluttering, tatty curtains. The windows were at waist level and most were open to allow the passengers some relief from the heat. Some of the buses were air-conditioned and didn't appear to be quite so crazy as the rest.

They just sat in the right-hand lane and honked every other vehicle out of the way. The overtaking and undertaking, as Stuart called the practice of passing on the left, caused Stuart to gasp in disbelief.

Situations which appeared to be heading for head-on smashes resolved themselves with inches to spare.

Anwar tapped Stuart on the arm. "Don't worry, they always drive like that."

Stuart shook his head. He had seen crazy drivers in Europe, Spain and France in particular, and also in South America, but these Indonesian bus drivers certainly took the first prize.

The road had been climbing steadily away from the flat coastal area towards the volcanic mountains. The scenery changed from the flat paddies to more steeply terraced gardens. Small rice paddies, no more than four or five metres long and a couple wide, stood one or even two metres above the next along the side of small valleys. The water cascaded from field to field and was moved across the small valleys in bamboo pipes. Stuart was even more impressed than he had been earlier in the day.

They ran on through a series of villages that seemed never-ending; it was difficult to see where one began and the last one ended such was the number of houses. These were punctuated by larger towns which resounded to frenetic activity of people moving and selling. Men organised the arrival and departure of numerous minibuses in various states of dereliction. Their whistles seemed to be part of their mouths as they blew furiously in an attempt to control the chaotic scenes. Most of the towns they passed through followed the same pattern.

The journey continued for the three hours Anwar had predicted. Then they arrived in a town, or rather city, of wide streets and grand buildings. Stuart noted the change of surroundings.

"Solo, or should I say Surakarta?" Anwar responded, noting Stuart's interest. "It's one of the cultural centres of Indonesia, along with Yogjakarta," he continued. "It is famous for batik cloth and being one of the centres of our independence movement in 1945." Anwar seemed proud, almost reverent mentioning the revolution.

Stuart looked around in silence. Finally the car made a left turn into the forecourt of a large white building.

"Hotel Djoglo," Anwar announced, "the best hotel in town," he continued, laughing a little.

Once inside the reception, Anwar completed the formalities for both of them. The driver unloaded the car and had a brief conversation with Anwar, then he left.

"You don't mind walking this evening, do you?" he asked Stuart.

Stuart shook his head.

"No, that's okay. No problem," he added.

Stuart's room was unusually large for a hotel room. It had a sort of enclosed balcony down one side. Stuart opened the door and went on to the balcony. It had no air-conditioning and Stuart felt a blast of hot humid air. He quickly closed the door and sat on the edge of the bed in air-conditioned comfort. He lay back and dozed for half an hour.

When he awoke to the sound of the telephone it was dark.

"Hello," he said.

"Hello, Anwar here. What time do you want to eat?"

"Give me fifteen minutes and I'll be ready."

Stuart showered and changed and in the estimated fifteen minutes met Anwar in the reception of the hotel.

They left the hotel reception and walked out on to the main road. Immediately outside the hotel, they came on a railway track running parallel to the road. Stuart had noticed it on the way in and wondered if it was still used. He stopped and looked left and right.

"It's OK," Anwar said, "these tracks haven't been used in a few years."

Stuart looked at the forlorn signal standing in splendid isolation a few hundred metres to the left. "Was it ever used?"

"Oh yes, up until quite recently these tracks were used by all sorts of trains, freight and passengers."

They crossed and walked down the road. The night was warm to Stuart's English body. It felt like the warmest English summer evening. It was what Stuart would have called 'close', meaning humid. Despite the oppressive feeling, Stuart felt reasonably comfortable. They walked for fifteen minutes.

Anwar made occasional comments about the buildings and the surroundings, but for the rest of the time they walked in silence.

They came to a small restaurant which Anwar seemed to know, ate a meal of local food and drank a couple of warm bottles of beer. Stuart was quite tired and after the meal was finished they walked in similar silence back to the hotel. The final words that evening agreed the time for the start the following morning.

The next morning the driver met them in front of the hotel at eight o'clock sharp. They drove for a little over half an hour to a small factory on the outskirts of the town. The offices of the factory were relatively well-appointed and fully air-conditioned. Stuart felt quite comfortable while they sat through a meeting with the owner of the factory and his various managers. He had met some of these before in the presentations on his first trip. Anwar provided the translations where necessary.

Stuart picked up the feeling of the meeting as it progressed and he concluded that it was positive. The smiles, whilst obligatory in Indonesia, seemed to be very genuine, and the conversation was not punctuated by odd or difficult questions. The conclusion of the meeting was simple. Stuart was to review and survey the factory and complete the work he had started on the basis of the data Anwar had first sent. They agreed to start that afternoon, after lunch.

Lunch was taken in a nearby Chinese restaurant complete with a few chilled beers. Stuart left the restaurant feeling happy and content. It was not the best start for the forthcoming afternoon. They left the restaurant at a little after one-thirty and returned to the factory. Stuart and Anwar, accompanied by the factory manager, set off on a tour of the factory.

The factory was like something from an English Victorian print. Ancient machinery, some from the UK in years gone by, had many operators moving quickly and skilfully among the whirling machinery. The noise was fantastic, clattering and banging back and forth in a rhythmical, never-ending chatter. Then there was the heat. Stuart had been in many factories around the world. The noise he had heard before, unlike Anwar, who visibly flinched at the cacophony, but the heat in this equatorial factory caught Stuart by surprise. His body felt sweaty all over in an instant.

The lunchtime food and alcohol only made the heat and noise seem more oppressive. Stuart started his tour nonetheless. While the factory was small, it was well organised.

The control of the materials was well in hand and the place was clean and tidy, at least as clean and tidy as any textile mill could be. All of the buildings were tin-roofed affairs, for walls were not necessary in the heat of Indonesia, the only function of the buildings being to keep the rain off. Security came from the large barbed wire-topped wall that surrounded the factory.

The staff moved around in the din, operating without verbal communication. They all stopped and gave a smile or nod of respect to the factory manager. To Stuart, the girls giggled in groups and gave shy smiles; the men looked respectful. Every so often some one would mouth, "Hello Mister", the universal greeting. Stuart smiled in the heat of his discomfort.

Stuart spent four hours in the sweating factory, wandering around in his own world, deaf to the noise. By the end of the afternoon he was a limp, sweaty being. He fell into the car for the short journey to the hotel. The next two days were the same. For these two days, Stuart was a little better prepared. He ate small non-alcoholic lunches and dressed in the lightest clothes he had. At the end of the third day he was beginning to get used to it all. The days were punctuated by odd meetings. Anwar hung around, guiding and translating where necessary. Occasionally he disappeared with one or other of the managers for half hour discussions. Stuart guessed some sort of negotiations were going on. He didn't ask.

Anwar didn't ask about the progress of Stuart's tour at any time during the visits to the factory. Instead he waited until they left Solo on the Thursday morning. They had been driving for half an hour or so with little conversation. Stuart sensed that Anwar wanted to talk about it. He waited patiently for his opening. Finally Anwar spoke.

"What is your opinion?" he asked cautiously.

Stuart continued to stare out of the window, considering his reply.

"They are not what I expected," Stuart answered, turning to Anwar.

"Better or worse?"

"Neither really, just different. They are well-organised and well-managed. All that old equipment is in, well, fantastic condition. It's a shame to throw it all out."

Anwar looked disappointed.

"So you don't think we can do any deal with them?" He paused. "I thought that they were the best hope for any sales."

"I didn't mean that we couldn't do any business, just different that's all. I will have to restructure the quotation and finance offer later, back in England."

He looked at Anwar's slightly confused face. Stuart smiled. "Don't worry, we will do something. I got the impression that they wanted to grow and expand and they've done all they can with what they have. I talked to the various managers while you were investigating. All of them were very positive about getting bigger and buying some more equipment. So I guess we had a successful time."

He settled down with a contented smile on his face.

## CHAPTER 10

## A JAKARTA WEEKEND

After his return to Jakarta, Stuart spent the remainder of Thursday afternoon and part of the evening working on a report of the trip. He took a light meal and slept early and well.

The following day, he worked in Anwar's office, refining and developing a revised offer. They finished quite late and Anwar invited Stuart for dinner at a small Indonesian restaurant. After dinner, Anwar left Stuart on the steps of his hotel at a little after ten-thirty. Stuart waved good-bye and started to climb up towards the main doors. He paused as he thought about The Inne to his left. He looked around at the steps and then back up at the hotel. One of the bell girls was holding the door for him. He smiled and pointed at the steps that led down to The Inne. He turned towards them, his mind made up.

Inside, the new Filipino Band were playing with slightly improved gusto, but still some way short of the Manila Seven Band's standard. Stuart recognised a couple of people standing by one of the barrel tables by the bar. He moved across and joined them, ordering a beer on the way. He chatted, as best he could in the noise, with the people about his trip and the general situation.

After his second beer, the band stopped and changed for the local all-male band. As Stuart watched the changeover he felt a nudge in his ribs. He paid it no attention. Many people had pushed past in the crowded bar and he had had many such nudges that evening already. But when the second one came, he turned and looked for the source of the nudge. He found himself looking down into Ita's big brown eyes.

"Hello Stuart," she said, smiling to reveal her set of white straight teeth.

"Hi," he said in a non-committal manner.

"When did you get back?" she asked.

"Yesterday," he replied.

"And you didn't call me?" she asked quickly.

"No, sorry I didn't," Stuart replied, looking down at his feet in embarrassment.

"No problem," she said, smiling again. "How was Solo? Did you enjoy?" she continued without any change of tone.

"Yes I did. I've never seen rice fields and volcanoes before," he said.

She laughed. "Rice fields are everywhere here, nothing special."

"I know, but I've never seen them before so it's special for me. You want a drink?" he said, remembering his manners.

"No thank you," she replied, holding her glass up. "You remember one glass a night is enough for me."

"Yeah, I remember." He smiled and turned to watch the band start up.

She moved round to stand on the opposite side of him, resting her glass on Stuart's barrel table.

He felt rather guilty about not phoning her but, he reasoned, why should he feel embarrassed and guilty? She was only someone he had met a couple of times. She had asked nothing of him and he nothing of her. There was no pressure on him. She was not a call-girl, he was sure of that, but what was she and what did she really want?

He looked down at her as she stood leaning against the barrel table. She was moving gently in time to the music. Her hair was what amazed him most. It was cut in a very simple style, maybe twelve inches below her shoulders, cut straight across. At the front it was cut in a fringe, not straight, but slightly uneven. For the rest her hair was black, coal-black, and shiny. It was so well-organised that he guessed she had had it lacquered. He bent down to talk to her, getting close to her right ear. He could not smell any lacquer on her, nothing except clean, freshly-washed hair.

"What are you doing tomorrow?" he shouted above the noise, atoning for his guilt at not phoning her.

She looked up at him and shook her head. Her hair moved like the slow motion sequence on a shampoo commercial. She reached up and held on to his left arm, pulling him down to her level.

"Nothing, no plan," she shouted in his ear. "Why?"

"I'll tell you later," he shouted back, gesturing at the band.

She nodded in her shampoo commercial way.

When the band paused for another changeover she looked at him with her head on one side. Stuart knew what she was waiting for.

"You like to go out somewhere tomorrow?" he said after a suitable pause. "Evening," he added.

She looked at him with a smile.

Again he was a little embarrassed. Her smile was a cheeky, naughty smile and her large brown eyes gleamed. For the briefest moment she reminded him of Frances, but there was a deep gracefulness in her that Frances had never exhibited. The brief excursions into the cheeky pouts were always followed by a return to the slightly distant graceful look.

"Well, I've only ever been here and a few restaurants," he said quickly. "I want to see some other places. You can be my guide," he added lamely.

She half-pouted back. "I thought you were trying to ask me to go out with you." She looked a little coy.

Stuart had decided that she was quite cheekily attractive when she behaved like that. It was a contrast with the graceful look. He shook his head rather too vigorously. "No, of course not. I just don't know where to go in Jakarta. And it's boring going around by yourself. All I ask is your company."

She nodded and smiled up at him. "Don't worry, I like to joke and tease," she said. "It's the Indonesian system: always laughing and joking."

He smiled back. One evening out to appease his guilty conscience which, he knew, had no real reason for existing. And, he convinced himself, it might be fun. The band started up again, rendering further meaningful conversation impossible.

When the band paused for a game with the audience, not, Stuart was glad to see, a repeat of the lambada incident, Ita stretched up to talk to him.

"What time tomorrow?" she asked.

Stuart shrugged his shoulders. "Eight o'clock. We can go and eat and then go somewhere else later."

"Better about eight-thirty or nine," she said.

"Okay, where?"

"In the front of the hotel," she replied quickly.

Stuart nodded his agreement. He felt quite safe. With his previous encounter, the Filipino singer, he had not felt safe or in control of himself in her presence. With Ita he had no doubt who was in control. They left together when the new Filipino band stopped at the end of their last set of songs. He watched her getting in the taxi as he climbed the steps to the hotel. She waved and smiled at him as the taxi left.

Stuart's Saturday morning was spent in Anwar's office, wearing the traditional Saturday clothes of jeans and tee-shirt. He worked at the data he had taken during his visit to the Solo factory. Anwar talked to him briefly about the coming week's visit to the cultural capital of Indonesia, Yogjakarta, known to everyone as Yogya. Stuart reckoned he could reduce the time needed, so they agreed to leave early on Monday morning.

Stuart spent the afternoon shopping for odds and ends for his family, something for each of his children and his wife. The act of shopping for them reminded him of their existence. He made a note to phone them when he got back to the hotel. He even considered phoning Ita and cancelling their evening out, but, he said to himself, he knew he was in control so he would go, just to see a bit more of Jakarta.

Even though Stuart knew little of Jakarta, he decided it was his job to find a restaurant for dinner. He had been to the Japanese restaurant with Anwar and one or two others, but none of them filled him with any real desire to go back. He scanned the pages of the *What's On* guide in his room. He noted three entries for the same restaurant, one as a 'typical English pub', one as a curry house and one as a European restaurant. Its name was The Fox and Hounds. It sounded moderately reasonable to Stuart although he doubted whether they would have any typical English beer to go with the 'typical English pub'. He noted the address on a bit of paper and got changed. He took a seat in the lounge close to the hotel, sitting in such a position that he could see people arriving. He ordered a beer and sat down to wait. It was a little after eight o'clock.

Ita arrived at eight-thirty-five. Stuart was impressed, since he already knew about 'rubber time', the Indonesian way of excusing lateness. She didn't see him behind the window, but stood nervously contemplating entry to the hotel. She looked around in all directions for Stuart but would not climb the steps to enter. He finished his beer quickly to spare her any further agony and signed his bill on the way out.

She looked relieved to see him as he came down the steps.

"I don't like standing here by myself," she said as he arrived. "Maybe the security man will get the wrong idea about me."

She was serious, Stuart could see. She did not want her reputation tarnished.

"Where do you want to go?" she asked quickly, anxious to be away from the front of the hotel.

"This place," Stuart replied, holding out his piece of paper. "Do you know it?"

She shook her head and the shampoo commercial flashed through Stuart's mind again.

"I don't know the place but this street is near the H.I." She read the address again.

"H.I?" Stuart asked, puzzled.

"Yes, the Hotel Indonesia. We'll go there and ask. It's very close, I'm sure."

"Taxi?" Stuart enquired.

She nodded and waved at the doorman. "Taxi Pak."

The door man smiled and nodded, making his way over to a discreet button which summoned the taxis.

The taxi came and Ita directed the driver. Ten minutes later they pulled up in front of the Hotel Indonesia. Ita asked the doorman for directions. He pointed down the side of the building. She thanked him and pulled Stuart by the arm in the direction shown by the doorman. They walked through the car park of the hotel, down the side of the hotel and parallel to the main road. On the left was an impressive traffic island with a statue atop a twin column stand. Cables carried rows of lights down from the statue to the circular base, where fountains played in a circular ring directed towards the centre. Stuart was impressed: it looked so different in the dark, almost beautiful, although the traffic was still heavy and air loud with the noisy hooting of horns.

At the end of the car park, they passed into a dark area shaded by trees. Stuart felt unsafe when they walked past a group of men talking in low voices and smoking.

"Drivers", Ita said after they had passed them, "waiting for their call."

"Over there." Stuart pointed to a garish sign which proclaimed 'Fox and Hounds Pub and Restaurant'. There were a number of other restaurants on the same street and the whole place looked lively and interesting. To Stuart, the idea of a pub and curry house all in one was quite something of a novelty. He was used to eight pints of beer and then a stagger to find the nearest available place; well, he had been in his younger days, since eight pints and a curry was something he had not done in a long time. It was more like a swift half and then wheeling the family into the restaurant nowadays.

"Are you sure that this is the place?" Ita asked, looking a little concerned.

"Yeah I'm sure. Come on," he said brightly, making to push her back with his hand but not actually making contact with her.

They crossed the road and Stuart opened the door and entered the dimly lit bar. A smiling waitress welcomed them over the threshold.

Stuart looked around and headed for the bar on the right. They had done their best to make the bar area look like an English pub. It was done in what Stuart could only describe as Indonesian mock Tudor. Black wooden beams formed a reasonable attempt at a Tudor setting. A number of horse brasses and English hunting pictures added to the effect. The bar was extremely small and with a low ceiling. It was crowded with Europeans, male and female, and a few local girls. Stuart pushed his way in and ordered two glasses of beer.

Ita looked slightly uncomfortable.

"What's the problem?" Stuart asked, noticing her expression. She shook her head. The shampoo advert flashed through Stuart's mind.

"Nothing. There is no music here?" she asked, puzzled.

Stuart shrugged his shoulders. "I don't know. It's usually like this in a pub in England."

"What do you do then?" she asked with an expression of concerned curiosity.

"Drink and talk," he said, and finished his first drink off with a single gulp.

"If we want to talk in Indonesia we stay at home, if we go out we go out to see something. Why go out to talk?" She paused to sip her drink. "So what do you talk about in English pubs when you talk?"

"Anything." He paused. "The weather."

She laughed.

"Where do you come from, originally? You're not from Jakarta, right?" Stuart asked.

"No, I come from Central Java, a small town. My Mum still lives there. My Dad is already pass away."

Stuart nodded his head in gentle respect. "You have any family – brothers, sisters?"

"Yes, three sisters, no brothers, and like every family here many uncles and aunts. Me and my sisters all work and support our mother. She has no pension and if we don't help she has nothing: the family system. It's the same in England?" she asked.

"Last time yes, now not so much. Everyone has a pension from the government."

She nodded. "It's good in England." She looked around quickly and then at her watch. "You hungry, Stuart?" she asked with her head cocked on one side.

Stuart smiled. He wasn't particularly but guessed that she was. He asked for the menu. They spent fifteen minutes deliberating over the choice of food. In the end Stuart chose because Ita had almost no idea what the food was.

The waiter called them five minutes later and they sat down to eat. Like every curry house in England, this Indonesian version also looked like the Taj Mahal, with each little bay topped with an onion-shaped cut-out in the wall. Stuart didn't like the look of the little booths and instead they sat in the 'European' part of the restaurant, done out to look like a baronial Highland mansion. Stuart sat opposite Ita and took another long look at her face as she sat playing with the first bits of food.

The food was good, Stuart had to admit as a curry 'expert', although his expertise was based exclusively on curries sampled in the UK. As he sat opposite Ita in the silence of hungry eating, he examined her face in discreet detail. Her eyes were brown, dark brown, dark brown pools of exotic luxury waiting for the unsuspecting to all fall into. The shape was of an elongated almond – he was tempted to say Chinese-shaped – but there was something different in the shape and arrangement. She had high cheekbones, like so many of the Javanese people that he had seen, and the outer corners of her eyes were slightly higher than the inner ones, giving her face that unmistakable oriental look. The mouth was turned up at the corners, giving her face a normally happy look without her needing to smile. When she did, the teeth revealed were beautifully white and straight. But it was the colour of her skin that Stuart noticed most. She had a little eyeshadow above her eyes and some lipstick on, but the rest of her face was that light nut-brown colour which almost every European white woman, and man for that matter, wanted to be. Not only wanted to be, Stuart mused, but quite literally died to be, spending money and risking skin cancer in chasing this elusive colour. And Ita had it completely naturally. Not only was the skin that colour, it was clear and unblemished. He could see no evidence of facial hair either, with the exception of her thick eyebrows and long eyelashes. 'These women have all the advantages,' Stuart thought. 'Clear golden skin, extra-white teeth, and thick, ever so thick, luxuriantly shiny black hair.'

"Not hungry?" she asked, noticing that he had stopped eating and was staring at her.

"Just resting," he replied, a little startled.

"What you thinking about?" she asked, realising that he was in some other place.

He raised his left eyebrow and smiled. "Nothing."

She regarded him carefully for a moment and then started eating again.

Ita ate well and announced at the end of the meal that she enjoyed it. Stuart considered the first part, his part, of the evening a success. As he asked for the bill, he looked at Ita. "Where to now? Stay here or move on?"

She looked at her watch; it was almost ten o'clock. "Move on."

They walked into warm night. "How far?" Stuart asked.

"We can walk if you don't mind," she said quickly.

They strolled back past the Hotel Indonesia, crossed the road and walked past a building site which proclaimed 'The Grand Hyatt' on its boards. On the other side of the main road were other hotels, The President and The Mandarin. The road was still quite busy but the traffic was moving reasonably quickly. They walked for almost ten minutes. Stuart was beginning to feel a little hot and sticky. Opposite a large McDonalds she turned down a dark roadway between two buildings.

"Is this right?" Stuart asked nervously.

"Yes of course." She tugged his arm. "Come on."

He followed meekly and nervously. They crossed a small bridge over a stinking water ditch which flowed darkly below. On the other side of the bridge was a sign which announced the Java Pub. A group of men hung round the entrance selling cigarettes.

Ita led the way up a narrow steel staircase. Inside the first-floor pub the first thing that Stuart noticed was the dark, slightly dingy nature of the place. It appeared to be almost a warehouse. The roof beams were visible and festooned with various placards and cards. The lampshades were made from red cloth crudely placed over wire frames and they gave a very poor light. The central bar had a small raised stage at one end. A waitress guided them to a small table on the right-hand side. They sat and Stuart ordered a beer. Ita wanted only orange juice. She had already had her one drink of the evening.

A band of three local men was playing on the small stage. They sang rock and roll songs from the fifties and sixties. They played with less professionalism and polish than the groups he had seen in The Inne, but they played familiar songs with gusto and power which made up for their lack polish. After a few songs, they retired and a second local group came on. This had four male musicians and a female singer. She was an attractive girl with an unusual voice and she blasted out songs with verve and enthusiasm. It was an altogether different type of place from the more sophisticated atmosphere of The Inne.

As time wore on the place began to fill rapidly, mostly with Europeans and a few local girls. The tempo of the music rose and people moved and clapped with enthusiasm and high spirits. At one point the singer began the old Frank Sinatra song, *New York, New York*. As she sang she stepped up and walked along one arm of the bar, ducking below the roof beams as she went. Stuart was really enjoying himself. He felt relaxed especially because Ita was not trying to do anything to him. They were enjoying nothing more than a good night out.

After a couple of hours, some time after one-thirty, Stuart was beginning to feel tired. He nudged Ita.

"You tired?" he shouted in her ear.

She shook her head. "No." She smiled up at him. "Later we go to disco, yeah?"

Stuart took a deep breath and nodded. It was Saturday night and he had no plans for Sunday so he could lie in. "Where?"

"Not far from here. We can walk," she shouted back.

For Stuart the idea of going to a disco at one-thirty was a bit unusual. At home, the pubs shut at eleven and the discos finished at two. Everything was that much later here. Still, there would be no kids to jump on him on Sunday morning and he wanted the full Jakarta nightlife.

They left the Java Pub and walked further up the main road, away from the Fox and Hounds where they had eaten earlier. At the end of the road there was a large roundabout with another statue and fountain on the far side. They turned left and walked down a smaller, badly-lit road. At the end they turned right through a mass of taxis and people milling around. Food stalls abounded and many locals sat, ate and talked.

"Come on," she said, leading a way through the mass of cars and people.

A little way down the street was a queue of people standing in front of a building which struck Stuart as being almost, well, alpine. At first, he could not rationalise these thoughts. Then he realised that it was the steeply sloping roof with huge eaves hung with lamps which gave this impression. A small balcony and whitewashed walls completed the illusion.

"Welcome to Tanamur," Ita said as they joined the queue. She pulled out her purse and paid while Stuart was admiring the front of the building.

"No," he said, surprised, "I'll pay."

She shook her head. "No problem." She held up her right hand up in an additional gesture of resistance to his intent to pay. "I have already. Come on."

She led the way up the narrow concrete staircase which led up to a small door. They were at the level of the small balcony that Stuart had noticed when they had arrived. Inside the door, Stuart heard, or rather felt, the music. It was not so much loud and deafening as low and rumbling, thumping into the pit of his stomach. The inside was like nothing Stuart had every seen before. It was crowded to the point of crush and the dance floor was covered with people gyrating in random time to the music. The bars were even more crammed with drinkers and talkers. The decor was the most unusual feature of the whole place. It wasn't like a warehouse – it was a warehouse. The walls and roof were rough concrete and a couple of roughly-built walls split up the bar areas. Atop the walls were precarious dancing stages with low floors built from rough steel sheeting and fences of bent steel bar. The dancefloor had four street lights at its corners, linked by what looked like telephone and electric cables in some bizarre parody of a street. The music was directed from what looked like a car sticking halfway up out of one wall. Occasional wafts of stage smoke were discharged from below the radiator of the car.

As they made their way down to the bar area, Stuart looked at the fellow customers. They were a mixture of locals and foreigners in roughly equal proportions of each and of male and female, with some he wasn't sure about. Some of the local girls gave Stuart a long sensual look with an occasional one winking.

Ita disappeared and returned with two glasses of beer from the entrance tickets.

"First drink free," she shouted at Stuart. "What do you think?"

"Busy!" he shouted back.

"Come on," she said. "Follow me."

She led the way past the bar and dancefloor to another, quieter bar at the back of the building.

Stuart drank the one glass of beer quickly and held on to the second. He surveyed the scene around him, the many beautiful local girls standing around in twos and threes, eyeing any man who looked in their direction. Groups of men, both local and foreign, stood or sat around eyeing them back, making the occasional approach in the age-old game of boy meets girl.

The record changed from something Stuart didn't recognise to something else he didn't recognise. Ita tugged his arm. "Come, we dance."

She obviously recognised the tune. Stuart followed obediently as she slipped through the crowds to the dancefloor. They danced for a few songs. Stuart felt the sweat on his brow as he moved in the crush of the floor. Ita, he noticed, was not in the least bit concerned by the exertions. They retired after about fifteen minutes. Stuart was surprised to find his glass of beer still on the bar where he had left it. He finished it in a single gulp.

The music changed again and Ita dragged him back to the dancefloor once again. They continued in this way, a short pause for a drink and then more dancing for a couple of hours. Ita, it seemed, had limitless energies and appetite for dancing.

Stuart glanced at his watch. To his surprise it was almost four o'clock. He had never been up this late partying in his life, even as a student. They had tried 'all nighters' as students but failed to stay the course. Stuart now realised that this was because of the early start and the quantity of alcohol consumed. Despite the late hour Stuart had drunk comparatively little of the weakish local beer and didn't feel in the slightest bit drunk. He was just beginning to feel tired. He nudged Ita who was standing close to his seat watching the dancefloor.

"You tired?" he asked.

She shook her head and Stuart noticed small amounts of sweat on her temples. She turned and looked at Stuart. She saw the tiredness in his eyes and the sweat on his face and the damp patches on his shirt. She took pity on him.

"Okay, come, we go now. It is time for close anyway."

She led the way through the crowd to the exit stairs. Many other people were beginning to move away and out into the still warm tropical morning. She led the way past the hordes of taxi drivers touting for business. She moved past those close to the nightclub and out into the main street beyond. She looked for a taxi which was not touting aggressively. Eventually she saw one she fancied and they got in. She directed the driver to the hotel.

"Sometimes they don't want to use the meter and want a lot of money," she said, "and then they want you to pay for them parking in front. All those men hanging around charge for arranging car park." She shook her head in a gesture of disgust. "This one is okay."

"How do you know?" Stuart asked.

"I can tell," she replied evasively.

The journey to the hotel was short. They didn't speak much. Stuart wondered what was about to happen.

"I take the taxi to my house," she said, interrupting his thoughts. "It's not far from here."

"Okay," said Stuart. "I will pay for the taxi."

He glanced at the meter and added some before giving the money to Ita.

She smiled. "Thanks."

"Thank you," he replied, "for a very enjoyable evening."

They rolled up the ramp to the hotel.

She smiled at him. "Bye Stuart."

He smiled back and climbed out of the taxi. He waved as the taxi left but this time she was not watching. He collected his key from reception.

"Good morning Mr Morgan," the male receptionist said as he handed over the key. Stuart smiled a tired smile and walked slowly to the lift. Pausing only long enough to put the 'Do not disturb' sign on his door, he flopped on to the bed and slept.

To his surprise, Stuart slept long and well. Usually, after a long night, he still woke early, usually earlier than normal. However, on this occasion it was eleven o'clock before he even stirred and twelve before he was up, washed and dressed. He had a light lunch and then sat by the pool in his shorts for a couple of hours. The sun was not too hot; as on most days in Jakarta the sun was slightly obscured by the haze of pollution. As he sat and watched the various people cavorting in the pool or, like himself, sitting and relaxing, he mused on the previous evening.

In some ways he was happy with the conclusion of the evening. Ita had made no demands on him, nor he on her, and she had even paid for some part of it. He had succeeded in going out for a good night out and nothing more. He had enjoyed himself and yet in some ways he was a little disappointed; more particularly, if he cared to admit it, his ego was a little disappointed. She had not asked him to phone her again or made any hint that she wanted to see him again. She had not touched him, other than to attract his attention or lead him somewhere. There had not been a good night kiss or even a handshake. The dancing, whilst long and vigorous, had not been accompanied by a slow dance; in fact every time the music had shown the remotest sign of slowing down she had quickly led him back to the bar. These all stuck in the throat of his ego just a little. Still, he consoled himself, he had enjoyed himself and he had seen something of Jakarta's nightlife.

When he analysed it rationally, he had no real desire to be unfaithful to his wife with this particular woman. He liked her well enough: her body seemed attractive, her face was quite pretty and she was pleasant enough company, but not, he convinced himself, the one to make a fool of himself over. He was not sure whether or not he would contact her again after he got back from his next trip. He decided to ignore the possibility and concentrate on his work. But his ego was still disappointed.

## CHAPTER 11

## GIN AND TONIC

Stuart checked out of the hotel before eight o'clock on Monday morning, deposited his suitcase in the hotel storage and met Anwar in the reception area. The morning was not yet hot as they left for the airport. The flight direct to Yogjakarta was slightly less unpleasant than the one the weekend before. The weather was slightly cooler and Stuart was better prepared for the heat. He wore his lightest shirt and trousers, with cotton socks and a pair of suede shoes.

Anwar arranged a taxi when they arrived and they went straight to the first factory, a large concern on the outskirts of the town. Unlike the one the previous week, this place was a different prospect. The offices were old and decrepit. The air-conditioning was provided by a number of old window-type machines pushed through various holes hacked in the walls and window frames. Few of them seemed to work properly and the smell of the clove cigarettes hung heavy in the air. The people moved with little enthusiasm and all the desks were piled high with paper and mess. It looked inefficient and badly organised.

Anwar talked with a small woman who sat close by the entrance. After a brief conversation she showed Stuart and Anwar to a small conference room and ordered tea for them. At least this conference room did not smell quite so much of burning cloves and the AC seemed to work.

Stuart looked at Anwar with his head slightly to one side. Anwar shrugged his shoulders in a silent conversation about the prospects. Stuart was, however, determined to reserve judgement.

The tea arrived and they sat down to drink. It was over half an hour before the man they had come to see, the director of marketing, appeared. He did not cut a particularly energetic figure. Throughout the morning they discussed what they wanted to do. The marketing director seemed to be thrown off-balance by the visit and he spent much of the time on the phone bringing other people down to the conference room to see who really wanted to meet Stuart and Anwar. This dragged on till lunchtime when they all broke for lunch.

In the afternoon, the whole scene was repeated until three o'clock when Stuart finally managed to start his talk. In their plan, it was to have started in the morning, with the afternoon being spent in and around the factory. There were so many interruptions for people coming in and going out, phone calls and questions that the whole presentation took until six o'clock. When Stuart and Anwar left the factory after agreeing to return the following morning, they were both drained and tired.

Anwar got them to a hotel in the centre of the town. The hotel was in a wide one-way street. Stuart looked up and down the bustling street, at the pedal cabs, the cars, the buses and the people, so many people moving slowly up and down the street entering the shops, buying from the roadside stalls or just looking.

Anwar nudged him. "Maliboro Street," he said.

Stuart nodded as if he already knew.

"Most famous street in Yogja," Anwar continued. "We can take a walk later if you want."

Stuart nodded again.

After an hour, the two of them emerged from the front door of the hotel and Anwar led the way into the crush. The number of people cramming the wide street was now even more than before. Stuart moved his wallet from his back pocket into his side pocket and kept one hand firmly on it as they pushed through the masses. Stuart had read in the hotel guidebook that Maliboro Street was 'almost European in its architecture and ambience'. Stuart looked around at the concrete-faced buildings all painted in white with varying degrees of weathering; at the vast numbers of small stalls selling so many things; at the brown faces of the people. He smelt the clove cigarettes; he smelt the heavy humid evening air. He heard the strange voices, the noise of the car horns and the click-click noise from the pedal cab drivers as they touted for business. Whoever had written the guidebook, Stuart concluded, must have been in a different Maliboro Street at a different time.

Stuart and Anwar drifted along in no particular direction. Stuart bought a few bits from the stalls: a belt for himself, some earrings for his daughter, tee-shirts for his wife and son. Anwar bargained aggressively for each item, walking away only to be called back for a new price by the stallholder. Stuart watched the game and enjoyed it. After more than one hour of the walk, Anwar pointed at his stomach. Stuart nodded and Anwar led him off down a small side alley.

Once they were off the main street, the noise dropped. The heavy tropical night air still hung on Stuart but, now that the crush was gone, he felt more comfortable.

They wandered along a small back road which ran parallel to the main street. Here was a new smell. A burning smell but not from cigarettes. It was a sweet smell, like burning sugar combined with roasting meat and charcoal. Stuart sniffed the air.

Anwar stopped. "Satay," he said simply.

"Satay?" Stuart asked.

"Yes, small bamboo sticks with meat cooked over a small charcoal barbecue. Very Indonesian. That's the smell."

Stuart nodded.

"You want to try some?" Anwar asked. "From one of the small stalls is the best, better than any big restaurant."

Stuart looked nervously at Anwar.

Anwar laughed. "Don't worry, the food is clean and good. Come on."

Anwar selected a stall and they sat down at some rough wooden benches. The satay came with rice, peanut sauce and sweet soya sauce, a thick black soya sauce that Stuart had never seen before. Anwar dug into the food with gusto. Stuart was a little more reserved. He picked slowly at the satay, trying the new tastes and flavours. After a few minutes he lost his reticence and began to eat more rapidly. It was good, he had to admit, and he was very hungry. They washed down the food with lukewarm Indonesian tea.

After a further walk, they turned back to the hotel. Once inside, Stuart and Anwar sat in the small foyer bar and ordered a cool beer each to take the edge off the hot night outside.

"What a mess," Stuart said, after half the beer had gone down.

"What? Yogjakarta?" Anwar asked.

"No, that's fine. No, it's that factory. Well, not the *factory* – I haven't seen that yet. Those offices and the people today – a complete and total mess. How do they compete? How do they make anything?" he continued.

"They are like so many old Indonesian companies. They operate in a closed market with little competition, with shared markets. They don't need to be efficient," Anwar answered.

"Okay, but why do they want to do something now?" Stuart asked.

"Well, some things are changing here. Maybe there will be more competition. Exporting is now the aim and they need a lot more to export." Anwar paused. "So maybe the time is right for some expansion."

"Do you actually think that they can organise themselves to expand?"

"With a little help from you and me, maybe." Anwar raised his glass and smiled.

The next day was spent trying to see the factory. At first no one could be found to guide them and then the man who came knew little about the machinery. Finally, shortly before lunch, they got in and walked about.

The factory was as decrepit and disorganised as Stuart's worst fears. The machinery, that which was working, was dirty and badly maintained. Guards and covers were off, string was in evidence holding things together and dirty oil pans littered the floor beneath the machines. The noise was not as intense as on the previous visit, a reflection of the lack of activity. Piles of cloth and yarn stood around in great heaps. The staff wandered around aimlessly and no supervisors were in evidence.

Stuart went to work as best he could, checking and recording the machine details, asking questions which their guide could not answer and trying to find some semblance of order in the layout and design of the factory.

By the end of the day, Stuart had a long list of questions and information requirements. Anwar set off to try to organise the information.

That night, sitting in the bar after a meal in the hotel, Anwar looked confused and upset.

"Hey," said Stuart brightly, "don't look so worried. These things happen. We couldn't know what a mess that place was going to be in, could we?"

"No, I guess not, but I feel it's my fault. I should have done some more research before you came," Anwar said despondently.

"Look," Stuart answered firmly, "I will get all the data and make some proposals. I think we have a chance provided that you can get their management to understand the realities of working for export, or even working at all. It's not been a wasted trip."

"I have to go back tomorrow evening, to Jakarta," Anwar said, looking at Stuart.

"That's okay, I can find my way around by myself if I haven't got finished." Stuart smiled, trying to cheer up Anwar.

After another frustrating day, Anwar left Stuart alone in the hotel to return to Jakarta. Stuart worked in his room for some time, then he watched a rather poor film on the hotel video channel before his eyes fell on the telephone at the side of the bed. He picked up the handset and began to dial his wife. Halfway through he stopped, he checked his watch, worked out the time difference and realised that she was probably out. He was about to put the receiver down when he noticed the small piece of paper that Ita had given him sticking out of the side of his diary. He pulled the paper out and without a further thought dialled the number.

The phone rang for a long time, so long that he decided to give it two more rings before he put the phone down. Halfway through the last of the those two rings, the phone was answered.

"Hello," a small female voice said, sounding a little out of breath.

"Can I speak to Ita?" he said slowly.

"This is Ita."

"Hi, it's Stuart," he said simply. "Have you been running?"

"No," she laughed. "Telephone always rings when I am in the toilet. Stuart, is that really you?" she said loudly and with much enthusiasm in her voice. "And where are you? In Jakarta?"

"Yes, it is me, and no, I'm not in Jakarta, I'm still in Yogja and I still will be until Thursday," he replied.

"Okay," she said, sounding slightly disappointed. "When can we meet again?"

Stuart was surprised by her forwardness. She had not wanted to arrange anything the last time they had met and yet now she was disappointed that he was still in Yogja and was keen to arrange a new meeting. The disappointment he had felt after their last meeting vanished, his ego somewhat appeased.

"Friday," he said. "Friday at eight o'clock in The Inne. Is that possible?"

"Yes, very good. Then we can eat, yes?" she replied.

"Yes, then we can eat."

"See you on Friday then and thank you for your telephoning." She hung up the phone almost before Stuart had a chance to say goodbye.

The following days were very frustrating for Stuart. He had to cancel his flight back on Thursday and book an early afternoon flight for Friday. He got the last bits of information just in time and he raced from the factory to the airport with little more than half an hour to spare before the departure time. He managed to check in, moved into the departure lounge and waited. The departure time came and went. There was no announcement and Stuart became worried. He looked at his fellow travellers. A few were looking at their watches, looking at the departure board and wondering. There were no other white faces in the lounge. Stuart suddenly felt very alone. He tried to ask an airport official what was happening but no one seemed to understand or know. Eventually a man tapped him on the shoulder.

"Are you speak English?" he said to Stuart.

"Yes," Stuart replied gratefully.

"The aeroplane is delayed maybe two hours because of problem," the man said. "You going to Jakarta, yes?"

Stuart nodded.

"I also go to Jakarta with same aeroplane as you, so I tell you what happen."

Stuart was glad to have found someone who could explain something of what was happening. The two hour delay turned into something more like four hours. A later flight to Jakarta took off before theirs, increasing Stuart's sense of frustration.

It was beginning to get dark when they finally boarded the plane. Stuart sat and sweated. The plane had been standing for four hours with no air-conditioning and the flight was full. Every seat was taken and the temperature soared inside the plane. Stuart felt the sweat running and prayed for take-off. Closing the doors was delayed by another half hour and Stuart thought that he was going to melt. The taxiing took an age and, whilst the air-conditioning was now on, it was not effective quickly enough to make Stuart feel any better before the plane took off. It was six-fifteen, more than five hours late.

The flight was short, less than an hour, and Stuart had no bags to collect. He raced through the terminal building and jumped into a taxi. It was seven-thirty. He wondered about Ita and whether she would be on time. He hoped not. The journey was slow. Stuart felt frustrated again but there was nothing he could do.

Eventually he arrived at the hotel, at eight-twenty. Checking in took an age and his big suitcase took even longer to arrive from the hotel storage. Stuart had to have a shower. By the time he got into the shower it was eight-forty-one. He was becoming really worried about Ita. He had a shave and general brush-up, threw on a set of clothes and raced down to The Inne. It was five minutes before nine when he finally pushed open the door of The Inne.

Ita was there. He saw her sitting on a bar stool at the side of the bar, her back towards him, talking with another Indonesian girl. He made his way round to where they sat.

As Stuart approached she looked up. He put on his best face and smiled at Ita.

"Sorry," he said with genuine sincerity. "The plane was late – very late, five hours or more."

She smiled back in a detached manner. She looked different. She waved her arm around.

"No problem for me," she giggled and sipped her drink. "We have been drinking these nice tonic drinks, me and my friend." Ita's voice was definitely slurred.

Stuart looked at the 'nice tonic drinks'. There was no doubt that it was a gin and tonic. Ita was on the point of being drunk.

With a single gulp she finished the remainder of her drink and turned towards the bar. She shouted and waved to attract the attention of the barman. It was so unlike the normally serene and graceful Ita. Two more 'nice tonic' drinks arrived, one for Ita and her friend. Her friend looked more in control and just smiled, with an evil glint in her eye, at Stuart.

Ita turned towards the stage and watched the band, bouncing her head in time to the music.

Stuart ordered himself a drink.

After fifteen minutes or so the band finished and Ita turned to face Stuart. Her face was flushed and her eyes had lost their deep pool impression: they looked hazy and empty. She smiled, tried to rest her arm on the bar and slipped off, spilling some drink on the way. She giggled uncontrollably.

Stuart took her arm gently. "Don't you think you had better stop and get some fresh air?"

"No way, I'm having fun. We've been here since eight o'clock drinking these nice tonic drinks," she slurred back.

"Those have got alcohol in," Stuart said firmly.

She shook her head violently. "No, they haven't."

Before he could stop her, Ita ordered another one to replace the one she had spilt. Stuart shook his head and looked at the other girl, who just smiled back again. He ignored Ita and watched the band start up again. After a while he felt Ita's hand on his arm. He looked round.

She smiled blearily up at him.

"Toilet," she mumbled. "I want go to toilet."

She moved unsteadily away towards the end of the bar.

Stuart recognised the symptoms. Quickly he asked for his bill and signed it before she came staggering back. Ita tried and failed to get back on the bar stool she had been occupying. She held on to his arm. "Please, I want go lie down."

Stuart held her arm and led her out of the bar. He glanced at his watch. It was a little after ten-fifteen. What a night out this was going to be. He half carried, half guided her out of the bar, carrying her small handbag in his left hand. He got a few strange looks as he left the bar. Getting her up the stairs out of the bar proved to be difficult. She could hardly walk, although she hadn't quite collapsed. Once at the top he tried to navigate the entrance to the hotel with some dignity, something which was almost impossible. He stopped to get his key, dropping his eyes so that he did not have to look the receptionist in the face.

Once in the room he sat Ita on the bed. She flopped uncontrolled backwards and sideways. She lay and groaned.

"What's the matter?" she slurred badly, trying to sit up. "Why the room not still?" She flopped back on to the bed.

Her beautiful eyes were a vacant, fuzzy mess. She was very drunk indeed.

Stuart considered what to do. Let her sleep, give her water, he wasn't sure. In the event the decision was made for him.

She sat up again very quickly and looked around. "*Munta mau munta,*" she shouted.

"What?" asked Stuart.

"*Munta,*" she replied, holding her hand to her mouth.

Stuart guessed the meaning of the word and pulled her up and directed her to the bathroom. She slumped to her knees and shuffled forward. Stuart lifted the lid of the toilet and put his left arm under her waist and across her chest, holding her right shoulder in his left hand. In this position he held her over the toilet. With his free hand, he gathered the black hair in a bunch and waited for the inevitable.

She heaved twice, making disgusting dog-like barking noises before anything actually came up. Then it really flowed. She heaved repeatedly until she was exhausted. Stuart reached across and flushed the toilet. He pulled her up and grabbed a towel to wipe her face. She looked terrible. She heaved again and he had to be quick to make sure that she didn't miss. She heaved two or three more times and then was quiet.

When Stuart was sure that she had finished, he pulled her up and dragged her backwards out of the bathroom. She flopped helplessly in his arms. He pulled her on to the bed and wiped her face down with his hanky. Her eyes kept closing and her head rolled around like a rag doll's. Slowly he lowered her on to the bed. He pulled off her shoes and put her legs under the covers. He brought a towel from the bathroom and rested her head on that, a precaution against further vomiting in the bed. She lay in the recovery position, on her left side, her eyes closed, her mouth open, already snoring a little.

Stuart sat in the chair and looked at her. He shook his head. He pulled one pillow off the bed and then settled down on the floor with the main heavy bedcover as his mattress. 'What a night,' he smiled to himself. Not quite what he had had in mind, probably not what she had in mind either, but what would be the result? That was still for the future. He looked at his watch. It showed almost eleven o'clock. Then he slept.

## CHAPTER 12

## BREAKFAST, LUNCH AND DINNER

Stuart was awakened the next morning by the diffuse sunlight shining through net curtains and through the gap between the two main heavy curtains. He sat up and rubbed his eyes and stretched a little. He looked around at the makeshift bed in which he found himself. For a moment he was confused as to why he had ended up on the floor. But then he remembered.

He looked across the wide bed towards the small lump on the far side. She was still there and still snoring lightly. Absently he scratched his hair, eventually running both hands through in an attempt to make it feel better. Then he rubbed the bristle on his chin. Rising to the kneeling position, he looked hard at the small mound that was Ita. She had not moved in the night. She lay in exactly the same position in which he had left her, atop the towel.

Stuart went into the bathroom and had a shower, hair wash and shave. When he emerged, she was still asleep. He sat on the edge of the bed and looked at her. Even in her slightly dishevelled condition, she was still undoubtedly very beautiful. There was a serene depth to her face. It could break out like Frances's into cheeky poutiness, but mostly it had a calm gratefulness which Frances's face had never had. There was something deeply serious about Ita which there had never been about Frances. It worried him and he shivered slightly.

After fifteen minutes of waiting for her to wake by herself, Stuart got bored. It was already some time after nine and breakfast would soon be over in the hotel. He wanted to get her up and out before too long. He opened the main curtain until the sunlight fell on her face. Then he pulled back the net curtain to allow the full force of the sunlight to fall on her sleeping face.

Then he opened a bottle of water and poured two glasses. One he drank straight down, the second he set, along with two paracetamol tablets, on the bedside table at her side, preparing for her inevitable hangover and headache.

After a few minutes, the sunlight began to have an effect on Ita's tightly closed eyes. They flickered slightly. Then with great speed she sat bolt upright and looked around with a strange mixture of panic and curiosity on her face.

"Where am I?" she asked.

"My hotel room," Stuart replied almost unnecessarily.

She looked around once more then put her hand to her forehead and flopped backwards on to the bed with a groan.

Stuart waited.

She lifted the covers of the bed gingerly and looked under. Her face looked a little more relieved when she realised that the only items of clothing she had lost were her shoes. Then she sat up more slowly and looked around a second time.

"Where did you sleep?" she asked.

Stuart gestured to the floor and his makeshift bed.

She looked down at his sleeping place and then back at him. "What happened last night?" she asked, still looking somewhat confused and afraid.

"Does *munta* mean anything to you?" Stuart asked with his head slightly on one side, his face about to break out into a laugh.

"Oh my God," she said slowly and quietly. "Was I really sick last night?"

"Oh yes, very very *munta*," he said, now unable to restrain his laughter.

She pulled her legs up towards her body and wrapped her arms around them, cuddling herself for comfort.

"Where?" she asked in a little voice. "In the bar?"

"No, fortunately not. I got you out before you collapsed and got you up here. Then you started shouting '*munta munta*' and I worked out what you wanted and managed to get you to talk to the big white telephone in the bathroom," he answered.

"What's the big white telephone?" she asked.

"The toilet."

She laughed a little, her fear and insecurity ebbing away as she heard the events of the previous evening, that she had got drunk, that she had come very close to making a total fool of herself or worse and that by good fortune had ended up with a real gentleman who had helped her and not taken any advantage of her situation.

Stuart observed her as she thought. He too wondered at the situation in which he found himself. How could he explain that a woman had spent the night in his room and nothing had happened? Whichever way he looked at it, it didn't look too bright.

"How do you feel?" was his next question.

This question, coupled with the declining fear and insecurity, allowed the other feelings to creep into her consciousness: the headache, the stomach pain and the horrible dry feeling in her mouth.

"Terrible," was her reply.

Stuart pointed at the glass of water and the two tablets on the table at the side of the bed. "For you," he said. "Paracetamol tablets – very good for headache and not bad on your stomach."

She quickly swallowed the tablets and drained the glass in a single gulp and then lay back in the bed.

"There's a bathroom with clean towels, hot water, soap, shampoo, deodorant – man's, I'm afraid – new hotel toothbrush..."

She sat up again and looked at him.

"...And a lock," he said finally.

She smiled at the last statement, for it reassured her that she was in the company of a man who could be trusted to behave decently. She lay back in bed again.

After a few more moments, she pulled herself upright again and, without a word, disappeared into the offered bathroom.

Stuart smiled to himself as he heard the door close, but, surprisingly, not lock. He could appreciate the worry that must have crossed her mind when she woke up – the strange hotel room, the man, not being able to remember – and now the confusion that she must be feeling as she felt relieved and safe again, because everything had worked out reasonably well.

She was a long time in the bathroom. Stuart always found the length of time that women had to spend in the bathroom one of life's mysteries and one of life's frustrations. When she came out Stuart was on the point of becoming angry, since breakfast would be close to finishing in the hotel.

"Come on," he said, trying to sound jokey. "Breakfast in the hotel will soon be finished."

She was brushing her hair with his brush. She stopped abruptly in mid-stroke and looked at him, horrified.

"Breakfast in the hotel?" she said quietly, but with an accent which left Stuart in no doubt as to the gravity of the suggestion. "I'll buy you breakfast," she said in a more normal voice, restarting her hair-brushing. "I'll go downstairs now and wait in the front. You come in five minutes," she continued in a brusque businesslike manner. She put the brush back in the bathroom and turned to leave.

"Mmmm," she said with an air of frustration, looking at her watch as she did so. "Can I use your phone?"

"Of course," Stuart replied.

She dropped her bag on the back of the desk chair and dialled a number and spoke quickly in her own language.

When she finished she looked at Stuart. "I should be at work – it's Saturday." She paused and sighed. "I told them I was sick in the head. Not too far wrong, yeah?" she said, with a smile returning.

This time she opened the door and left.

Stuart waited the required five minutes and followed.

She was waiting outside the entrance not looking at the hotel or anyone in the area. As Stuart came closer, she started walking away without acknowledging him.

Now he understood the reason for her horror in the bedroom. Her reputation was at stake: to be seen eating in or leaving the hotel with a strange European man on a Saturday morning would make her look like a call-girl or prostitute, which she clearly wasn't. He respected her wishes and walked on the opposite side of the road down the hotel drive.

Once out of sight of the hotel, she crossed to join him, looking at him with a smile. "Thanks very much for what you did for me last night and this morning. I could have got myself into a lot of trouble last night in that bar, drunk like that."

"I guess it was my fault for being late really," Stuart replied, trying to find the inevitable reason that this woman would use to blame him for her own actions in the manner that his wife always sought to find a reason to push the blame on to him.

"No, not really, being late is part of the system in Indonesia. It was my friend really. She give me those nice tonic drinks," she replied, much to Stuart's surprise.

"Gin and tonic drinks," he corrected her. "Each one is as strong as a glass of beer, maybe more, and you had four or five. It's no wonder that you *muntaed*," he said, bastardising the Indonesian word with an English ending.

She laughed and slipped her small arm into his right arm, giving a squeeze and looking up at him with a smile. "Thanks again. Come on, now is time for *sarapan* or at well past ten o'clock more like *makan siang*. That's breakfast or lunch to you." She smiled again, revealing her perfect white teeth and her big brown eyes, now pools of deep seriousness once again. She tugged his arm again. "Come on," she said. "Over there in that."

She waved and gestured at a small orange three-wheeled contraption which Stuart had seen many times in Jakarta but in which he had never ridden.

"In that?" he said incredulously.

"Yes, of course. I'm taking you for a Jakarta breakfast so must go in Jakarta transport," she laughed, most of her normal composure regained after the bath and paracetamol.

In the back of the tiny contraption they were forced to sit tight together, legs touching, shoulders nudging as the vehicle lurched around. It was noisy, very noisy. The driver appeared to be sitting on the engine, which must have been a scooter-type, air-cooled single cylinder judging from the noise and heat. The floor where Stuart rested his feet felt hot even through his shoes and he could not imaging travelling far or driving one of these things all day. The driver seemed unconcerned by any of this and he simply held his course as he navigated rather precariously around the large triangular garden in front of the hotel.

After ten bone-shaking minutes, during which Stuart was sure that a collision was inevitable on two occasions and during which conversation was impossible, they stopped. Gratefully Stuart climbed out and Ita paid the driver. They had arrived close to the unimaginatively named Japanese Restaurant to which Anwar had brought him on his first visit. As on Stuart's first visit, the street outside was crammed with stalls and small eating places. Ita wandered around until she found one that looked suitable. They sat down.

It was hot and the sweat trickled down Stuart's back as he sat. No breeze broke the still air to offer any release from the heat. Ita seemed unconcerned. She ordered some food which quickly appeared and, Stuart had to admit, it tasted really quite good.

Ita paid with a handful of small change from her pocket when they had finished and they sat and looked at one another in the mid-morning heat.

"What now?" he asked. "What else constitutes a Jakarta breakfast?"

"I don't know. How much of Jakarta have you seen?" she replied.

"Nothing."

"Okay, you remember you did ask me to be your guide," she said, her cheeky face tilted to one side, "so follow me."

And with that she jumped up and led Stuart away through the maze of tables.

The rest of the day was a blur for Stuart. They queued for half an hour in the heat to ride a small lift to the top of a tower from where they got a hazy view of not very much. Ita explained that this was 'Monas' or Monument Nasional, the first president's contribution to the Jakarta skyline. In the air-conditioned basement were a set of dioramas giving Indonesia's history. Stuart and Ita started in the middle and worked backwards and then forwards, giving Stuart an interesting if unconventional view of Indonesian history. From there they crossed to the Nasional Museum, which Stuart found interesting but hot.

In the middle of the afternoon they got in a taxi and went down to the Blok M shopping area. Ita pointed out a green Marks and Spencer sign from the window of the taxi. "It's the best," she said with awe in her voice.

"No, not really," Stuart replied, using the same manner in which Anwar and Ita had replied to Stuart when he had found the paddy fields so unusual. "There's one in every town in England," he continued.

"Really?" She sounded genuinely amazed.

He nodded in affirmation.

She shook her head in disbelief. "It must be so nice in England," she sighed.

They played and walked around Blok M for a couple of hours. Ita tried various things on and refused to allow Stuart to buy anything. Then she went to the toilet and Stuart used the opportunity to buy the item of clothing over which she had deliberated the longest. She seemed surprised and grateful when he presented her with the gift on her return.

They had a late afternoon snack in McDonalds, the latest, crowded craze in Jakarta. Ita said she enjoyed it, but Stuart wondered if rice would not have been more appropriate.

They finished and looked at one another, the first real time they had stopped for the whole day.

Stuart smiled. "What now?"

Ita shrugged her small shoulders. "I don't know."

She reached round the chair for something, then her face suddenly contorted in a look of shock as she looked around. "My bag! Where is my bag? I thought I put it here, on the chair."

Stuart looked at her. "You haven't had a bag all day, except the carrier bag with the new clothes in."

"You sure? I know I had my bag with me last night. I don't remember having it or losing it though." She looked worried. "My keys and everything are in it."

"It must be in my room," Stuart said, trying to calm her. "But I don't remember seeing it. Come on, let's go back and check."

Quickly they moved out into the street and caught a taxi. She didn't speak on the journey back.

"You want to wait?" Stuart asked, remembering the morning.

"No, no problem at this time of the day," she replied.

Stuart collected his key and led the way to his room. In the room, she found her bag straightaway hanging from the back of the chair where she had left it after making the telephone call. She looked relieved. She checked the contents and then disappeared into the bathroom. When she emerged after what seemed to Stuart an age later, she had brushed her hair and, from the sound of it, had a shower as well.

Stuart excused himself and went into the bathroom. Once inside he felt so hot from the day's exertions that the only cure was a quick shower. He emerged feeling better.

She was sitting on the edge of the bed, sitting on her right leg, which was curled under her bottom. The room was almost dark except for the light from the television and the partially opened bathroom door. She was staring intently at the television. He passed between her and the set to retrieve a glass of water which she poured for herself, standing on the small coffee table. He drank it down in one.

He looked at her as she sat engrossed in some violent American police story, and, as if drawn by a magnet, he moved slowly towards her and sat on the bed next to her. She didn't react to his presence. He looked at her profile: the smooth concave shape of her nose; the way, unlike a European face, in which her mouth was not in the same vertical plane as her forehead, with her mouth slightly forward so that the concave nose fitted into her face rather than being a lump stuck on, as with a typical Western face. Then there were those long eyelashes, thick eyebrows and full lips. He looked away to the television, anxious not be caught staring. Then he looked back at her, at the curiously flat profile of the back of her head, at the hair, that thick, shiny, black river which flowed so smoothly over her shoulders and down her back. He wanted to touch that hair so much, just once, just to see how it felt. The desire became an uncontrollable urge and, almost subconsciously, he stretched out his right hand and gently, ever so gently, stroked her from the back of her head down over her shoulders and on to the end of her hair on her upper back. Even at this stage it was just to touch – he didn't see it as the first step to anything, for he still had no desire, no plan, no ulterior motive for the touch. It was one of innocent discovery.

She reacted to this contact slowly, turning her head towards him, but keeping her eyes on the television. Then she flicked her eyes round in a blink and looked up at him. In the dim light of the television he gazed deeply into those deep brown pools of sensual serenity and, without a moment's hesitation, dived straight in and abandoned himself. They held the stare for a moment, moving closer bit by bit, their heads tilting slightly in opposite directions, until her eyes closed and their lips touched ever so slightly, ever so gently, in the first kiss. It was a dry, inactive kiss with no movement, not much more than a touch really. She pulled away a little, but Stuart didn't move.

Her tongue flicked around her lips, moistening them for the next, inevitable, kiss. This one was a little more active, a slight movement of the lips before he pulled away and flicked his tongue around his lips. The third one was a full kiss. Both of them tilted their heads further away from the vertical and pressed harder together, their lips merging in a moist movement of pleasure. They held this kiss for what seemed like an age. Stuart half broke away but her right hand found the back of his neck and she pulled him in and refused to let him go. Her hand left his neck briefly and the television went dead. There was a gentle thud as the remote control hit the floor. Her hand returned to its former position.

Slowly, as the kiss intensified, his left hand moved and rested on her waist and she pulled him gently and slowly down until she lay on the bed and he was half over her body, kissing with a passion that he had not known for a long time.

Then he broke the kiss: suddenly he remembered where he was and who he was. Visions of his wife, Ralph and Colleen flashed before his eyes. He rolled over completely and lay on his back trying to catch his breath, steady his mind and attempt to try to climb out of those dark pools. He moved more of his body on to the bed to support the middle of his back, which was hanging off the end with his feet resting on the floor.

Ita did likewise and interpreted Stuart's pause and movement in a totally different way. She slowly unbuttoned his shirt, starting at the top and working down, opening the shirt wide and gently stroking his exposed torso with those small delicate hands. They made an erotic trail over his body. He opened his eyes and looked up at those pools of dark brown serenity and slipped helplessly back in again. She lowered her head and the kiss began again. Her hair fell about his face, surrounding him with its glossy blackness. Her smell wafted over him, the exoticism of her absorbing him in the age-old Asian magic.

She had not tucked in her tee-shirt at the waist after her visit to the bathroom and it rode up easily under Stuart's left hand.

He found her skin for the first time. It was so smooth and cool – he had felt nothing like it before. Gradually, as the kiss continued, his hand moved slowly up the smooth skin of her back, around the curves of her spine, up and up until it touched the strap of her bra. At this instant the memory of his family flooded back and he realised where he was and what he was doing again. Again he pulled back, breaking the contact with her.

She sat up and looked questioningly at him. In a single movement she lifted the tee-shirt off, and Stuart could just see the outline of her bra in the near darkness of the room. She moved down again kissing his lips, which resisted for an instant.

He felt her nipples, hard and erect, pushing into his chest through the material of her bra as she thrust against him. His hand moved round her back and in an instant the bra was undone. She lifted her chest to allow the bra to move and he felt her nipples directly against his skin.

Her right hand moved down his torso until it touched the top of his jeans. She slowly undid the belt with her hand, then slipped the single top button undone and eased the zip half down. As she did so, Stuart's feelings reached upwards, higher and higher: he had not felt so sexually alive in years.

This was a new experience for him. It was a mature reaction, not the one of a schoolboy or university student with overactive hormones, but the reaction of an experienced man. Again his wife and family flooded in amidst the arousal and sheer animal lust that ran through his body. He knew that he had to stop, to push her away and stand up. He half succeeded in pushing her away and sitting up. She sat up too, looking at him, her breasts outlined against the small light coming in from the half open bathroom door.

Instead of continuing and standing up, he looked at the outline. He looked at the hair flowing down her shoulders, imagined the brown eyes and dived in for the last and final time. He leaned forward and put his mouth to her nipple. She arched her back and neck, gripping his hair and falling backwards on to the bed. Stuart was now on top and doing the pushing. He kissed each nipple in turn, tasting her, smelling her skin and feeling the smooth body that lay beneath him. His left hand reached down to the button at the top of her jeans. It came undone and the zip came down with ease.

She sat up and slipped her jeans off, and he did likewise. Now they were both naked except for knickers and underpants. She lay back on the bed and invited him. He needed no second invitation: he had abandoned himself to her completely and his wife had gone from his mind. He began to kiss her nipples again, each in turn, until they were both equally hard. She moaned slightly as he did so, eventually pushing his head away and lower. He moved down her smooth, flat, firm stomach with gentle kisses until he came to the top of her knickers. They were only white cotton ones, plain and the normal, standard shape, the sort of knickers which would not raise the slightest interest in him when worn by his wife, but now they were the sexiest knickers that he had ever encountered, the object of more passion that he had ever felt and the gateway to something more exotic than he had ever dreamed of.

First he sniffed. Nothing but clean woman. Then he eased down the top, kissing the gradually exposed flesh, looking for the hair. Her hair was a long time being revealed. When it was, he kissed and nuzzled it, pulling her knickers further and further down. Eventually he pulled them off in a single swift movement. She moaned a little and moved her body in a longing, aching manner in anticipation of what was to come. Her legs opened for him and his lips moved around the edge of her small neat patch of hair, coming closer and closer. She reacted to this teasing by moving her hips to try to make contact with his mouth, but he avoided her until he was ready. When he was he touched her and she went still. She was ready for him, very ready, and he kissed her with an overwhelming lust. He wanted to eat her, to drink her in and absorb her passion into his.

After what seemed only a few seconds, she pushed him away and on to his back. Her small hands ran down his torso and over his underpants, gently caressing and teasing him. She pulled back the waistband of his underpants and released him. Her fingers seemed so cool, so gentle, against him. The feeling was unbelievable: he thought that he was going to explode. Her head descended towards his groin and she took him in her mouth and now it was his turn to moan and arch his back. After a few delicious seconds he had to push her away otherwise the explosion would have happened.

She lay back on the bed waiting for him. For a second he was confused. What about protection? For her against pregnancy, for him against anything she may have? He paused, and she looked at him expectantly. Then he was back in February, packing his suitcase for his first visit to Indonesia.

He smiled and stood up and moved over to his open suitcase. In the corner pocket he pulled out the packet of three condoms and turned to face her. As he moved back towards the bed, he realised that there was no going back, that he was about to be unfaithful to his wife for the first time. Somehow, up to this point, he did not feel that he had been unfaithful. Despite the fact that he was in a hotel room with a naked Indonesian woman, and that they had just done things considered by many to be more intimate than making love itself, he did not feel that he had yet really been physically unfaithful. Mentally the step had been taken a few minutes ago when he had kissed her for the first time, but now the absolute undeniable physical unfaithfulness was about to start. He was not going to stop, he knew that.

She looked at the packet and nodded in agreement. He slipped a condom on and then knelt on the bed at her feet. Slowly he kissed her feet, then up her calves, across her knees, then up her smooth firm thighs, past her hair, up and on over that smooth, flat stomach and those erect nipples until he found her mouth again. They kissed and held each other in a long embrace as he searched gently for the way in. She moved in response, positioning herself to accept him. And then he was there.

He felt the warmth and the smoothness begin to embrace him. He pushed slowly deeper, slowly, until he was all the way in. She moved slowly to help him and then he really had committed adultery, been unfaithful to his wife for the first time, mentally, physically, in every possible way. This flashed quickly through his mind as he luxuriated in the strength and depth of his feelings, the emotional ones as well as the sheer physical pleasures which were now engulfing him, and then the thought was gone. Her legs opened wider and her calves looped over his and she pulled him in close. He sensed that she did not want to be 'banged' or 'hammered' in a rapid, violent way, more that she wanted a slow, sensual coupling. This suited Stuart, for too much movement and the explosion would bring all these lovely feelings to a dramatic end in an instant.

They moved together slowly with the deep rhythm of two bodies in harmony. She broke off the kiss and pulled his head to one side. He could hear her breathing in his left ear and he could smell and feel her hair all around him.

Then she was breathing more rapidly, almost panting, in short, shallow breaths. Her movements were getting faster and he changed the pace to match without thinking. He was not actually 'thinking' about making love: he was not conscious of doing this, or moving like that; he was not conscious of, or worried about her feelings. He knew, somehow, that he was doing everything right for her, for him. He had never experienced this before. Usually, so much of the time making love was spent worrying about movement, position, whether the woman was enjoying it, whether he could hold out for long enough, but now all those anxieties were gone and they were just doing it in complete harmony. He could feel the feeling rising within him, and she too seemed to be breathing harder and faster.

Then she gripped him hard, her right hand on his buttock, her left on his neck. She held her breath and pushed her groin hard against his and remained still. She moaned, "Mmmmmm," then resumed her movement very slightly.

He felt a tightening in him and he knew that he couldn't stop himself. He moved out and in again for the last time and she shuddered all over her whole body. Her legs moved up and down his calves.

He felt himself heave and his buttocks tighten in orgasm.

"Oh God," she half shouted. "Oh God," again and finally, "I come, I come," her voice fading as she stopped moving and held herself tight against him.

Both of them were taut in the final throes of orgasm. And then they relaxed, slowly, him settling down on her, she going limp and allowing her arms and legs to fall away from him and her head to loll to one side.

Making love, and having the woman orgasm during it, had never been so easy for Stuart. He pushed up with his left hand and looked at her. Her eyes were closed and her hair dishevelled around. Her whole body glowed with exertion and pleasure. Gently he rolled off. She gasped a little as he did so, but made no other movement. She lay still, inert, almost sleep-like.

Then Stuart slept.

Stuart woke with a little start. Ita stood by the entrance of the room, dressed, hair combed, bag in hand. He was still naked, the condom still in place.

"Bye, I have to go," she said with a little embarrassed smile. She turned and was gone.

Stuart fell asleep again, this time for almost half an hour. When he awoke he felt strange. What had just happened? At first he felt as though he had been dreaming – a very realistic dream of the erotic and the exotic, of the smells and tastes of Asian woman, but a dream nonetheless. He lifted his head a little and looked down his naked body, the condom still in place. It had been no dream. He sniffed the air – he could smell her exotic presence in the room, on his body, on the bed.

Slowly, he sat up and scratched his head, collected his thoughts and went into the bathroom. He put the condom in the waste basket, wrapped in tissue paper. Then in a detached, almost zombie-like manner, he showered, dressed and wandered out not really knowing where he was going. Almost automatically he headed for The Inne. He ate and drank without enthusiasm: it was merely sustenance, something to fill his stomach and some time.

As he stood watching the gyrations of the Filipino band in front of him, he thought about the events of the early evening. He tried, and partially succeeded, in convincing himself that nothing had happened. It had after all been a dream. The alcohol lulled his brain and allowed him to believe in the dream. He felt nothing. There was no physical change in him, no visible sign of his adultery – his nose hadn't grown or his hair changed colour – so it became easier to convince himself that nothing really had happened. Once the Filipino band had finished their second set of songs, he paid his bill and left.

Back in the room, he stood with his back to the wall, leaning against it with his hands behind his back, looking at the bed. It had been made up by the chambermaid and the cover folded back, so he could not see any impression of the evening left on the bed. Then he went into the bathroom and looked hard at himself in the mirror. He pulled his tongue out and checked the appearance of it – no change. He glanced furtively into the waste bin, but it was empty. Nothing had happened, he was sure.

He took his clothes and climbed into the bed. He closed his eyes, preparing to sleep. As he did so, he could smell her again in the bed. It was there, definitely, a combination of perfume and body. It could only have been a very faint odour, but the smell brought everything flooding back into his mind. He opened his eyes and looked for her. He closed them again and smelled her. He stretched in the bed and rolled over, hunting for the strongest smell, wanting to find her again. But she was not there. Only the merest, faintest hint of her presence still hung around in the fading, faint smell. As he looked and smelled, he drifted off into deep dreamless sleep. Tonight the dreams had been real.

# CHAPTER 13

# SURABAYA AND BACK

Stuart spent Sunday in a sort of daze. He rose late, still unsure of what had happened the previous evening. Now that even the smell of her had left the bed, he was more uncertain than ever whether or not he had actually had the experience. He ate an unenthusiastic brunch, swam a little, tanned a little, fell asleep in front of the TV and waited patiently for Monday to arrive.

He and Anwar had a plan to visit the last of the three factories on the list in East and Central Java, close to the second city of Indonesia, Surabaya. They were due to leave reasonably early on the Monday morning, not so early that Stuart needed to go to bed at nine the night before, but he did anyway.

Anwar was as prompt as usual. Stuart had been waiting for almost an hour after waking around five-thirty. They left for the airport, Anwar chatting enthusiastically about the prospects for the trip. Anwar's enthusiasm washed over Stuart and he remained slightly bemused. He had managed to arrange a visit to a fourth plant of which Stuart had not heard in the Surabaya area. That meant that the trip would be prolonged by a few days, meaning that Stuart would not get back into Jakarta until Friday and he was due to fly out on the Sunday. He wondered about the prospects of seeing Ita again.

The flight was short and uneventful. A modern 737 carried them to the Juanda Airport of Surabaya and they sat in the small business section at the front. From the airport, they travelled by car along a toll road dual carriageway, heading inland towards the mountains.

It was only when they entered the largish factory set almost on the road that Stuart began to wake up and come out of his reverie. They were conducted into a large boardroom which smelled badly of stale clove cigarettes. Here they had a long meeting, punctuated by lunch and tea in the afternoon. Then they drove back to Surabaya.

The following day was spent in the factory, examining the machines, cataloguing and discussing the company's needs. Stuart wasn't hopeful. They were well-organised and heavily into the competitor's equipment. Stuart felt that the smiles were just politeness. Anwar felt the same way too.

On the Wednesday, they journeyed even further into the country to a rundown-looking building set well away from the road.

"This place!" said Stuart incredulously, with more than a little annoyance in his voice.

This was the reason they would be late back to Jakarta; this rundown factory was the reason Stuart might not get to see Ita again. The prospect of not being able to see her made him want to see her all the more. Before it had occurred to him that he might not see her again before he left, he had been worried by the prospect of seeing her and what was going to happen. Now such worries had vanished.

"It's not quite what I expected either," Anwar confessed, looking out of the window. "Should we just go?"

"Mmm, yes, why not," was Stuart's slightly hopeful reply. "Who's that?" he continued, looking at a figure half running towards them from the front door.

"Oh, I guess he's the owner, Mr Puriadi, or Chan to his associates. He has seen us – we can't go now," Anwar said, dashing Stuart's hopes of an early return. "He's an interesting character," Anwar continued. "He's fifth-generation Chinese here, with an Indonesian name of course, but most people call him by his real Chinese family name, Chan. He's the black sheep though. He married a Javanese woman rather than a Chinese one so his family stuck him out here in this little backwater," Anwar said. "The main family is very rich and powerful in Indonesia. They have a huge conglomerate of companies, all controlled by the old man, Chan's uncle."

"How do you know all of this?" Stuart asked.

"Oh, you find these things out. He contacted me last week by phone after our visit to Yogja and I did some checking," he replied.

"But if he's the black sheep stuck out here, how can he have any money to expand or buy equipment?" Stuart asked, puzzled as the slightly fat, balding Chinese man approached.

Anwar smiled. "Trust me," he said enigmatically.

Stuart shrugged his shoulders and followed Anwar's lead out of the car and into the heat of the mid-morning sun.

"Ah, good morning, so glad you come," Mr Chan said, mopping his brow and shaking Stuart's hand at the same time. "So glad. Please." He gestured towards the building and then shook Anwar's hand.

Stuart was afraid of a hot, stale office which would be greatly uncomfortable for the next few hours. The approach to the entrance did little to reduce that opinion. The outside of the building was, well, ramshackle.

Mr Chan led them through the first set of doors into a surprisingly cool interior. There were a number of potted plants, some clean new-looking armchairs and a small wooden carved table which Stuart fancied for his living room at home. The walls were all clean and painted in designer grey with a dark pink border. The lights were hidden and discreet.

Past the second set of doors they entered the office proper. Here it was just as cool and clean and even carpeted with a deep rich pink carpet which felt very luxurious underfoot. A secretary sat at a modern office desk tapping into a computer. She was elegantly dressed and elegant in herself.

She smiled at them as they passed. "Good morning gentlemen," she said in almost unaccented English.

"My receptionist, secretary, accounts, everything," Chan said. "And my wife," he added almost as an afterthought.

Anwar nudged Stuart gently in the ribs. Stuart smiled back at him.

They continued through into the main part of the office, past two more girls sitting at computer screens. A new printer stood by a large photocopying machine. All the equipment was new and up-to-date. The decor of this part of the office matched the standard of the reception area. Stuart was impressed and confused. Nothing about the exterior would have given the slightest hint of the interior. They continued through a large door and into Chan's own office. This was modest in size and discreetly furnished in the latest style.

"Nice office," said Stuart, impressed.

"Don't worry about the outside," Chan said, laughing. "One day I fix. Never judge book by cover, yeah," he said, laughing loudly to cover his embarrassment.

Stuart and Anwar smiled in response.

"Please sit down," Chan said, pointing at the chairs.

"Me, I'm Mr Puriadi, but call me Chan," he said, offering a business card to each of them.

"Stuart Morgan from Ormistons."

"Anwar from here and there."

Chan laughed. "Of course, Mr Anwar, I know you by your reputation."

They handed their business cards over and sat down. Chan picked up the phone and jabbered quickly into it. As he sat down opposite Stuart and Anwar, his wife came in. She was even more beautiful and elegant standing up than sitting down. She moved with the tall, slim gracefulness so common in Javanese women. She put the tray of tea down on the table and smiled at them. Then she left without a word.

"Now," said Mr Chan, "let's start."

He handed them some papers each. They were computer printouts produced to a very high standard.

Stuart was again impressed. He flicked through the document and saw the name of Ormistons well represented. In fact most of the machines were Ormistons, all very old and some very very old. He couldn't recollect any deliveries to this part of the world before, even for spares. He was confused. He examined the production figures and he could not reconcile the machines to the production.

Chan smiled at them. "Okay?" he asked enthusiastically, like a schoolboy waiting for a teacher's approval.

"Well," started Stuart. "I can't quite reconcile the production figures with your list of machinery."

Chan looked a little disappointed. "Yes I know, this wrong."

Stuart smiled in satisfaction.

"This too low, I miss some production."

Stuart was jerked out of his smugness. "What's too low?"

"The production. We lost some this month from the breakdown. Last month is better," Chan replied.

"How can you get all that from these old machines?" Stuart asked in disbelief at the already high figures being, in fact, low because of breakdowns.

"We go two twelve hours for six days. I pay good wage, two times the rest – I get good staff, they work hard, we get good production," he said, looking from Stuart to Anwar as he spoke.

"Where did you get all these old Ormistons machines from?" Stuart asked.

"I have friend, far family. He live in South America and I visit him. He showed me the factory with the Ormistons machine and I talk to them. They say that Ormistons the best: never break down, never wear out. So I start to look. Then I find going for scrap so I buy, bring here and throw out my newer machines from India and Germany and now..." He waved his arm round the room at the new furnishings. "But my problem spare parts. Now we have none of some type, you know."

"Okay," said Stuart, "I'll make some recommendations for spare parts. We can still make most for these old machines."

"I no want recommendations, I want spares. You look today, get me price tomorrow, I order tomorrow," he said almost angrily.

Stuart glanced at Anwar, who smiled and winked. Stuart held up his hands. "Okay, no problem. Let's start."

And with that they moved into the factory.

The factory was, Stuart had to admit, good. Despite the outside appearance, the inside was clean, tidy and organised and, above all else, buzzing with activity and motion. He checked the machines over, investigated the spares problems, identified models and years and wrote a long fax back to his office. He demanded a reply by the following morning.

They left some time after six and it was a two hour drive back to the hotel. Once back, they didn't go immediately to their respective rooms, but sat in the lobby bar and drank a beer or two. They chatted excitedly about the prospects.

"You see, you must not ignore any potential customer. Things have a habit of surprising," Anwar said. "I must admit that I thought that we had gone to the wrong place when we arrived, but, well there you are. He's the best prospect for business here, by far," he continued.

"I can see why he wasn't bothered about becoming the black sheep of the family," Stuart replied, thinking along a totally different track from Anwar.

"What?" Anwar asked, confused.

"Well, his wife. I think I would become the black sheep of my family for a wife like that," he said with smile.

Anwar laughed. "Yes, she is something of a woman. Very Javanese and very clever, so people say. My contact said that she is the actual brains behind the operation. He's a good fixer and dealer but she makes the long-term plans. The office, one hundred per cent her I would guess: the computers, I bet she specified and he went and haggled the dealers down. So who buys them? Him or her?"

There was a pause in the conversation. Stuart had been meaning to ask Anwar, in a roundabout way, about Indonesian women in general and now seemed like a good opportunity.

"I've been wondering..." he began hesitantly, "about Indonesian women."

Anwar stopped drinking and looked at him.

"In the wider cultural sense, not just because there are so many beautiful ones," Stuart continued.

"Well... in the 'wider cultural sense'," Anwar said with a smile, emphasising Stuart's euphemism of the wider cultural sense. He guessed that Stuart was probing for information because he had seen, met or liked some woman somewhere and he wanted to find out the ground rules. "Well," he continued, "it has been said that there are only two types of unmarried Indonesian women, virgins and whores."

"Isn't that a bit extreme?" Stuart replied, a bit shocked at the directness of Anwar's reply.

"No, I don't think so, not in the country areas at least. In the more 'civilised'" – he said the word with a curious tone, indicating that he did not entirely agree with the proposition that the cities were more civilised than the country – "big cities it is less true and there are girls, women who are unmarried, have boyfriends and are not virgins, just like the West, but a lot of them have a sorry sad tale to tell about something and they collect in the cities because maybe they can meet someone who doesn't mind if they're not a virgin." He looked at Stuart as he said the last few words.

"You mean like a foreigner," Stuart said, picking up the implication.

"Yes, like a foreigner. They see the TV and have some idea about foreign cultures. So they hope that they will be able to meet the man of their dreams who won't worry about the sad story. Unfortunately, they often slide into prostitution. So many of the sorry tales are to do with foreigners. They make all sorts of promises when they work here on two or three year contracts and then disappear, leaving a girl with a ruined life." Anwar stopped and ordered two more drinks.

"You sound bitter about us foreigners," Stuart said defensively.

"No, not really," Anwar replied. "For every one sorry tale due to a foreigner there must be ten due to some equally unfaithful Indonesian man. It's just part of life. But remember that – many foreigners don't."

They both sipped their newly-arrived beers.

"In the wider cultural sense", Anwar continued, slightly mocking Stuart's phrase, "women here are dominated by men. Most are Muslim, eighty-five per cent maybe, and strict enforcement of the Muslim law pushes women into veils and the home. Here, it's much more relaxed: women work a lot. I like to employ women – they generally work much harder, learn quicker and are much more reliable than the men. Most men want a big office, a big salary and nothing to do, at least at the middle levels. At the lower levels, the working levels, the men are very good, but in an office they seem to change."

Their conversation was interrupted by a page for Stuart. His office was on the phone, disbelieving his fax. On his return, they ate a quick meal in the coffee shop and then retired to sleep. It was just before ten.

Stuart sat in his room, looking at the telephone. He picked up the handset and dialled Ita's number. It was a long time being answered and it was not Ita who answered.

"Can I speak to Ita?" he said loud and slow in true foreign fashion. Something unintelligible came back so he simply said, "Ita."

The phone went quiet and Stuart was on the point of replacing the handset when a small voice came on the line.

"Hello, Ita speaking."

"Hi, it's Stuart. Sorry it's very late to telephone you. Did I wake you up?" he asked.

"No, not really, I was in bed but not really asleep yet. Where are you?" she answered.

"In Surabaya, in my hotel room."

"Alone?" she asked.

"Of course alone. Why do you ask?" he replied, a little puzzled.

"No reason. When are you coming back to Jakarta?" Her voice sounded unsure, nervous even.

"Tomorrow, late probably." He paused. "You alone too?" he asked, returning the question.

"Mmmm, of course. I just quiet waiting your calling me," she said in her little voice.

He wanted to reach down the telephone line and hug her small frame to his body, to protect and hold her. He felt frustrated at the distance.

"We meet on Friday, okay?" he said.

"Mmm yes, because tomorrow you tired, yes?" she replied.

"Yes, what time. Seven or eight?"

"Seven," she replied straightaway. "When you go home to England?" Her voice sounded even smaller and more emotional.

"Sunday evening," he replied quietly.

She was quiet.

"Hello Ita, are you there?" he asked after a short while.

"Yes I am. See you on Friday, I want to sleep now. Bye," she said quickly with a detectable sadness in her voice.

Stuart barely had time to get a goodbye out before the phone clicked dead. He felt a surge of unhappiness flow through him. It would be some two days before he could see her again and then only for a couple of days, for then he was on his way home. He tried to sleep but couldn't. He had a drink from the mini bar and then tried again. With still no luck, he set off downstairs to the pub-like place in the basement. He watched a singing group until some time after one before he returned to his room and only then was he finally able to achieve the condition of sleep.

The following day was a blur. It was all action from the moment he picked up the telefax pushed under his door from head office. They went to Mr Chan, discussed prices, delivery and further work for his spares. In the end Stuart came away with the promise of an order for almost fifteen thousand pounds worth of spares and a plan to overhaul and update two machines at a later date. New machines were also talked about. They left well after seven in the evening, caught the last flight and Stuart sank gratefully into his Jakarta hotel bedroom at well after eleven. He was elated to have a real prospect of an order, elated to be back in Jakarta and elated that one of the two days to meeting Ita had now passed. Sleep was no trouble on this evening.

## CHAPTER 14

## REUNION

Stuart waited nervously in the lobby of the hotel, trying to stand still and not succeeding. He glanced at his watch every few seconds watching the hand move round towards seven o'clock. He hoped that she was going to be on time. In the event, she wasn't far off, for it was only a few minutes after seven when she walked up the ramp towards the hotel. He saw her and went through the doors to meet her. They met halfway up the steps.

She looked shy, he was flushed with nervous embarrassment. They exchanged smiles but no words.

She turned and set off down the steps. Stuart followed.

"Did you walk here?" he asked to break the ice when they were at the bottom of the steps.

She shook her head. "I don't like to arrive here by taxi. In the front, I mean – it's too public."

They continued in silence. Once at the bottom of the ramp and out of sight of the hotel, she slipped her arm into his and squeezed. They both felt better for the physical contact, but nervousness pervaded the atmosphere.

'Before you actually made love with someone for the first time', Stuart thought, 'there are two possibilities. You knew it was going to happen: there was a sense of anticipation, a courtship of months or only hours, but you knew.' Or sometimes it happened without planning, as it had between him and Ita.

He honestly had had no plan in his mind beforehand. He had been prepared to leave her in the afternoon, and but for her bag being missing, she would never have come back to his room again. He had helped her out of her problem in the bar with the drink, and, had they not made love when they did, Stuart reflected, they would probably never have done so. It was the combination of the previous evening, her embarrassment and her gratitude for his behaviour, the day touring Jakarta and, most of all, the moment. Had they not made love they would have become good friends, Stuart knew. But now they had, even if

Stuart was still believing it was a dream. Now he could not deny his feelings at the sight and touch of her. The game had changed irrevocably: after that first unplanned time, the transition back to mere friendship was practically impossible to make. The problem now was the next step. To continue and do it again or to stop, realising that it was a one-off occurrence. The thought of this made them both nervous and both understood, without speaking, the other's feelings. A silence fell between them.

They walked along, not something that Stuart wanted to do too much in the warmth and stickiness of a Jakarta tropical evening.

"Where shall we go?" he asked after they had walked a few hundred metres or so. "Eat?" he added.

"Yes, eat. Eat like what?" she asked.

"You choose. I will eat anything – I'm hungry. Our office was so busy today to get everything finished. We may have an order from Indonesia," he replied.

She looked at him with a surprised expression. "That's good. An order, so this mean you will come back?"

"Mmm, yes, I think so."

Her small arm squeezed his again and she seemed a mite happier and a mite less nervous.

"Chinese, I want Chinese food," he declared brightly, trying to throw off the tension. "Come on, let's get a taxi."

"No taxi, not necessary over there." She pointed to an office building not far away. "That's one of the best Chinese restaurants in Jakarta."

She led the way and they walked.

The Chinese restaurant, The Summer Garden, was located on top of a five-storey office block. Like so many restaurants in Jakarta it was actually part of an office block. There was no 'restaurant area' as in most cities. Instead each office block had its own, at the top, in the basement or on top of the car park. It made choosing a place to eat quite difficult. You had to decide in advance rather than being able to browse. The fact that they were able to walk to this one was unusual. Inside, it was cool and large, with a low ceiling so you did not have the feeling of eating in a barn. Stuart liked the place immediately, especially the large Chinese dragons which guarded the entrance.

They sat at a small table by the window. A large menu appeared. The specials consisted mainly of ridiculous items at vast prices, such things as 'Three kinds of animal penis double-boiled in ginseng'. Stuart smiled. He knew that many Chinese men were obsessed with size and performance. He imagined some middle-aged businessman with a bulging midriff eating this, because at these prices no young man could afford it, and then trying to pretend that he was an eighteen year old sexual athlete with some young girl.

He showed the menu entry to Ita who laughed and hid her face behind the menu.

They ordered and the food was good. Whilst Stuart tucked into pork and chillies in pancakes, broccoli in sauce, rice and some form of chicken, Ita picked and nibbled in a slow deliberate manner, not really eating very much at all.

"What's the matter?" Stuart asked.

"Nothing, it's okay. I'm not so hungry at the moment." She smiled weakly.

Stuart made his best attempt to eat all the ordered food and almost succeeded. The waiters cleared the plates and Stuart paid the bill and they left. Stuart had enjoyed the food, but felt disappointed because Ita had obviously not liked it so much.

"Don't you like Chinese food?" he questioned her as they left.

"Oh yes, very much, but not today. This evening I'm... I don't know, maybe I'm...well." She could not or did not want to express the way she felt.

"Where to now?" he asked.

She made no reply. Stuart was becoming a little angry with her.

He led her back towards the hotel. She followed meekly without speaking or touching him. It was only just after eight-thirty and Stuart fancied doing something. The hotel was a good place to start: a taxi to somewhere else or The Inne. As they approached the hotel, he moved towards the entrance to The Inne.

For the first time in the evening, she exerted some positive influence, nudging him gently towards the main door of the hotel.

He paused and looked at her. She did not look back but carried on walking up the steps. He followed a short distance behind and collected his key.

She had disappeared, on past the lifts and into the toilets close to the cake shop.

He went and stood by the lift. He knew what she was doing, behaving discreetly.

The doors of the lift opened and he and two other people got in. Almost as the door closed, Ita stepped in. The other people got out at a lower floor than Stuart's, much to Ita's relief.

She stood in the opposite corner, not looking at him, just staring ahead. She led the way out of the lift, walking quickly and turning in the opposite direction to Stuart's room.

He shrugged his shoulders, wondering if all this was really necessary, and went to the door of his room opening it quickly, then she was there and inside.

He shut the door and turned round to see her sitting on her leg, on the bed, head down, her hair falling around, covering her face. She had already taken off her shoes. He stood in front of her.

"What's the matter, Ita? Why don't you want to go out?"

Her shoulders shrugged slightly and her head shook a little.

He put his hand under her chin and lifted her face up. She resisted a little and even when he could see her face, her eyes still looked down; there were tears on her cheeks. He lowered his head so that his eyes were level with hers.

She still avoided his eyes.

"Hey," he said softly.

She finally looked at him, her eyes a little red and wet. Her hair was hanging down around her face and her sad eyes peered out from behind the black strands: she looked child-like and innocent. Stuart reached forward with his hands and held hers as they lay on her lap. She looked at him directly with those big brown eyes, dark pools of mystery. He leaned forward and kissed her on the forehead and then lightly on the lips. Her reaction surprised him greatly. She moved her hands off her lap and on to the back of his head, holding tightly and drawing him back to her as he pulled away after the kiss. She engaged their lips with a ferocity that he had not seen in her before. The previous time had been all gentle love and subtlety. This was animal passion.

She kissed him hard and lay back, pulling him with her. She breathed heavily through her nose, almost snorting in passion as she did so. She rolled him over on to his back and climbed on top of him. He was surrounded by hair yet she continued the kiss, leaning her full weight on top of him.

After what seemed an age she stopped and sat up. She pulled the tee-shirt over her head and shook her hair into a falling cascade. Stuart was reminded of the shampoo adverts and he smiled. As he smiled she suddenly covered her bra with her arms.

"The light," she said quietly.

Stuart managed to reach the switch and the room was plunged into darkness. She leaned down and undid the buttons on his shirt, then, standing by the bed, undid his belt and trousers, pulling them off. He slipped his shirt off while Ita lowered her jeans. It was all so quick, so unlike what he was expecting from her. She moved over to the suitcase and pulled out the remains of the three pack of condoms and put them on the bed beside them. Then she climbed back on board, lying on top of him.

She resumed kissing, not quite as ferocious as at the start, but almost. He felt the smooth coolness of her skin against his chest, the inside of her thighs against the outside of his as she moved her hips around on his groin. He ran his hands up and down her back, feeling the curve of her spine, the valley in the centre and two small mounds of muscle up either side. He reached her knickers and ran his hands over her moving buttocks. He passed his hands back up her spine as far as the bra strap and then back down. On the second approach to her bottom he pushed his hands gently under the waistband of her knickers and began to ease them down. She raised her bottom to help him. He managed to push them far enough down to allow him to explore the cleft of her bottom. Her skin was so smooth: there were no lumps, pimples or hair to upset the flow of his hands over the flesh. She obviously enjoyed the touch and her kissing and breathing increased in intensity.

His hands worked back up and found the still-fastened bra strap. It remained fastened only a second longer. She lifted her chest momentarily to allow the bra to move away, letting her breasts touch his chest. Then she sat up, breathing heavily. She lifted the bra off and pushed her hair back. She slipped off him and removed her knickers completely. Then she eased his underpants down, releasing him. She smiled and gently caressed him with one delicate hand. The second found the space between his legs. Here she massaged him gently, around the edge of his hair, under, over and around. Coupled with the first hand, it was almost too much for Stuart to bear: it came dangerously close. He was on the point of saying something when she stopped, sensing his condition. She picked up one of the remaining condoms and skilfully unravelled it over him. Then she put her leg over him and sat on his stomach. With her hands on his shoulders, she manoeuvred herself until he was positioned at the entrance. He felt the warmth around him and as she pushed down, he felt it engulf him. She pushed hard until their hair met. She shuddered slightly and pressed down hard on his groin. Then slowly she began to move around and around, in a circular motion, punctuated by a few longer linear motions all the way out and then slowly all the way in, her breathing all the while increasing in its intensity. She bit her lower lip and moaned slightly. He reached up and began to kiss one nipple and hold the other breast. She moaned more at this treatment and her motions atop him became more intense and rapid. She started breathing in little pants, then holding her breath before snorting it out in a sudden gasp. Her eyes closed tightly, she screwed up her face, she held her breath for longer and longer periods. Somewhere down in Stuart's loins the feeling was rising, but in the face of her display of passion it was lost to him. Then she began to moan, quietly at first, then louder as she exhaled after holding her breath. Then she gripped his shoulders hard, and began to move violently on him.

"Oh... Ohhh my God!" she almost shouted. "Oh my God!" The second time a little quieter. She arched her neck and shook her head from side to side.

"Oh God, I come!" she said finally, shuddering and shaking from the exertion. She let out a long breath and began to breathe more normally. She let her head fall forward, her hair reaching down to his face. Then she slowly relaxed her grip on his shoulders and the pressure on his groin. She let herself down on to his chest, resting the side of her face against his trunk.

She was quiet and silent for more than a minute. Then she sat up and asked him, "You too?"

Her eyes were bright and lively again.

"I'm not sure," he said truthfully.

"Not sure, why?" she asked, puzzled.

"Because I was watching you. It's like nothing I've ever seen before."

She gave an embarrassed laugh. "You are the one who is like nothing else," she replied. She climbed off him and examined the condom, quickly removing it. "Yes!" she said with a laugh, "Definitely." Then she jumped up and moved towards the bathroom with great speed.

He listened to the shower going, knowing that she was washing again. He could not help but feel a little disappointed with it this time. She had been so sensual and erotic the first time. They had moved in perfect harmony. This time she had, well, screwed him good and proper. She had taken her pleasure in great gulps, leaving him with almost none. He had had a vague feeling of coming himself but it was lost in the intensity of hers. He guessed that this was the way most women felt after sex with an uncaring man: slightly frustrated and disappointed.

She came out of the bathroom wrapped in a towel. "Okay, you wash now," she said, ordering him into the bathroom. He went like an obedient schoolboy. 'So,' he thought, 'Anwar thinks that this is a male-dominated society!' He washed and walked back into the bedroom naked.

The lights were still off in the bedroom, so the only light came from the small concealed light in the entrance. She was in the bed, under the sheet. The towel was at the side of the bed and her knickers lay undisturbed on the floor: she was naked under the cover. He climbed in beside her. As he lifted the sheet to get in he caught a quick glimpse of her body in the very low light. In that short second he saw her nipples, dark against the rest of her body, but little else. He wanted so much to see her. She cuddled up to him and he felt the naked cool smoothness of her body against his. She rested her head on his chest. He stroked her hair with his right hand, following the strands in the cascade they made as they flowed over her body and his. She nuzzled him contentedly, like a cat being stroked. Maybe she would have purred if she could have.

Her right hand moved up and down his chest and over his stomach, slowly, ever so slowly, getting closer to him. She avoided all contact, stroking the inside of his thighs, tops of his thighs and the edge of his hair. She shifted her head and body further down the bed and swept the sheet off their bodies. Stuart realised that she was not satisfied with making love once and that a second time was definitely in the offing. He was, much to his surprise, already rising to the occasion. It was many years since he and his wife had done it twice in one night, or even on consecutive nights. She shifted again, moving her head closer until he felt her breath against him. Her right hand continued to play on his skin, down around his groin, along his thighs, between his legs, but never actually touching. He felt an erotic frustration building in him: he wanted her to touch, just once, but she didn't, she just teased. Then, when he was on the point of asking her, she reacted. Instead of touching, she kissed lightly and gently. Then she licked along, around and over.

His right hand had been stroking her side and back, along into the valley of her waist, up and over on to her thigh, and now it stopped on her thigh. He gave a little tug in his direction. She understood and stopped her activities for a moment, moving her body round, lifting her leg over his chest and lying down on his chest, her face in his groin, his face close to hers. She resumed her kiss and then took him in her mouth. He leaned forward and put his face into her, smelling her, tasting her, wanting to swallow her, to drink her in. She was already ready for him, wet and smooth. She responded to his kiss quickly. She stopped kissing him and tensed, then she shuddered gently.

"Oh... I come," she said quietly. "Just a little bit," she added, sounding slightly embarrassed.

Then she rolled off and found the last condom. Again she fitted it with skill. This time she lay on her back, legs apart, waiting for him. He knelt at her feet and began to kiss his way up her body. Over the knees, up those smooth firm thighs, past the neat bush of black hair, up over the stomach, heaving with rapid breathing, and up past her hard nipples. He kissed each one in turn before he found her mouth and kissed that. He didn't enter straightaway, but rather waited on the edge, allowing her to feel him, allowing him to tease her. She moved and tried to find him, but he kept just out of reach. Her face contorted in frustration. She moaned a little and tried again. This time he let her find him, just the end. She gasped as she felt him enter her. Then in a single strong push he slid all the way in. Now she really gasped and groaned. "Ohhh God," she hissed as he pushed again. "Don't stop. Please don't stop!" she pleaded.

He was able to move fairly rapidly without any risk of an accident. He felt wonderful. She moved in rhythm, greedily gulping down the sensations. She started panting and holding her breath in turn. She was close, he knew that. He pushed himself up off her, his hands on the bed beside her shoulders. He looked down his body to the area of activity. He could just see himself disappearing into her and the sight filled him with a surge of passion: he pushed harder. Her legs were wide apart, her calves linked over the backs of his knees, offering him no escape. She let out a long-held breath. "Ohh... God!" she almost shouted, then again, "Oh my God!" The second time she did shout. "Don't stop! More!" she pleaded again.

Her eyes were tightly closed, her head rolling from side to side. She gripped the sheets with her outstretched arms, tugging and pulling the sheets into folds of cloth. Then both her hands flew to his buttocks, gripping, pulling him in and in as she screamed a little through clenched teeth, "I come, again, now!" And as he thrust in again, her whole body was taut. Her hands moved up his back and she lifted her upper body from the bed, and kissed him, then broke off the kiss to shout, "Ohhh God, I come again!" Then she dropped back on to the bed and was still, quiet except for the now subsiding rapid breathing.

Stuart looked down at the small brown body beneath him in sheer wonder. Were all Indonesian women like this? If so, no wonder so many European men got married here. He looked at the beads of sweat appearing in the valley between her breasts, on her brow and above her top lip. What passion, what enjoyment, total abandonment to pleasure and the sensations of the flesh, of the body, of sex and lust. He felt quite awed and not a little jealous of her.

After a minute she opened her eyes and looked at him in the low light. Her whole face was softened and slightly dreamy. She raised her eyebrows in question. He shook his head. She looked surprised. He rolled off her and she turned over on to her stomach, lifting her bottom slightly. He knelt behind her and put his hands under her middle. He lifted her slightly and she pushed her bottom higher. Using his left hand as a prop on her bottom, he guided himself into her. As he pushed in, feelings that he had never had spread along the length, into his groin and loins. It was tightness, smoothness and pressure in all the right places. Not the feeling, for he felt in no danger, but just sheer pleasure. He moved in and out slowly. She sank back on to the bed and he lay on top of her, his legs wide apart. He moved and she moved in a sleepy, gentle motion. Then he pushed back up into the kneeling position and watched himself disappearing into her. It was so erotic, almost detached from reality. Here he was watching himself disappear into this beautiful woman, feeling these sensations running up and down his body, while she lay sleepily with a satisfied expression on her face.

It was getting too much for him. He put his hands on her buttocks, smoothed his hands over them and gripped the sides of her hips. He was aware of the feeling rising in amongst the other sensations. He moved harder and quicker and she sensed what was happening and raised her bottom higher, allowing him to plunge deeper. Then he felt it coming. He pushed deeper one last time, pulling her hips while he pushed, and the muscles tensed four times, giving him four delicious bites at this particularly ripe cherry. As he finished he shook uncontrollably and lay down on her back, twitching. Then he rolled off and lay at her side gasping. She turned her head to him and smiled. The disappointment of the early evening gone, he lay with his eyes wide open staring at the ceiling, blowing out deep breaths in an attempt to calm down. Never, never in his life had he experienced anything like that before.

They both dozed a little in the dreamy, relaxed world of post-orgasmic humankind.

## CHAPTER 15

## CONFESSIONS

Stuart dozed a little. He was wakened by the light going on. He looked up dreamily. Ita was sitting at the table, on one leg as usual, looking at something. She had obviously washed and was dressed in her long tee-shirt and knickers, the rest of her clothes neatly folded on the back of the chair.

She turned to him when she heard his movement. "Wash," she said simply. "Off you go."

He went obediently. He showered all over, including washing his hair, and put on a fresh lot of aftershave. He came out and found a clean pair of underpants and a tee-shirt, the same style of dress as hers, and went to see what she was reading.

She was actually reading the room service menu. He looked at her and she looked up at him and smiled.

"I'm hungry," she said.

"But we've had dinner, or did you forget?" he replied, a little smile on his lips.

"No, I didn't forget but now I'm hungry for food. Last time I was hungry for something else," she laughed, slightly embarrassed.

He shook his head. "What do you want?" he said.

"Just this." She pointed at an item on the menu.

"Nasi goreng," he said reading slowly.

"Yeah, just fried rice."

"Nothing else?" he asked.

"Tea?" she replied, looking up at him.

"Okay."

He ordered the food. While they waited she looked quietly through the rest of the menu, then through the directory of hotel service and the instructions for international telephone dialling. Stuart simply watched her. Her face was now devoid of the little make-up that she usually wore. Her hair was swept over her right shoulder as she leaned on her left arm, turning the pages with her right. He examined the nose, its gentle concave shape;

he examined the dark eyebrows and the long eyelashes; he examined the colour of her skin: it was brown, a beautiful shade, enhanced by the soft incandescent light of the table lamp. She really was quite beautiful.

The doorbell jerked him out of his reverie, and he realised that it was room service and that he had no pants on.

"Just a minute," he shouted as he struggled to the door, pulling his pants on at the same time. Ita slipped quickly into the bathroom, closing and locking the door. The waiter came in, holding the tray high at shoulder height. He placed the tray on the small coffee table. He stood up and presented Stuart with the bill to sign. He looked curiously at the small jeans looped over the back of the chair and the bra folded neatly on top. His eyes flicked down to the small pair of shoes under the chair. He smiled at Stuart with a raised eyebrow. Stuart handed him the bill back with a large tip tucked discreetly inside.

"Thank you, sir," the waiter said, smiling. "I hope you both enjoy your meal."

Stuart smiled an embarrassed smile and could not look him in the eye. He was sure that it would be all over the hotel in minutes, but he hoped that the tip would help.

Once the door was closed with the 'Do Not Disturb' sign on, Ita re-emerged from the bathroom. She sat down at the coffee table and demolished the large plate of fried rice, the three sticks of satay, the piece of chicken, the prawn cracker and two pieces of bread. She finished off with a glass of water and then poured tea for both of them.

He looked at her in amazement. "Feel better?"

"Much," she said, dabbing her mouth with the large serviette.

"You know," he began, "usually you take a woman out, buy her dinner, see a show, go to the cinema or whatever and then come back and make love. You, first it's make love and then let's eat or whatever."

She smiled. "I was so nervous tonight – I never like that before. So afraid you didn't want me, I just wanted to make contact with you again, to touch you, to join together again, so I couldn't eat. I not eat all day, so of course I hungry now."

She laughed again. "Just minute." She disappeared into the bathroom.

Stuart moved the teacups on to the bedside table and turned off all the lights except the one on the bedside table. Then he removed his tee-shirt and climbed into bed, propping himself up in a sitting position on the pillows.

She came out of the bathroom and sat on the opposite side of the bed, her back towards him. She lifted her tee-shirt off and revealed the smooth brown back which he had been stroking not long before. Its colour was like that of her face, brown and even. No bikini line, no shoulder strap marks, no spots or marks to blemish the silkiness. He wondered if she was going to turn round and give him the longed-for view of her breasts, but instead she skilfully slipped under the covers without facing him and slid across the wide expanse of the bed to get close to him. She snuggled in against his chest and wrapped her right arm around him. They were silent: only the faint noise of the air-conditioning broke the silence.

During the ten minutes of silence they both absorbed the feelings and sensations of the evening, tried to rationalise the feelings, the passion and the pleasure.

Stuart broke the silence. "Will you sleep here tonight?" He paused. "Please, I'd like that very much," he added.

"Yes, I want to, I want to wake up with you," she replied softly from his chest without raising her head. "But I have to go to work. I must leave about six-thirty."

Stuart reached over for the telephone and booked a morning call for six. He drank half a cup of tea and then settled down to stroke her hair.

"Your job?" he asked after a few strokes. "What kind of job is it?"

"I'm a secretary. Well, more like a personal assistant really, I do everything for my boss: expenses, typing, accounting," she replied.

"Do you use computers?" he asked.

"Oh yes, Lotus 1-2-3, WordStar, we use a lot of computers. I been trained for three months and I have a laser printer, Hewlett Packard," she continued.

Stuart was reasonably satisfied that she was genuine. Anwar's 'virgins and whores' statement kept running through his mind. Ita was clearly neither, so what was she? What was her reason for being with Stuart now? Whatever the reasons, he knew that he wanted her to stay the night with him, to sleep next to her, to feel her body close to his. He hoped that the conversation they were now starting would lead to some of the answers.

After a while, she began, "How much do you know about Indonesian women?"

"Not much. I know you, I know Mr Anwar's wife a little, I've met girls downstairs. But actually *know* about them – I know very little." He paused. "Except that most of you are exceptionally beautiful."

She dug him in the ribs at the last comment. "No, silly, I mean culture of Indonesia and women and girls and men."

"You tell me," he responded.

"Okay. Well, some things are very important here, you know, things that girl possess and can lose." She paused, waiting for Stuart to find the correct answer.

He didn't reply.

"That can be lost very easily and destroy a girl's life," she said, prompting him.

"You mean virginity," he answered after a suitable delay.

"Yes, I mean that. To be a virgin is very important if you want to be married. If you not virgin it's difficult. Most people think if not virgin then you must be..." She paused. "Well, like..." she stopped.

"Like a call-girl," he helped out.

"Yes." Then she stopped again and she raised her head. "Pass me some tea," she said quietly. As Stuart reached for the tea, she sat up and wrapped the sheet around her body. He was still denied his glimpse.

She took the teacup and saucer and held both and the sheet while she drank. She put the cup down on the bed beside her.

Stuart felt that Anwar's sad story was about to be revealed.

"How old am I?" she asked Stuart next.

"Twenty-two or three," he replied. "I've no real idea, it's so difficult to judge the age of Indonesian people."

"I am twenty-eight, not married, never married and..." she paused and looked down, avoiding his eyes, "...obviously not a virgin." She looked up again, meeting his eyes with a slight smile.

Stuart looked at the small lady before him. All through his life, since he was a spotty teenager, women and girls had wanted to tell him their secrets, their problems. He was a good listener, discreet and not a gossip. He could be trusted and women seemed to know it. Here was another one about to do the same. And more than any other woman who had told him her life story, he wanted to know Ita's secrets and Ita's reasons. He smiled at her. "Why?"

"Why is a long story," she answered, picking up the cup and saucer.

"It's early, I'm not tired and I am a good listener," was his soft, gentle reply.

She let out a long sigh and put down the cup and saucer again, shifting her legs into a cross-legged position, arms folded to support the sheet around her breasts. "I was seventeen, in secondary school, a good one, Catholic. They were all organised by the Dutch and are still the best. Anyone can go – Muslim, Christian, it doesn't matter. I was top of my year, the best in the school. I was set for a scholarship for one of the government universities. And then..." She paused and looked down, away from his eyes.

"And then," he prompted, but she remained silent. "And then," he said again, "you fell in love, right?"

She nodded her head slowly in agreement. "It was worse than that. I fell in love with a Muslim boy and all my family are Catholic, or Christian, Protestant or similar. One of my uncles is a Pendatar, a priest, in the Baptist Church. So my family definitely would not have approved."

"I suppose that made it all the more exciting or... well, that's not the right word, made you want to continue with it against your parents' wishes," he said.

She regarded him with an expression of admiration. "Yes," she said, "when I look back on it, that was a big part of it. No one else understood that. How did you know?"

He smiled. "Teenage rebellion. Most young people feel that they have to defy their parents, go against their will and establish independence."

"Not here." She shook her head. "Not like that here – we must obey and follow our parents." She sipped the last of the tea and handed Stuart the cup. "He said, my boyfriend, that it didn't matter to him – he was going to become a Catholic or whatever, because he wanted to marry me. My parents said I was too young, that I must go to college first and become qualified, that my prospects were so good that I had to wait. That just made me more keen to stay with him."

Stuart nodded in agreement.

"Then I was so determined to marry him. He said he was too. He said that we should make love before to prove our love to each other. After a few weeks of his pushing, urging, he talking about nothing else, I agreed, I consented. It happened outside, near to his house on some waste ground." She stopped, her eyes filling with tears.

Stuart pulled a hanky from under his pillow and handed it to her.

She smiled in thanks and dried her eyes. "He was brutal," she continued, "absolutely awful. Sometimes I still dream about it." She paused again and looked down.

"You don't have to tell me," Stuart said tenderly.

She shook her head. "I have to tell someone – it's been more than ten years."

He looked at her in amazement. "Ten years without saying, without saying anything to anyone?"

She nodded her head.

"How, why, how could you keep this inside you for so long, until now?" He looked sadly at her.

"I don't know. I've hidden it from view from everyone. I never had a girlfriend I wanted to tell. All the boyfriends, even the Europe man who want to marry me, I never tell him – I was afraid that he would not love me any more." Her eyes filled with tears again.

"Not even your mother?" he asked.

"Especially not my mother. It would break her heart if she knew," Ita replied.

"So why me?" he asked. "Why tell me after all these years?"

"You are different, you already married, happy married. You are a good man, a kind man, like no man I ever meet before," she said, looking directly into his eyes.

"I'm not so good. In fact I must be very bad to my wife – I have been unfaithful to her, with you," he answered.

"That doesn't make you a bad man," she said.

"You try to tell my wife that," he replied with a smile.

She laughed a little through the tears. She dried her eyes once again and returned to her story.

"He was nice at first, gentle, then once most of my clothes were open, his eyes filled with a hazy wild look and he held my arms out wide, he forced my legs apart with his knees. I tried to shout but he pushed his mouth over mine in a kiss, he bit my lips and made them bleed. He pushed himself on to me, into me. The pain – oh God, the pain was awful. I was so shocked that I couldn't even scream." She paused and the tears now ran down her cheeks unchecked. "He was in me, pushing, grunting, dribbling from his mouth all over my face. Then he shouted and was still. He climbed off me and sat next to me and lit a cigarette. I was in such pain. It was hot, like burning. I put my hand down," she gestured towards her groin. "It was wet with blood, with other stuff." She shook her head. "Then I tried to sit up but he looked at me and said 'I've not finished yet', and then he was in me again. Three times in an hour, each time more painful than the last. I fainted the last time from the pain. Then he left me, told me to wait because we had to leave separately so it would look right." She stopped to dry her eyes.

"I lay for another hour, in too much pain to move," she resumed her narrative. "Then I tried to get myself together, pulled my clothes on and got home. I got in the house and washed and then I bled for four days. I told my mother it was menstruation and she believed me although it was only three weeks since the last one. I told her that I had pain in my stomach, so I drank strong *jamu*."

"*Jamu*?" he asked.

"Traditional medicine to make sure I was not pregnant. It made me so sick I was off school for ten days." She paused to look at Stuart, whose own eyes were beginning to fill with tears.

"And do you know," she shook her head in disbelief at what she was about to say. "Do you know", she repeated, "I still wanted him. Even after that I still thought I loved him. I went to find him as soon as I could. He met me and I asked about getting married. He laughed. How could he marry a Catholic, how could he marry a girl who was not a virgin, who had been with other men? He said that for the last ten days I had been with every boy who wanted it. Everybody in his school knew about the dirty, little Catholic prostitute. Then he said that I hadn't really been a virgin, that I had waited for menstruation so that I could bleed and look like a virgin to trick him into marrying. I was so shocked I walked home in a trance. At home I sat down on the bed and my mother came in. She told me that my boyfriend's father was next to the imam in the mosque, he wanted to become an imam himself and would not allow his son to marry a non-Muslim and if I became a Muslim many of my family would throw me out. My parents were worse than his, stuck in their ways. Even if he had been a good man they would never have let me marry him. I cried in my mother's arms; this let me release the emotion. She thought I was just sad because of that. She didn't know, she has never known the real reason. I spent two days in bed and she fed me like a baby." She stopped for a moment.

"And then?" Stuart prompted gently. This was like no other story any woman had ever told him. He sat and the tears welled in his eyes as she spoke.

"And then", she continued, "I went back to school, worked very hard, went to Gadjah Mada University in Yogja, did very well, but I knew I could not make the right marriage to get me in a good job, so I came to Jakarta and, well, here I am," she smiled, her story almost told.

"Did you ever see him again?" Stuart asked.

This question brought a smile to her lips for the first time since the narrative had begun, then she laughed and nodded her head. "Yes, I saw him once, two years ago. I was home visiting my mother when I saw him. He recognised me, but I didn't see him at all. He was tall and still so handsome but when he smiled his teeth were blackened from too much cigarettes. He never stopped smoking. He had some job in a factory. His wife wore the Jailbab Muslim headdress. She was quite pretty, I could see that even though she wore a chador. She held one child and two more stood in her wake. He was proud because she was pregnant again. He said that I had not changed since I was at school. He looked at me with an expression of disappointment in his eyes. I told him that I was not married, that my job came first. Then I told him how much my salary was, then his eyes opened wide and his mouth dropped. Then I said goodbye." She smiled at the memory. "I am happy. I found out he was not good man before I married him, even if he took my virgin away from me."

Her ability to find something good out of what was a brutal rape and deflowering at the tender age of seventeen amazed Stuart.

She was silent.

He looked at her as she sat, the tears drying on her cheeks, his hanky clutched in her hand. She pulled her knees up in front of her and rested her chin on them, wrapping her arms around them. She stared ahead, her story told, her emotion gone.

It was Stuart who broke the silence. "Why me? Why tonight? Why only tonight that this comes out?"

She didn't answer immediately, but continued to stare ahead. Then she looked at him. "Because you release my emotion, when we make love, it came out. It has never been like that before. Never." She stopped.

She went back to staring ahead. After a minute or two she resumed. "After I come to Jakarta, I think I am not virgin, maybe I should find boyfriend. I did, we made love, it was good after a while. Then I find out that European men don't worry about being a virgin before married so I looked for a nice Europe man. I had a European boyfriend for three years in here. I enjoyed making love with him very much, not like tonight, but good. He wanted to marry me, then his contract finished so he went back. At first he sent me some money, then that stopped and I heard nothing else. That was two years ago. Since then I have no boyfriend."

She moved across the bed and touched Stuart for the first time since the narrative had begun. She held the hanky to his eyes in turn and then held on to the hanky very tightly. She cuddled close to him, her body cool in the comparative chill of the air-conditioning. He pushed the pillows down to the sleeping position and turned out the light. Then they lay in silence, touching. No further words were necessary, for everything had been said. They just lay, emotionally exhausted and physically satisfied. After half an hour they were both asleep.

## CHAPTER 16

## SATURDAY LUNCH

The wake-up call came through as required at six o'clock. Stuart groped for the phone with his left hand. A cheerful voice said, "Good morning Mr Morgan, it is six o'clock and this is your wake-up call."

"Okay, thanks," was all that Stuart could manage in response. Ita lay next to him, her body close to his, an arm wrapped round him. He looked at her, eyes still closed, quiet and peaceful. A gentle smile came to her lips, she stretched slightly and then opened her eyes.

"Hello," she said, looking at him. "Good morning." She giggled a little to hide her shyness at waking up with him.

For Stuart it was the first time in twelve years that he had woken up with a woman other than his wife. "It's six o'clock, Ita, and good morning," he said with a smile.

She smiled back, squeezed him once and shuffled across the bed to where her tee-shirt lay. She got her tee-shirt on, denying Stuart any glimpse of her naked body, and then she disappeared into the bathroom.

He got up and pulled open the two sets of curtains. Even at six o'clock, the sun was shining brightly and it hurt his eyes a little. He sat down again and looked around, absently scratching his head.

Ita was not long in the bathroom. She came out and slipped on her jeans and shoes, grabbed a piece of stale bread from the leftovers of the previous evening's food and turned to leave.

"Saturday, right?" she asked between chews.

"Yes," he replied.

"Okay, I finish work at twelve, you?" She continued to chew the lump of stale bread.

"An hour or so is all I need at work, no more," he replied.

"I will be here." She pointed at the room door. "One o'clock. We go out for lunch." She nodded her head, prompting Stuart.

"Okay, one o'clock," he replied.

"Got to go." She walked over to him, kissed him on the cheek, chewed the bread once more and left.

Stuart stood up and looked out of the window. The traffic was still thin, for the main rush would not start for another half hour or so. He put his right hand on the curtain pelmet above his head and leaned his head against his outstretched arm. For a moment he stood still, trying to comprehend what had happened. It had been, quite simply, the most incredible night of his life. It was not the night he had enjoyed the most, since that had to be the night he was on the winning team in the university UAU final. It was not the night with the longest sexual marathon – that was at the age of nineteen when anything less than five was considered not par for the course – not even the most emotional, for him at any rate, as he had had some very emotional experiences in the past, although he reflected, usually alcohol-enhanced. No, last night was the most incredible night for different reasons.

Somehow he felt as though he had touched the soul of another human being in a way that no one else had ever touched that person's soul. He felt as though he had, by being the first person to share her experience – and he had no doubt that he was the first – become closer to her than to anyone else, his wife included. He knew that Ita had some special, very special, feelings for him, but how and why? Love at first sight? Hardly. They had met a number of times and he didn't think that Ita had had any more plans for making love than he did, which was none, when they first met. No, it was just one of those things, a meeting of two minds and bodies at the right time and place. He didn't want to change anything or alter the moment in any way. He turned back to the bed and lay down on his stomach, searching for her smell amongst the dishevelled sheets.

He slept for another hour and a half until the more reasonable time of eight o'clock. Then he showered, dressed and had a long breakfast with plenty of coffee. When he returned, the bed had been changed, the room cleaned: her memory of her presence was gone except in his memory.

Stuart entered Anwar's office a little after ten. It was in its usual Saturday morning relaxed mood, with jeans and open-neck shirts the order of the day. Even the normally well-dressed Anwar had no tie on.

As Stuart entered the office, Anwar smiled broadly. "Good morning Mr Morgan! It looks like we have an order – only spares, but it's better than nothing, in fact it's better than I think we could have ever hoped for!" He waved a piece of fax paper at Stuart.

Stuart took the paper without speaking and read it carefully. It wasn't actually an order, it was a request for the ordering procedure, methods of payment and a list of spare parts totalling more than fifteen thousand pounds. Stuart smiled. "It's not an order yet," he cautioned.

Anwar refused to let Stuart dampen his enthusiasm. "Oh, come on, it is as good as one! Old Mr Chan is going to order this stuff, believe me, and some more later. All you have to do is to come up with a good proposal for future supply, financing. I'll send you Chan's order within two weeks. Okay! So no more doubt." He looked hard at Stuart. "This spares order will just about cover my expenses," he laughed.

Stuart smiled back. "We have anything to sort out before I go back to the UK?" he asked.

"Not much, so we can have an early and long lunch break," Anwar said.

Now Stuart was confused. How could he refuse lunch with Anwar? What could he give as an excuse? "Well actually," he began shakily, "I have other plans for today."

Anwar regarded him with his head slightly to one side, an eyebrow slightly raised.

"Yeah, it's just some people that I met and we are all going home this weekend, so we wanted a last lunch together," he continued in an unconvincing tone. "Perhaps tomorrow?" he added in compensation.

"Sorry, family day tomorrow, all arranged." Anwar gave a slightly flustered smile.

They looked at each other in an embarrassed silence, each discomfited at their mutual inability to accept the invitation.

It was Anwar who broke the silence. "Come on, we have some things to arrange about Mr Chan and your next visit."

Their business was completed within half an hour and Stuart said his goodbyes to Anwar and the staff.

By eleven-thirty he was back in his room. He changed, and spent an hour by the pool, coming back up with half an hour to go before Ita was due. He showered and dressed in jeans, running shoes and a tee-shirt. Then he sat down to wait. His wait was not long as Ita appeared a minute or so before the appointed time.

She almost bounced into the room as Stuart opened the door, quite unlike her earlier graceful movements.

"Hi, Hello," she said brightly, reaching up to kiss him on the cheek. She put a plastic bag down on the chest of drawers, rummaged around and pulled something out. "Before we go, can you do this?" She held a small camera in her left hand and something in her right.

Stuart took the camera and looked at it. It was a very old Kodak Instamatic, a largish square lump, battered and well-used. Stuart laughed. "What's this for?"

She looked confused. "For take photograph."

"With this?" he laughed again, looking at the camera with amusement. Then he looked at Ita. She looked upset: her brown eyes had a look of child-like hurt, as if she felt that she had been told off for doing well.

"This my camera. I bought it when I was at school with my money, but for a long time I didn't use it." Her voice was small and hurt.

Stuart realised the significance of the camera and the effect his amusement had had. Immediately he changed his attitude.

"Let's have a look," he said softly, taking the film from her still outstretched hand. He opened the back of the camera. It was a little dirty and Stuart started to clean it with a tissue.

She watched him attentively, like a small child waiting for a toy to be repaired, her head bobbing around to get the best view of what he was doing.

He checked the operation of the shutter: it seemed to work reasonably well. She went over to the bag and rummaged round a second time to find another packet.

"I bought these as well." She handed him a packet of flash bulbs. "Here." She flicked up a flash section on the camera.

He looked at it carefully. "There must be a battery somewhere – this is an electric flash." He searched and found a small compartment door on the bottom. He opened it to reveal two old, salt-encrusted batteries. He pulled them out with care. "We need some new ones of these too," he said, tossing the old ones cleanly into the waste bin. He cleaned up the battery compartment, scraping the terminals with his small key-ring penknife. Once finished, he loaded the film. She pulled her handbag from within the plastic bag, and they were ready to go.

Downstairs, in the hotel drugstore, he bought two batteries, loaded them and the camera was ready.

"Where are we going?" he said as they walked towards the door of the hotel.

She smiled and walked backwards in front of him. She held a key in her right hand. "I got a car," she said triumphantly.

"Your car?" he asked as she returned to his side.

"No, from my office friend," she replied in a tone which indicated that it was a stupid question.

"You have a license?" he asked nervously.

"Yes, of course," she answered in a similar tone to that used before. She led him to a small, well-used Toyota Starlet parked below the main ramp in a small parking area.

He sat in the passenger seat while she busied herself with the preparations for driving. He felt nervous.

"Sorry," she said, "no AC, so maybe a bit hot."

Stuart smiled and nodded, trying to hide his nervousness from her.

Then they were on the move. She drove quite slowly, but competently enough for Stuart to relax after ten minutes or so. She didn't speak at all as she drove, her concentration was complete. At first they struggled through the Jakarta traffic. Stuart felt very hot in the small car. Now he knew a little of how the truck drivers and bus passengers must feel in their non-air-conditioned transport. But presently they reached a dual carriageway of motorway standard, a toll road. Ita took a ticket and they bowled along at a reasonable pace.

"Where are we going?" he said, as the driving became easier for her and her concentration relaxed a little.

"Out for lunch," she said without any further explanation.

At the end of the motorway, Ita paid a toll and they started along a normal two lane road. They drove though a series of villages and towns which, like so many towns and villages Stuart had seen in the other parts of Java that he had visited, seemed to run into one another, with little to show where one ended and the next began. As they moved further on there were many large villas, hotels, restaurants and other places of entertainment lining both sides of the road.

"What is this place?" Stuart asked. "Why all these discos and stuff?"

"This is a holiday area for people from Jakarta," she replied, not taking her eyes off the road. "People come here for the weekend from Jakarta. The air is fresh, the weather cool – it's a good place."

"Okay," Stuart said, satisfied.

The road was busy and twisty, and many trucks and buses came careering in the opposite direction. Stuart realised that as they were climbing, the rest, coming in the opposite direction, were descending. Stuart wondered about their brakes for a while and then tried to put it out of his mind, because there was no point worrying about it. Along the way they passed a police station. Outside were a number of cars, one bus and a truck, all with various amounts of crash damage. Stuart tried even harder to put their brakes and driving habits out of his mind. Ita continued to drive with care and caution. She was cut up a number of times by some crazy overtaking manoeuvres, but she remained a lot calmer than Stuart would ever have had he been driving.

Eventually, as the road climbed higher and the wind pushing in through the open windows became cooler, the last village stopped and was not replaced by another one. The road became even more twisty as it snaked up the side of hill. All around the road were small bushes, all of the same height, all cropped to flat tops. They carpeted the hillsides and valleys in a smooth green roll. Stuart looked with interest at the new scene.

"Tea garden," Ita said, noticing his interest.

"Tea, as in drink?" he replied.

She laughed. "What else is for tea?"

"I have never seen it growing before," he said, "only in packets ready to drink."

"We can stop there later. It's part of my plan," she said mysteriously.

"Plan?" he asked, looking at her concentrating profile.

"After lunch," she answered.

The road snaked up the hillside in a series of tight twists and sweeping bends, with high banks of red tropical soil on one side and sometimes precipitous drops on the other, and all the while the tea bushes marched in regimented rows up and down the flanks of the hills and valleys. At one point they passed a section of road with a central reservation. Into this central reservation a footbridge descended. As the road swung left beyond the bridge, Stuart looked back. An enormous house stood on a shoulder of the hill with what must have been a fantastic view of the valley below. The footbridge led from the house and Stuart guessed that the house belonged to the owner of the tea garden.

Ita glanced at him. "That's the manager's house, for the tea garden. Gunung Mas, the Golden Mountain, is the name of the garden."

Stuart was amused by her calling such a huge plantation a 'garden'.

"It is the biggest tea garden in the world," she continued, ignoring his amusement.

"If it is so big why have I never heard of it at home?" He asked the obvious question.

"Ah," she replied with a superior, knowing tone in her voice. "That is because it is such good tea that we drink it all here and don't have anything left for export." She looked at him and smiled.

"Watch the road not me," said Stuart as she looked at him.

She laughed again.

Stuart looked at her again. There had been a definite change in her since the previous day: a lightening in her behaviour. She was not so serious: she laughed much more easily. Her eyes still had the deeply sensual look, but behind this the deeply serious look was supplemented by a gay levity. It was quite a change. Stuart realised at that moment that what had happened the night before, a night that seemed an age ago now, had been really as serious as he had felt at the time: it was the first telling of her awful story. The ten year suppression was over – another human being knew what she had been through. He felt strangely privileged with the information. He smiled to himself and looked at her again.

She knew that he was looking at her and smiling. "*Apa*?" she spoke in Indonesian, a little unnerved by his attention and smile.

"Sorry?" he asked

"Sorry, I mean what. What are you laughing and looking at?" She glanced at him as she drove.

"Watch the road!" he repeated sternly.

She flicked her eyes back to the job in hand.

"I'm not laughing at you, I am smiling because you look so happy," he said without a trace of embarrassment at what was really, for him, quite a soppy, sentimental line.

She just continued to look ahead and smile.

They continued to climb past a cluster of houses and a group of stalls selling fruit until they came to a big restaurant on the right side of the road. She pulled over and parked the car close to the entrance.

"Lunch," she announced with a note of triumph in her voice. She led the way in, disregarding a waiter who tried to show them to a table inside the large building, and went straight to the outdoor balcony which overlooked the valley and the snaking road. They sat opposite each other looking over the balcony. The ground was about thirty or forty feet below the balcony and below that it sloped away steeply to the tea gardens below.

"Nice," he said simply.

"You like?" she said, looking at him with the gaze of a child desperately seeking approval from a teacher, her brown eyes big and wide.

"Yes, I do, it's quite fantastic up here, the view is... well, just tremendous."

She smiled back, happy that her choice had been approved.

"What's the name of this place?" he asked.

"The restaurant?" she asked.

"No, the area," he replied.

"This is Puncak," she said.

"Oh, this is Puncak," he said as if he had just seen the light.

"You know already?" She looked a little crestfallen.

"No, of course not, but some woman I talked to on the plane the first time I came here mentioned that it was a nice place to go."

A waiter came and they ordered a drink and read the long menu. Stuart couldn't decide, for there was too much choice. "You choose," he said, taking the easy way out.

She nodded in agreement.

She put her bag on the table and took out the old camera. In the open bag, Stuart could see his hanky, the one that she had used the night before to dry her eyes, to dry his eyes, neatly folded inside. The monogrammed 'S' in the corner revealed it to be one of a set of six bought by some aunt a few Christmases ago. They were good hankies, Irish linen with the blue 'S' embroidered in one corner, hardly the most exciting present of the year, but somehow very relevant and crucial to the situation in which he found himself. She was trying to frame a picture of the vast expanse of scenery which lay before and below them.

"Here," she said, handing him the camera, "you try, I can't do it."

He took the camera and tried to frame the immense scene in the tiny viewfinder. The camera was – almost any camera would have been – inadequate for the task. He lowered it and looked at Ita instead. She was looking at the view, her chin resting on her left hand, her hair swept behind her right ear. He framed her instead of the scenery. He framed the concave profile of her nose and the rest of her face against the roof pillar behind her and snapped.

She turned and looked at him, an expression of mock anger on her face. "I meant take a picture of the garden, not me."

He snapped her again.

She grabbed the camera. "Here, you are no good," she said. She took one photograph of the scenery then turned the camera on him. The first time he was looking into the valley, unaware that she was taking a photograph of him, and then he swung round, pivoting his chin on his left hand and raising his left eyebrow at her; she snapped again.

He tried to grab the camera off her but the food arrived to interrupt their game.

Stuart had to admit that she had chosen well: lamb satay on a sizzling hot plate, vegetables with peanut sauce, barbecued fish, white rice and the fiery red sambal dish of ground chillies and shrimp paste. She ate with her fingers and he attempted to emulate her with moderate success. The food was quickly finished and Stuart washed his down with beer, Ita with warm, milkless tea. Then they just sat and watched the view.

"You finish?" she asked after about ten minutes of watching the view.

"Yeah, okay," he replied, turning his eyes from the view to her. "Where to now?"

She smiled. "For a cup of tea."

The bill arrived and Stuart was able to grab it first, and paid the equivalent of less than five pounds. It was incredibly good value.

She led the way out of the restaurant and across the road and down the hill a short way. There was a series of stalls selling mainly fruit and vegetables, but also some trinkets and small bonsai-type trees. Stuart paid the fruit and trinkets little attention, but the small trees caught his eye.

"How much?" he asked the man.

The man held up five fingers.

"Five thousand?" Stuart asked.

The man nodded and smiled.

Stuart though that this was cheap, less than two pounds, but Ita breezed up and shook her head.

"Five thousand is far too much. Maybe you should offer only two," she whispered in Stuart's ear.

Stuart held up three fingers and the man quickly handed him the plant. Stuart looked surprised.

"What am I going to do with this?" he asked, looking at the small, but admittedly beautiful little tree. "I can't take it home. Would you like it, Ita?" he said, offering her the plant.

She looked at it with her head on one side. "If a present from you, of course I like to have it," she said, "but three thousand is too much. But you agreed and now you must pay."

Stuart paid and the man looked happy.

Ita carried her tree and Stuart carried the bag of fruit that she had bought and they crossed back into the car park. She carefully arranged the tree in the boot on a piece of paper and put it in one corner to stop it sliding about. Then they drove off down the hill again.

Just above the point where the last village finished and the tea garden proper began, Ita turned off the road and drove down a small tarmac road to a parking spot. At one side was an open-sided building, on the other a number of people selling barbecued corn on the cob. A few small horses and their owners stood around touting for business.

"Okay," she said as she locked the car, "now we go for walk in tea garden."

She led him further along the road before turning off down a small unmetaled track. They walked in silence, occasionally nudging shoulders or catching hold of an arm to provide support on the uneven ground. Stuart liked the cool fresh feel of the mountain air. It was such a relief from the hot, sticky environment of downtown Jakarta. The exercise and walk were good. Apart from the odd swim in the hotel pool, he had had almost no exercise in the last month. They walked on through the rows of tea bushes, past a group of pickers who looked nothing like the dainty ladies in saris normally seen in the idealised pictures of tea gardens. They wore big bamboo hats and thick rubber gloves, and passed comments in loud raucous voices.

Ita smiled as one comment came in their direction.

"What did she say?" asked Stuart, breaking the silence of the last forty minutes.

"Nothing," Ita replied, still smiling.

"Oh, if it's nothing, why the big smile?" he said.

"She just said that I am a small woman with a big man and that I must be easy to get satisfied." She stopped walking and looked up at him, her eyes wide.

Stuart smiled. "Do you agree?" he asked with a raised eyebrow.

"What do you think?" she replied, her eyes even wider.

He laughed a little and one of the tea pickers made another comment which brought forth another peal of equally raucous laughter. Ita smiled again and then started to walk on.

After another half hour of silent walking, they stopped and sat on a low wall.

"Enough?" she asked, fanning herself with her hand. "I think far enough. We go back, yes?"

"Okay," said Stuart, glad that she wanted to return, since even the cool of the mountain area was hot for his English constitution after more than an hour of walking. They turned and Ita led them back a different way. They had been climbing all the way on the way out, and now it was easier to descend back to the car.

Back at the car, Ita led him into the open-sided building. "Now for the cup of tea," she said.

At a small counter a small, smiling girl stood waiting for their order. In a short menu under the glass of the counter, the selection was tea of different types from the Gunung Mas gardens.

"Coffee please," said Stuart.

The girl looked confused. "*Tidak Ada*," she replied, shaking her head.

Ita kicked Stuart. "You come in the tea shop of the biggest tea garden in the world and ask for coffee?"

He grinned back. "Tea please."

The girl smiled, realising the joke.

The tea was brought to one of the bare wooden tables at the edge of the building. It was good tea, served with milk. Stuart asked for a second cup and then asked to buy some packaged tea. He choose two types, one in a fancy red and yellow pack, the other in brown paper. He bought two of each, one to take home to England and one to give to Ita.

Ita bought them both a third cup just before the girl started to close up the shop. Then Ita bought two barbecued corn on the cobs and they sat on a wall in the gathering dusk, eating the corn and watching the tropical night fall.

As soon as it was dark, they got in the car and drove back to the city. The journey back took longer than the outward one, and it was after nine o'clock by the time they reached the hotel. They had dropped the small tree and the tea off at Ita's house. Stuart hadn't gone inside as Ita said that the car had to be back and there was no time. Then they left the car at its appointed place and got a taxi back to Stuart's hotel.

"I take a shower, no problem?" she said, once they were inside the room.

Stuart shook his head. "No problem."

She disappeared for ten minutes and reappeared washed and in a change of clothes. She wore another loose, large tee-shirt, black with some logo, tucked baggily into the top of a pair of white, very tight jeans. She noticed Stuart's interest and gave a playful twirl. "Okay, you like?" she asked.

"Mmmm," he said, admiring her from the back as she went to the mirror to brush her hair. "Very much I like," he said, aping her sometimes broken English. In fact, she looked absolutely gorgeous in the jeans. She had an excellent figure, and all of it firm and smooth.

"You wash now!" she commanded and Stuart dutifully obeyed.

It was almost ten by the time he had finished. She had put her make-up on and stood waiting for him.

"We eat now?" she asked.

"Okay, where?"

"Downstairs, The Inne. It's Saturday night and time for enjoy," she replied.

Downstairs, in the heat, smoke and noise, they found a table to one side and ate a light meal. The new Filipino band had improved to the point where they were almost good, and Stuart enjoyed their music and the music of the Indonesian change band.

They left at one o'clock, both tired, both ready for sleep. They slept, naked except for knickers and underpants, intertwined and cuddling.

## CHAPTER 17

## SUNDAY AND DEPARTURE

They both slept long and hard, tired from the walk, the late night and the emotional outpouring of Friday night. Despite the fact that the curtains were not fully closed and a shaft of morning sunlight must have been penetrating the room for several hours, it was well after ten before Stuart opened his eyes. He rubbed them in turn with his left hand and craned his head forward to see the still sleeping form of Ita, wrapped around his torso. He smiled to himself and stroked the black hair with his right hand.

She moved slightly at his touch, then began a full stretch of her legs and free arm. She opened her eyes and moved up Stuart's chest, resting both her arms across and putting her chin on her interlocked fingers. The big brown eyes looked into Stuart's. Those deeply serene pools, with their seriousness and intensity, looked straight into Stuart and into his heart. 'The eyes are the window of the soul,' thought Stuart as he continued to look and remember some quotation from his schooldays. He had seen right into Ita's heart and soul and was pleased. At the same time, he felt that she could see into his, that she could see things of which he was not sure, that she could divine what he thought and felt and what his actions would be, even though he himself, in his direct conscious mind, did not know. He smiled at her as a way of breaking the look, uncomfortable now that she knew what the future held and what he would do and he didn't.

"What now?" he asked when he could stare no longer.

"Wash," she said abruptly, and then, equally abruptly, she moved across the bed, grabbed her tee-shirt and slipped it over her head, denying Stuart yet again his much yearned-after glimpse of her naked body.

She disappeared into the bathroom.

Stuart respected her privacy and allowed her to shower and wash without going into the bathroom himself. When she emerged, he went in and when he had finished she was sitting on the edge of the bed fully clothed, hair combed and make-up finished.

He felt rather shy, standing there with only his underpants on.

She turned and laughed. He became even more shy and grabbed some clothes.

"What's the matter?" he asked once his polo shirt was over his head and more or less on.

"Nothing," she said, fighting back a further laugh. "You look..." she paused. "Well... sweet. Like a little boy, all round and pink." She laughed again.

Stuart wasn't sure how to take the comment. So he pulled a small boy face and pulled on his jeans. He decided at that moment that he had to lose some weight: he was getting slowly fatter as time went on and now, for some reason, appeared to be the right time to take himself in hand and sort out his slight paunch.

She had turned back to face the television.

"Come on," she said. "Let's go."

She stood and switched off the television.

"Where?"

"Eat?" he suggested.

"You want to swim? I brought my costume," she asked.

"In the hotel pool?"

She shook her head.

"I know a place we can swim and look around all day. We can eat as well."

"Where?"

"Not far, called Ancol," she said.

He remembered that it was his last day and he was due to check out at four in the afternoon.

"How far? You know I have to leave today."

"Yes, I know."

Her brown eyes saddened a little.

"But that's later, we got the rest of the day."

She brightened up almost immediately.

"Let's go."

They collected their swimming things and put them in a plastic bag. They turned to leave, then she turned back.

"I almost forgot," she said, picking up a small, black plastic case. "The film – we can get the picture today, one hour only, across the road near the hotel." With the plastic film case clutched in her right hand, they left the room.

They crossed the road and went into the small photographic shop. Ita arranged everything, including two copies of all the pictures.

"One for you and one for me," she explained.

Outside they got a taxi for a ride that lasted half an hour. They went into the Ancol Dreamland swimming pool and separated to change.

Stuart was first out. He slipped into the lukewarm water. The pool was crowded with Sunday families: children splashed and climbed everywhere, leaping off the sides, off the diving boards and down the two waterslide chutes. He watched the women's changing room exit for a sight of Ita.

She wandered out tentatively looking left and right for some sight of Stuart.

Unlike most women who were walking around the pool, she did not have on either a dressing gown or towel wrapped round her. She didn't seem shy about her body at all and walked with grace and dignity. She wore a one-piece suit with high-cut legs. It was the nearest that Stuart had ever been to seeing her naked. He watched her closely from his body-down vantage point in the pool. She turned away from him and walked towards the shallow end of the pool. Her back he had seen before, but he had never seen her bottom in anything like as little clothing. She had kept her body mostly covered from his sight even though his hands and mouth had touched and explored most of it in minute detail.

Her back sloped in towards her waist from both sides in a smooth curve, unhindered by rolls or lumps of fat. The curve merged into the line of her bottom, curving gracefully back in the opposite direction to the tops of her thighs, again all unencumbered by fat or dimples or any other of the things which would have affected an Englishwoman of her age. There was a gentle curve of the spine in the other direction, from front to back, and this curved back into a neat tuck under at the top of the back of her thighs. Her bottom was a lovely shape. Her upper thighs were smooth and sleek, and on the inside they just met at the top before they curved out a little and joined her body. Stuart was amazed at her figure. He knew that she had a reasonable shape, and that it was firm, but the sheer beauty – he was tempted to say perfection – of her back view was a surprise to him.

He could have watched her all day, just walking to and fro.

But she turned when she could not see him from the shallow end and walked towards him.

He had the opportunity to appreciate her front view. Her stomach was almost flat. It had seemed flat when she had been lying down and he had been exploring it, but there was a little bulge at the front. Her breasts, he already knew, were small, but this didn't detract from her appearance at all. All of this, the back and the front, were enhanced by a skin colour of rich golden brown.

She walked with a smooth easy gracefulness and gentle roll of the hips. She actually walked right past him and he was tempted to let her continue so that he could get another glimpse of her rear view, but instead he splashed her to get her attention. She smiled at him without appearing surprised, turned and walked to the edge of the pool and dived straight in. She swam across the pool using breaststroke, diving beneath the water on each alternate stroke and breathing on the other. She turned and swam back to stand by Stuart.

She smiled. "Shall we swim?"

He shrugged his shoulders. "Yeah, why not?"

They swam across rather than along the length of the pool to avoid the diving board jumpers at one end and the children at the other. After five times across Stuart was feeling the pace, but Ita showed no sign of slowing. He struggled to keep up for another two times, then suggested that they try the waterslide. After one long queue for each of the two slides they gave up and returned to swimming. Ita did another five times across, Stuart another two. Then they lay in the water by the edge of the pool and talked, played, joked and generally fooled around with each other. They sat out on the edge, trailing their feet in the water. Then it was time to finish swimming and eat.

They ate in a small stall outside the swimming pool, on the edge of an art market. After they finished, they strolled around the stalls looking at the various works. Some quite took Stuart's eye, but he had no way of getting them home. He bought some small things to take home as presents, something in particular for Colleen.

Ita knew what he was doing and for whom he was buying for. She went very quiet and offered no comment when he showed her the things he wanted to buy.

He glanced at his watch. It was already two-thirty, time to go.

She looked up at him with her brown eyes sad. She nodded: she understood the glance at the watch. She led him in silence to the taxi rank and spoke only to direct the driver all the way home.

They entered the hotel. Stuart grabbed her arm.

"The photographs," he said.

Her face brightened in an instant.

"The pictures!" she said excitedly. "Come on, now."

She turned and almost ran out of the hotel. She quickly led Stuart by the hand across the busy main road back into the small photographic shop. She paid and opened the small packet. They sat down in the corner of the shop and looked through the twenty-four pictures together. The ones that Stuart had taken of Ita, especially those that for which she had not posed, were good, despite the simple camera.

Stuart thought that, as usual, he looked like an idiot.

"You look good in some," he said, holding the first one that he had taken on the restaurant balcony, "but me, I look like an idiot, a moron."

"No, you look very handsome. In this one." She held one that she had taken when he was eating corn on the cob in the tea garden. "And this one." She handed him another.

"Don't get them mixed up – we've got two sets," Stuart said as he handed hers back.

"Sorry," she said, biting her lower lip and looking up at him with childlike innocence.

He smiled. "Come on, we must get back. I haven't got much time."

They returned to the hotel and Stuart packed.

She sat on the bed very quietly watching his steady progress. She waited until he had almost finished before she spoke.

"When will you come back, Stuart?"

"I am not sure. A month or two maybe. It depends on Mr Anwar really, not me," he replied, trying to be as accurate as he could. He pulled out a business card and held it out to her. "This is my work address," he said. Then he took it back and carefully wrote his home address and telephone number on the back. "And this is my home address. If you want to write, then..." he paused, embarrassed by what he knew he had to say.

"I know," she interrupted. "I write to the work one, yes?"

He nodded his head.

She put the card carefully in her bag alongside Stuart's monogrammed hanky.

"I will write to you," she said quietly. "You write me also?" she asked.

"Yes, of course I will write to you. I will tell you everything about England and my life," he said extravagantly.

"Some things I don't want to know about," she said in a little voice.

He realised his mistake and quickly and quietly finished his packing.

They left the room and carried the bags between them, Stuart's suitcase, his flight bag and Ita's plastic carrier bag.

She held on to his arm all the way down in the lift and to the cashier's desk. She stood in silence while he paid. Outside, they took another taxi for the airport. They sat in the back of the smoky-smelling taxi in silence, her small hand in his, gripping him tightly.

They arrived in good time.

"I must go and check in," he said. "In there." He pointed beyond the glass partition. "If you are not a passenger then you can't go in there."

She nodded and he left and disappeared inside.

He checked in and gave the possibility of leaving straightaway without any goodbyes a thought, but only a passing one. He could still see Ita standing waiting for him beyond the glass, so he came back out into the warmth of the Jakarta evening with one and a half hours to go to departure.

They sat in a small bar and each drank a glass of coke but they did not speak. She looked at him with those big brown eyes, now tinged with sadness behind the seriousness, the deep sensuality missing, hidden by the emotions of the moment. After one silent drink they stood and left. They stood in front of the entrance.

She stood in front of him and pushed her arms around his waist, looking up into his face. Her eyes were beginning to fill with tears. She bit her lower lip hard to fight them back, but it was no use – a tear ran from her right eye down her smooth brown cheek and away.

"Stuart," she began slowly and in her small voice. "Stuart," she repeated louder and more firmly. "I don't know why this is like this," she said. "Why you and me to meet and then..." She shrugged her shoulders. "Well, then to say all my life to you, I don't know why you were the one."

She squeezed him round the waist and he put his arms around her.

"When I first met you, I have no idea about you. I just thought you were so funny dancing. I had no plan or idea for anything. I never had a plan for you and me. If I not got drunk that time then maybe nothing, but now, after the first time and then again, I cannot stop. You are so different to anyone I met before – you are very good man." She squeezed him again and stopped talking.

"I don't now why either," he said after a pause. "I have no idea also and I've never done anything like this before. I have always been close and faithful to my..." he paused, not wanting to say 'wife' in front of her.

"I know, I can feel your character. This is why something with us is different," she replied and then fell silent again.

Stuart had no idea where to go from here, what to do, what to say or how to carry on or stop. He knew that he would have to leave very soon or his plane would go. He squeezed her.

"I have to go – my plane is ready for boarding."

"I know." She paused. "Stuart... I..."

He looked at her, into those brown eyes. He stroked her hair.

"Stuart, I love you," she said quietly.

He looked down at her. Such few hours they had spent together, such a short time – and now she had said the ultimate, Stuart almost knew that she would, almost knew she had to say it after what had happened. He squeezed her again and then eased himself away from her and picked up his flight bag. She smiled at him though the tears ran down both cheeks. He leaned forward and kissed and waved goodbye but no more words were said. He passed the glass door and the security check again and looked back as she stood waving slowly towards him. He kept his eyes on her until his walk took him out of her sight. Then he couldn't see her any more so he stepped back and caught sight of her again as she was walking away, Stuart's hanky in her hand, her head bowed. And finally he lost sight of her in the crowd.

He walked briskly to the boarding gate, found his seat on the plane and sat numb until take-off, then, as Jakarta and Indonesia fell away, he too cried.

## CHAPTER 18

## A BARBECUE

Some three weeks after Stuart got back to England, he walked into his house after work on a rainy Friday afternoon in late May. He was quite late because he had been working hard, partly because he had to and partly because he hadn't had quite such a nice time at home since he had returned and any excuse to stay out was used. As usual Catherine was in the kitchen preparing food. He dropped his briefcase in the hall and wandered in.

"Hello," she said curtly, without warmth, simply fulfilling the politeness of ordinary conversation.

"Hi," he replied and turned to the fridge and took out a bottle of white wine. It was already opened; Catherine had a glass on the side of the sink. He poured a glass and sat down at the pine kitchen table.

She began to speak without turning to face him. "You haven't forgotten tomorrow, have you?"

"Tomorrow?" he asked, puzzled.

"Ann and John are coming, and you had forgotten, hadn't you?" she continued, still facing the sink.

"No, I hadn't forgotten. It's a barbecue, right?" he said with a sarcastic laugh.

"Yes, and don't be like that," she said with irritation in her voice.

"It's pissing down," he said, the wine contributing to the lunchtime alcohol in his system, making him more garrulous.

"It will not rain tomorrow," she said with determination. "And you had better behave."

"I don't know what you mean," he said.

With that the conversation finished and he took his wine and went upstairs for his second bath of the day.

He did, of course, know exactly what she meant. His 'coming home' feeling was still with him. He had been, in her words, 'a complete pain in the arse' since he had come home. They had struggled to make love twice in the more than three weeks, and they had barely spoken in a reasonable manner. He stayed at work for long hours, justifying it on the basis that he was starting a new business area and it was necessary to put in long hours. He also went to the pub after work a lot more, sometimes two or three times a week. He told her that she had to understand the position he was in and the opportunities which he could make for himself. She had started by humouring him and trying to understand. Even the worst case of 'coming home' in the entire time that he had been working had only lasted a week. After the week had passed she stopped attempting to understand him and got angry, the kids got upset and Stuart stayed the same. By the end of the second week she gave up being angry and they settled into a cold peace. This state had now lasted for more than a week.

Catherine's new technique was now to shame him into submission by inviting their oldest and closest friends round for a barbecue. He couldn't possibly continue to be rude and inconsiderate in front of them, and, once the mood was broken, she hoped, it would stay broken. Stuart had forgotten the barbecue. Ann and John were their oldest friends. Stuart had been friendly with John at university; he was two years older than Stuart and it was he who had encouraged Stuart to apply for the job with Ormistons. He wasn't actually Stuart's boss, but he was now in a management position higher than Stuart and he was widely respected throughout the company.

Stuart took his second bath, two baths a day was the second visible sign that something was different since he had got back, and it was one that his wife had not really noticed. The main visible evidence of change was his weight. He had lost some while he was away – the heat and the food had contributed to that – but he had continued to lose weight since he had come back. He was now more than a stone lighter and this was despite the increase in the alcohol consumption which had also occurred since he had returned. He had no real perception that his food intake was lower; perhaps his appetite was less. He wandered downstairs, washed and changed.

Colleen met him at the bottom of the stairs. He smiled at her. She was the only one of the family with whom he had maintained a reasonable relationship since he had come back. She held his hand and led him into the front living room. They sat down on the sofa, she still holding his hand.

"Daddy, what's the matter with you and Mummy?"

"Nothing, my darling," he replied. "Daddy's working hard and it makes him tired and sad."

"Okay," she said simply. She gripped his hand tighter and snuggled into him. She was the only one who really affected him.

Their son, Ralph, had always been his mother's favourite as a son and the firstborn. Stuart was, and always had been, the dutiful father. Feeding and changing nappies, taking them to school, reading stories and generally doing everything he should. And yet he had never really felt that close to Ralph. Ralph had always gone to his mother, never his father, and when there was any dispute, as now, Ralph sided automatically with his mother and cut his father off. Colleen was close to her father, but she was confused when there was conflict: she wanted and needed both her parents. Stuart gave her a squeeze.

"Don't worry, my darling, Daddy will always be here for you." But he wasn't really sure what he meant when he said it.

The Saturday, in accordance with Stuart's prediction of the previous evening, dawned wet and raining. He looked out with a sense of satisfaction at the prospect of the miserable day ahead. However, he was soon disappointed and Catherine vindicated in her confidence when the rain stopped before eight and by nine in the morning the sky was clear, with the sun coming out while they ate breakfast.

"Okay, you," Catherine said, pointing at Stuart. "I want the garden tidy, the barbecue ready and the drinks sorted."

"I'm going for a bath," he protested.

"You had a bath last night," she said.

"Well, I want another one," he said truculently.

"Okay, but just remember the things – the garden, the drinks and the barbie. I am going out to get the rest of the stuff. You kids," she continued, turning to the children, "don't bother your father and play quietly."

"Mummy," Ralph protested, "I want to come with you."

"Okay, get your things and come on."

She turned to Stuart, "I'll be gone for about three or four hours. Just make sure everything's ready when I get back."

And with that they left.

Stuart finished his bath and came back downstairs; Colleen had gone to her friend's house next door. He glanced at the weather. The sun was now shining brightly in an almost clear sky, the British weather up to its usual tricks. The only thing predictable about the English weather was that it was unpredictable. Stuart considered the possibilities for the day. He pulled on his shorts, a tee-shirt and the battered training shoes he used for gardening. First, he cut the grass front and back. It took him almost two hours to cut it, clean the mower and put all the clippings in the compost bin. He trimmed the edges and was preparing to start on the borders when Colleen came back from her friend's. She stood watching her dad while he collected the necessary tools.

"Daddy, I'm hungry," she said as he knelt down to begin the weeding.

"Okay, I'll make us both a sandwich and a cup of tea," he said, smiling at her and glad of the break.

Inside the kitchen, he busied himself with the food while Colleen sat and watched. They sat together with tea and sandwiches.

"Daddy," she began quietly in between bites, "do you love Mummy?"

"Yes, of course Daddy loves Mummy, and Colleen and Ralph," he replied automatically.

She went quiet, satisfied with the standard reply, but Stuart realised that it was exactly that – a standard reply. He silently questioned its validity, and looked at Colleen. One thing was for sure, he loved his little daughter.

"I love my little Colleen the most," he said with sincerity.

She smiled back. "I love my Daddy too," she said and took another bite of sandwich.

When the sandwiches were finished, she stood up. "Can I help you in the garden, Daddy?" she asked.

"Of course, come on," he said, and led the way out into the garden. They spent the next hours together in the garden, cleaning and weeding the borders and the vegetable patch. As the time wore on Stuart felt happier than he had at any time since he had got back.

Catherine and Ralph returned very late, at four o'clock.

"You've been busy," she said with a smile. "The garden looks great." She surveyed the back garden. "Where's the barbecue?" she asked, her head on one side. She was on the point of being annoyed.

"Okay, it's not quite ready. Well, it isn't ready at all. We've been busy with the rest, haven't we, Colleen?" he said, putting his arm round his daughter.

"Fine, but just make sure it's ready for cooking by seven. Okay?"

Stuart nodded. "It will be."

Stuart set to work with the pile of bricks which stood behind the shed, building a makeshift barbecue on the edge of the lawn away from the house. They had a steel sheet with holes and ridges that Stuart had brought from work and a large grill bought from some kitchen shop. Stuart used the metal sheet for the charcoal fire and the grill for the food. It was a large cooking area and they had cooked for more than ten guests on it. The only problem was the amount of charcoal it took to fire it. They had had to buy a smaller one for family barbecues. But tonight, with Stuart, Catherine and the two children, Ann and John and their three, they needed the full size. Stuart laid the wood and charcoal ready for use.

Inside the house he selected two bottles of red and two bottles of white wine. He stood the red wine out and put the white in the fridge. Several cans of beer and soft drinks also went into the fridge. Stuart checked the quantity of ice in the freezer and chopped some lemons and limes. Then he had his second bath and came downstairs still dressed in the same shorts but with a clean tee-shirt.

"Stuart, aren't you going to change?" Catherine asked in a pained voice.

"Nope, I'm not. It's a barbecue with our best friends, it's hot and I'm doing the cooking, so no, I am not changing," was his brusque reply.

"Okay," she said in resignation, not wanting to fight and disturb his slightly improved mood.

He went into the garden and finished his gardening and then put the tools away.

Ann and John, plus children, arrived early and well-dressed. Ann went into the kitchen to help Catherine and the children disappeared to play with Ralph and Colleen. John stood like a spare part on the paving outside the back of the house. He was dressed in a polo shirt, light-coloured slacks, white shoes and a rather effeminate-looking cravat. Stuart eyed his dress and thought that it had Ann written all over it.

"Like the cravat," he said with a raised eyebrow.

"I've got my shorts in the car, but Ann said you would all be smart," John replied, looking at his shoes.

"Go and get them and change," Stuart said quickly.

"I can't. I'd have to go past her in the house to get changed and she'd stop me." He looked worried.

"Listen," said Stuart in a conspiratorial manner, "I'll go in the house, get a bottle of red wine and two glasses, and you get your shorts and change in the shed." Stuart pointed at the small wooden shed towards the back of the garden. Both of them set off on their respective missions. When Stuart got back out, John stood with his ex-army shorts on, the same white socks, shoes and polo shirt, still with the cravat.

"Loosen the cravat, John," said Stuart, handing John a glass of red wine. He set the bottle down beside the roughly built barbecue.

Ann came out of the house. "Stuart!" she shouted, "Catherine wants to know when the barbecue will be ready for the potatoes to go in."

"Give me forty minutes," he shouted back.

"Oh my God, John, what have you done?" Ann almost screamed across the garden.

"He's given in to the heat of the cooking and the sun," said Stuart, trying hard not to laugh.

"Oh... Oh!" She could not speak and went back inside.

"Looks like trouble for you later, John old son." Stuart could not stop himself laughing out loud. "Sometimes I actually think that you are henpecked."

They lit the barbecue and nurtured the small flames, carefully building the lumps of charcoal around the areas of flame. Once it was going well, they built up a pile of charcoal on top in preparation for making a full-width fire.

Ann came out of the house with the potatoes wrapped in silver foil. She was dressed in a tight skirt and blouse, with high heels that sank into the grass as she walked. She looked very unsteady as she walked towards them.

"Ann," said Stuart in a voice of slight admonishment, "this is a barbecue, not a dinner party at the bloody Rotary Club."

She looked slightly embarrassed. "Sorry, I'll ask Catherine for some more suitable footwear."

Stuart winked at John.

Ann went back in the house, and Stuart and John were left to tend the fire, drink and ponder.

"How's the garden?" John asked.

"Okay. You want to see?" Stuart replied.

"Yep, come on."

They walked down the garden, past the roses climbing the wooden frame and into Stuart's vegetable plot. They looked at a few things, and ended up at the end of the garden.

John turned to face Stuart. "Listen," he began, "Ann said that Catherine came round the other day and cried all over her." He sighed. "She said that you were being a pain ever since you got back from your last trip. She's worried why it's taken you so long to get back to normal."

Stuart was shocked at this revelation: he hadn't realised that he had pushed Catherine so far, or that his behaviour was so obvious. Now he felt shy at having been exposed in front of his best friend.

"What's the problem?" John continued. "I know you have often been pissed off when you come home but not as long as this." He paused and had a drink of his wine. "Is it a woman? Is that the reason?"

Stuart shrugged his shoulders.

"Look," John said in a quiet voice, "ever since I started going away I've... well, I've basically shagged my way around the world. Before I was married, and since, although not so much lately."

"Does Ann know?" Stuart asked.

"No, not from me. But I think she knows, when I get back and I have, well, had a bit – I'm much more romantic and loving. It sparks my life up sexually and I'm like a new man for a few weeks. She has asked me why I'm so, well, randy after some trips and not others."

"What do you say?"

"Hormones."

"Hormones!" Stuart laughed.

"Yeah, women don't have the monopoly on hormones, you know," he replied defensively.

Stuart laughed again. "Hormones," he said to himself. "Doesn't she say anything?" he asked in a normal voice.

John shook his head. "It's one of those never spoken about things. We are very close, the kids are fine, I'm a good husband when we are together. Provided it doesn't come home to roost and I don't catch anything, it's no problem," John answered with a disarming shrug of his shoulders. "But you, Stuart," John continued looking at Stuart, "you never could have a good fuck and walk away from it, could you? Even in university you never had a one night stand, except for 'The Lump' when you were pissed at the flat party."

Stuart laughed at the memory of that awful night.

"You always had to fall in love and take things so seriously. While the rest of us were at it all over the place with anyone, you had how many girlfriends at university?"

"Counting The Lump?" Stuart asked.

"Yes, four, wasn't it?" John said.

Stuart nodded.

"And then all those business trips when we went off and did whatever, you were always the one who left and went back to the hotel. We envied you: your strength of character and the strength of your marriage and I suppose the weakness of our own marriages. But I never let these... well, flings or fucks on the side upset my relationship with Ann. I always kept them separate. There was never any feeling – it was just, well, physical satisfaction and curiosity. But you, well, you could never fuck without emotional involvement, you always had to be in love, and when you were or things went wrong you were a complete pain in the arse." He paused and looked at Stuart. "Is that what's happened now?" he continued.

Stuart said and did nothing.

"Have you met some piece of South-East Asian tail that's captured your heart? You wouldn't be the first. I hear that they are all beautiful out there. Is that what's happened?"

Stuart remained silent.

"Come on, Stuart, you know what's important: them in the house – Catherine, Ralph and Colleen. Anyone else met on a business trip is nothing. None of them – not the type you would meet in any bar in any hotel, anywhere in the world, at any rate – none of them are worth it. Believe me," John implored him.

Stuart remained passive. He didn't nod his head or shake his head, for to have done either would have admitted something to John that some of what he was saying was true. To remain passive was the only way to avoid giving anything away.

John looked at Stuart, shook his head and had another drink. Then he bent down and examined the lettuces at his feet. "Nice, coming on well," he said.

Stuart stared at the back of his head in wonder. He had just delivered a carefully rehearsed speech on a very delicate subject and now, the speech over, he simply reverted to a normal topic of conversation. Stuart couldn't do that; maybe that's why he couldn't just 'have a good fuck and walk away', as John had put it. Stuart found it difficult to switch off things in which he was involved emotionally. If he had been delivering the speech to John, he would have had to continue until John had admitted or at least responded. But even though Stuart did not say or do anything in response, John's speech affected him deeply and he thought hard and long for the next half hour while they stirred the fire and drank the rest of the well-warmed red wine. By the time he put the potatoes in the midst of the charcoal, he had made his mind up to try, at least, to be normal and behave better.

The result of his resolution, made as he plopped the potatoes in the fire, was that he should become the life and soul of the party. They finished both bottles of red wine and had to get a third; the two bottles of white also disappeared. The patter was good, the jokes were quick, and John, Ann and two of their children had to get a taxi home as neither of them was fit to drive. The third child stayed with Colleen. Stuart promised faithfully to return the car and daughter the following Sunday morning.

He and Catherine tided up the garden and doused the barbecue. He went upstairs first and flopped on the bed with just his underpants on, too lazy to change into his pyjamas. He fell into a half-sleep.

Catherine came up and undressed in front of her half asleep husband. She stripped right off and crawled, naked, up the bed. She pulled Stuart's underpants off and applied her hands to him, stirring him from his half-sleep. She pulled him over when he was ready and they began to make love.

Stuart, in his half-asleep, alcohol-moderated condition, closed his eyes and all he could think of was Ita. As he moved his hands over Catherine's body, it was Ita's smooth brown skin he was stroking, not Catherine's pale white ample flesh; it was Ita's brown nipples, not Catherine's pink ones that he kissed. Somehow he lost himself in Ita's memory. He felt as though it was her underneath him. Somewhere in his dream he came, the alcohol reducing sensations to a minimum. He opened his eyes and saw that it was Catherine with whom he was lying, not Ita. Catherine lay with her eyes tightly closed, biting her bottom lip, her legs moving up and down the bed slowly. He looked at her ample body and her pink nipples and felt a sense of disappointment. Catherine, on the other hand, was not at all disappointed. She opened her eyes and rolled on to her side to face Stuart, her eyes glassy and misty.

"God, that was good," she said, still squeezing her legs together to extract the last bits of sensation. "I haven't come like that for years," she continued.

Stuart looked at the ceiling and felt nothing but disgust and embarrassment. He had satisfied his wife while actually making love for the first time in years and the reason was the presence of Ita in his mind. He turned over and presented his back to her.

She cuddled him and they slept.

# CHAPTER 19

# A GAME OF CRICKET

The insistent and unwelcome ring of the bedside telephone brought Stuart out of his Saturday morning sleep a few weeks after the eventful barbecue. He groped around for the telephone, eventually finding the handset.

"Hello," he mumbled in a barely awake state.

"Stuart?" an excited male voice came down the phone.

"Yes," Stuart replied.

"It's Harry Wilson from the cricket club. Your game's cancelled tomorrow," the voice said.

"You woke me up at seven-thirty on Saturday morning to tell me a cricket match on Sunday is cancelled!" Stuart almost shouted down the phone, in disbelief that even a cricket fanatic like Harry Wilson would ring him up at seven-thirty in the morning. Stuart prepared to drop the phone on him.

"Thanks very much, Harry, and goodbye," he said brusquely.

"No listen," Harry said. "Today the first team is playing away at Madisons. The second team has a cup game and has borrowed a couple of players from the first team and the third team tomorrow is still on so we need some more for the first team game today."

"Me?" Stuart said incredulously. "I play for the fourth team on a good day, I've played once for the third team and now you want me to play for the first team against the best team in the league?"

"Yep."

"You're nuts! I'm not the twelfth man, am I?" Stuart asked, worried that he would go all that way and end up sitting out, umpiring and making drinks.

"No, at the moment you are tenth man and I can promise you a game. Anyway your batting is, how shall I say, durable if not prolific and I just want to avoid us being humiliated by them. You're a good fielder as well and believe me you'll get a lot of practice today, so don't worry. Start is eleven, be there by ten-thirty. You know the place?" Harry said in a rapid-fire voice.

"Yes."

"Okay, see you there. I'm captain of the first team for the day so we are both out of our depth," he added with a laugh.

The phone went dead. Stuart scratched his head. It was a good one and a half hour drive to Madisons' ground. He would have to leave by nine or before. He checked the time again: just after seven-thirty. He looked at his still sleeping wife, scratched his head with his other hand and lay down again for a little rest; after all, he had one and a half hours to get ready.

The little rest turned into more than an hour. It was well after eight-thirty when he awoke for the second time.

"Shit!" he shouted as he jumped up. "Damn and blast!" he continued to curse as he stood shakily.

"What's the matter with you?" Catherine said angrily, in newly-awakened confusion.

"I'm late! I've overslept for cricket," he said as he wandered round the room looking for something, as yet undefined.

"It's Saturday – you play tomorrow," she said, sitting up and staring unbelievingly at her husband as he rolled around the room in his underpants looking for something. "And what the hell are you looking for?" she said with angry exasperation at his undirected careering around the room.

He stopped and looked at her. "Harry just called – I'm playing for the first team today," he said, looking at her with his head on one side as if she should have known.

She flopped back in the bed. "Okay, I'll do the kids today. You go."

Stuart washed quickly and collected his kit, grabbed a slice of toast and rushed out to his car. He backed out of the drive and then remembered that he had no money. Stopping the car in front of the house and leaving the engine running, he dashed back into the house and grabbed his briefcase. He laid it on the dining room table, undid the combination lock and extracted his wallet. He pushed the case closed and left it on the table, turned and rushed out again, calling a quick goodbye for the second time.

Only when he was in the car and driving did he have a chance to reflect on what had happened. Stuart loved cricket. He was not so good – he never had been – but he loved the game and would always turn out. He batted, as Harry had said, 'durably'. He could be relied on to hang around, especially against the sort of attack that most fourth teams could muster, but against a first team – and not just any first team, the best in the league – he was not confident of his ability. He was good at fielding: he had a good accurate arm and could reach the stumps on most grounds from the boundary. He had been involved in running out more people than anyone else in his club. He could also catch; not slip catches, but open field catches, on the run and usually one-handed. As for his bowling... Well, he was a useful sixth bowler if one of the others failed. He smiled as he drove. The first team! The first time he had ever been asked for anything higher than the third team and that was only once. This too would probably be only the once.

For Harry, who was the regular third team captain, it was a tremendous honour for him to be asked to captain the first team. He had been on the edge of the first team a few years ago as a captain and batsman but had never made it. Stuart knew, however, that Harry would rise to the challenge: he was a shrewd captain, always doing the unexpected, the unusual. He was good enough as a captain almost to get into a team for that reason only. If he had been a bit of a better player, he would have been the first team captain. His batting was good on a good day, but he was far too inconsistent against a good attack to keep his place as a batsman, especially when the first two teams had able captains who were also good in other departments as well. Harry was also over forty and had resigned himself to playing at a slightly less competitive level.

Stuart arrived at the ground at almost exactly eleven o'clock. Harry was rushing around with his pads on.

"Where the hell have you been?" he shouted at Stuart as he wandered over towards the pavilion with his kit bag in one hand and his bat in the other.

"Sorry, fell asleep again," he shrugged.

"Okay, okay," Harry said irritably. "We're batting, I'm opening with George, and you're number eight so get changed quick." Harry turned and rushed back to the pavilion as the opposition took the field, one of their number muttering about forfeits for the late arrival on the field of play of the batsmen.

Stuart did as he was told and changed, slowly dressing to make sure he looked the part; even if he was out first ball at least he could look the part and frighten the opposition. He appeared at the pavilion door, fully kitted out in whites and pads, his own, ready for a little batting practice. He owned all his equipment. When he reached the bottom step there was the unmistakable sound of a falling wicket, the cheers of the fielding side, the groans of the other members of Stuart's team. Stuart squinted at the returning batsman. It wasn't Harry or George, the other opener – it was someone else, the number four bat.

"What's happening?" Stuart asked.

"We're being bloody hammered. Fourteen for three in the seventh over," the scorer said from his seat on the edge of the grass next to the pavilion. "It's a total bloody disaster." He turned to look for the next batsman. "Come on, get them bloody pads on!"

"I'm left-handed, I need left-handed pads," whined the number five batsman standing limply by the club kitbag.

"Get some pads on!" shouted the scorer, rapidly losing patience.

"Two minutes to change a batsman and I'm counting," came a voice from the field of play.

"God, that's all I need," said the scorer under his breath, "A flamin' expert on the rules of the game."

"Come on, you'll lose another wicket in twenty seconds," the owner of the voice said in a gleeful tone.

"Stuart, you're padded up – go on in, get going," the scorer said, looking at the still-standing number five.

"What, now?" said Stuart, disbelievingly.

"Yes! Get a bloody move on or we'll be fourteen for four in ten seconds," the scorer said in the tone of an exasperated schoolteacher.

Stuart tucked his bat under his arm and walked forward on to the field.

In the middle, Harry stood leaning on his bat, one leg crossed over the other with a faraway look in his eyes. Stuart joined him in the middle of the wicket.

"So?" Stuart asked.

"Who's changing the order round?" was Harry's first question.

"No one. There was no one else padded up except me, and some dickhead on the boundary started blabbing about the two minute rule," Stuart said by way of explanation.

"Okay. Well, it could be worse – you might just be the best player for this situation," Harry said, standing up fully. "I just want to last the full forty overs."

"New batsman at the wicket," someone shouted.

"Okay," Harry said, turning towards his end. "He's bowling fast and straight, nothing else. Just don't try to have 'im over the boundary in the first over, that's all."

Stuart nodded nervously and walked down to face the bowler. Every cricket innings that Stuart played had had a series of stages: avoid the golden duck, avoid the duck, reach double figures, score the first boundary. He ran through these as he walked.

"Middle," he said to the umpire.

"That's middle," came the reply.

Stuart marked his ground.

"Right arm over five to come," the umpire advised.

Stuart hunched low, his bat at forty-five degrees to the ground. He held it loosely, with 'soft hands'; any edges would drop quickly to the ground instead of flying to one of the three slip catchers standing guard. It was a good policy. The first ball touched the outside edge and flew straight towards second slip, but it fell well short. Stuart stood, relieved that the first hurdle was over.

"Lucky batsman!" came the voice from behind the stumps.

'All I need,' thought Stuart. 'A talker behind the stumps.'

The second ball found the middle of Stuart's bat and rolled slowly back towards the bowler. It was accompanied by a further set of 'Ooohs' from behind the stumps. The next two sailed untouched past the outside edge of Stuart's bat. He watched them go with care. On the last delivery, the bowler dug the ball in short and it reared viciously at Stuart. He tried to duck, but the movement was not fast enough and instead he slipped and fell in a large undignified heap, losing his hat and bat in the process. The ball sailed over his head. He heard the unmistakable sound of laughter behind the stumps. But despite this he was still there, the over finished.

Stuart and Harry converged for the mid-wicket conference. "Keep it there," was all Harry said.

Harry made a couple of runs off the third ball of an otherwise uneventful over. Then Stuart faced up again. The first ball was a good length and it rose to waist height. Stuart managed to get his bat on it, rolling his wrists and pushing it out on the on side.

"One run!" Harry shouted clearly. They ran and Stuart's second stage had been passed. He relaxed a little.

Stuart had pushed his way to seven singles by the end of the fourteenth over. The score was up to thirty-four, the biggest stand of the innings. Stuart stood facing the final over of the opening bowler who had taken all the three wickets to fall so far and caused Stuart to end up on the floor during his first over of batting. The bowler was becoming frustrated by Stuart's dogged determination and persistence. He worked himself up for one last over. He steamed in for the first delivery and let fly. The ball was always going down the leg side. Stuart shuffled across and flicked at it. He missed, but his body obscured the ball and the ball sailed past the diving keeper for four. The umpire looked at Stuart and hesitated.

"Byes or leg byes?" he asked.

"I didn't touch it with anything," said Stuart.

The umpire signalled byes.

"You bloody touched that with your pads! I saw it!" shouted the wicketkeeper. "Them's leg byes, not byes against me! Leg byes!" he continued, shouting at the umpire and Stuart.

The umpire shook his head. "I think them was byes," he confirmed.

The wicketkeeper wandered back to his post, muttering under his breath.

Harry winked at Stuart.

The next ball was in the same place. Stuart missed it and this time the keeper had it. The third ball was well outside the off stump. In his effort to bowl fast and blast Stuart out, the bowler's direction was wandering. Stuart hung his bat out to catch an edge, which he did. The ball skittered wide of the only remaining slip, right through where second slip had been only an over before. It hit the boundary rope with great speed. The first boundary and his double figures arriving in the same instant. Harry winked again. One more ball whistled past the outside edge. The fifth delivery was dug in, short and hard. Instead of ducking, Stuart faced up to the ball and swayed to the offside, swinging his bat round in a near horizontal arc, rolling his wrists as he did so. He made contact with the ball high up on the splice of the bat, near the handle, but it didn't matter: the fast delivery and Stuart's hefty swing put enough pace on the ball to ensure that it bounced once and then crossed the boundary rope. His second four in the over.

The bowler cursed, the wicketkeeper was silent and Harry winked again. For his final delivery, the bowler concentrated hard. His speed was less and his direction correct. Stuart, for his part, became very cautious. He had had two pieces of luck and now he had to survive. He pushed forward defensively with hardly a swing of the bat. Some cricket bats, and Stuart's was one, had a 'sweet spot', a part of the bat off which the ball flew much faster without any apparent effort. The last delivery struck this spot and flew off the bat, slightly to the on side of the stumps, at great speed. The despairing bowler flung himself in the direction of the ball, but missed. Harry jumped to avoid the ball and turned to watch as the ball sped over the boundary for Stuart's third four of the over.

There was a small ripple of applause from the other members of Stuart's team. Harry and Stuart met in the middle for a conference.

"What's that for?" asked Stuart, referring to the applause.

"Fifty up," replied Harry, his face a little more satisfied. "We've got 'em rattled."

They continued to bat for the next fourteen overs, steadily building on the foundations that they had laid. The fifty partnership came up; the overall score was ninety-five for three; the run rate more than three an over. Stuart was the dominant player, with Harry on thirty-six to Stuart's forty-two, close to his highest ever score. He was within sight of his first ever fifty. He turned to face the start of the thirtieth over.

The bowler was a slow off-spinner. He was difficult to hit hard, and Stuart pushed a single. Harry pushed another and then Stuart managed a couple off the fifth ball to bring him to forty-five. The last ball came down; it was well tossed up and slower. Stuart put his left leg down the wicket and dropped on to his right knee. He swung his bat in a fast, full-arm stretch arc, making contact with the ball with the sweet spot of his bat. He almost fell over as his swing continued in the follow-through. The ball took off, climbing into the sky, curving high over the head of the square leg umpire, over the head of the backward square leg fielder and bouncing some ten yards beyond the boundary rope. Stuart stayed on his knee, watching the curving flight of the ball and loving every second of it. Such a hit gave the most tremendous pleasure. He looked at the umpire whose arms were raised aloft signalling the six. His team members applauded. Harry walked down the wicket and patted the still-kneeling Stuart.

"Good on you. That's your fifty up, lad. Now we've ten overs left – let's see if we can't get to one sixty at least."

Stuart nodded his agreement and went back to his end.

He managed a single during the next over and then stood to face the off-spinner again. He swept the first ball for four, and applause broke out for the hundred partnership. The third ball went for four in the same way as the first, taking him to sixty.

Then he hoisted his second six in exactly the same place as the first. It wasn't hit quite so well as the other, but it cleared the rope just the same. The next ball Stuart pushed out squarish on the on side.

"One run!" he shouted to Harry. He reached the other end.

"One more!" Harry shouted.

Stuart turned and obeyed blindly; it was Harry's call after all. He watched the throw coming in like a slow motion replay. He lunged forward, stretching his bat out and running it along the ground. He made the white line, but could hear the crash of the wickets breaking and the rising shouts of "Owzat!" from the fielding side.

He looked across agonisedly at the square leg umpire who was squatting low to get the best view. He stood up and glanced at the other umpire before raising his finger. Stuart was out, run out for sixty-seven, his highest ever score, his longest innings. He dropped his head, tucked his bat under his arm and turned towards the pavilion. He thought the decision harsh, very close, but he walked without protest. Harry smiled at him and raised a thumb in a salute of congratulation. It was a long walk back, but his team mates were all standing, clapping, cheering. They patted him on the back, shook his hand, gave him a seat. He sat down, exhausted now that it was over. The rest went back to watching the game.

Stuart took his gloves off, removed his pads and box, had a drink of water and then wandered over to the scorer. He checked the details of his innings. The score was one hundred and twenty-seven for four; they had put on one hundred and thirteen and Stuart's was the highest score.

"Good knock, lad," said the scorer. "Just what we needed. At least we've not been humiliated," he added.

"What do you mean?" asked Stuart, worried by the defeatist tone of the man's voice.

"Well, we won't win but at least we've given 'em a good game," he replied.

"Let's wait and see, eh?" Stuart said, slightly angry.

The scorer went silently back to his book.

In the remaining overs three more wickets fell and another forty-two runs were added to the score, taking them on to one hundred and sixty-nine for seven. Harry was not out at sixty-one, the pillar of the innings. He set straight to with the team in the interval.

"I know them's got the best batting line-up, but they've got the best bowling as well and look what happened to that. So, come on, let's try our best. Now no beer in the interval – I want us all sharp."

He paused as the team turned away to prepare for the coming session. "Stuart, come 'ere, lad," he said, motioning to Stuart.

Stuart followed him obediently to a corner of the pavilion veranda.

"Now, I've only got three real bowlers, plus a fourth who's not bad on a good day, and, well, you and George to make up the fifth," he said, holding Stuart's arm.

Stuart shook his head.

"So my plan is like this," he paused, justifying his plan before he revealed it. "Because they have only got a low score to go for, because they think we are no good, they're goin' take it easy at first, not push it, so I figure we put you and George on first, get through eight overs and... well, you never know."

"I'll get bloody hammered all over the ground," said Stuart in disbelief. "You know what happened last time I bowled."

"No, don't worry. I'll take you off the first time you get hit for a boundary," he continued.

"Then I'll bowl one over for you," Stuart said with a shrug of his shoulders.

They wandered out to defend their team total of one hundred and sixty-nine. One of the opening bats was the chatty fielder, the one who knew all the rules. He opened and took his guard against Stuart's opening over. Much to Stuart's surprise, his opening over went according to Harry's plan, with the batsman treating Stuart with caution, a single being the only result. His second over was a maiden, the third yielded three; off the last ball of the fourth the chatty batsman stuck a good four and Stuart shook his head at Harry. At the other end, George was holding his end up well. At the end of the eight overs, the score was a mere twelve runs. George continued for another four until the end of the fifteenth over; the score had progressed to thirty-four. By the end of twenty overs, the opening pair was still together and the score had, ominously for Stuart's team, moved on to seventy-three. The rate was accelerating and the two batsmen were making a marked and careful job of bringing their team to victory.

The first ball of the twenty-first over was delivered to the chatty batsman who drove it, a little uppishly, through the off side towards Stuart. At first Stuart thought that he would be content with making a good stop and saving the single. But as he watched the flight of the ball he realised that he could make an attempt at a catch. It was the first even half-chance his team had had. He lunged forward, diving with his arms outstretched, and took the ball half an inch off the ground, his knuckles grazing the surface of the grass. He rolled over onto his back, the ball clutched tightly in his hands. He looked around triumphantly from his vantage point, flat on his back.

To Stuart's surprise, the batsman was still standing, resting on his bat.

"You picked up off the ground, lad," he shouted at Stuart. "It was bump ball, right, umpire?"

The umpire made no move.

"You're out, well out!" Stuart said incredulously as he got to his feet.

"No, lad, it was a bump ball – you picked it up after it bounced," the batsman said again.

"Look at my bloody hands," said Stuart, showing the green stains on his knuckles.

"Sorry lad. Bump ball, right, umpire?" the batsman asserted again.

Stuart shook his head as the umpire said nothing and the batsman stood firm.

Harry came over to Stuart and patted him on the back, taking the ball out of Stuart's still tightly gripping hands.

"What can we do?" Harry asked Stuart. "Even when we get 'em out they still don't bloody walk."

"Give me another over," said Stuart, releasing the ball to Harry.

The next over, Harry tossed the ball to Stuart. The chatty batsman was facing. Stuart marked out a run-up a good two paces longer than the previous one. His first two deliveries were wide down the off side. He glared at the umpire, daring him to call them wide and he didn't. The third was a half-volley which was promptly dispatched for four runs. On the fourth ball, Stuart took an extra two paces and charged in even harder. In the final stride he put all the effort in, but as his arm came over he held it back, imperceptible to the watchers, but back nonetheless. The batsman, seeing another half-volley approaching, put his foot down the pitch and swung his bat. But he was too early: when the ball bounced, the bat was already past it, the ball was underneath the bat, the bat was through its stroke and the batsman was turning his head, his ears were filled with the sound of the ball hitting the top of the off stump. This time he had no option – he was out.

Stuart didn't punch the air or give any sign of enjoyment at the dismissal; he merely glared hard at the batsman as he walked away.

The new batsman scored a single off his first delivery and then Stuart was faced with the second opening batsman. Stuart gave him the same delivery as he had the chatty batsman two deliveries before. This time the batsman made contact, but at the wrong time. The ball lofted high and easily into the hands of the mid-off.

In the space of three deliveries, Stuart had changed the face of the game. He bowled another over, the twenty-fourth and then Harry brought on his two best bowlers for the last sixteen overs. The opposition still only needed seventy-two to win, not much more than four an over – very easily achievable.

Within three overs, however, the two best bowlers from Stuart's team had removed both of the new batsmen for three runs. The position of the opposition was suddenly becoming a little bit dangerous. But they still had only sixty-nine runs to get, with six wickets in hand, a rate of just over five an over in the thirteen overs remaining. The odds were still with the batting side.

After four more overs, during which the two new batsmen played themselves in, the number five batsman began to make his presence felt. He hit eight off the tenth last, leaving forty-two to win with nine overs remaining, exactly six an over. At the start of the next over, the burly number five put a really high ball up, a real steepler, the sort of ball that goes so high it comes down with snow on – and it was heading in Stuart's direction.

He threw off his hat and took off after it, thinking only to stop the boundary, but as he ran and looked up and over his left shoulder, he realised that he might be able to make a catch out of it. He stuck out his right hand and lunged forward, diving as the ball came from behind him. The ball struck his fingers and somehow, despite the speed, it stuck. He fell forward, knocking the ball out of his hand as his right elbow hit the ground, but the ball's trajectory was kind to Stuart and his left hand seized it before it fell to the ground. He rolled over and sat up in a continuous move from the initial dive to catch the ball. He held the ball triumphantly aloft as the number five tucked his bat under his arm and walked, acknowledging the catch as he went.

The next three overs saw a slowdown in the runs so that with four overs left, the opposition needed thirty-one runs, over seven runs an over. The number six was now the danger for Stuart's team. Carefully he played and guided the ball, making a run a ball and waiting for the final push. With two overs to go Madisons needed fourteen. The first ball was pushed firmly by the number six batsman towards Stuart through the off side. Stuart ran in hard towards the striker's end, picking up the ball on the run. The non-striker was running towards the danger end, the natural end at which Stuart should throw, given the angle of his run. But Stuart didn't throw at that end. Instead he threw sideways, at ninety degrees to his run and towards the non-striker's end, where the number six was ambling home, feeling safe. To run him out the ball had to be a direct hit. Not only had Stuart thrown awkwardly, but he only had one stump at which to aim. However, as is the nature of the game, his aim in the brief instant between success and failure was perfect: the number six was run out by a good yard.

The rest of the over was a maiden. At the start of the last over Madisons still needed fourteen and on the last ball five runs, but they managed only a single. Stuart's team had pulled off one of the most amazing victories of the season, of many seasons.

Harry patted Stuart on the back, smiled and said nothing: there was nothing to say. On their way back to the pavilion, their team mates and the supporters formed a short avenue for him and Harry to walk down, clapping and shaking hands, patting them on the back.

Stuart had top scored with sixty-seven, taken two vital wickets, held a vital catch and made a run-out at a crucial point of the game. At every juncture in the game when the opposition had been getting the upper hand, Stuart had pulled it back with a piece of brilliance such as the bowling or a session of sustained concentration such as the batting.

Harry told him so in the bar afterwards. They paused only long enough to remove their spiked shoes and drank, still dressed in cricket whites.

Madisons number five batsman, their captain, congratulated Harry on his victory and Stuart on his catch. The rest of the team sulked at the opposite end of the pavilion bar.

On his way to the toilet, Stuart bumped into the chatty batsman.

"You were out back there, you know," Stuart couldn't resist digging at him.

"No way lad. Good try an' all but no." The batsman still clung to his story.

"You may know the rules but you can't play the game, mate," said Stuart quietly, almost under his breath.

"What's that?" the batsman asked angrily.

"You 'eard," said Stuart, raising his voice again.

At that point Harry wandered past.

"What's this about those fellers who know all the rules but still can't play the game?" he asked Stuart. "Oh 'ello Bill, didn't see you there. Good game. Pity about the dropped catch, mind – could have sworn it was good," he continued, beaming at the chatty batsman.

The batsman let out a "Humph" and walked off. Harry winked at Stuart. "He's well known for that sort of thing. He argues with every umpire when he's out. Still, you 'ad your revenge."

"But", said Stuart, "he never gives up. He still tried to pretend I didn't catch it."

"'Ave a drink lad and forget it. We won and that's what counts." Harry patted him on the back again.

Stuart downed the first two pints of shandy in very quick succession before taking his first pint of beer. This went down more slowly. The conversation was of the day, of their remarkable play and the victory. The members of the opposing team slunk off one by one with not much in the way of goodbyes. Stuart had a second pint of beer and some sandwiches which had thoughtfully been provided by the opposition but hardly touched by them. The time flew past and it was after nine when he wandered out, dumped his stuff in the boot of the car and began the long drive home.

It took him less time to get home than it had on the way, but it was still past ten and going dark in the early summer dusk.

The house looked strangely dark when he arrived. He couldn't see Catherine's car or any lights on. Still, her car could be in the garage and they could be still sitting out back in the warmth of a nice summer's evening. He parked his car in the drive and let himself in. He dropped his kitbag on the floor of the hall and glanced sideways into the dinning room. His briefcase was open on the table. He was momentarily surprised to see it there. Normally he kept it underneath the desk in the small upstairs office room. But then he remembered taking his wallet in the rush of the morning departure and was reasonably satisfied. Still, he couldn't remember leaving it open. He shrugged it off. There were far more important things to think about, such as sixty-seven runs and two wickets.

He called hello through the house a number of times but got no response. He made his way through into the kitchen and checked the garden, but it was empty. There was no note left for him, which Catherine would normally leave if she had changed her plans. He shrugged his shoulders again and filled the kettle. While the kettle was boiling he prepared the teapot, his favourite mug and two slices of bread which he fitted in the toaster but did not switch on. When the kettle boiled and he had poured the water, he pushed on the toaster. This old habit resulted in both tea and toast being ready at the same time. The toast popped up and he poured the tea. As he poured, he became aware of a presence behind him.

Turning his head, he saw Catherine leaning against the doorpost in a position similar to that she had adopted the night before his first trip to Indonesia. For some reason that moment flashed through his mind as he returned to his tea.

"Brilliant game!" he said, taking the toast and beginning to butter it generously. "Sixty-seven runs, two wickets, an unbelievable catch and a direct hit run-out," he continued.

No response came from Catherine.

He continued, oblivious. "I was the star of the team! Me and Harry won the game between us, his captaincy and my individual brilliance." He tried to make the story a little too fantastic to elicit a response.

Still none came.

Finally he turned and sat down facing her with a cup of tea and plate of toast. He looked at her questioningly. Her face displayed no obvious expression except hardness.

"Fabulous game," Stuart started again. "Best I've ever played in my life! If I never play again I can go to my grave happy after that performance! One for the grandchildren," he continued in his enthusiasm.

His wife remained unmoved.

He took a bite of toast, lowering his eyes as he did so.

His wife moved her arm swiftly from behind her back, casting something on to the table in front of him.

Stuart looked up at her and then down at the pile of paper on the table. There were four letters, each with a neatly typed envelope from Ita's company, each with a consecutive number in the top left corner, each with gaudy Indonesian stamps on the right.

The contents of one had spilled out revealing Ita's neat handwriting. A few photographs of Ita and Stuart were visible as well. Stuart surveyed the pile and remembered his untraceable feeling that something was wrong when he had seen the briefcase open on the table. He had shut it, but he had not closed the locks as he always did to prevent just such a discovery. The letters themselves were innocuous enough. Ita had not filled them with masses of gooey 'I love yous' or anything like that, but, combined with the photographs, it was going to take some explaining. Stuart searched for an idea; none came.

"Oh," he said finally, looking up at his wife. The pause and the initial exclamation had sunk him before he started. He was guilty of something and she knew it and he knew it. Had an explanation come straight out, that she worked for Anwar, that she was his public relations girl or something and it was her job to accompany Anwar's guests, then he may have stood a chance, but the pause and the 'Oh' had destroyed that possibility. One of those brief instants in which a life changes had occurred for Stuart.

"Is that all you have to say?" Catherine said, still leaning on the door frame. "Oh?" her voice rising in anger.

"You want some tea?" he replied rather foolishly.

"God, you're impossible!" she almost shouted back. "Where are my cigarettes?" she said in a lower tone, moving away from the door and towards the rows of kitchen cupboards and their drawers.

Catherine had smoked on and off, mostly off, since Stuart had known her. He hated it when she smoked and not just because he was a confirmed and lifelong non-smoker. She had a way of smoking which was more than a little reminiscent of the boys behind the bike shed era of early adolescence. She held the cigarette low down between index and middle finger, not high up like most women. She often left the cigarette in her mouth while she talked or talked while blowing out smoke. At the end of the cigarette she often held it between index, middle and thumb, with the lighted end in towards the palm of her hand like some tramp trying to get the last drag from his dwindling cigarette. All in all, nothing could be more guaranteed to make Stuart angry than the sight of Catherine smoking.

She found a packet and peeled off the wrapping, quickly shoving a cigarette in her mouth. She left it there, dangling, while she searched for a match. Then, once lit, she leaned back against the cupboards, legs and arms crossed, and took a long, heavy drag. The smoke made Stuart feel as though he was the aggrieved party. He felt angry.

"You often go rooting through other people's belongings?" he said in a slightly haughty tone. "Looking for things?" he continued.

"Stuart, I'm your bloody wife," she said, blowing smoke out as she spoke. "I should be able to go through all your things – you shouldn't have any secrets from me."

The conversation paused. Neither one knew which way to go.

Catherine spoke next. "I suppose that you..." She paused for another pull on the cigarette. "Well... fucked this little teenage tart," she continued, spitting the words out and again blowing out the smoke as she spoke.

Stuart shrugged, slightly surprised by the venom in Catherine's voice.

"I'm not going to answer that. If I say no you won't believe me, if I say yes then I'm condemned out of my own mouth." He paused for a bite of toast. "She wasn't a teenager and she certainly wasn't..." He hesitated, not wanting to associate Ita with the word 'tart'. "Well, she wasn't... you know," he said, avoiding it.

"This explains a lot," Catherine started. "All the moody behaviour when you came home last time. You were lovesick for some bit of Eastern fanny." Catherine's language could degenerate at an alarming rate when pushed: the middle class veneer of polite society was ripped away very easily under stress. "Come to think of it, all those other times when you have been moody, maybe all those times were because you had been... well, humping your way round the world. Oh, what a bloody fool I've been. I was the understanding wife, holding her husband's hand, consoling him when he came back from those oh so difficult business trips abroad, when all the time you were getting it away with any bit of skirt that you happened to find." She paused for a drag on the cigarette.

"No, this was the first time," Stuart said and immediately regretted it, wanting to bite off his tongue.

Catherine seized the words. "So you are admitting that something" – she paused, not wanting to have her worst fears confirmed – "happened," she said in a low voice.

Stuart looked at his toast and took a small bite. "Look." He began searching for the right words. "It wasn't some drunken orgy or anything."

"Oh, and I suppose that's supposed to make me feel better, knowing that you had to think about it first before you did it with her. If it was some drunken binge I might have been able to, well, excuse it." She paused again.

"No, I suppose it wouldn't make you feel better," he said, staring ruefully into his tea.

The conversation stopped again.

"So," Catherine began again, and pulled hard on the cigarette. "So you actually expect me to believe that this was the first fling you have ever had?"

Stuart nodded.

"So you are definitely admitting that you ... that you did it with her?" she asked again.

Stuart remained still.

"Oh come on," Catherine said, with an edge of annoyance in her voice. "I know you did, and your refusal to admit it only makes things worse." She glared at him, but when she got no response she took another pull on the cigarette and continued, "So if this was really the first time then I guess I don't really know how to feel and what to say. I've been sitting upstairs for four hours waiting for you to come home, running every conversation through my head, but..." She paused. "Pour me some tea," she said brusquely as Stuart sipped his.

He obeyed and walked over to her, handing her the cup with one hand and making as if to put his other hand on her shoulder.

"Don't!" she said fiercely, cringing away from his touch.

He placed the cup on the table opposite his and sat down to resume his tea-drinking.

After a minute of silence, she sat down opposite him to drink the tea.

"Ashtray," she said in the form of a command, not a request.

He silently obeyed even though the ashtray was nearer her than him.

"But", she began again, "now you're here I don't know what to say." She stubbed the cigarette out and took a sip of tea. "I'm hurt," she continued, placing the cup down. "But more than that, I'm bloody furious with you. After all these years you have to do this. What were you doing? Male menopause come early, had to prove you could still pull the birds? What?" She paused and lit her second cigarette and blew the smoke in his face.

He stared through it, unresponsive.

"I thought we had a good relationship, a good marriage, but now... well, everything's..." she stopped, lost for words.

"Where are the kids?" asked Stuart, suddenly realising that they were absent.

"What? With my mother," she answered angrily.

"We had, we have," he corrected himself, "a good marriage. There's no reason for..." He paused. "These trials make a good marriage stronger."

She regarded him closely. "So the husband having a quick fling makes a marriage stronger?"

"Or the wife," he added quickly.

They both paused, with little more to say.

"Are you going to go back?" she asked quietly a few minutes later.

"To Indonesia, you mean?" he replied.

"Yes, of course I mean that," she answered, slightly irritated.

"Yes, I have to. It's my market. I've got to develop it – it's the best opportunity I've had since I joined Ormistons. I have to carry on," he replied in a soft voice, trying to placate her.

"Will you see her again?" Catherine asked quietly. "Of course you will," she continued, answering her own question. "You will see her just once, just once to tell her that you have a wife, two children, and you must stay with them, and you love them."

Stuart shrugged his shoulders.

"You agree?" she asked.

He nodded once.

"Okay." She stubbed out the cigarette in a gesture of finality. "And you sleep downstairs tonight. I don't feel up to having you close to me."

He nodded again. She stood and left the room, leaving Stuart to finish his tea and toast in state of shell-shocked disbelief at the events of the last half hour.

Stuart's greatest achievements on the cricket field were destined never to be mentioned in the family again.

## CHAPTER 20

## GOING BACK

In the weeks which followed that extraordinary Saturday, the situation between Stuart and his wife very quickly reached a state of tense stalemate. With the children, they behaved more or less as normal; when alone there was little said.

The night of that Saturday Stuart had spent on the living room sofa. Catherine had sent the children to her mother for the night after she had discovered Ita's letters in Stuart's briefcase. They had returned on Sunday afternoon and Stuart was graciously allowed back in the bedroom on Sunday night. He had, however, slept on the floor. He slept on the floor for the next three nights, before Catherine allowed him back in their bed. Despite the fact that he was in the marital bed, there could have been a six foot brick wall between them for all the contact or warmth there was. There had been no sex, not even the hint of sexual contact since that night.

Stuart knew that the situation would remain so until he had been back to Indonesia to 'finish it', to end the relationship with Ita and to tell her what was what. A letter would never satisfy Catherine in this respect. Stuart longed for the call to come from Anwar to end this awful state of limbo. It finally came three and a half weeks after the Saturday, and Anwar gave him less than a week's notice of the trip in the fax message that Stuart received. Stuart read the fax with a mixture of relief and apprehension: relief that the time was at hand and apprehension at what might happen. The day he found the fax on his desk he could not concentrate on his work for the rest of the day. He paced about the office and was touchy and short with people, all very uncharacteristic of him. When the time came to go home he was even worse: he shouted at the other drivers for their minor traffic errors or their impatience, all, of course, from the safety of his own car.

When he got home, he fumbled with the key in the lock and dropped the key, his fingers shaking in nervous anticipation. He walked in the house and dropped his briefcase in the dining room and went though into the kitchen where Catherine was making a pot of tea. He stood at the door. She turned slowly to face him, looking steadily at him.

"You're going back?" She paused. "Yes, of course you are," she continued, answering her question herself.

He nodded once and then sat down.

"I can read you like a book, you know," she said quietly. She put the teapot down by the sink and lit a cigarette from the packet on the table. She inhaled deeply and blew the smoke towards the ceiling. Then she sat down opposite Stuart and looked at him again.

"Just remember, Stuart," she said, waving the cigarette around as she talked. "Just remember what I said the other week: you see her once, you tell her what your situation is, you have a wife, children, and that is that." She paused for a pull on the cigarette. "Because if you don't do that – if you once..." She paused again, not wanting to mention any word associated with making love. "Well, even touch her," she continued, "I will know. The second you walk through the door I will know."

Stuart nodded again. Here, in the familiarity of his own kitchen, the situation was easy to deal with. He would meet Ita and tell her – that would be that. His wife would know if he didn't and his wife was more important. He knew that he didn't have time to send a letter to Ita to tell her that he was coming back. Maybe the best thing was not to tell her, just to arrive, meet her and finish it. He reasoned that this was best.

When the evening meal was finished and Stuart had finished supervising the children doing the washing and drying up, he went into his small office room and opened his briefcase to check through a few papers. He saw Ita's letters, now up to number eight, and rethought his strategy. At the very least he owed her a message to tell her that he was coming, he reasoned. He took a blank sheet of paper and handwrote a simple fax message to send to her office. He put it in his briefcase, left the work and went back downstairs for a drink.

The following day Stuart realised that he couldn't send the fax from his office. He remembered that there was a small shop advertising fax messages somewhere near the Arndale Centre in the centre of Manchester. At lunchtime, he drove into the centre and parked the car in the main car park. He found the shop with ease and in a minute the fax was sent for a few pounds. He pocketed the transmission report and wandered out. On his way back he stopped to buy some flowers and chocolates for Catherine, roses and a continental assortment from Thorntons, her favourites, as a sort of peace offering. Further down the shopping centre, he passed Marks and Spencer. He remembered Ita and her mentioning Marks and Spencer in terms close to religious reverence when they had passed a sign advertising the Marks and Spencer shop in Jakarta. He turned and went into the shop, intending to buy her some small thing. Purely by chance he entered in the ladies section, in particular the lingerie department. He pondered and wondered for a brief minute what Ita's slim body would look like in M&S's best. Then, almost without thinking, he picked up a shiny cream bra, a pair of matching ordinary knickers and a pair of matching thong knickers. He paid quickly and slightly furtively and then left.

On the actual day of departure, Sunday, Stuart and his wife were more tense than usual. They barely spoke but exchanged knowing glances, looks and glares. When the time came for him to leave, Catherine and the children went to Manchester's Piccadilly Station to see him off. He kissed Colleen, shook hands with Ralph and kissed Catherine lightly on the cheek.

She looked at him hard. "Just remember," she said slowly, "I'll know."

Stuart nodded, for he had no doubt about that. "Bye kids," he said as brightly as he could amid the apprehension. "Bye darling," he said to Catherine.

Then he turned and walked to the train. He took a last glimpse and waved at his family, wondering what the future held in store.

On the train to London, the strain of the past few weeks got to him. He drank more cans of beer than was really good for him at the start of a twenty-four hour journey. In the airport he drank some more, so that by the time the flight was available for boarding he was quite merry. He drank the pre-dinner drink, the wine with the meal and then the proffered port wine, calling for a second little bottle of the port. In this state, it was an easy job for him to plan the conversation with Ita: what he would say, what she would say, how easy it would be to say that it was all over, that his wife and family were more important. With these thoughts in his mind he fell sideways on to the two unoccupied seats next to his and slept for most of the way.

When he arrived in Jakarta for the third time, he was quite well rested and, apart from a not entirely unexpected headache, he felt reasonably well. It was after nine in the Jakarta evening when he wandered past the smiling customs officers and into the warm blanket of humid tropical heat. He looked around for the hotel man in his pink cap. He saw him and made his way over. He gave his name and said that he would get a taxi rather than a limousine. He turned towards the taxi rank and there stood Ita, dressed in loose-fitting jeans and a big tee-shirt.

Her hair was longer than before and it seemed shinier, if a little less like the shampoo advert, the extra length making it less controllable. Her eyes, when he looked into them, seemed bigger, browner and deeper than before. More than a hint of happiness was visible in them, along with the ever-present deep sensuality. They stared at each other for what seemed like an age before she extended her right hand to shake his.

"Hello, Stuart, welcome back," she said quietly as he extended his hand to shake hers.

It struck him as a rather curious gesture for two people who had been rather passionate lovers the last time they had met, but then he had remembered that she was not prone to expansive gestures of affection in public.

"Hello Ita," he said eventually. "You look..." He paused, wondering what he should say rather than what he wanted to say. "...You look better than I remember," he said finally, what he wanted to say winning over what he should say.

She let go of his hand and turned towards the taxi rank.

During the journey Stuart wondered about starting his prepared speech, about his wife and children, but he couldn't. He decided that the back of a taxi was an unsuitable location for such a delicate matter; perhaps the quiet of his hotel room was a better place. He put the thoughts out of his mind and talked of other things.

Once in the familiar surroundings of the hotel foyer, the thoughts of his mission with Ita went further from his mind. He checked in and she followed discreetly to his room. She hid in the bathroom while he let the bell boy bring in his bag. Then she sat on the edge of the bed, one leg dangling over the side, the other tucked up in a display of loose-limbed flexibility that Stuart found a little disconcerting, especially, he rather unromantically thought, as this came from the traditional Indonesian habit of squatting on the toilet; children were not so much potty-trained as squatty-trained. He smiled to himself as she flicked through the television channels.

He looked at her, in profile, her hair, definitely longer, smooth, black and shiny as before and as irresistible as before. Her face, with its gently concave nose, those full lips, slightly parted, showing a glimpse of her white, straight teeth.

"I'm going to take a shower," he said, his contemplation finished.

"Okay," she said, not turning her head from the television.

He showered, shaved, washed his hair, cleaned his teeth, put a bit of aftershave on and dressed in nothing but the hotel white towelling dressing gown. He came out of the bathroom clean and pink. His suitcase lay on the low chest of drawers, open. He could see the wrapping paper of her Marks and Spencer present. He picked it up and walked over to her.

"Here," he said, holding it in front of her, to distract her from the television. "This is for you."

She looked up. "Oh, for me?" she said with what seemed like genuine surprise. She took the small package and tore one corner open. Her eyes lit up with a cheeky twinkle when she saw what the contents were.

"Marks and Spencer," he said.

"Really?" she said with increasing delight. She didn't open the packet any further but stood up and went to the bathroom. Stuart sat on the corner of the bed and continued her activity of flicking through the television channels.

He heard the toilet flush and the washing water flow. She was a long time coming out of the bathroom. Stuart was beginning to wonder, again, why women took so long in the bathroom when the door opened and Stuart got a surprise as big, but in the opposite sense, as that he had had on that extraordinary Saturday a month before.

Ita walked towards him dressed only in her new present. It was the closest that Stuart had ever been to seeing her naked. The bra and knickers, the ordinary ones, fitted her perfectly.

He almost gasped at the picture he beheld. She had brushed her hair so that it hung down with some at the front, but most at the back, reaching to the level of the bra strap. Her brown skin seemed to glow in the kind light of the incandescent bulbs in the hotel room; the shiny cream lingerie set off her skin in a perfect combination. Her figure and shape appeared as Stuart had remembered them in so many thoughts and dreams.

"What do you think?" she asked playfully, turning a full circle.

Stuart watched her, admiring the way the shiny fabric followed the immaculate curves of her bottom, curving slightly in to the fold between her buttocks. All he could muster was a little, "Fine."

"Only fine?" she said, facing him with her hands on her slim hips. She tossed her head petulantly and walked back into the bathroom.

Stuart was a little disappointed, thinking that he had upset her. He was about to say something, and made to move towards the bathroom when she emerged for the second time.

The second time she emerged, she was wearing the bra and thong knickers.

If Stuart felt that he had had a big surprise the first time, it was nothing to the surprise he felt the second time she emerged. From the front, the thong knickers curved up gracefully from the centre, around the join between her legs and body, riding high over her hips up towards her waist, emphasising the length of her legs and the curve of her body. Stuart's stomach had a sick feeling ache of sexual anticipation, something he had felt only twice in the last ten years – and both times had been with Ita.

"Well?" she asked again.

"Turn round and I'll tell you," he replied in a quiet voice.

"No," she answered, a little shyly. She walked past him and stood in front of the mirror, admiring herself by standing on her tiptoes and turning to the left and right.

While she did this, Stuart admired her back view. The waist-high side straps visible from the front continued over her hips and down towards the valley between her buttocks. The two straps widened into a triangular-shaped piece of cloth which covered the area where the valley of her buttocks merged smoothly into the small of her back. The third side of the triangle ran down and disappeared into the valley, a small glimpse of it being just visible in the small gap at the top of her legs. These three lines of cloth framed her buttocks to perfection. The effect on Stuart of this picture quite startled him, and he stared open-mouthed. The small movements she made as she admired herself in the mirror only served to make the vision more complete.

"Well?" she asked again, without looking at him.

"Perfect," he mumbled.

She turned to face him, brushing her hair behind her shoulders. "One nice thing about this bra", she said, when she was facing him, "is that it unfastens at the front."

Stuart watched and realised that he was about to get what he had been denied before: a sight of her naked breasts.

She slowly moved her hands to the centre of the bra, skilfully undoing the clip and opening the bra cups outwards like two doors, sweeping the bra down her arms and on to the floor in a single motion. Her breasts were before him. They were not too big, a perfect A cup; he had chosen the right size. They were the shape and size of small upturned saucers; they stood firm like the rest of her body. Her nipples were dark brown in colour, set against the lighter brown of her skin; they stood up a little because of the chill of the air-conditioned room and, Stuart hoped, some rising sexual excitement. Stuart was not disappointed with his first view.

Stuart looked at her from her feet to her head. She looked quite unbelievable. As he met her eyes, she pushed her shoulders back a little, her breasts out a little and repeated her question. "Well?" she asked in a low voice.

"Absolutely perfect," he said a little louder than the last time. He stretched out his arms towards her, and she moved forward to allow him to reach her. His hands came to rest on the top of her hips, on the bands of cloth that formed the knickers. Slowly he pulled her closer until he could reach forward with his mouth and then he took her right nipple in his mouth and kissed for a moment. He repeated the kiss on the left one. Ita moaned a little, arching her back and putting her hands on his head, her fingers in his hair. His hands moved slowly along the bands of cloth, down and backwards around her back, until his hands met in the middle of her back. He moved them back in the opposite direction until they reached the highest point of the cloth on her hips. He then followed the line of the bottom edge of the cloth. His hands moved back and down, this time tracing across her buttocks towards the valley. His hands joined together where the thinning cloth strip disappeared between her legs. He ran his hands out horizontally along the line of juncture between leg and buttock until he was once again on the side on her hips. He moved his hands back up to the bands of cloth and repeated the circuit a number of times.

All the while he kissed and sucked her hard nipples, each one in turn. All the while she stroked his hair and breathed a little heavier.

After a few more circuits of her knickers, he grasped her buttocks gently in his hands, squeezing and massaging them. Then he returned to the knickers on her hips. Slowly he peeled them down the sides of her hips, along her thighs until they fell away to her feet. He stopped kissing and she pulled away just enough to reach down and undo the tie-belt of the dressing gown. She pushed it off his arms and away on to the bed. He ran his fingers up the inside of her thighs and along the outer edge of her hair. She let out a small moan as he deliberately failed to find contact with her most sensitive parts.

He stood slowly and pulled her towards him, embracing her in his arms. She tilted her head up and they began a long kiss. When they broke, Stuart felt totally overwhelmed by her. She was so... well, not erotic really, but exotic – exotic was the word, Stuart decided. It was not just her shape or good looks. It was all the other things: the almost hairless body, the smoothness of the skin, the rich warm brown colour, the darker pieces, the high cheekbones and the white teeth, the hair, the luxurious hair, the trim petite neatness of her body and, most of all, those eyes, their shape and set, sloping ever so slightly from the outside to the inner corner, the deep pools of sensuality that they became whenever he looked into them. He stared at her.

"What?" she asked, looking at him with an enquiring face.

He smiled and shook his head once, leaning down again and taking up the kiss once more.

Slowly, by degrees they backed towards the bed, sat on it, lay on it and moved into the centre of it side by side, half on top, half underneath, as they kissed and stroked each other into a state of high emotion. Breath was short, sometimes even snorted through the nose, eyes closed in a lost world for just the two of them. Ita rolled fully on top of him, broke the kiss and manoeuvred herself on to him. She held herself up with her hands resting on his shoulders.

He felt the warmth spreading as she pushed him in deeper. He gasped a little, she gasped a lot. She pushed her knees out wider and sank lower towards him, biting her bottom lip as she did so. When she was satisfied with the position she began to move, slowly, deliberately, extracting the sensations and pleasures of the moment.

Stuart felt the warm tingle in his groin as Ita sank down on to him. It was more than four weeks since the Saturday night and it was a week before that when he and Catherine had last made love; more than five weeks without any sexual release, even a dreamed one. He knew that he would not last long in this encounter, but he knew he didn't have to worry. With Ita he never worried or thought about what was happening; whatever he did was right for them, whatever she did was right for them.

She dropped her head forward and enveloped his face in her hair. She gasped and groaned with more intensity. Stuart felt an unstoppable tide rising in him. He tensed and pushed his buttocks together, pushing himself up towards her, trying to get deeper inside. She pushed down harder on him, taking a deep breath and holding it in. Stuart didn't need to move: the muscles deep with his groin tensed and contracted, giving him a brief explosion of pleasure. He groaned out loud.

Ita stiffened and let out her held breath. "Oh God, I come," she whispered at the end of her exhaling breath. She took another deep breath and relaxed her taut muscles.

Stuart allowed himself to relax slowly, sinking back on to the bed. For Stuart it was an orgasm of release, a release of almost six weeks of pent-up sexual frustration. It had been physically satisfying, but not fully emotionally satisfying.

They remained joined together, he still firm within her, she not wanting to release the warm feeling she had deep within her. They looked at each other and smiled.

"No condom?" Stuart said, suddenly worried.

"No problem," she smiled back. "I can count and it's safe now."

"Sure?" Stuart said, still a little worried.

"Sure," she replied affirmatively. "It's so much nicer without the condom, yes?" she continued.

Stuart nodded.

When she did eventually relinquish her hold on Stuart and lay down beside him, Stuart was still partially firm, the length of time of the softening reminding him of the length of time since his last sexual encounter.

With only five minutes of rest, Ita rolled on to her side, propped her head up on her left hand and looked at Stuart. Her right hand began to stroke his chest. She worked her way down his body, on to his thighs and up the insides of his thighs towards the centre. His legs were slightly apart and she was able to move very close to him without actually touching anything. He moved his hips a little to try to make her make contact but she skilfully avoided his efforts. He moved his legs a little further apart and she began to stroke and massage between his legs. Stuart felt the same sick sensation of sexual excitement rising in his stomach as she did so. When Stuart was approaching frustration, she moved her small delicate hand lightly over him and gripped him gently. Her hand felt cool against his heat.

She moved her hand only a few times before she rolled on to her back. Stuart rolled on to his side and propped himself on his right arm and looked down at Ita's body. She moved her legs up and down the bed slowly, opening and closing herself, revelling in the anticipation of the feelings to come. She squirmed around, arching her back and lolling her head from side to side. He stretched down, brought his left hand up the inside of her thigh and made one pass of his fingers through her moist hair. She moved to try to get a second touch but he denied her. Instead he rolled over and put his left leg between hers, allowing his hand to rest on her breast. Slowly he moved more on top of her, sliding his right leg over to lie between her widely spread legs. They nuzzled together, making contact and sliding easily together. The warm and secure feeling was spreading through both of them as they joined again.

Ita wrapped her lower legs over Stuart's, holding him into her. He pushed himself up on to his hands and manoeuvred his hips to get deeper. She lay back, eyes closed, with a distant smile on her lips.

Stuart and Ita moved together for quite a while in a symmetrical rhythm with little apparent effect on either of them. But slowly her breathing quickened. Then her head rolled from side to side, slowly at first, but then more rapidly. Her hands spread out wide, gripping the sheets. Stuart realised that she was building to another awe-inspiring climax. He could feel her legs tightening on him, her movements becoming more intense, pushing against his groin. He lowered himself down on to her and kissed her lips. She responded with an open-mouthed kiss of great passion, almost hurting his lips. It did not last for long, for she broke the kiss and hugged his body to hers, his face buried in hair, her short tight breath rasping loud in his ear. She moaned, quietly at first, then louder, holding her breath in between, letting it out in short rasps. She gripped Stuart hard.

"Oh God," she whispered. "Oh God," again, louder, with the next breath. Then she took a long breath in, held it with her whole body tense. "Oh God!" she shouted out loud. "I come! Ohhh! I come!" she shouted a little less loudly as the orgasm subsided. She released a little, some tension relaxed, but not all.

Stuart felt her contractions on him and he felt the storm rising in his groin, spreading outward from the centre. He began to move in and out with longer strokes, coaxing the feeling, building it up. He closed his eyes and gripped her hard. Her body tensed again as he moved with more desperation, moaning and groaning as he did so.

"Oh God, I want come again!" Ita shouted in Stuart's ear. "Don't stop! More, push more!" she shouted and demanded in her need.

Stuart let out a long low moan as he lost himself in his pleasure, his loins moving of their own accord, the feeling now over most of his body, the centre in his groin intense and unbearable. He screwed his eyes tight shut. "Ohhhhh God, my darling Ita," he hissed out through tightly clenched teeth, and his orgasm came in four waves of muscular contraction.

She bucked and jerked beneath him, gripping tightly; as he came, she let out a final cry, "I come again. Oh God, I come again!" Her body was completely taut against him, both lost in their own world of simultaneous orgasms.

For two minutes, which seemed like hours to both of them, they held the tight grip of orgasm. Then slowly, almost imperceptibly, they began to relax away from the tension, wilting down, like a plant without water, on to the bed. Her arms fell away to the side, her legs uncoiled from his, his grip on her shoulders and head loosened and his head dropped to the pillow. When he slackened enough, he slipped out of her almost without noticing it, then he lifted his hot, perspiring and satisfied body up and off her equally perspired and satisfied body and looked down on her. Her eyes were still shut; sweat had broken out along her top lip and in the valley between her breasts.

He rolled off and lay alongside her. Stuart dozed off into a half sleep filled with beautiful images of Ita and their sexual passion so recently enjoyed. He luxuriated in the feelings of warmth now fading through his body.

He was awakened from his reverie by a sharp slap on his stomach.

"Come on," Ita said with a dreamy smile on her lips. "Wash time." She stood and led the way to the bathroom.

Stuart swung his legs down and sat on the bed. He scratched his head absently before standing, a little shakily, and following her into the bathroom.

Ita was rifling the contents of the guest bathroom pack, looking for a shower cap. She tucked her hair up inside the polythene cap and looked ridiculous. She stood with her hands on her slim naked hips and looked at Stuart.

"What's so funny?" she demanded.

"Your hat," he replied.

She didn't reply and stood in the bath, turning the shower on and closing the curtain.

He followed her in for his second shower in less than an hour.

Ita took the soap and began to wash herself. She had not done much when she turned to Stuart. She began to soap his chest, then his groin. She reached round him and soaped his bottom, running her hand between his legs and massaging him much as she had done earlier in the evening, and, although the soap and water gave it a very different feeling, the effect was the same. Stuart felt himself, amazingly, rising again.

He took the soap and returned the gesture, soaping her breasts and fondling her hard nipples. He soaped her hair and rubbed his fingers through and over her, exploring her warmth with his wet fingers. She groaned a little. Then he dropped the soap and grabbed her in a passionate soapy embrace. She ripped off the shower cap, allowing her hair to fall and become wet in the embrace.

They were just too different in height to make love standing up face to face. So Ita turned round and presented her bottom towards Stuart. She gripped the substantial metal soap-holder set high in the wall by the shower. Her body leaned forward into the stream of water, so that it bounced off her head and back and on to him. She pushed her head forward so that it cleared the shower and all the water fell on the small of her back. She raised her buttocks, offering herself to him. He took hold of her waist with one hand and guided himself into her with the other. When he was in the right place, he held her waist with both hands. Then he pushed himself fully in. She moved herself to facilitate the best position. He watched himself go in. He gasped at the strength of feeling still possible after already making love twice. She pushed against him, steadying herself with her hands. He moved in and out in long expansive strokes, feeling sensations different again from those he had experienced earlier that evening. It was now a total erotic experience, making love in a shower – one of his greatest fantasies which had never happened before – and with a small brown lady of almost unimaginable exoticism. He lost himself in his real-life fantasy and came quickly and loudly to his third climax of the night.

He looked at Ita as he withdrew; she turned to face him.

"Ohh, that was good," she said, looking a little flushed again.

"Did you..." He paused, a little embarrassed. "Well, you know."

"Mmmm, I did. Not so strong as last time but different," she said. "Now let's finish our shower," she resumed in her typical matter-of-fact way.

Stuart, as usual, was the first to finish in the bathroom. He wandered out and dressed in tee-shirt and underpants. He turned off the bedroom lights and lay in bed under the sheet, staring at the ceiling. He reflected on his mission: not to touch Ita, to tell her. How impossible that mission, so confidently planned in his mind in the safety of his own kitchen, now appeared when confronted with the real live Ita.

It might have been easier if she had not been so reserved at the airport. Had she rushed up to him and professed undying love in loud emotional terms, he might have pushed her off and began the process in his mind to carry out his mission, but he felt a little hurt that she had not done so. Maybe he felt, well, jealous that she had someone else and she was in control, wanting to play down the previous events between them. That had undoubtedly affected him, made him want to be close to her just to prove that he still could: the male ego still demonstrating its power. He supposed that coming out of the bathroom dressed in a dressing gown was also not too smart a way of starting his mission, nor giving her such a present, although he was somewhat shocked by the response that it provoked. She had reserved showing her naked body to Stuart until exactly the right time in their relationship: when it was most likely to fail and stop, she had revealed herself to him. She knew, Stuart guessed, that he was desperate for a glimpse, for a sight of her body. He had tried often enough to see her but she had been so skilful at hiding herself during their previous encounters. He had watched her closely in the swimming pool and she had known how closely. Possibly, he thought, until he had seen her he could not stop the relationship. Even though he had now seen her, the chances of him stopping it were almost non-existent. The previous hour had cemented them together very firmly.

Stuart's thoughts were interrupted when Ita came out of the bathroom and dressed in her tee-shirt and knickers. She switched of the remaining lights in the hallway and bathroom and slid quietly into bed next to Stuart. She snuggled close to him, wrapping an arm and leg around him. After a minute of relaxation, allowing their bodies to diffuse into each other, Stuart started his mission, or rather he tried to say what his mission should have been.

"It wasn't supposed to be like this," he began quietly.

"Like what?" she replied sleepily.

"Like this." He hugged her to him. "Like this, in bed, making love."

"Why?" she asked, still sleepy and unconcerned.

"Because I wanted to say stop, to say we cannot carry on, that I have a wife and two children and I cannot have you as well." He paused.

"So?" Ita asked, still unconcerned.

"Well, doesn't it make a problem for you?" he asked, having said what he wanted, surprised at the total lack of response.

"You have wife in England, not here. Here you have me, I have you. You have no one else in Indonesia. I don't know your life in England. It does not bother me or worry me – I close it from my mind. You the same, yes?" she said in the same sleepy tone.

"No, it's not the same for me. I cannot forget you when I go back – I cannot isolate this part of my life when I'm in England. You dominate my thoughts, my dreams. I think of you, your face, your hair, your body. Everything about you floods back to me all the time. It's very difficult for me. For you, you can concentrate, you can remember – you don't have anyone else to be with if you don't want. I have no choice. I must stay with my wife, I must stay with my children and all I can think about is you." Stuart was saying much more than he should, much too much, straying far from his mission, but he couldn't stop now that he had started, even though his mission was in tatters, a total failure. "You have a choice: you can stay by yourself. I can't," he repeated, his voice a little cracked with emotion.

"I didn't want to make a problem for you with your wife," she said in a small, shy, almost apologetic voice. "I just want you when you're here. It's all I need. It's enough."

"I find it so hard, Ita my darling," he said, his voice even more emotional than before. "Sometimes when I make love with my wife I close my eyes and can see only you." He squeezed her gently.

"I'm sorry, Stuart," she said quietly, "but my life, my chance of a normal life here was destroyed when I was young. Since then I have tried to make a life for myself: I go to school, I get a good job, I have a career, but until now, until you, no love, no one to open everything to." Now her voice was beginning to show some emotional strain, but she controlled it well. "So all I ask from you, Stuart my love, is for you to be with me when you come here, for you to keep coming back, for you to write to me, to share a little of you with me." She stopped.

"Ita," Stuart said after a pause.

"Yes?"

"I love you," he said simply.

She squeezed him by way of reply and then they slept.

# CHAPTER 21

# MR CHAN AGAIN

The next morning, Ita was up and washed before six-thirty. She told a sleepy Stuart that she had to go home and change before work and asked for him to call her with his plan. Then she was gone with a single peck on the cheek. She left him with two more hours of delightful memory-filled half-sleep before he had to get up.

At first, the events of the evening seemed to have been a dream, a feeling not unlike the one he had had after their first sexual encounter. He was not sure if it had really happened, but, as he slowly woke up, the tender nature of his groin and the unmistakable smell of Ita's perfume and Ita on the bed convinced him that everything was as he had dreamed it.

He ate a quick breakfast and took a taxi to Anwar's office. Anwar positively bounced into the reception to meet Stuart.

"Well, hello Mr Morgan, and how are we today?" he said in a very impressive imitation of an upper class English accent.

"Okay, just a little jet-lagged," Stuart lied.

"Come into my office." Anwar led the way back.

Some of the staff, especially Anwar's secretary, recognised Stuart and smiled at him. He smiled back, enjoying the recognition.

They sat in the two easy chairs, waiting for an obligatory cup of tea to be brought. When it arrived, their conversation began in earnest.

Anwar leaned forward and patted Stuart's knee. "Well, how is England and Ormistons? You look so well, full of life," Anwar continued. "Very full of life, almost blooming with happiness." The twinkle in his brown eyes was easily visible to Stuart. "You must be glad to be back."

Stuart nodded, looking Anwar in the eyes. "Well, England is not so bad. It's the summer – time for cricket, barbecues and the like. Even so it's still an awful lot hotter here," he said.

"Okay," Anwar said loudly. "Business first. Tomorrow we go to Surabaya to see Mr Chan and a few other factories. Your fame has spread quite quickly and we have a lot of publicity visits to make. Can you still remember your presentation?"

"Of course I can, no problem for me. How many times?" Stuart said.

Anwar shrugged. "Maybe four or five times."

"You have been busy," Stuart said, leaning back to admire Anwar.

Anwar gave a smile as if to say it was nothing. "Because I told you, we can work together, you and I, we can. Now I have an office for you. I have a pile of letters, faxes, papers for you to go through over the rest of the day. Then tomorrow, mid-afternoon, we will leave and tonight you will come to my house for dinner."

Stuart tried to take all this in. At the end he had only one question. "How long will we be away?"

"Be back Saturday afternoon or evening," was Anwar's reply.

"Okay, I'll catch up on my reading and then we can have a little lunch; I know your wife's cooking and I want to be able to do it justice."

"Good man!" Anwar almost shouted.

Stuart felt so overwhelmed by Anwar's obvious enthusiasm for Stuart's return and his genuine affection for Stuart. All Stuart could manage was a smile.

He stood to leave Anwar's office and then remembered something. "Oh, er, speaking of Mr Chan, whatever happened to the spares order that you confidently predicted last time I was here?" This time the twinkle was in Stuart's eye.

Anwar looked embarrassed. "Well, I think our Mr Chan will tell us when we see him." He said it with such finality that Stuart knew not to probe further.

In his new office, already labelled 'Ormistons Representative', his first job was to telephone Ita at work.

She answered the phone. "Hi Stuart," she said when she recognised his voice, her voice seeming so faraway and small.

"I'm going away to Surabaya tomorrow, back on Saturday," he said.

"Okay, no problem. What about tonight?" she asked.

Stuart wondered about that. A long time as it had been since the previous sexual encounter before last night, he was not sure whether his tender groin could respond and, even if it could, whether or not it would be a painful disappointment after last night.

"Well, I have to go out to dinner with Anwar," he said, in a slightly defensive tone, playing down the prospect of meeting Ita.

She remained silent on the other end of the phone; she understood his tone.

"So I guess we could go out later, after. How about we meet at The Inne?" he replied to fill the silence.

"Yes," she said brightly. "What time?"

"Ten-thirty, eleven. And don't drink any of those nice tonic drinks," he said.

"Urukk!" She almost retched down the phone at him. "No way! See you later. I have to go, I'm very busy today, sorry."

"Bye," Stuart shouted as the phone went dead. He stared at it for a moment. She could be so abrupt sometimes, so matter-of-fact, while all the while he expected her to be lovey-dovey and gooey. It was these contrasts which so intrigued him and kept him so interested in her.

In the end, no lunch was taken by Anwar and Stuart. Anwar had another appointment and Stuart was engrossed in his reading. He went back to the hotel in the mid-afternoon for a rest and change of clothes. Anwar's car picked him up at eight o'clock.

Stuart presented Anwar's wife with a present from the UK. He was glad that he had not had lunch since Anwar's wife had prepared a sumptuous feast of Indonesian food. There was fish in a yellow sauce; some hot spicy beef in a coconut milk sauce, not unlike a curry but with a subtly different taste; there was fried, thin, stringy chicken which tasted far better than any fried chicken he had tasted before; there was fried rice, plain rice, noodles, spinach-type vegetables with chillies, blanched vegetables with peanut sauce and of course the inevitable sambal chilli sauce. Stuart ate until he could eat no more. Anwar pushed him, offered him more, cajoled him, but he had to admit that he was full, and very delicious it had all been.

After the plates had been cleared by the housemaid, Anwar and Stuart sat down together with a cup of Javanese coffee each.

"You know," Anwar began quietly, "those spares from Mr Chan turned into a bit of a problem."

Anwar put his best anguished look on to convince Stuart.

Stuart nodded in agreement.

"You see, after you went back, he started to call me up and ask for more discounts." Anwar repeated his anguished look. "And well, I didn't want to ask you over the phone, in case..." He paused again. "I was worried that you would think that I was trying to get some more money or something."

Stuart shook his head. "I wouldn't think that. If we can't trust each other completely then we should stop doing business together," Stuart said, a little annoyed that Anwar had delayed telling him in the UK and that the order was delayed as a result.

"Well, you'll see when we visit Mr Chan this week. He will want some more discount off your prices – be prepared." Anwar took a sip of coffee.

"I was expecting something like that," Stuart said, "so no problem."

Anwar smiled at Stuart. "You see, you and I can do business together. Now there is full trust between you and me, yes?"

"Yes there is, there has to be."

"I don't want to deal with anyone else in your company except you," Anwar said, looking Stuart in the eye. "Okay, you understand?"

"I understand," Stuart said with equal seriousness, not wavering in returning Anwar's look. "But if that spares order is delayed any longer then someone else will come because they will think that I can't do my job," he continued, in the same serious tone.

Anwar looked at him with an expression of genuine alarm. "Really? Is it that serious? If it is then I'll give the discount from my commission, no problem." He looked quite agitated.

Stuart tried to continue the game, but his face broke into a smile.

"This joke, right?" Anwar said, realising the game.

Stuart nodded and they both laughed.

The rest of the evening passed quickly in good-humoured joviality until it was time for Stuart to leave, 'to make sure he recovered from his jet-lag' as Anwar said, at ten o'clock. He watched Anwar's car go from the top of the steps before he turned and disappeared down the steps into The Inne.

The same slightly less proficient Filipino band was playing and the place was reasonably full. He looked in vain for Ita. After he had convinced himself that she wasn't there he took a bar seat and ordered a beer. He drank one and then a second, feeling quite tired and full. He checked his watch. It was almost eleven and he really was beginning to feel jet-lag or something. He was about to go when a familiar smell wafted into his nostrils amid the smoke and beery smell of the bar. He turned round and saw Ita was standing beside him, dressed in white jeans and a dark blue tee-shirt, her hair simply brushed back over her shoulders.

She looked up at him and smiled. "Hi," she said, laying her hand on his arm.

"Hello Ita, want a drink?"

"Mmmm," she replied, pursing her lips together and nodding her head, her eyes looking up at him like a wide-eyed child. She looked so cute and impish, her serious eyes more mischievous than ever before.

"You want to stay here tonight?" he asked her quietly.

"Mmmm," she replied again in the same way.

Stuart felt a little worried: his nether regions were still feeling tender after the previous night's exertions. Her behaviour since coming into the bar filled him with fear of what she might do to him once they got upstairs. He decided that a few drinks and a long session of watching the band was in order. However, Ita finished her one drink of the night quite quickly and he could not face another on top of Anwar's wife's food, so they left after less than an hour.

Once in the room they cleaned their teeth and completed the normal pre-sleep formalities in an almost routine way: there was absolutely no hint of a sexual advance from her. He got in bed first. She stood looking at herself in the mirror for a while before stripping down to her knickers in a very matter-of-fact way in full view of Stuart with the light on.

She knew that he was watching and she looked at him and smiled. The lights went out and she slid into the bed alongside him. She cuddled close and wrapped a leg and arm around him, closed her eyes and made as if to sleep.

Stuart was surprised and grateful.

After a few minutes, during which Stuart almost dozed off, he felt her arm tighten against him. He thought the worst, that she was making the first stage of an advance, but to his great surprise there came the unmistakable sound of a loud fart. The tension in Ita's arm relaxed and she settled down against him again.

"Ita, was that you?" Stuart said in disbelief.

"Well, was it you?" she said sleepily.

"No."

"Well, it must have been me."

"Do all Indonesian women fart in bed?" he asked incredulously.

"Don't you fart?" she asked, squeezing him.

"Not in public," he replied.

"You're not public, you're Stuart," she replied, lifting her bottom a little and farting again just for effect.

He began to laugh uncontrollably, his body heaving, until he almost fell out of bed. When his laughter subsided a little he tried to speak.

"Here I am with an oh-so-polite Indonesian, well Javanese, woman, the most beautiful woman I have ever met, with whom I have had so much passion, whom I love and who now lies here and farts in bed. So romantic!" He laughed again.

"You finished?" she asked sleepily as he subsided after a further minute's laughter.

"Mmmm," he said, still giggling a little.

"Well, I know how to make you laugh now," she said. "All I need do is fart."

And with that they both drifted off into sleep.

Ita left at six-thirty the next morning. Stuart checked out and went to Anwar's office for nine. They left for Surabaya at two in the afternoon, everything having a friendly familiarity about it for Stuart: he felt at home. They checked into the same hotel in Surabaya, had a pleasant evening meal and retired early.

The following morning, Thursday, they left early in a hired car. Anwar directed the driver to the small isolated factory of Mr Chan's, a difficult place to find, but it was their second time and they found it easily. The driver of the car showed some reluctance in diving off down the narrow pot-holed road. The road had got better. There was some evidence that a grader had been at work filling the biggest holes and levelling out some of the small mountains which obstructed progress. The factory, however, looked the same as they approached.

Once they were close, they realised that a small area in front had been paved with small bricks to make an arrival area. Along the front, small gardens had been formed with a number of shrubs and bushes. A coat of paint had been applied and the outer doors had also been replaced. They entered and felt the cool waft of efficient air-conditioning. The entrance hall was like before, in its cool efficient grey. Through the second set of doors, they entered the main office.

Chan's beautiful Javanese wife sat at the wide modern reception desk.

"Hello Mr Morgan, Mr Anwar," she said in her smooth graceful English. "Nice to see you again." She extended her hand to each of them in turn. "I'll get my husband."

Anwar nudged Stuart. "The boss," he said quietly.

"You told me this was a male-dominated society – the men rule," Stuart whispered back.

"Don't believe everything people tell you," Anwar laughed.

She returned. "My husband will be here in a minute," she said, guiding them to her husband's office.

They sat to await his arrival. A tea boy came in with four cups of tea and set them on the table. Anwar nudged Stuart again. "She's joining us this time. Now we'll see who's boss," he whispered.

Mr Chan bustled in a moment later. "Hello Anwar," he said, grabbing Anwar's hand. "Mr Morgan," he said, turning to Stuart and shaking his hand firmly and rapidly. "Please sit down. My wife is coming to join us."

Stuart nudged Anwar and Anwar smiled.

They sat and Mr Chan's wife glided in to join them with a cardboard file in her hand. She sat opposite Stuart and looked at him and smiled demurely, casting her eyes down as she smiled.

Stuart looked at her face, the black hair, the brown eyes and the high cheek-bones, and suddenly Ita came flooding back into his mind. He was looking at Ita not Mr Chan's wife. Suddenly he missed Ita very much and he wanted to rush out and go straight to her, he wanted to abandon his meeting and run. He felt a nudge in his ribs as Anwar tried to bring Stuart back into the present world. Stuart realised that he had been staring at Mr Chan's wife. He smiled, a little embarrassed, and bent down to retrieve his briefcase.

"Okay, we start?" said Chan.

The rest nodded.

"Okay, first I want to say about the spares. This price too high – I tell Anwar already I want discount. What you think, Mr Morgan?" Mr Chan said in his rapid-fire English.

"Well, maybe we can give a discount, but you've already delayed buying them for so long. That's very risky. What if you had had a breakdown? Any discount would have been swallowed up in lost production," Stuart replied.

Chan shifted uneasily in his seat and glanced at his wife.

She looked at Stuart and give a knowing smile.

"Okay," Stuart began, "five per cent if you order now, today." He already knew the mark-up on the spares prices and five per cent still left a very large profit on the sale.

Chan glanced at his wife again and she gave an almost imperceptible nod.

Stuart noticed and tapped Anwar's foot under the table.

"Okay, I give you order today, no problem," Chan said hastily.

His wife passed him the file. He opened it and shuffled the papers. "Err, we want to decide about the old machines here. Maybe we want to repair or buy new. What you think?" he said, looking at Stuart.

"You have the prices I gave last time for rebuilding those two old ones you have and I can get you the price of one new one which could replace them with capacity to spare," Stuart replied, knowing that even that machine was one of the smallest in Ormistons' range.

"Okay," said Chan. "You get me price, send price and then we discuss. I have this list of more spare parts."

He pushed a list to Stuart. There was more than the value of spares which he had promised to buy a few moments earlier.

"If you give me five per cent again then I order from you today also," Chan said, looking down at the table.

"You see, we don't want to have a breakdown because we lose production," his wife spoke for the first time, "and until we have enough spares to keep going we depend on you to give us the good price and delivery."

Stuart was surprised at her directness. He guessed that they had had some troubles, a breakdown or two, while her husband had been trying to get a discount out of Anwar. Stuart smiled to himself: 'Penny wise and pound foolish'.

"You see, Mr Morgan," she continued, speaking slowly and gracefully, "before we met you, we had no access to spares. We relied on what came with the machines and what repairs we could do by ourselves. But of course the machines are never as good when they use the defective parts; quality and production suffer. So now we want to have a good spares policy and keep our production and quality good." She smiled at Stuart. "You agree?" she asked almost unnecessarily.

"Of course he agree – he is salesman for spares," Chan said loudly, but good-humouredly, finishing with a laugh.

"Yes, I do agree." Stuart smiled at both of them. "It's widely known that skimping on spares always affects production and quality. We can advise on the correct type and number of spares to carry so that you don't tie up lots of money in them."

"Okay, okay," said Chan, holding up his hand, "I know when I'm beat." He laughed again.

Stuart and Anwar looked at each other. Both of them knew that they had a good customer in the making.

They ate lunch with Chan but not his wife. She stayed behind to produce the orders. It was she who read Stuart's copy of Ormistons' 'Terms of Sale' at great length and she who actually signed the order. Stuart and Anwar left with more than thirty thousand pounds of spares orders in the bag, the original fifteen thousand plus the order Chan had given them that morning.

In the late evening, Stuart and Anwar sat in the bar of the hotel, drinking an after dinner beer.

"You know," said Stuart, "we've got the making of a good customer there, old Mr Chan."

"I know, and I think his wife is the one to concentrate on, the one who will get the expansion plans through. Mr Chan's a hard worker, an improviser, but he cannot stop being a Chinese street trader. He always wants his discount, to try and save a bit," Anwar said. "He can't resist it." Anwar smiled at Stuart. "Still, his wife seems to like you – she looked at you a lot. And you at her, if I might add." Anwar paused.

"Yeah, I know. I'm sorry about that, but she is rather beautiful and, well, she reminded me of someone as well." Stuart paused and then realised the enormity of his admission. "A friend I had at university," he added quickly.

"You have many Indonesian women in your university then?" said Anwar with a cheeky smile on his face.

Stuart could only manage a shy smile in response.

The next day they visited another factory a good way from Surabaya, two hours by car in fact, but adjacent to the main road. It was a large rambling factory, well run but with too much of their competitor's equipment in place to give them much hope of a sale. On the Saturday they visited a small concern in Surabaya, too small to be of real interest, but the managers were extremely keen. Stuart and Anwar agreed to make some proposals for the smallest size of machine in Ormistons' normal range. Then on Saturday afternoon, they left Surabaya for the return trip to Jakarta.

# CHAPTER 22

# MY STOMACH ACHE

Stuart arrived back in the now familiar reception of the Kedutaan Hotel. He checked in with speed: his details were on the computer and all he had to do was sign. Once in his room, he stripped off for a cooling cleansing shower and then sat on the bed, naked but for a towel, and phoned Ita at her home. The phone rang for a long time.

Eventually a voice answered. "Hello?"

Stuart knew it wasn't Ita.

"Hello, can I speak to Ita?" he said in his best Foreign Office voice, slow and loud.

The voice babbled something unintelligible.

"Ita, please, Ita," he said slowly and even louder.

The phone went quiet; Stuart wondered if he had been cut off, but he could hear faint voices and other noises so he held on. Eventually, he heard slow footsteps coming towards the phone.

"Hello," a small voice said, definitely Ita's, but small and weak.

"Hi Ita, it's me, Stuart," he said brightly, wondering at the weak-sounding voice on the phone.

"Oh hi," she replied, a little brighter. "When you get back?"

"An hour ago," he replied. "Tonight, can we meet, go out? You eaten?" he asked quickly, his voice sounding like that of an excited schoolboy.

"No, sorry, not tonight, Stuart. I have my stomach ache," she said, returning to her weak voice again. "Maybe tomorrow we meet, okay?"

Stuart was quite shocked; in fact he was so stunned that he could hardly reply. "Okay," was all he could manage, and with that Ita said, "Goodbye," and the phone went down.

Stuart was upset. For the last two days since he had seen Chan's wife he had thought of little else but Ita. He was so keen to get back to Jakarta, so excited at the prospect of meeting her again, of making love, of sleeping close to that smooth exotic body, of looking into her big brown eyes, of tasting her exotic fruit, that this news was very upsetting. His chin crumpled a little and he sniffed; he almost cried. He was very shocked at his own reaction to Ita's unavailability.

After ten minutes or so, he stood and finished his bathroom duties. He dressed and sat on the bed, flicking idly through the television channels. Then he had an idea. Jumping up, he rummaged through his briefcase and extracted one of Ita's letters. He carefully wrote her address on the back of one of his business cards and left the room. Downstairs, in the hotel lobby, he bought a small box of expensive chocolates and a nicely arranged group of orchids in a cardboard and plastic box. Then he got a taxi in the front of the hotel. He waved the card at the driver.

"I want to go here," he said in the usual manner.

The driver nodded. "*Tau Aku Tau*," he replied excitedly. "*Jauh jauh dari sini*, far long way," he said in halting English.

"Okay, *tau juah tau*, no problem," Stuart replied jovially, and they were off with a big smile from the driver.

They drove down the tree-lined avenue Stuart now recognised as Jalan Jeneral Sudirman. They passed the shopping area where Stuart had bought presents for his children. They passed close by Anwar's house and kept on going. The driver talked in his few words of English all the way, observing Stuart in the rear-view mirror. Stuart tried his best to reply slowly and in very simple English. The driver seemed to understand and gave him big smiles and laughs.

They arrived after almost an hour's driving, in a smallish street, well-lit, with many houses of different sizes and designs clustered together along both sides. He looked left and right for the numbers. They were neither odd and even on separate sides nor were the numbers consecutive on each side. It took two passes down the street and one question by the driver before Ita's house was identified. Stuart looked along the road; it wasn't far from the main road as he remembered, and a number of the small three-wheeled *bajaj* were visible. He decided that it would not be a problem to let the taxi go. He paid the driver, complete with a big tip, and stood in the street, alone for the first time in Jakarta outside the confines of the hotel, Anwar's office and the big department stores, away from taxis, away from safety, away from the English language.

He glanced nervously up and down the street, but there was no hostility in the faces of the people, only smiles. He felt reasonably safe and in control.

Stuart stood in front of the house which he had identified as the one with the correct number. He had forgotten what the house looked like as he had only seen it from the confines of the car after their trip to Puncak. It was a two-storey house, painted in streaked and stained white, with a number of feeble lights in each corner of the roof, under the eaves. It butted up to the houses on either side as close as any terraced house in England. To Stuart's eye it looked a little shabby, but the only thing with which he had to compare was Anwar's rather palatial spread. He tried the gate but it appeared to be locked. He tried to push it a few times, again without success. A number of small children had gathered around him.

"Hello mister," the tallest of them said to Stuart.

Stuart smiled back. "Hello," he said, and they all giggled loudly. One of them pointed up at something.

"*Ini*, mister," he said, pointing again. "*Itu*."

Stuart looked and saw a small push button, the bell. He smiled again. "Thank you."

They all laughed again as Stuart reached round to push the button.

A small woman appeared from a door alongside the garage, dressed in a white overall and rubber flip-flops. She approached Stuart.

"Ita," he said loudly.

She nodded and unlocked the gate, allowing Stuart into the small driveway. A car stood in the drive, parked close to the garage door; it was the same one that had taken Stuart and Ita on their Saturday afternoon adventure to Puncak some months ago. The woman led him past the car and to the front door of the house proper. She pushed it open and silently offered entry to the house.

She showed Stuart a seat in the entrance hall. The hall was hot and the air still and slightly fetid with the warm damp smell of decay. The area was lit by a single low-wattage fluorescent bulb which cast a lurid white light, emphasising the starkness of the room. The chairs were old, slightly musty, wood-framed affairs which would have been uncomfortable to sit in for a long time. The floor was concrete tiles, roughly laid and uneven, but they appeared to be cleanly swept despite the smell. A small glass-topped table stood in front of the chair, complete with a vase of plastic flowers and plastic doily. Stuart felt a little uncomfortable.

The woman disappeared up the stairs and knocked lightly on a door. Stuart heard a brief conversation before he saw Ita peering at him from the top of the stairs.

"Is that you, Stuart?" she asked, scarcely able to believe that it was.

"Yes it is," he replied, a little nervous that he had disturbed something.

"Come up, don't sit down there, come up quick," she replied quickly, dispelling Stuart's fears.

He made his way up past the woman who glanced at him a little severely. He entered Ita's room and she closed the door.

"It's so good of you to come," she said, reaching up to kiss him. "I'm so surprised! I not ready – my room is a mess, not tidy."

"No problem," he said in his softest tone. "Here, these are for you." He offered her the chocolates and flowers.

"Oh Stuart, thank you so much. They're beautiful and I love chocolates. Here, have one." She offered the box to Stuart.

He shook his head. "No, no, these are for you, for when your stomach ache goes. I hope you will be better soon."

She laughed a little and held her stomach. "It's not like normal stomach ache," she said.

For a brief second Stuart thought about the unprotected sex of a week ago and his mouth went dry.

"I get it every month at the same time," she continued. "Menstruation, you know."

"Oh," said Stuart in a loud voice indicating that the penny had dropped. "I see. Then open the chocolates and we can eat them together."

She smiled and nodded. "You want tea?"

"Yes thanks, no sugar."

"No milk also, okay for you?" she asked.

"Yes, okay."

She left the room to organise the tea. Stuart quickly wandered round and looked at the photographs on the small chipboard and wood-effect paper dressing table which stood in one corner. There were pictures of Ita, of Ita and a number of other girls, and of Ita with an old woman dressed in traditional costume. There was a single faded black and white photograph of an Indonesian man. Stuart looked at the face. It bore a striking resemblance to Ita, so he guessed it was her father. There were no other photographs of men in evidence. For some reason that Stuart could not place, he felt better at this discovery: a surprise visit to Ita's house and no obvious evidence of any other men in her life. He continued his circuit of her room. Her room was large and again lit with a cold white fluorescent bulb. There were two other doors in the room besides the one through which they had just entered. One seemed to lead to a bathroom, while the second glass-panelled door next to the room's only window led to a small balcony which looked out at the back of the house. On a small chest of drawers which stood close by this door, under the window, was the small bonsai tree that Stuart had bought on that trip to Puncak. It stood on a small white embroidered tablecloth. The tree appeared to be well looked after.

Against the opposite wall was the bed, a large double, with a small bedside table and bedside light. There were two chairs to complete the furniture. The floor was the same type of concrete tiles as downstairs, but there was no smell of decay as there had been downstairs. Stuart wondered if they used damp-proof courses in house construction, as the house smelled very much like the unmodernised Victorian house in which he had lived as a student.

Ita reappeared with two cups of tea on a small wooden tray. She set them down on the bedside table. Stuart looked at her as she did this. She looked frail, her shoulders stooped a little, her movements constricted and tight, quite unlike the Ita to whom he was used. Her hair looked to have lost its shine; her skin seemed to be dull and less radiant.

"Does your..." He paused. Menstruation was not something he talked about with his wife: it was almost a taboo subject in many English households. "...your menstruation", he continued, trying not to sound embarrassed, "always give you such pain and problems?"

She nodded. "In here, in Indonesia, we get a day a month extra holiday for menstruation if we need it, but if we don't use it we get a bonus. Why, in England not like that?"

"No, not really. Most women try to carry on as normal. In fact some women have a big emotional problem, some sick and some no problem – it depends," he said.

"For me not much of a problem, but I feel tired, upset and then for one day, that's today, I get a bad stomach, but I worked today. I cannot wash my hair until it's finished. So." She pulled her hair a little by way of example.

A silence fell on them for a minute or two. Stuart looked around the room. "That tree is still going, still alive."

"Of course," she said in mock anger. "From you, so I look after it very good, give it water, stand it outside in the rain, talk to it, give it new earth, everything," she laughed. "When you are not here that is you." She laughed again, pointing at the tree.

He laughed. "You're crazy, you know?"

She nodded and some of the sparkle came back to her.

They sat and talked for a long time, about Stuart's job, about Indonesia, about each other. Ita told him that she shared the house with five other girls and that the woman who had opened the door was the housemaid. The car belonged to the boyfriend of one of the other girls. Stuart excused himself to the toilet once. The toilet was a wet-floored Indonesian squatter, with a traditional tiled water container which Stuart thought was a bath. He couldn't imagine bathing in it but he guessed that they managed somehow. The bathroom smelled and looked clean.

Ita yawned once and Stuart glanced at his watch. It was eleven o'clock. "I have to go, Ita. You're tired and I don't want to give you a problem with your menstruation."

"No problem, you can stay as long as you like, but you must be tired after being in Surabaya. I will call a taxi for you." She shuffled slowly out of the room. She came back a few minutes later. "It will be ten minutes."

"Tomorrow?" Stuart asked, looking at her as she sat heavily on the bed.

"Mmm. I want to see you because I think that you will go away again next week, yes?" she asked.

"I will be going on Monday, to Solo, to Yogya, for the whole week, maybe until Saturday or maybe even Sunday or the week after."

"Okay, I will call you in the morning and then we can see. But now you come here," she said, patting the bed beside her.

Stuart obeyed and sat beside her. She put her arms around him and hugged him tight.

"My darling Stuart," she sighed gently. "My darling," she repeated.

He smiled and hugged her back.

She kissed his cheek, and then he turned to reach her mouth. They kissed a long slow gentle kiss: a kiss of affection and love rather than lust. They continued to kiss until the noise of a car horn in the street below signalled the taxi's arrival.

They stood up and Ita wrapped her arms around him, he around her. They kissed again, and suddenly the closeness of her body to his, pressed against his, the kiss, the week's separation became too much for him. His heart began to beat very fast, his face flushed and his stomach got that sick feeling again.

Ita seemed to sense this, for she put her hand down to his groin and massaged him through his jeans while they continued to kiss.

Stuart's breath became shorter; he tensed as she stroked. Then he felt himself tense and his groin tingled and the feeling spread outwards from the centre. She gripped him hard through the cloth and in a second he exploded, groaning quietly as he felt the surge.

"Ohh," he said weakly. "Ohh, that was a surprise."

"You enjoy?" she asked questioningly.

"Mmmmm," was all he could muster.

"Your taxi's waiting. We talk tomorrow on the phone, yes?" she continued, reverting to the matter of fact.

"Okay, I'll see you tomorrow, Ita." He kissed her again and turned to leave.

She saw him to the door. "Bye my love," she said as she stood with her arms folded, leaning against the door.

"Bye Ita, I love you," he said quietly, almost out of her earshot, and left for the taxi.

He sat in the back seat of the taxi, his legs apart, with the sticky warm wetness spreading around his groin, a lovely satisfied feeling in his body. Ita was full of surprises. When he got back, he went straight upstairs, worried about any visible evidence of Ita's activities showing on his trouser front. In his room he stripped off and washed his underpants through in the sink before settling down in bed with the television on. He slept some time just before one.

He didn't manage a long sleep; he was up and about by eight. He wondered whether or not to call Ita, but he decided to wait for her call. He didn't eat any breakfast. He lay about the room, neither really in bed nor out of it, clad only in his underpants. He switched the television on and half watched, drifting in and out of sleep. The telephone's ring pulled him back into something like a fully awake state. He sat up and answered.

"Hello Stuart." It was Ita's voice and she sounded more lively than last night.

"Hi, how are you feeling?" he said, trying to wake up.

"Better, much better," she said. "What do you want to do?"

"What can you do? We can't go swimming, we've been to Ancol, we've been around the museums, we've been to Puncak – what else is there left to do?" He was actually trying to be funny, amusing, but Ita misinterpreted his meaning.

"It's all right if you don't want to go out with me. I understand, we cannot make love so you don't want to see me." Her voice was small and faint.

"Ita!" he said loudly, but tenderly. "Ita, don't! I didn't mean that! I just mean that we have to think of something a little different for today, that's all. I do want to see you. I thought of nothing else except you while I was away. I wanted to come back so much," he said.

She was quiet on the other end of the phone.

"Ita," he said, trying to coax her to speak again, "are you still there?"

"Yes," she said quietly.

"It's nine o'clock now. Shall I come to you, or do you want to come here?" he asked.

"Can I come to see you?" she asked in her same quiet hurt voice.

"Of course, of course," he said in his most friendly voice, "Please, as soon as possible, you come."

"Okay, I will come now. Bye," and the phone went down.

Stuart busied himself washing and dressing. He went downstairs to wait for Ita, not bothering with breakfast. He wandered around the hotel lobby waiting for her to show up . He had dressed in shorts and tee-shirt, for it was hot and he wanted to be comfortable.

She came within thirty-five minutes of the phone call. She too was dressed in long shorts and a polo tee-shirt with loose sandals on her feet. She smiled up at him as he waved to her, pushing open the hotel door.

"Hi," he said, taking her hand and making as if to kiss her, but she pulled away and signalled with her eyes. He remembered her reluctance to be too close to him, to show too much affection in public. "A taxi?" he asked, leaving go of her hand.

She nodded, and the doorman signalled for one to come.

Once inside and on the move the taxi driver asked Ita something and Ita replied. Stuart looked at her.

"Where are we going?" he said brightly. "A surprise?"

She dug him in the ribs. "You like boats?" she asked.

"Yeah, they are okay, I suppose. I've never really thought about it, why?" he replied with a non-committal shrug of his shoulders.

"But you like them a bit. You would like to see some, yes?" she replied in a pleading voice.

"Yes, I would like to see some," he said brightly again, realising how easy it was to upset her normally, and how much more easy it would be to upset her in her present condition.

"Good," she smiled, happy again.

They rode for quite a way, past streets which held fleeting remembrances for Stuart.

"Are we near Ancol?" he asked.

She nodded. "You already know Jakarta, yes?"

"Not really, I just recognise some bits," he replied and gave her small hand a discreet squeeze.

She smiled and looked out of the taxi window.

They approached the main area of Ancol, with its huge nightclub and the funfair. The driver turned left and away from the entrance. They ran alongside a wide stagnant area of water, Stuart was not sure if it was a river, lake or canal. They turned down a number of small streets and ran through an area of rundown small warehouses. Trucks and lorries plied in and out of these frail-looking timber and corrugated iron structures, in some chaotic version of business and trading. Despite the look of the buildings, there was an obvious air of frantic activity: so many people, loading, unloading, driving, directing and all on a Sunday in this heat. Stuart was more than a little amazed at the scene. They rounded a corner away from this activity and took a sharp right turn beneath a white painted gate. Stuart paid the taxi and they stepped out into the warmth of the mid-morning sun.

Stuart put his sunglasses on and took Ita's arm in his and together they began to walk towards the boats. As they got closer, he could see that the boats were not boats or ships anything like those he had been expecting to see. They were sailing ships, real wooden-hulled sailing ships, with masts and white sails. He was amazed: another surprise in this country full of surprises. Each boat was made in the same basic pattern, but the size and detail of each of the hundred or more boats which stretched out into the distance along the quayside was different.

Stuart approached the first one of the line. It was moored at about forty-five degrees to the quayside. Two long bending wooden beams ran out from the quay to the side of the ship. Over these precarious planks the ships were being unloaded. Each boat was a graceful curve from stem to stern. The high front prow rose up to terminate in a long jib mast. Amidships, the curve came close to the water level. The free board appeared minimal, but the vessel was wide and, since the main cargo appeared to be wood, Stuart guessed that they were pretty stable and safe. At the wide high-rising stern, a bridge and accommodation section was formed. It too followed the graceful curve of the main hull: nothing on the ship, apart from the masts, appeared straight, everything was curved and shaped. They looked so graceful and beautiful ranged along the quayside.

Scores of men laboured to unload the boats. Each man had a lump of foam or cloth on his shoulder and they navigated the precarious, bending gangplanks with ease, carrying loads of sawn timber on the pad of cloth. Huge stacks of timber laid on the quayside, all of it hardwood – teak and mahogany. The smell of the timber's rich oils hung in the air. Traders scurried about, counting, marking timber, arguing and supervising the loading of sections of timber on to the fleet of small trucks which plied the space between the wood piles and the ships.

Stuart stopped to look, but Ita tugged his hand. "Come on, there are so many of them, all the way over there."

She pointed into the distance and they walked. A number of other tourists passed by, some taking photographs and handing out 'smile money' to the hard-working dockers. An adventurous couple negotiated the gangplank of one ship and explored the inside of the ship. Most of the boats had rusty exhaust pipes sticking out of some part of the superstructure, indicating that they had engines as well as sails. They walked the full length of the quay, maybe a mile, and every space was taken up by one of these magnificent vessels, every one unloading or loading, some being repainted, others scrubbed down, every one still in commercial service. It was quite a shock to Stuart to see the extent of the trade. These were not a few industrial relics working in some museum fleet, this was not the Tall Ships Race setting off from the Albert Dock in Liverpool – this was real life. These ships and the people were working, competing in a modern world of supertankers and containers, and surviving.

"Impressive," he said to Ita.

She squeezed his arm. "Good, nice boats?" she asked, pleased as a child at having got her homework right.

"Mmmm," he said, "wonderful. It's fantastic, unbelievable."

They reached the end of the quayside and looked out over the blue-green sea. A slightly cooling sea breeze blew in and took the edge off the heat. They looked out, arm in arm, her head resting on his shoulder. Stuart was quite overwhelmed by the beauty of this scene and of Indonesia. His chin crumpled and his eyes moistened. She squeezed him as if she understood his feelings.

Then they turned and began the walk back. By the boat nearest to the entrance a man stood with a number of small models of the boats. Stuart had not seen them before and tried to direct Ita towards them.

She resisted.

"What's the matter?" he asked, puzzled by her reluctance.

She pushed him away and into the shadow of a pile of timber.

"I wanted to look at those, maybe I want to buy one." He was confused and if Ita didn't explain herself quickly that confusion would turn to anger.

"I know you do, but if they see you the price will be double or more," she said, by way of explanation. "Which one you like?"

"I don't know, I cannot see them from here," he laughed.

"Okay, you go over, choose one, pick it up and then walk off down there." She pointed towards the entrance gate. "When you are out of sight I will go and buy it for you."

Stuart followed her instructions and examined the model boats alone. There were two main types, painted and varnished. Like the prototypes, no two were the same. Eventually he settled on a white-painted one with blue lines. It was quite small and he guessed that he would not have so much trouble with it on the aeroplane on the way back. He held his chosen boat aloft and then set it down slightly to one side.

"How much?" he said slowly.

"Fifty," the man said. "Good boat."

"Too much." Stuart turned to walk away.

"Okay sir, how much? Forty? Yes, forty?"

Stuart shook his head and walked away.

The man ran after him. "Okay, thirty, mister, thirty."

Stuart shook his head and continued on. When he was by the gate he stopped and sat down, concealed from the seller's vision, but able himself to see what was happening.

Ita moved out and selected another boat, not the one Stuart had selected, to bargain over.

Stuart tried to signal to her but he was too far away.

She talked and gestured with the man and eventually she walked away. He ran after her with the wrong boat, but she resisted. Then she walked back and almost casually picked up Stuart's chosen one. In a few seconds the deal was done and she walked away with the prize.

"What was going on?" was Stuart's first question when she reached him. "I thought you had got the wrong one."

"No, I knew which one. First I got his price level. If I had chosen your boat it would have been too obvious. But I chose the bigger one, so he wouldn't suspect. Then I got his price down low, but I told him that it was still too expensive for me. So he offer me a smaller one, yours. I got the low price," she said with a satisfied smile.

"How much?" Stuart asked. "He wanted fifty from me, but that came down to thirty without much pressure."

"I got it for eleven thousand," she said with a smile, "and don't try to pay me for it. It's a present for you."

They left the quayside and found a taxi. It was almost twelve o'clock and Stuart was feeling hungry. "Lunch?" he asked.

Ita nodded and then spoke to the driver who nodded and set off. They drove through the old part of the city, past the railway station and through the crowded trading district of Glodok, which was busy even on Sunday.

They rolled up into the grounds of a big hotel.

"The Jakarta Intercontinental," Ita announced, as they swung around into the main entrance. "They have lunch and jazz on Sunday," she said, leading Stuart in through the main doors and up an escalator.

They did as well: an Indonesian jazz band complete with a singer, played and sang the five per cent of jazz that Stuart actually liked. The food too was good, the buffet extensive and inexhaustible. After two hours of eating and drinking, punctuated with long inter-course rests, Stuart and Ita left and returned to the Kedutaan Hotel.

They went up to Stuart's room and lay down and watched television in silence. They watched two films until after seven o'clock, Ita curled up against Stuart on the big double bed. It felt so comfortable, so complete, so close. Stuart was beginning to realise that he was deeply involved with Ita. What would happen when he got home to face Catherine? Even to think Catherine's name brought a shudder to him. He knew that he couldn't lie to her, that he couldn't cover it up. He didn't want to but he knew that he had to think what to do with her.

As long as he came back to Indonesia he knew that he would continue to meet Ita, that their relationship would get stronger. Somewhere in this situation something would have to give, something would have to break: Ita, Stuart or Catherine. Whatever happened, Stuart's children, Ralph and Colleen, would come off worst; that was the way it happened. They were always the victims. He had to stay with them, he knew, but what of Ita? He looked down at the small form curled up against his body for warmth and protection. Ita who had had such a life so far and was now so heavily involved with him, how would she react?

Ita interrupted his thoughts by sitting up and stretching. "I have to go, I'm sleepy and I want to go home to rest." She switched the television off.

Stuart offered no resistance: he needed some time to think. "Okay, I will call you when I know my plans."

She smiled and stroked his face. "Good."

"Thanks for today. It was, well, fabulous. I really enjoyed the boats, and that", he pointed at the wooden model on the table, "is my little tree."

She laughed. "Good night Stuart my darling." She kissed his lips gently and then turned to leave. She opened the door.

"Bye Ita, see you soon, take care," he said with feeling. He reached down and kissed her again and then she was gone.

He sat in the half-lit silence of his room. He held his head and, as earlier in the afternoon, his eyes moistened, and then he cried properly, for the first time in years, for what reason he didn't really know. He took a whiskey from the minibar, drank it and slept cradling the little bottle in his hands.

# CHAPTER 23

# BOROBUDUR

Stuart checked out the next morning and made his way to Anwar's office by taxi. The day was busy because he and Anwar had much to discuss about the forthcoming visits, and they didn't manage to leave the office until the late afternoon, only just managing to catch the last shuttle flight to Semarang. They stayed overnight in the Jasa Rakyat Hotel, which was set in a beautiful location on a hilltop to the south of the city centre. Stuart would have liked to stay longer but they had to leave early in the morning for Solo.

The first factory on the list was the factory that had most impressed them with sales possibilities on Stuart's second trip. That was, of course, before they had been to Mr Chan's place. They were well received and were presented with a copy of an enquiry document for a number of new machines.

Anwar and Stuart checked into the Djoglo Hotel in the centre of Solo for their second visit. They were both tired and didn't leave the hotel, preferring to eat and drink within its confines. In the bar, after a reasonable meal, Anwar sat musing, looking into a glass of fruit punch.

"What?" asked Stuart.

"Nothing really," Anwar replied.

"No, go on, what's on your mind?" Stuart urged.

"Well, it's just that I knew about those documents – the ones for the new machines that we got today – several months ago, before you came for the first time. I had already met your Mr Jackson and I was trying to do some investigation into the background." He paused and sipped his drink.

Stuart looked at him with interest.

"And I tried to get them to issue them to me, so that we could bid – open competition. But do you know they wouldn't! They refused – they said that their orders were not open to competition." He turned and looked at Stuart.

"That's progress," said Stuart. "If we bid."

"You must! Whatever you do you must bid," said Anwar forcefully. "They've given you the documents, so if you don't bid you might as well go home now and not bother coming back."

"Okay, when we bid, we might just be being used as a test price, to push the German prices lower," Stuart replied.

"Yeah, and that's just what you wanted to do last week, or have you forgotten – when we went round that big factory near Surabaya?" Anwar pushed.

"Yes, but I will not get much support back home for too much of that, not if every factory tries it on. We have to be selective," he said, looking at Anwar.

"Mmmm," was Anwar's reply.

"And that is your job, to tell me which ones to bid with force, which ones not to bother with too seriously. Everyone has limited resources, so I'm just signalling a warning, that's all." He went back to his drink while Anwar sat in silence, reflecting on the conversation.

The next day they visited another factory, new on Anwar's list. Again it appeared to hold out little prospect, but Stuart agreed to spend a day or so doing a survey. He spent Thursday in the factory and went back on Friday for a further meeting. On Friday afternoon, Anwar dragged a reluctant Stuart round a second new factory, which they visited again on Saturday morning, staying until after lunch.

When they finally left, Stuart was quite exhausted. It had been a hectic week.

"Where to now?" he asked Anwar as they sat in the back of the car preparing to leave the factory.

"Do you want to get back to Jakarta this weekend?" Anwar replied.

"Can we?" Stuart asked with a hopeful tone in his voice.

"Maybe, but I doubt it. There's not too many flights, it's late afternoon and we have to drive for at least three hours to get anywhere to catch a flight," Anwar replied, sounding distinctly disinterested in the prospects. "I'm not bothered. I told my wife that we may miss the weekend." He looked at Stuart. "And have you got anything to get back to Jakarta for?"

Stuart looked at Anwar's questioning and slightly cheeky face.

"No," he said with a smile, "I haven't."

"Okay, then we shall go to Yogjakarta and I will show you the real culture of Java, the history of the Javanese," Anwar replied with relish.

Stuart had suspected that Anwar wanted to spend some time alone with him, outside the confines of business and work. Stuart was beginning to realise that the relationship with Anwar was becoming strong and an important part of the potential business dealings between Ormistons and Indonesia. Whatever Stuart's personal desires for wanting to get back to Jakarta and to Ita, he wanted to build a good relationship with Anwar, one on which he could count in the future. It was one of Stuart's strong points that he could pick up on such feeling and act correctly: he had an uncanny knack of fitting in and forming good relationships. The one with Anwar was developing in a way that even Stuart was finding a little surprising.

Stuart knew that Ita would understand, that anything which was good for Ormistons' business in Indonesia was good for Stuart and Ita. He settled down to enjoy the rest of the weekend with Anwar, exploring the cultural past of Java and the Javanese.

The car took three hours to reach Yogjakarta. Stuart was very tired when they arrived but after a shower he succumbed to Anwar's infectious good humour and they went walking in the crowded streets and byways of the city centre. Stuart bought a few bits and pieces. He enjoyed bargaining and knew a few numbers to allow him to pretend to be bargaining in Indonesian. They ate in a small backstreet restaurant, satay and rice with beer served over ice, 'on the rocks' as Stuart joked.

Then Anwar wanted to go the disco in the hotel and Stuart felt that he had to oblige. It wasn't too full but Anwar threw himself on to the dance floor with gusto, leaving the exhausted Stuart in his wake. Anwar almost, but not quite, seemed to meet a woman and danced with this particular girl for longer than the rest, and later they sat together, all three, and talked, Stuart sitting on the edge as an observer.

By one-thirty Stuart wanted to go to bed, but Anwar was still very much active. Eventually, at two o'clock, Anwar relented and they left. As they went through the door, Anwar turned and passed some quick message to the woman with whom he had been dancing. Stuart began to wonder at all this – the overt familiarity and the secret signals. They agreed a time for the morning, not too early, and then separated at Stuart's door.

Stuart closed his door and listened to Anwar's footsteps moving further along the corridor. He was just beginning to turn towards his bed when he heard the distinct sound of footsteps, trying to be quiet, passing his door, in which direction he wasn't sure. Stuart smiled to himself: either Anwar was back on the prowl, back to the disco or the secret liaison was being realised. For Stuart, sleep was the only thing on the agenda.

The next morning, Stuart woke as early as usual. He lay around for an hour before washing and going down for breakfast. As he sat in the small coffee shop, the woman with whom Anwar had been dancing slipped quickly past and out of the door, dressed in the same clothes as the night before. Fifteen minutes later, Anwar came down.

"Well, good morning Mr Morgan," he beamed in expansive good humour.

"You got out of the right side of the bed this morning, then," Stuart said with a wicked smile.

"What?" Anwar asked with an expression of shock on his face.

"It's just an expression: if you're grumpy and bad-tempered you must have got out of the wrong side of the bed, so if you are as happy as you are, then you must have got out of the right side," Stuart explained in the manner of speaking to a child.

"Ohh," said Anwar, his expression of shock dissolving. "So long as it's the right or wrong side of the right bed, yes?"

Half an hour later they left the hotel, Stuart in his shorts, tee-shirt and sunglasses and Anwar in a light-brown, short-sleeved, safari-type suit. They took a *becak*, or pedal-powered taxi to the Kraton, the palace of the sultan of Yogjakarta.

The Kraton was a rather ornate corrugated iron-roofed building. Stuart was a little surprised at this, having been brought up on British castles and palaces, built of stone and brick. Anwar explained the history: the basic fabric and carvings were centuries old, only the roof was new. Outside, they visited the museum of the carriages of the sultan. Here, a number of small horse-drawn carriages, ornate and plushly furnished, slowly decayed in the heat and humidity, well cleaned and dusted but not kept in the sort of conditions that would ensure their preservation for a great length of time. Faded black and white or sepia photographs displayed the use of the carriages for ceremonial occasions. After so many sterile National Trust and other British museum displays, with everything preserved in aspic, everything with its little notice, everything catalogued, Stuart found the almost haphazard storage of so much history refreshing. He became more interested when Anwar found an old groom, who had worked in the stables with the Sultan's horses all his life, to act as a guide.

From the Kraton, they had a refreshing bottle of water and then took another *becak* to the Water Castle. On the way they passed through the bird market, a dense and closely packed area of shops, mostly filled, as the name suggested, with caged birds. Anwar explained that some songbirds were sold for vast sums of money, thousands of dollars. Their songs were recorded and sold hundreds of thousands of copies.

"Birds", Anwar explained, "are very important to Javanese men."

"Really?" said Stuart smiling.

"Why, why what's so funny?" Anwar asked as the *becak* rattled along.

"Do you not know what bird is slang for in English?" Stuart asked.

Anwar shook his head.

"For a young and attractive woman. So birds are important to Javanese men! I should hope so." Stuart laughed again and nudged Anwar's ribs.

"Yes, okay," said Anwar, a mite embarrassed.

With that they were silent for the rest of the journey to the Water Castle.

The Water Castle was more or less untouched by modernity. It remained very much as it had been left when the sultan last used it. It was kept clean and in good condition, but again no real attempt had been made to 'preserve it' or return it to its 'original' condition. It was decaying in accordance with its fabric. The stonework was, however, somewhat more durable than the wood and cloth of the Kraton's carriages.

Anwar found a guide and translated for Stuart. The main feature was a large pool, now devoid of water, around which was a stone wall and a promenade area. The promenade area had a number of large and ornate stone vessels which had once held exotic plants to give shade. On one side was a tall structure, from where the sultan could observe the maidens bathing. After he had selected one, the guide explained, she was brought up to one of the bedrooms. The bedrooms were small and slightly claustrophobic. Each bedroom had a stone bed, quite short and narrow. Stuart looked out through the small window and tried to imagine a pool full of semi-clad, or even naked Itas swimming and playing and of having his choice of any of them. There were two smaller pools, one reserved for the sultan himself and the other for queens and princesses.

Further into the Water Castle, their guide led them along a dark and humid tunnel. Light came from a few jagged holes in the roof where, due to the ravages of time, the roof had collapsed inwards. Ferns grew in around the edge of these makeshift skylights, casting a diffuse light. Water dripped. The floor was uneven and they had to proceed with caution. At the end they came to a circular chamber whose walls climbed upwards and inwards to a circular opening which admitted a gentle and soft light. This was the 'circular well', the guide explained. In the centre was a platform which could be accessed by four sets of wide stone steps. Around the walls were two levels of galleries similar to the one where Stuart and Anwar now stood. They stood in the upper one and there was a lower series of more numerous but slightly smaller ones. Originally, the lower tunnels had been filled with water, as had the three pools of the main part of the castle, and the symmetrical set of four stone steps would thus have been partially submerged. Stuart tried to imagine the past scene in the now decaying well. Some change in the water levels had drained them all and left them dry, probably saving them from complete collapse. Stuart was amazed by the complexity of the system, the adventurous nature of the builders and how such a castle must have looked like a place of the gods to ordinary people. He was, yet again, surprised and impressed.

From the Water Castle, they passed some small batik workshops where groups of people painstakingly produced batik prints, the hand-painted ones. Stuart had to stop and buy a small piece for framing. They sat and ate a light lunch at a mobile stall, a *'kaki lima'*, Stuart remembered.

Then Anwar directed them back to the hotel.

"What now?" asked Stuart in the air-conditioned comfort of the hotel lounge.

"A cold beer," Anwar replied, "a very cold one."

Stuart laughed and agreed and they drank one in silence. Anwar glanced at his watch. "Come on," he said jovially, his good humour continuing. "I now want to show you the 'wider cultural sense' of Javanese history." He laughed and patted Stuart's arm.

"Okay," replied Stuart, "I'm all for the wider cultural sense."

The car had arrived, as if by magic, at the front door of the hotel. They got in and were whisked away. The journey took more than an hour, almost one and a half, and it was mid-afternoon when the car pulled into a large roughly-paved car park. They stepped out into the heat and Anwar led the way across the car park and past the row of ramshackle stalls selling food and trinkets. They started to walk up a wide path which sloped upwards towards a distant hill.

"Where are we?" asked Stuart.

"Borobudur," Anwar replied in a deep and mysterious voice.

"Borobudur?"

"Yes, it's the largest Buddhist temple anywhere in the world," Anwar said with some pride.

"Buddhist? I thought Indonesia was mostly Islamic?" Stuart asked.

"Yes it is, but not far from here we have some very large Hindu shrines. Bali is almost completely Hindu, and we have Buddhists and Chinese Confucians."

"Catholics," Stuart interrupted.

"Yes, Catholics," Anwar repeated slowly. "And Protestants and Baptists and every other religion," he continued, picking up the pace of his speaking. "Are you Catholic?"

Stuart shook his head.

"Do you know any Catholics here?" Anwar asked, curious that Stuart should mention one particular religion.

Stuart shook his head in embarrassed silence.

The conversation faltered and paused: Stuart was embarrassed and Anwar conscious that he had touched a raw nerve, or at least a sensitive spot, in Stuart.

Stuart's silence could not be contained as they approached the main part of Borobudur.

"God, it's unbelievable!" he said excitedly as they got closer. "I've seen nothing like it before."

The whole square basic shape of Borobudur rose before them. Above the biggest base square rose tier upon tier of smaller squares, each forming a balcony or gallery overlooking the one below. On the top level were a series of bell-shaped domes silhouetted against the sky. The scale of the temple amazed Stuart.

"This is Buddhist, right?"

Anwar nodded in confirmation.

"So many religions side by side," Stuart shook his head in disbelief, "and living in peace together." He became slightly carried away by the more sentimental side of his nature.

"Well, not exactly in perfect harmony," said Anwar, trying to bring Stuart back down to earth. "People are still people and I'm sure that they have as many problems here as in England," he continued.

"Mmm, I suppose so, but here it seems different, here by all this." He waved his arms at the magnificent structure that grew ever closer as they walked.

Anwar smiled and allowed Stuart his fantasy.

They mounted the base level of the temple and walked around each gallery before ascending to the next level. Each gallery had carved walls and friezes depicting the complete history and teachings of Buddhism. Stuart was fascinated and they lingered long on each level, Anwar patiently allowing Stuart to look for as long as he wanted. The top levels were circular, not square like the lower levels. Two statues of the Buddha sat gazing serenely over the Javanese landscape. There were many buddhas, seventy-two, Anwar informed Stuart, but most were hidden in the stone bell-like constructions which they had seen from below. These were perforated to allow the seated buddhas within to see out. On the top level, Anwar completed a couple of circuits before sitting down in a particular chosen spot and glancing at his watch.

Stuart joined him after a final tour of the uppermost level of the temple. For a while they sat in silence.

"Not long now," said Anwar after about ten minutes or so.

"For what?"

"Sunset. It's the most beautiful time to be in this place," Anwar said, looking at Stuart, "and tonight is going to be a good one, I can tell."

Stuart looked out towards the sun, still high in the sky by English standards, but definitely on the way down in the tropical sky. As they sat and watched, the sky close to the descending sun began to change to a gentle orange glow. As the sun set on the horizon, the glow spread outwards along the horizon and upwards and over their heads. Stuart was sure that he could see the sun moving, but it was painful, even with sunglasses on, to look directly at the sun for long. The glow increased in intensity, the colour deepening from light orange to a vivid red at the centre; the range and extent of the colours in the sky was so great that it was not possible to take them all in without swinging the heads from left to right, from the horizon to directly above.

As the sun approached the horizon, its colour became the strongest, the most brilliant shade of deep orange that Stuart had ever seen. The surrounding sky was every shade of red, orange and crimson. As the disc of the sun crossed the horizon, its strength seemed to be at its height; on the point of exit, it gave its greatest show. Anwar nudged Stuart and pointed at the bell-shaped edifices and seated buddhas behind them. They were caught in the orange glow of the sun's dying rays, the light giving them a quite different appearance from before: the harsh stone edge was gone and buddhas appeared almost lifelike, the serene smile more visible, more expressive.

Stuart could now definitely see the disc of the sun moving, descending, becoming absorbed in the body of the earth. And then it was gone, its whole disc below the horizon. The sky continued to display its orange, red and crimson shades in a slowly fading glow of past glory. Soon that too was gone, the sun was down, the sky was rapidly darkening to full darkness and the sounds and feel of the tropical night were all around them.

Stuart had never been out in the Indonesian countryside in the dark before.  It felt strange, a little oppressive at first, the quietness, the heat and the gentle sounds from a distant mosque floating on the night air.

He and Anwar for a long time watching the gathering darkness.  They sat in silence, each in a private world of admiration of the splendour of nature.  Stuart felt slightly overwhelmed.

Anwar waited until it was completely dark before he put his hand on Stuart's arm and gently squeezed it.  He nodded in the direction of the car park and then they made a move.  Stuart stopped a couple of times to listen, to take in the atmosphere as they descended the galleries from the upper levels to the rough path that led to the car park.  Once again Stuart had been surprised and amazed by Indonesia.  Every turn he made, every new place he went, all had their surprises, their hidden facets, their beautiful side.

# CHAPTER 24

# RETURN TO JAKARTA

Late on Tuesday afternoon, Stuart found himself wandering through the domestic arrival hall of Sukarno Hatta Airport yet again. He was alone. Anwar had left Stuart on Monday evening, and Stuart had spent Tuesday looking round yet another factory. More contacts, more studies, more recommendations, more slim chances. He steered a course for the public telephones and dropped a one hundred rupiah coin in the slot. He telephoned Ita's number. He had not been able to get through to her on Sunday or Monday and he wanted to see her as soon as possible. His scheduled departure day was Wednesday, the next day.

Ita answered the phone. "Is that you, Stuart?" she asked excitedly.

"Yes, it is."

"You still in Yogjakarta?" she asked, a little worried that he was.

"No, Sukarno Hatta, on my way into Jakarta," he replied, much to her relief.

"Oh good. You didn't call earlier?" she asked.

"I tried, Sunday and Monday, but no reply." He pondered the plan for the evening. "Shall I come to your house now, straightaway?"

"Can you? You don't mind?" she replied.

"No, I'd like to, very much."

"Okay, see you soon, maybe an hour, yes?" she said.

"Yeah, I guess an hour. Until then, bye."

"Bye Stuart," she said quickly and dropped the phone.

Stuart arrived in Ita's street just over forty-five minutes later. He paid the driver and rang the bell and was surrounded by the same horde of children.

"Hello Mister."

"Hello there," Stuart replied, smiling at them.

They descended into a fit of giggles and ran off.

The housemaid showed Stuart into the house and Ita rushed down the stairs to meet him. She was quite her old self: the eyes were gleaming, the hair with its shiny lustre restored and she bounced and hopped in excitement at seeing him.

"Stuart, oh how are you?" she said after she had given him a kiss in the privacy of her bedroom.

"Fine, but I think I'm probably smelly. I spent the day in a hot factory and then flew back to Jakarta. Can I have a wash?" he asked.

"Mmm, yes, of course. You have a towel?"

He shook his head.

She pulled a small, thin, yellow towel from a drawer in the chest of drawers and handed it to him.

He stripped off and wrapped the towel round himself, a little shy with Ita standing in front of him fully clothed. He went into the bathroom, hung up the towel and looked at the tiled tub.

"Ita," he shouted, "what do I do?"

She put her head round the door. "You use that," she said, pointing at a red plastic scoop hanging up by the door.

"How?" he asked rather stupidly.

"I'll show you," she said, perfectly seriously.

She picked the scoop up and dipped it in the tub of cold water. "Like this!" she said with great glee, flinging the scoop of water over Stuart, who had, too late, realised the nature of his foolishness in asking her how.

"Shit, that's cold!" he shrieked. "You horrible girl!" he continued, still shouting and cuddling himself for warmth.

She just laughed, loud and long. "Well, you did ask me," she managed after the laughter subsided.

Stuart shook his head and took the scoop.

Ita retreated rapidly from the bathroom, closing the door.

After the shock of the first scoopful, he had to admit that using the scoop was a quick, refreshing and easy way to have an all-over wash. It was also very economical on water. He used only a few inches of water from the tiled tub to first wet himself, and then to rinse himself. He washed his hair as well, shaved and cleaned his teeth, all using the little red scoop.

He emerged, pink and clean, with the towel wrapped round his middle. Ita had organised a cup of tea for them both and turned out the main fluorescent light. The room was filled with the much kinder light from the bedside lamp. He sat on the bed, his back propped up against the headboard, his legs stretched out, still clad in nothing more than the small towel. He drank his cup of tea.

Ita sat on the other side of the room looking at him in silence. She had lit a mosquito coil in one corner. Its highly pungent smell wafted around the room giving it, to Stuart's uninitiated senses, an extremely exotic temper. As Ita looked and Stuart looked back, the air between them become alive with feeling: the tension, the anticipation mounted and Stuart felt the light, fluttery feeling rising in his stomach, his heart beginning to beat a little faster.

For a few minutes more, she just continued to sit and look at him at him with those big, brown eyes. She continued to look until Stuart was on the point of screaming out and demanding that she came to him, when, like so many times before, she reacted at exactly the right time.

She stood, slowly and deliberately. She brushed her hair back with both hands and looked at Stuart with the most blatant sexual promise that Stuart was sure he had ever encountered. She put her hands on the waistband of her jeans, undid the button and slid the zip down, the noise seeming to echo around inside Stuart's head. She pushed the jeans to the floor. Then she lifted the tee-shirt up and over her head, and dropped it on the floor beside the jeans. She rearranged her hair again. She stood for a while to allow Stuart to admire her, to admire the Marks and Spencer bra and knickers she wore.

He watched and admired.

Then she removed her bra, undoing the front fastening slowly and then sweeping the bra back and off her arms in a single swift motion. She dropped it to the floor.

Stuart felt his heart beat faster, felt himself bursting out from the confines of the towel, felt himself pumping with every beat of his heart. He felt light-headed, hot, sick in his stomach.

Then she rolled the knickers down the side of her thighs and she was naked. She stepped out of the knickers and walked forwards to the foot of the bed. She slid her small hands up his shins, over his knees and on to his thighs.

Stuart felt as if he were about to die.

She pushed the towel off the last bit which Stuart's erection had not been able to dislodge by itself and lowered her mouth over him.

Watching her do it was the most erotic thing he felt that he had ever seen. He gasped and moaned almost immediately.

"Stop," he breathed as she made her second stroke along his length.

She did so and looked at him.

He shuffled down the bed and lay flat.

She turned around and lay on him, her head towards his feet, his face close to her. Then he lifted his head up to her and began to kiss her in the most intimate way.

Her head dropped down and again, absorbed him into her mouth.

Ita was already very moist and Stuart lost himself in her, lost himself trying to drink her, to eat her, to taste and absorb her, to become part of her. His hearing went a little deaf, his head swam, the light-headed feeling grew stronger and he felt as though he were floating above the bed. The feelings coming from his groin were like none he had ever had before, even with Ita – this was special, different. Nothing was going to stop the climax; he couldn't, he let her continue while he continued. He felt his buttocks tense, his legs open a little, his knees pushing down to the bed while his bottom pushed up. He was coming. He plunged his face into her again, the taste, the smell of her heightening, enhancing his own feelings.

She moved and tensed herself as he pushed and kissed harder.

And then it was there, it seemed as though all the muscles of his body tensed and contracted in the first explosive surge. He stopped kissing her for a second and let out a loud gasp.

She took her mouth off him after the first contraction, but her small hand still massaged him through the rest.

His head lifted again after the first surge and his kiss resumed. She groaned and tensed and then relaxed, falling limp on his body, her hand still. He let his head fall slowly back to the pillow and his hands fall away from her hips and bottom. She slid slowly sideways off him and on to the bed. Both were breathing heavily and deeply.

Ita was the first to move; she went into the bathroom and Stuart heard her cleaning her teeth. When she came out, he went in and washed the sticky mess that was his groin. When he came out, Ita was lying on the bed, face down, her face resting on its right side, arms around her head with her hair flowing out across the pillow. Her skin seemed to glow and shine in the light, its very golden light brown colour entrancing him; it seemed not to be real. He sat on the edge of the bed and stroked her back with his left hand. It was real, it felt so silky smooth to his touch. Almost without realising, he began to massage her left shoulder, then his right hand joined in on her right shoulder.

"*Minyak,*" she murmured.

"Mmm?" he replied softly.

"Oil," she said again, a little louder, "in the cupboard."

He reached down and opened the small bedside cupboard. Inside were a number of small bottles. One had the word 'Minyak' visible. He took it out, cautiously opened it and smelled the contents. It smelled of some spice that he couldn't place. He poured a little on to his fingers and rubbed it between thumb and forefinger. The oil felt smooth and sensual. He dribbled a little on her back, her back shivering slightly as the cold oil fell on it. He started on her neck, on the two bands of muscle that ran up either side of the spine and into the skull close to her hairline. He ran his thumbs up both sides together in a smooth, hard motion. Then he worked from her shoulders, from the muscles over her collarbone, round and up on to her neck, to the hairline. She grunted contentedly as each massage stroke was completed.

He shifted his attention lower, to her back and shoulder blades, adding more oil and working in and around the tendons and muscles close to the edge of the shoulder blades. On the right-hand one, he found a little knot of hard muscle or tendon which jumped under the touch of his fingers. Ita squirmed as he pushed it.

"Sorry," he said gently, and continued more gently with both hands on the offending area. After a few minutes, the knot lessened and he resumed on both sides, massaging hard again.

"Too much sitting in front of the computer," she murmured.

"Mmmm," was Stuart's only reply as he busied himself with continuing to massage her. He worked lower and lower down her back, eventually shifting his position on the bed. He started to massage her whole back, starting from the small of her back, just above her bottom, running up the two cords of muscle, around the shoulder blades, over the collarbone and finally stopping just below her hairline. Sometimes he went up the middle of her back, sometimes he spread a little wider, running up her sides, over her ribs and skirting her armpits. On odd occasions he went even wider still and brushed her breasts with his fingers. And all the while he looked at her, at the golden skin, now glistening with massage oil, made smooth and sleek by the polishing of his hands. And all the while he drank in the exoticism of the situation: the mosquito coil smoking in the corner; the smell of the spice in the oil; the smell of Ita; the heavy warmth of the humid tropical atmosphere, so different from the air-conditioned comfort of the hotel room; the noise of the small lizards that ran over the walls and ceilings as they signalled to each other; the noise of the larger geckos as they called to the night air – all so exotic, all so intriguing, all so overwhelming for Stuart. He was lost in a fantasy world of his own creation, but the fantasy under his fingers was real.

After some twenty minutes of massaging Ita's back, Stuart moved to the bottom of the bed and oiled her calves in turn. Slowly he smoothed the fingers and thumbs of both hands into her left calf. He massaged the back of her knee and then her thighs, stopping short of her bottom. He repeated the massage on her right leg, noting the absence of anything but the wispiest of hairs over the whole extent of her legs. When he had finished both legs and was happy with the result, he sat astride her legs, with his bottom on the back of her knees. He dribbled oil on her bottom. Now he applied both hands to her buttocks and the tops of her thighs. He ran his thumbs inwards along the join between thigh and buttock, allowing his thumbs to disappear into the gap between her legs, further in with each pass. Then he pushed his thumb and hands up over her buttocks, massaging and kneading them firmly and symmetrically. Then he went back to the join line, easing his thumbs in further and further, closer and closer to her.

Her bottom began to move ever so slightly in time with his massage, her legs opening slightly, her bottom rising up.

Stuart saw her response and slid his hands over her buttocks, up her spine, over the shoulder blades and along her arms, lying down on her back as he did so, until he eventually reached her hands. He grasped both hands and they interlinked their fingers. He lowered his mouth and kissed her cheek.

"No condom," he whispered in her ear.

"No problem," she replied quietly. "Still safe."

Then she smiled, her eyes shut tight.

He nuzzled her hair and took a heady draft of the mixture of scents. Then he pushed himself back into the sitting position and manoeuvred himself into the right position. Ita's bottom was raised slightly and he eased himself into her with a slow deliberate motion. He let out a long breath as he moved deeper, Ita tensing and moaning a little. He lay down on her back again once he was inside, and they both relaxed to enjoy the sensations of the moment. The oil on her body, on his body contributed to a wider sensual sensation than that generated by intercourse alone. Their whole bodies became smooth and lubricated like the most intimate parts, sliding together as extension of the activity in their groins. It had now become an almost unbelievably sensual erotic experience. Stuart pushed himself back up and put his hands on her hips. He lifted her and pulled her towards him, pushing deeper, spreading his knees wider and feeling the smooth slide of his inner thigh against the outside of her buttocks. Feelings inside him rose again and he had the start of a sensation deep in his groin which was beginning to spread outwards. He leaned forward again and linked fingers with her.

She clenched her fingers tight against his. She held her breath and then let it out in a long, loud snort before gasping a new breath in to hold it again.

"Ohh God," she said quietly on the next breath. "Oh God, it's coming," she said again.

Stuart was now on the point of no return: he held himself still and tense, holding his breath against the moment.

Ita held her breath and then pushed back at him hard. He slid in a little further, she groaned loudly, and a sudden explosion of sensation in Stuart's groin forced him to moan loudly and uncontrollably as his orgasm surged. Ita's hands gripped his and she let out a long, almost whistling breath, and a little-voiced exclamation, "Oh God, I come."

Then she was still, then she was quiet. Stuart lay down gently on her back and attempted to catch his breath and wait for the sensations running through his body to subside.

They remained in this position for some time, each reluctant to disengage from the position that had given them so much pleasure. When Stuart finally rolled off her and lay on his back, the oil that had felt so erotic, so fantastic a few minutes ago now felt sticky and uncomfortable. Ita went into the bathroom and washed. She came out with a towel and wiped down Stuart's oily body. Then he slept.

When he awoke, almost an hour had passed. He lay naked underneath the white sheets of the bed. Ita was nowhere to be seen. He lay back and relaxed again. When she had not appeared after ten minutes he became a little alarmed at her absence. He looked around for his clothes. He could see them neatly folded on the back of one of the chairs. Ita's clothes were similarly folded on the other. He was just starting to get up when the door opened and Ita came in with a tray. She was dressed in a long, thin dressing gown made from something shiny. It clung to her body and revealed that it was all she was wearing. She set the tray down on the bed by Stuart.

"Hold it," she said.

Stuart obliged, and she lifted the two glasses of water off the tray and on to the bedside cabinet. On the tray was a single large plate filled with steaming noodles and vegetables.

"Mie goreng," she said, "or fried noodles in English."

"Did you make these?" he asked.

"Mmm, well, with a little help from the housemaid I did," she replied, handing him a fork.

They tucked in with relish, Stuart realising how hungry he was and Ita in her post-orgasmic eating mood.

"Make love and then eat," Stuart said in between mouthfuls.

"Yes of course. I can eat any time, but to make love with you like that is rare, so I must make sure to make love first. If you eat first, maybe you fall asleep, or you fart in the middle of it." She laughed at her own joke.

Stuart shook his head: so much humour was common throughout the world.

When they had finished and washed it down with a glass of water each, Ita looked at Stuart in a questioning way.

"What?" he asked.

"It's after ten o'clock. You want to go to the hotel or..." she paused.

"Or stay here with you?" he replied, finishing her sentence for her.

She nodded.

"I'll stay here," he said.

She leaned forward and kissed him, then she removed the plate, glasses and the tray from the bed and took them out of the room. When she returned, she slipped the dressing gown off and climbed, naked, under the sheet and entwined herself round Stuart; in a minute they were both asleep.

The next morning Stuart awoke in an empty bed. He looked around and found his watch on the bedside cabinet. It was just after six-thirty. He flopped back on the bed. 'Why did Ita have to wake so early?' he thought to himself. Every time they had slept together Ita had always been up first, usually up and away. The door creaked open and Ita pushed her way in with a tray. On the tray was a single large plate of fried rice, two forks and two glasses of water.

"What's that?" he asked, pulling a face at the sight of so much food so early in the morning.

"Breakfast," came the obvious reply. "Fried rice, the Indonesian speciality, nasi goreng," she continued, setting the tray down on the bed beside him.

She offered him a fork and, just to be polite, he ate some. It was good and tasty, he had to admit, but he couldn't really raise the enthusiasm to eat much so early.

Ita ate heartily. "Breakfast is the most important meal of the day," she said between mouthfuls. "You should eat."

He shook his head and lay back. When Ita had eaten her fill, she drank a full glass of water. She offered the second to Stuart.

He shook his head.

"What then?" she asked, with her small child expression.

"Tea," he replied.

"Of course," she replied smiling. "Tea."

She stood up and took the tray.

Stuart drank the cup of milkless tea quickly when she returned.

"Come on, wash," she commanded, and moved into the bathroom.

The naked Stuart followed her.

She had already removed her dressing gown and stood coiling her hair up on top of her head. She picked up a toothbrush and pushed it though the resulting bun to secure it.

Stuart quietly picked up the small red scoop and filled it from the tub. Ita was engrossed in sorting out her hair. He threw the scoop over her.

"Stuart!" she shouted. "Don't! Stop it!"

She twisted and tried to move out of the way as he filled the scoop a second time. "Don't you dare!" she said through clenched teeth, her hands still trying to push the toothbrush through her bun. "Don't, No!"

Stuart menaced her with the scoop, grinning widely. He slowly let the scoop fall to his side, relaxing his threat.

Ita too relaxed and completed fixing her hair. She dropped her arms to her side, and Stuart flicked the second scoopful over her.

"You!" she said, struggling to find an English word to express her feelings. "You! Stuart, you're like a little boy."

He laughed. "You did it to me last night! We're even."

"Okay finish, now give me the scoop and I want to finish the wash you started." She stood facing him, her right hand outstretched, her left resting on her hip.

Stuart looked at her as she stood and her beauty swept over him again. She looked too good to be real. He handed over the scoop meekly.

"Thank you," she said firmly. She put the scoop in the water and made to pour it over herself, but, almost inevitably, she threw it over the still-dry Stuart.

He knew it was coming and he refused to flinch, or duck. He just smiled. "Thank you, I wanted a wash."

With that, they both washed and rinsed in co-operation rather than attempting to extend the game any further.

Ita slipped the dressing gown on again and disappeared downstairs as Stuart came out of the bathroom. When she came back, Stuart was dressed, apart from his shoes.

"I've arranged for a taxi, in half an hour. My friend takes me to work."

"Okay. Er..." He paused. He had to tell her that he was due to leave Indonesia that evening. "You know I'm leaving today, for England?" he said quietly.

"Yes, I know," she said in her small voice. "I'm going to take the afternoon off, to come with you, if that's all right."

She looked down at her feet.

Stuart walked over to her and lifted her face to look at his.

Her eyes still looked down.

"Yes, of course it's okay. I will have to be at the airport at five," he said, trying to meet her eyes.

"You come here before, then we go," she said, still looking down.

"Yes."

She looked up and smiled, a sad smile, but a smile. "It takes an hour from here, so come at four."

He reached out and hugged her to his body. She slipped her arms around him and nuzzled into his chest.

Stuart's taxi came and he went first to the Kedutaan Hotel. He approached the reception desk.

"Hello Mr Morgan," the receptionist said with the usual smile. "I thought you were staying here last night, you were down in our computer to check in."

"Er yes, I had a change of plan," he said, not wanting to look her in the face. "Are there any messages for me?"

"I'll check. No, none," she replied, looking down at the computer. "Are you checking in now?"

"No, I'm not. My suitcase is still here, in your store."

"You want it now?" she asked quickly.

"Can I collect it this afternoon, before I leave?"

"Yes, no problem. Where are you going?" she asked.

"Home, back to England."

"When are you visiting us again?" she asked, looking hurt that he was leaving.

"Soon, very soon," he replied, smiling back. He liked the hotel very much; the friendly staff made the place.

He left and got a taxi up to Anwar's office. Anwar was in the reception area.

"Good morning Mr Morgan," he said, scanning Stuart's casual clothing. "Get back all right last night?"

Stuart nodded.

"Hotel okay, no problems?" Anwar continued, a twinkle in his eye.

"Mmmm," Stuart replied.

"And you're leaving today, right, this evening?"

"Yes, I want to go from here about three."

"Okay, no problem. We discuss this morning, have a lunch and then you can go."

Stuart nodded and followed Anwar into the main office.

# CHAPTER 25

# DEPARTURE OR NOT

Sitting in the back of the taxi on the short journey back to the hotel from Anwar's office, Stuart tried to sum up the future work and rationalise his programme for returning to Indonesia. He had a number of competitive bids to sort out, some other offers, such as the ones for Mr Chan, and of course, Mr Chan's spares order to process. The amount of work was unlikely to take less than six weeks to complete, if everything went well, given that there would be some delays, some distractions. He guessed that eight weeks, say a round two months, would be about the right length of time. This consideration was more for Ita's benefit than any other reason, because he knew that she would ask and he wanted to be ready with a realistic answer.

He wandered into the hotel, where his favourite receptionist was on duty.

"Mr Morgan!" she said brightly. "You didn't stay here last night," she continued cheekily.

He shook his head. "I've come for my suitcase," he said with an embarrassed shrug of the shoulders.

"You are going back today, to England?" she asked.

"Yes I am."

"We will all miss you. When will you be back?"

"A couple of months, I think," he said with a sense of *déjà vu*: it was almost a re-run of the conversation earlier that morning with one of the other receptionists. "Any messages?"

She shook her head.

"Okay, I must go."

She extended her hand to him. "Bye bye, Mr Morgan. Please come back soon." This time there was genuine feeling in her voice and expression.

He collected his suitcase from the hotel and got a second taxi to pick up Ita for their journey to the airport. The drive was slow, slower than he remembered, but it was still before four when they pulled up outside Ita's house. He asked the driver to wait and pressed the bell. Ita wasn't quite ready and he spent five fretful minutes waiting in the musty hallway.

"Come on," he said with a smile to disguise his impatience. "We're late."

"Okay Stuart," she said, kissing him on the cheek. "We will get there – it's only five past four."

They got in the taxi and left. She sat close to him, touching his leg and holding hands, squeezing occasionally.

The road from Ita's house back towards the city was busy. The further they went the busier it became and the slower the cars moved, stopping altogether for minutes at a time. Stuart became more agitated as the stops grew longer and the movements forward a shorter distance each time.

"What's the matter?" he asked, his voice rising in annoyance.

"Don't worry, my darling," Ita said, trying to soothe him, to calm him, "we've got time."

As the halts got longer, however, even Ita's happy optimism faded. She became quiet and shrank away from Stuart, losing contact with his leg and leaving go of his hand.

"*Machet*," the driver muttered under his breath. "*Maacheet*," he repeated, drawing the word out.

"What does that mean?" Stuart asked.

Ita shook her head.

The driver pushed the car forward, easing it into a small gap on the left, one wheel in the gutter. He turned down a small side street and suddenly they were moving again. Stuart sat back and relaxed for a second. They drove on at speed down small roads, round tight bends, in between people and cars before emerging a few hundred metres further down the road they had just left.

The driver banged the steering wheel with his hand. "*Wah doh machet terus*," he said loudly.

"What's he saying, Ita?" Stuart asked as Ita sat in the corner, close to the door.

She looked at him bleakly. "It means stuck, something like that, jammed."

"Oh great, that's all I need! My first traffic jam in Jakarta on the way to the airport, twenty-four hours of travelling ahead and I have to sit here in this bloody taxi with hardly any AC and sweat myself stupid." His voice rose in anger as he spoke.

Ita shrank further away into her corner.

Finally, some time after five, they reached the main road which led to the toll motorway to the airport. There was still about six or seven kilometres to go before they reached the toll road but Stuart felt a little easier. He sat back and checked his watch again. Twenty past five. He said a little prayer.

They moved a bit quicker along this bigger road. Then, as they approached a set of traffic lights, all the vehicles seemed to slow at once and stopped. Horns blared loudly, but nothing moved. Stuart could see that the traffic lights were green but still nothing moved. They sat and he fumed. Suddenly, people seemed to be moving all around them, alongside the taxi, moving towards the lights. Drivers got out of their cabs, people hung out of the windows of the buses, their driver wound his wind down and shouted to someone in the crowd. He smacked the steering wheel again and muttered something.

Stuart looked questioningly at Ita.

"Crash," she said quietly. "At the red lights."

"Shit!" Stuart said loudly, causing Ita to jump a little. He flopped back against the seat in defeat.

Sirens announced the arrival of the police and other services. But still they did not move forward. It took almost forty minutes before the cars began to move again. It was exactly six o'clock. One hour left to departure. It was still possible for Stuart to catch his flight if they could clear the traffic lights quickly. Their forward progress was initially good, moving half the distance to the lights in a few minutes, but then they got stuck again as cars and buses from the left side tried to come across to their side to get round the crash site. The 'me first' attitude of all the drivers caused a whole series of little jams as no one gave way. Each took minutes to sort out, and progress became sickeningly slow. At the junction itself, the crash soon became visible. An overloaded truck, probably crossing after the lights had changed against him, had been hit by a small jeep-type car. The damage was not so bad to either vehicle, but the truck had shed its load all over the intersection and all over the jeep. The police and some medical people were trying to get one person out of the jeep, fighting through the truck's shed load to do so. Stuart had never seen so many people standing and watching. There were thousands, all stood round, with more arriving all the time. They created a second traffic hazard, worse than the original crash.

The three or four lanes of Stuart's direction and the same number of lanes from the other direction were both reduced to one lane each. Cars to the left of their taxi pushed across to get round the crash. Four lanes at right angles squeezed into one and then these two opposing streams tried to cross each other. The result was complete chaos. Drivers tried to sneak round the jam, to get in somewhere else, but all that did was to lock in those in the centre of the jam even more firmly, so that no one could move forward or back. The noise of the horns was deafening. The police seemed more concerned with protecting the lorry's shed load from being stolen than with directing the traffic chaos all around them.

"Look at them!" shouted Stuart in frustration. "Why don't they wait? Why can't they see they're making it worse by going round? Are they all stupid?"

Ita sat quietly looking out of her window at nothing in particular, hiding her face from Stuart.

Stuart glared at the driver of a truck which blocked their way, his way blocked by a car trying to get in front of Stuart's taxi. The driver grinned around at everyone; he laughed and joked with the driver of their taxi.

"Look at him! He just thinks it's bloody funny!" Stuart ranted, his temper lost.

It took Stuart's taxi more than half an hour to cross this one intersection. His rage settled to a silent fume.

Beyond the intersection the road was clear. The driver pushed on with speed, swerving and dodging the cars and lorries in a manner that Stuart would have found alarming if he had not been so angry. But the watch on Stuart's wrist showed that they would probably lose the battle with time. They entered the toll road with less than fifteen minutes left. It was no use. The driver tried, but even on the toll road slower traffic seemed permanently to be in the outside lane, always blocking progress.

At the airport Stuart jumped out even though his watch told him it was too late – he had to try, maybe the plane was late. He left Ita in the taxi with some money to pay. He rushed in and stood breathlessly at the Singapore Airline check-in, smiling hopefully, holding his ticket.

"Flight closed sir," the woman at the desk said, glancing at his ticket.

"Left already, already take off?" he persisted.

"Not yet take off but closed."

His heart leapt. Maybe there was a chance. "I have a connection to England, please."

She shook her head. "Flight closed."

"Please?" he pleaded.

She picked up her radio and babbled for a moment. She shook her head. "Already doors closed and taxiing. Sorry."

Stuart's shoulders sagged. He was suddenly aware of how hot he was, of how sweaty and tired he felt from the taxi ride, from the frustration and now the let-down. He had missed the flight. Dejectedly he turned and shuffled out into the heat again. Ita was standing waiting for him, looking lost and sad.

"Gone?" she asked.

He nodded. "Please look after my bags. I want to rebook."

He moved slowly back inside and over to the ticket window. "Can I get another flight to Singapore tonight?" was his first question.

The girl looked at his ticket and shook her head. "I'll have to cancel your reservation to London," she said after tapping on the computer for a minute.

"Okay. When can I get to London?" he asked.

She pondered for a while, tapping the computer, shaking her head, tutting.

Stuart looked on anxiously.

"Not until Saturday, leaving Saturday evening, seven o'clock," she said, her deliberations complete.

"What?" he almost shouted. "Saturday! It's only Wednesday! What am I supposed to do?"

"Sorry," she replied stiffly.

"Okay, I'm sorry," Stuart apologised. "Business, first class?" he asked in a more reasonable tone.

"Problem is from here to Singapore, all airlines full all classes until Saturday. Is common problem for us. I will wait list you. Where are you staying?"

"The Kedutaan Hotel," he said.

"Okay, you're confirmed on Saturday, same flight numbers as today, wait listed on Thursday and Friday." She pushed the tickets back to Stuart.

He went back out to join Ita.

"Saturday," he said, "I can't leave until Saturday – everything's full."

Ita received the news silently.

He led the way to a taxi and directed the driver to the hotel. Ita followed silently in his wake and sat in a corner of the back seat, as far away from Stuart as it was possible to get in the confines of the small car. The journey back was uneventful, fast even. The intersection where the crash had occurred was already cleared. They sped back to the hotel in fifteen minutes less than an hour, one of the quickest journeys Stuart had ever had from the airport; the irony was not lost on him.

Stuart led the way into the hotel and up to the reception desk.

"Well, hello Mr Morgan." It was the same receptionist to whom Stuart had talked to a couple of hours before. "I thought you were leaving today, for England."

"I was," he said in an exasperated tone, "but the road was so busy I missed my flight."

She nodded. "So I understand. You're the second person to check back in today because of that."

She busied herself with checking Stuart in. He signed and collected his key.

"Oh," she called after him. "A message for you."

"For me?" he said, confused. How could anyone know that he was here?

"Mmm." She handed him a small piece of paper.

"Please call Mr Anwar urgently," he read out loud; the time written on the message was four-fifteen.

They went up to the room, Ita following a step behind, still silent since the airport. He opened the door and threw down his bags. She sat in the chair in the corner by the window, staring at her feet. She didn't even try to move and hide as she had always done when the bell boy brought Stuart's small suitcase.

"I want to make some calls," he said, sitting on the bed.

She made no response.

First he dialled Anwar's home number.

"Oh Stuart, thank God you got my message! Where are you – the airport?" Anwar said, obviously relieved.

"No, in the hotel. I missed the flight. There was a crash and a hell of a traffic jam."

"Oh, that's good, well, I mean, not the crash but because you're still here," Anwar said.

"Why?"

"Because Chan rang. He wants us to go to Surabaya tomorrow – he says it's very urgent, we must go. He wants to see us in the afternoon and then for dinner," Anwar said.

"This serious?" Stuart asked, a little annoyed for no reason that he could think of.

"Mmmm yes, it is serious, I think it's something very important. You can come? When is your new departure date?"

"Saturday, everyone's full until then."

"That's common," Anwar replied. "It's the flight to Singapore that's always full."

"Yes, you're right, that's the problem. I can come tomorrow, no problem," Stuart replied. "Nine in your office?"

"Yes, nine o'clock is fine. We'll stay the night there, okay?"

"Okay." Stuart dropped the phone after a goodbye each. "One more call," he said to the silent and almost comatose Ita; she had not moved since she had sat down.

He dialled his home number. "Hello Catherine, it's me," he said, recognising his wife's voice instantly.

"Where are you?" she asked icily, no other greeting being offered. It was the first time that he had called during his trip.

"Still in Jakarta. I missed my flight – there was a car crash."

"Are you hurt? Were you involved?" Catherine said with concern in her voice, immediately allowing twelve years of knowing and loving Stuart to come to the fore, to burst through all the other things she had been feeling about him since that fateful Saturday at the thought that he could have been hurt.

"No, it was someone else, another car, not our taxi," he continued. "It's just as well I've been delayed, as I've got to go on another visit tomorrow, a very important one."

"When will you be leaving then? Tomorrow?" she asked hopefully.

"No, not until Saturday."

"Saturday!" she shouted down the phone.

"Yes, there are no flights until then," he said, as calmly as he could. "First, business or economy on any airline: they're all full. I'm wait listed for tomorrow and Friday, but I'm not hopeful."

"Okay," she said in a quiet voice. "Is everything else okay?"

Stuart knew what she meant. He looked over at the silent woman by the window. "Yes, everything is okay, according to plan," he lied, as he sat in his hotel room looking at Ita. "Everything's okay. I have to go – I've got to meet the agent again this evening for a talk about tomorrow," he lied again, surprised at how easy it was with a phone and twelve thousand kilometres between him and his wife.

"Okay, bye Stuart."

"Bye," he repeated and the phone went dead.

He looked up and looked at Ita again. "Ita," he said calmly, "you okay?"

She gave no response.

"I want a quick shower then we go out, yeah?" He tried to sound bright.

When she still did not respond, he stood up and crossed the room to her. He knelt down in front of her and put his hand under her chin, attempting to raise her face to his. She didn't resist, but wouldn't look him in the eye.

"What's the matter, Ita darling?" he asked in a little boy voice, looking up at her with his head lowered, his eyes like a child's looking up at an adult, trying to curry favour.

She refused to look at him.

He tried again and she glanced at him, her lips pulled in, her eyes red, tears streaking her face.

Stuart thought that she almost laughed, or at the very least smiled. But she turned her head away again and the moment was lost.

"What do you want to do?" he asked again, still in his little boy voice.

"I," she said quietly and hesitantly, "I want to go home." She paused. "Now," she said a little more forcefully.

Stuart stood up and back, suddenly tired of trying to get through to her, tired of everything around him: the heat, which left him so uncomfortable now; the delays; the stupidity of the other drivers – their attitude, their smiles and jokes at the chaos they created; the missed plane; the lies on the phone to Catherine. He gave up.

Ita stood and walked towards the door, glancing at him once, her eyes full of sadness. "Bye Stuart," she said and was gone.

He had a sudden urge to run after her, but he seemed rooted to the spot. He didn't move.

After a few minutes he showered to wash the heat and stress away from him. He felt numb and tired. He lay down to sleep, but sleep would not come. After an hour of tossing and turning, he gave up and got dressed. He left his room and went straight down to The Inne. He sat on a stool and drank beer without a thought of Ita, or anything else for that matter, until the barman waved his bill at him: the music had finished, the bar was closing. Stuart had gone through ten glasses. He stood, wobbled slightly and tottered off to bed, and this time sleep came directly.

## CHAPTER 26

## MR CHAN'S REWARD

After substantially less than twelve hours in the hotel, a slightly tired but more or less otherwise unaffected Stuart checked out. Anwar was in his office pacing nervously in a manner that Stuart had never seen before. It made him realise the seriousness of what Chan must had said to Anwar. He didn't start any conversation or try to communicate with Stuart other than to say hello. Stuart decided to wait and let Anwar be the initiator of any conversation.

They left for the now familiar drive to the airport, the third time that Stuart had passed that way in the last sixteen hours, and he was fed up of the journey, the stops, the jams, and the way most of the local drivers merely laughed at the chaos, and the jams. Still, in Anwar's white Toyota Crown, the air-conditioning worked, the ride was comfortable and the driver behaved in a more reasonable manner than most taxi drivers. For the whole journey to the airport, to Surabaya and to Chan's isolated factory, Anwar remained in his pensive, uncommunicative mood. He was the second uncommunicative Indonesian with whom Stuart had had to deal in the space of the last twelve hours.

They arrived at Chan's factory at lunchtime. Chan's gracefully beautiful wife, ever-attentive despite the fact that they had interrupted her lunch, showed them into the main meeting room and provided tea.

"My husband is around the factory. He will be back soon," she said as she brought in the tea, handing a cup to Stuart and Anwar with her right hand as required by Indonesian etiquette.

Stuart was glad of the tea. It was better than that served on the aeroplane and he was now feeling the thirst effects of his ten glasses of beer the night before. He drank quickly but noticed that Anwar left his untouched. On the table in front of them were three cardboard boxes, each fastened and sealed with wide parcel tape, each wrapped with coloured nylon string.

Anwar stared at them for a long time. He pushed one gently, assessing the weight by its resistance to being moved across the smooth table top. It was obviously heavy, obviously full of something. Anwar allowed himself a little smile. Still he did not reveal anything to Stuart.

Chan bustled in. "Hello Mr Stuart, Anwar," he said, extending his hand to each in turn. "Sorry late," he continued in his typically clipped Chinese English. "Looking round factory. I always do this in lunchtime. You want to eat, drink?"

"We have a drink already from your charming wife," Stuart said in a gentle and respectful voice, "and for me, I prefer to sort out the business first and eat later. If I can do both at once maybe it upsets the stomach," he continued with a smile, trying to lighten the atmosphere a little.

Chan laughed heartily. "Yes, my wife very good woman, and I agree, we business first and tonight we have dinner together, yes?"

"I think that that is the best plan," Anwar said quietly. They were almost the first words he had spoken that day.

"Okay," said Mr Chan, "this for you to look at." He waved his hand at the boxes. "You take away from here, you look, you copy, *in secret*," he added forcefully, "then tonight I come to your hotel, we have dinner and I take back."

Anwar nodded and Stuart looked from one to the other, confused.

"Business finish." Chan laughed again.

Three men appeared and carried the boxes out, one each, to Chan's waiting car.

Stuart and Anwar checked into the hotel, and all the boxes were delivered to Anwar's room. After a quick wash and brush up, Stuart joined Anwar in his room. Anwar had ordered tea and they waited for it to arrive before they attacked the three boxes sitting on the floor. Stuart was desperate to ask Anwar what it was all about, but he held back, convinced that the boxes would show him what was going on.

Anwar sat back in the chair and sipped his tea, offering the first opening to Stuart. Stuart untied the string carefully, wrapping it into a ball for later use. Then he took out his small key ring penknife and sliced easily through the layers of wide brown tape that covered one of the boxes. He gingerly opened it and peered in.

"Well?" asked Anwar as Stuart looked in.

"Well, it appears to be full of files or books and papers," he replied.

"Take them out and let's look," Anwar said impatiently.

Stuart removed the uppermost file, sat on the bed and opened it. At first he was confused. It appeared to be an offer document from Ormistons' main competitor, the German company. Then, as he read further he realised that that was exactly what it was.

"Well?" asked Anwar for the second time. "Is it of use to you?"

"It would appear to be an offer, a tender, for some machines for..." he shuffled through the pages "...for Chan's factory, from our German friends." He shuffled through some more pages. "And," he continued, "it seems to have all the price and technical schedules of the German machines, the financing offer, everything."

"It is useful to you?" Anwar pressed again.

In Stuart's hands it was an almost priceless document: he knew the competition's price, he knew the technical offer, he knew the financing offer, and they could now put together a competing offer, knowing that they could undercut, knowing that they would beat the competition in all areas. It increased their chances of breaking into the market one hundredfold.

"Could be of use, I suppose," Stuart said with a non-committal shrug of the shoulders.

"Could be?" Anwar almost shouted, sitting up in surprise at Stuart's response.

"Well, okay, in the right hands, like mine, such information gives us one hell of an advantage in making our offers to Chan." He could not stop the smile coming to his lips.

Anwar relaxed and settled back down to enjoy his tea.

Stuart examined the rest of the contents of the first box. All of it related to offers made to Chan by the main competitor, the offers dating back several years. The offers were undoubtedly attractive and Stuart could not help wondering why Chan had not taken any of them up over the last few years.

Anwar left his tea and began to open the string on the other two boxes. Stuart went to work with his knife to open the tape. Inside each of the other two boxes were similar sets of documents, offers and tenders by the Germans, and some others from an Indian manufacturer, not only to Chan's company, but to other factories all over East Java. The range of the offers covered a large proportion of the Germans' complete production. With this information Stuart and Ormistons could undercut in almost every area and make life very difficult for the German company. He smiled and shook his head at the treasure trove that Chan had handed them.

"You want to copy?" Anwar asked.

Stuart nodded and Anwar disappeared out of the door.

He returned a minute or two later. "All arranged. We can use the machine in the business centre, alone, unobserved," he reported. "Now how much do you want to copy?"

"All," Stuart replied hopefully.

"What, all of them?" was Anwar's response.

Stuart nodded.

"Oh come on, you must be able to reduce it – that will take us hours," Anwar replied. "Here" – he tossed Stuart a yellow block of sticky labels – "mark the sections. I'll get busy with the copying. Now let's go."

And with that, they started to pull the documents to pieces, on Stuart's direction, and copy them. It took them more than three hours to do even the reduced amount that Stuart wanted. He had reduced the volume from three boxes down to one. Anwar produced a fourth box and some parcel tape and they carefully rebound the original documents and stacked them back in the original three boxes. Anwar punched holes in the newly copied material and made neat files of it for Stuart. Then they packed it into the fourth box and bound it up with tape.

"Okay, good job done," said Stuart when they had finished. It was six-thirty. "What time is he coming?"

Anwar shook his head. "Don't know. He'll call when he arrives."

"Right, I want a shower and a change. If I don't hear from you in the meantime, I'll see you downstairs at, what, seven-thirty?"

Anwar nodded. "Take your box, then it doesn't get mixed up with the rest," he said as Stuart turned to leave.

Stuart manhandled the heavy box downstairs to his room. He sat and looked at it for a while and his good spirits returned as he considered the use he could make of it and how much their chances had improved. He showered and changed and then sat to watch television for a while. Then he noticed the telephone, switched the television off, picked up the handset and dialled.

"Hello," a small voice at the other end said.

"Ita?" he asked.

"Yes. Stuart, is that you?" she replied, her voice loud and full of happiness.

"Yes, it is. How are you?"

"Fine, I'm okay. Where are you?"

"In Surabaya, I'm..." he replied.

"When are you coming back here, to Jakarta?" she said, interrupting him.

"I'm coming back tomorrow and then leaving on Saturday," he said, giving her the full plan.

"I'm so glad you called me," she said, her voice small again. "I was worried that after last night you wouldn't, that you would just leave."

"No, of course not. I missed you last night. I wanted to run after you, but I couldn't," he said softly.

"I'm glad you didn't. You were so angry with me! You were so upset that you couldn't leave Indonesia. I was very upset." She paused.

"I was never angry with you – I was just angry with all the cars, the traffic, the delay. I don't like to miss flights. But I was never angry with you. I'm a stupid European with a temper. Sometimes I cannot control it. But I was not angry with you."

"You sure? I thought you were angry with me and everything in Indonesia," she said.

"I was, for a while, but never with you. Now it's all gone. Everything in Surabaya is good," he said, trying to be bright.

"And then", she said, continuing in her small voice, "your other life came too close to me."

"Er yes, the phone call. It was very stupid of me to do that," he said, his voice defensive. "I should not have done that to you."

"No, you not stupid: I am too sensitive. I know your other life and I can forget it most time, but last night it came too close to me, and I could not cope with it – after you being angry, everything was too much for me. So I had to go." She sniffed a little, as if trying to hold back the tears. "But then I was worried if you don't call me again, or we not to meet before you leave. So I'm so glad you call me now."

"Oh Ita, I could not leave Indonesia without seeing you again after last night. I will be back tomorrow afternoon. Shall I come to your house?" he asked.

"No. Can I come to your hotel, straight from my office?" she replied. "About six-thirty or seven, that okay?"

"Fine, see you tomorrow, Ita my love, tomorrow."

"Bye Stuart, bye." And the phone went dead.

Downstairs in the lobby bar a few minutes later, Stuart joined Anwar, who was already seated and halfway through a fruit punch. Stuart ordered the obligatory beer.

"No sign?" he said.

Anwar shook his head. "He'll be here."

"What's behind all this?" Stuart asked after his first long mouthful of cold beer.

"What?"

"That lot upstairs."

Anwar paused before he answered. "Well, let's just say that I'm not the only one here in Indonesia who is trying to get at the dominance of our German friends. And I do spend time visiting these people when you're not here."

"Oh?"

"Monopoly is good for no one except the holder of the monopoly: simple business sense," he shrugged.

"I know that," Stuart said, "but why after so many years? Why start now?"

"All it takes is someone to try," Anwar replied simply. "If you had tried before, a few years ago, maybe you would have had success then." He paused for a sip. "Why didn't you? I mean try earlier to break into this market?" He looked hard at

Stuart, who offered no reply. "I mean you are so big in South America, in some parts of Africa, India especially, so why not try here?"

"Everyone likes a monopoly for himself," Stuart replied slowly. "Many years ago, many companies decided to spilt the world up and stop competing head on in every market."

"A club?" Anwar asked.

"Sort of. A cartel is the usual name."

"So I ask you now, why should you now decide to come into this market at this time?" Anwar replied.

"Well, some of us don't agree with such, what shall I say, arrangements. We believe that it's bad for business in the long term." He shrugged his shoulders. "It makes you lazy about giving good prices, good service or good products – development suffers."

"So who benefits?" Anwar asked, a little puzzled. "Your description makes it sound like nobody gets anything from a cartel."

"Well, that's not quite true. If they hold up, the people and companies involved can make big profits by not fighting, but you all have to hold it together for it to work."

"And someone isn't?" Anwar asked. "Should I say, playing the game, yes?"

"That's right – someone's not, and you and I are going to benefit."

"Your company," Anwar said, ignoring the last part of Stuart's sentence.

"Here of course yes, but in other places, no."

"So you mean they attacked you, in your, how shall I say, protected markets?"

Stuart nodded.

"So you want to get at them here?"

"And other places. But it was a hard job for me to persuade our management to even try. They wanted to patch things up, to reset the arrangements so things could carry on as before." Stuart laughed.

"So from your approach here, you and I will benefit, and I hope Chan and the others too. I want you and your company to give us a full commitment here, not halfway as a way to get your little club back in order."

"Well, not from me, that's not my idea. We may not have been the ones to break the arrangements and we may have lost out in some other areas, but we are not going to give up until we win. And with Mr Chan and the Indonesian textile mafia we might succeed here."

Anwar laughed. "Don't say that in front of Chan – the Indonesian textile mafia." He laughed again. "That's not a bad description though." He finished his fruit punch drink and ordered two beers. "You see, you have to understand that Chan's an old-fashioned trader, like most Chinese businessmen. He likes to deal, to trade and play one off against the other. He doesn't have much idea about long-term planning."

"You said that before. Do you think that his wife is behind this?"

Anwar nodded. "It seems, Mr Morgan," said Anwar smiling, "that you have scored a success with Mrs Chan. She likes you and believes that you can offer them a good deal." He patted Stuart's arm. "But I'm glad I understand more about your reasons. I might have been a little nervous if I had not known you first, but you and I, we understand, yes?"

Stuart nodded. "But our reasons are the same as yours," Stuart answered.

"How?" asked Anwar, a little surprised.

"Remember what you told me when I first came, that the agent of the Germans was encroaching on some other business area, right?"

"Ohh yes, I do remember. Yes, I suppose you are right."

"I was worried about that at the time. I have never told that to my office – they might have run away if I had." He laughed. "But now I agree, Anwar, you and I do understand each other and I trust and believe in you."

Anwar nudged Stuart in the ribs. "Chan," he whispered.

Stuart looked round and saw the suited figure of Mr Chan looking around the reception area.

Even though Chan had come to their hotel, he had done the inviting so the choice of restaurant was his. He had chosen the hotel's own Chinese restaurant; indeed, he chose the food as well, allowing Stuart and Anwar only to choose their own drinks. During the meal, which was large and served over a long period of time, they talked of nothing but generalities, of the food, the weather, the political situation in their respective countries. Chan was a typical Chinese host. He forced food on his two guests, spooning bits from each new dish into the bowls of Stuart and Anwar, waving away any idea that they may be full. Only when the last dishes had been removed and replaced by a plate full of sliced fruit did their conversation turn to business.

"Okay, Mr Morgan, we finish eating, now we talk business and you don't get the stomach ache, yeah!" He laughed loudly at his own joke.

Anwar and Stuart nodded and smiled politely.

"Now," he continued in a quieter, almost embarrassed manner, "my wife ask me to give you this."

He looked at Stuart and passed over a large brown envelope.

Stuart took it and glanced at Anwar.

Anwar raised his eyebrows.

"I can open it now?" Stuart asked.

Chan nodded. "Please you open."

Stuart opened the envelope and extracted a sheaf of papers. The first one was on Chan's headed paper addressed to Ormistons. Stuart glanced quickly through and realised that it was a specification for an order for a whole range of machines, similar to those in the documents enclosed in the boxes upstairs. It was Chan's complete expansion plan rather than the one small machine for which Chan had already required a quotation.

"Thank you for the opportunity," Stuart said as he handed the envelope to Anwar.

"I hope", Chan said slowly, "that you have enough information to make us a very good offer. You understand?" he said, looking straight at Stuart.

"Of course."

"Okay, good. How long will it take to make the offer?"

"For a complete package with everything, two months."

"Why so long? Usually one week?" said Chan.

"No, not if you want the best offer. Give us time and we will give you what you want."

Chan nodded, he understood.

Then Chan asked for the bill. The meal was finished, the business concluded. Anwar went to his room and arranged for the three boxes to be brought down.

"You see," Chan said slowly when they were alone, "my wife is the planner of our business. She bought all the computers, made the office nice. I said no, not necessary, not important, but she made me do it. So we did."

"And now?"

"What you think? She got the factory under control, the costs, everything, and we started to make more money. Then she want to make the machines work better so when I heard that Ormistons is in Indonesia, I find out where and call you to come here. My wife want the spares, but I want the discount." He laughed to cover his embarrassment. "So now she wants that we buy machines from you, but I want the best price. So..." He paused.

"So," responded Stuart, "so we can give you a very good offer?"

"Good, good, this good." He bounced a little in his chair in his excitement.

Anwar returned. "Everything is loaded in your car."

Chan stood up. "Okay, see you next time, Mr Morgan." He shook Stuart's hand vigorously. He and Anwar walked to the car together, leaving Stuart alone.

Stuart moved into the lobby bar and took another beer, watching Anwar see Chan off, a few words and gestures being exchanged before the two men shook hands.

"Everything okay?" Stuart asked when Anwar returned.

"Fine, everything is okay."

"What is really going on?" Stuart repeated the question from earlier in the evening. "Why did he wait until now to give us the full quotation?"

"For effect, he wants us, you in particular, to feel privileged, so that you have some moral debt to him. Don't forget he's a street trader with a factory." Anwar smiled.

"Yes, he told me about his wife and things, that he was reluctant to change and modernise. I think he likes the sweatshop image."

Anwar smiled. "Maybe so. Now, tomorrow, what time shall we depart for Jakarta?"

## CHAPTER 27

## FATE IS SEALED

By noon of the following day, Stuart and Anwar were speeding along the toll road from the airport to the centre of Jakarta. Stuart felt better than he had felt on this particular journey for a long time, certainly better than the previous three times he had passed along the toll road. He had Chan's precious box in the boot of the car, he had Chan's quotation request in his briefcase, the prospect of returning in two months and, on top of all that, the thought of meeting Ita later that evening. He smiled to himself: he was happy again with Indonesia, with the business and with Anwar. He was looking forward to meeting Ita very much. He had missed her after that abortive, but serendipitous trip to the airport. He was allowing himself to believe, after the phone call to his wife, that he could handle the situation in England, that he could lie and run two lives, one there and one here. He smiled again.

In Anwar's office they discussed the future work that they both had to complete before Stuart's next visit. The time scale was looking very much as if it would be the two months previously estimated by Stuart. He left by three o'clock and checked into what was rapidly becoming his favourite hotel of all time: The Kedutaan. Once safely in his room, with Chan's cardboard box standing next to his suitcase, he fell asleep for more than an hour.

When he woke up he wandered down to the swimming pool to shake off the inevitable leaden feeling he always got when sleeping during the day. He swam in the company of a couple of Indonesian girls. They watched him while he swam. When he looked at them they turned away and giggled. When they swam he watched them. One in particular had a slim, supple body, like Ita's, with no spare fat evident. He thought of Ita and the swimming pool last time. He thought of her stripping off in front of him the day he had arrived and he had had to lay the towel over his groin to cover his embarrassment. As he sat and thought further, his erection became almost painful. He ordered tea and tried to stop the thought process that was causing him so much delightful discomfort.

Later, when he had sufficiently recovered and darkness and the mosquitoes were beginning to make sitting by the small pool no longer pleasurable, he made his way back to the room. He showered and changed into the regulation jeans and tee-shirt. He had just finished when the door bell went. He walked, barefoot, to open it. First, he looked through the small peephole. He could make out a widely distorted Ita, fidgeting nervously in the corridor. He opened the door to let her in. Once in the small corridor that connected the door to the room proper, he got another shock.

She had come straight from work, so she was in her work clothes, her working appearance. Her hair was tied back, simply, with a towelling-type band which was at shoulder level. The hair was not tightly restrained, hanging down gracefully at the sides, curving backwards and over her shoulders, just touching them, to be contained within the band. She wore more make-up than he was used to. She had a coat on, a cream, crumpled, linen-type coat, with padded shoulders and a wide wrap around the front. Under that she had a black, high-necked blouse which fastened at the back and Stuart thought, looked as if it were made from silk. Her skirt was black, slightly shiny and tight. She wore black high-heeled shoes. He gaped, his mouth open.

"What's the matter?" she asked, standing in front of him.

"You look so different, so sophisticated. I've never seen you with a skirt on before," he replied weakly.

"You don't like?" she asked, her head on one side, looking coy.

"Very much I like," he said, imitating her slightly distorted English.

"Well, give me a kiss," she said in a deep sexy voice, her eyes misty and inviting.

He leaned forward to kiss her. With her wearing high heels and him in bare feet, there was not much difference in height: he was almost at her eye-level. Her eyes closed slowly, her head tilted and they kissed.

He heard a small thud as her handbag hit the floor. Her arms lifted and intertwined around him, her right arm at the back of his neck, the left around his waist, pulling him closer.

The kiss became a long passionate embrace and his hands fell to her waist, wandered inside her cream, buttonless jacket, riding over her slim hips, across the material of her skirt. They closed their bodies together in the embrace, melding, merging into a single being.

Their breathing became short and snorted through the nose as the kiss continued. Stuart found the button and zip at the back of Ita's skirt. The skirt came undone easily, falling away to the floor where Ita kicked it away. His hands went to her buttocks where he found the Marks and Spencer thong knickers. He ran his hands around the edge of the cloth, down and into the valley of her bottom, moving outwards along the base of her bottom in a symmetrical motion of both hands. The feel of her skin, the feel of the cloth, framing her bottom in his mind's eye to absolute perfection, made his passion rise higher as he kissed her.

Her left hand moved from his back and on to his groin, massaging though his jeans, then fingering his belt, flicking the large buckle undone with a finger. She deftly moved the zip down and then undid the button. By moving and jiggling his hips, Stuart contrived to make the jeans fall away to ankle level. Further downward progress was difficult.

The kiss continued unabated.

His right hand rode up under her blouse which, by the feel, confirmed his earlier assumption that it was silk, pushing, searching for her bra, searching for a breast to massage, a nipple to touch. He found them all in quick succession, and as he touched the nipple, her breathing snorted again, her lips pushed harder into Stuart's mouth.

Stuart moved his right hand down from the breast, his left hand still on her buttock, and passed it down over the front of her knickers. A moan emanated from her as she kissed and felt his hand close to her, a sound of complete abandonment to her passion.

He slipped his hand inside the smooth material of her knickers. She snorted and clenched her eyes closed. His hand moved down, through the hair, down and into her. She was already wet, very wet. He passed her finger over her once; her whole body shuddered as he did so.

He transferred both of his hands to the outside of her hips, rolling and easing her knickers down. They fell to the floor and she stepped one leg out of them.

Her hand slipped inside his underpants and gripped him hard. It was his turn to gasp in the passion of their embrace. His underpants fell to the floor to join his jeans around his ankles.

Slowly they sank to the floor, first kneeling and still kissing.

Eventually she broke the kiss and lay back. He followed her down, his mouth close to her mouth, and then the kiss resumed as his body's weight pressed on to hers. Her legs spread wide, her knees against the wall on one side and the wardrobe on the other.

They needed no thought, no guidance as the groins met and joined, sliding into preordained positions with no resistance. As he entered her, they broke from the kiss, and gasped in unison. She linked her calves over the back of his knees. He was still a little restrained by the jeans around his ankles; indeed both of them were still semi-clothed.

Once linked, once joined, groin to groin, the kiss resumed and their snorting and passion became a little more controlled. They began to move in harmony, searching out the feelings, the rhythm to produce the ultimate sensations. For them, for these two people, no thought was necessary, no reason: it all happened without the need for thought. Stuart could feel the sensations spreading out from his groin – it was not going to last very long.

Ita broke the kiss.

"Oh Stuart," she whispered. "Oh Stuart, my darling," she said a little louder, as they moved and pushed together. "Oh Stuart... Oh Stuuuuart!" she almost screamed as her orgasm arrived.

It was the first time that she had ever said Stuart's name at the height of orgasm.

He heard her voice and he felt the contractions against him and this heightened his sensation to the point of unbearableness. His whole body went stiff as his muscles contracted to release him step by step from the tension. He came in a number of waves in the midst of Ita's contractions. "Oh Ita," he muttered on the last contraction. "Oh Ita, I love you," he whispered as the sensations drifted away, drifted down and were gone, but for the memory.

They remained tense and interlocked for some time, pressed close in the post-orgasmic search for some further feeling there, but always elusive and never found. Slowly they relaxed, but didn't uncouple. They lay together, relaxed and intertwined.

Eventually, Stuart stirred himself as he felt himself slip out. He sat back, kneeling. Ita levered her body up, supporting herself on her hands. Stuart looked at her: the cream jacket was still in place, the silk blouse ruffled, the front-fastening bra hanging down below the level of the blouse. Her make-up was smudged and distorted, her hair askew. Her knees flopped outwards, her feet slid together, one still with the knickers wrapped round. She looked unbelievably sexy to Stuart as she looked up at him and smiled. He stood and offered her a hand which she took, to help her to stand. They divested themselves of all remaining clothing, Stuart stumbling around trying to get his jeans off. Then they lay on the bed and cuddled and dozed.

As usual, Ita was the first to move. When Stuart woke, she had gone. She was in the bathroom. He found her, naked, washing her thong knickers out in the sink. She had removed most of her make-up and brushed her hair, allowing it to fall around her in a black waterfall. She smiled at him in the mirror.

"I've been wearing these all day," she said, holding the knickers up so that they formed a Y-shape in front of the mirror. "And I have been feeling so..." she paused, a little embarrassed, "so much that I want to make love." There was probably a word in her own language that would have expressed exactly what she wanted to say, but in English she struggled. "My bottom so bare against my skirt," she said, looking at him, "so nice. Can you get me some more like this?" she said, holding them up again.

He nodded and cuddled her from the back.

She squirmed a little to get away from him. "Get away, you are dirty. Wash," she commanded.

He obeyed.

When he had finished, Ita had left the bathroom, her knickers over the shower curtain rail. She was dressing again. She had brought a pair of spare knickers in her handbag, ever the practical person. She dressed again in her work clothes, then put her make-up back on, the naked Stuart watching her all the time. When she had finished she turned to Stuart.

"Are you going out like that?" she said, laughing.

He shook his head. "I'm just waiting to see how you look before I dress," he said.

She laughed again.

He dressed smartly: trousers and a short-sleeved shirt. It was his turn to be watched.

"Very nice," she said as he finished.

He pouted and strutted around in a grotesque parody of a catwalk display.

"Stop it," she laughed. "I'm hungry."

"I forgot," he said. "Make love, eat. Correct?"

"Yes," she replied decisively.

"Okay where? We both look very smart, so how about the posh Italian restaurant in the hotel."

"What's posh?" she asked.

"You know, posh," he said as if it was obvious. "Well, like high-class, you know, sophisticated."

She nodded in agreement. "Sounds good to me," she replied, and they went downstairs.

Stuart was interested to see how Ita would behave in such European surroundings, to the strange food on the menu, a different way from that to which she was used. They sat and Stuart ordered some wine as his first step. Ita looked through the long menu and made her own choice without asking Stuart for advice. He was impressed. The wine arrived first, Bordalino, a thick Italian red, one of Stuart's favourites even if, in Jakarta, it was something over thirty pounds a bottle. He tasted it and pronounced it good. Ita also took a glass and sipped it gingerly.

The meal came: starter, main course and sweet. Ita drank her glass of wine and Stuart the rest of the bottle. They revelled in the food, the conversation, the closeness that they felt for each other. Stuart was pleasantly surprised at Ita's behaviour. She seemed completely at home in the midst of such a European setting. The meal finished and they retired to the bedroom and slept.

The following day, as usual, Ita was up and away first, leaving Stuart sleepily in bed. He agreed to pick her up again at her house, somewhat earlier than the previous attempt. He slept for another hour and then took a long bath. Breakfast was another long affair, with four cups of coffee and a complete read of the local English language newspaper, *The Jakarta Post*. He called Anwar and agreed that there was nothing which demanded Stuart's presence in Anwar's office that day. They said goodbye on the phone.

Stuart frittered away the rest of the morning and early afternoon in shopping and reconfirming his tickets for that evening's flight.

He packed and left the hotel to collect Ita at around two-thirty. He arrived at Ita's house at three, more than an hour before they had agreed and Ita was already ready. They had tea and a snack while the taxi driver waited, his meter running. They left for the airport well before four and had no delays *en route*. The journey was as quick and efficient as any journey could be through Jakarta's clogged streets. They arrived with something over two hours to wait for Stuart's flight.

After he had checked in, they went and sat in the same small bar where they had sat the first time they had separated at the airport, the time of Ita's tearful acknowledgement of her feelings for Stuart. Now he was faced with an entirely different Ita.

She sat, her elbows on the table, her head down, drinking coke through a straw. She looked up at him, her brown eyes full of playful happiness, an impish, almost childish quality to her face in this position. She smiled at him as he looked at her.

"You look happy," he said

She nodded once, not taking her mouth from the straw.

"Why so happy? Because I'm going home? You are happy because I'm going home?" he continued.

She shook her head twice, again still not disengaging from the straw.

"Well, why do you feel so happy? Last time we were here, in this bar, you were not so happy."

Finally she took the straw from her mouth. "Because last time I didn't know what the future was with you, if you would come back, it you would still want me. I was worried, but now..." She lowered her head and took up the straw again without using her hands.

"But now?" he said, prompting her for further explanation.

She left the straw again. "But now I know you better, I trust you completely to come back to me in the future. I will never forget that," she said, her playful eyes now deadly serious. "You will not abandon me now, Stuart, whatever happens." She sucked her straw again briefly. "Will you?" It was not a question.

"Whatever I can do for you, I will, Ita my darling," he said quietly as she went back to her straw. "If I know what is happening, what the situation is, I will do what I can," he smiled, trying not to get too emotional himself, although Ita appeared not to be worried or upset.

The conversation paused.

He looked at her as she continued to sip her coke. She was really quite beautiful in her exotic, South-East Asian way. He was sure, sitting here looking at Ita, that he would not abandon her: he would attempt to support her life, her emotional condition, in whatever way he could. The chance of his coming back was very good, since the market was on the point of providing some orders; his relationship with Anwar was very important to the future success and it was getting stronger with every meeting. He smiled to himself as he considered the situation. He felt confident that he could deal with the situation at home, with the situation in Indonesia. He knew, sitting opposite Ita as now he was, that he would not abandon her.

When Ita had finished her coke, Stuart stood up to leave. "Come on, Ita, I have to go."

She looked sad. "So soon? You have almost an hour before your aeroplane takes off."

"No, barely forty minutes, and last time I was the last one on the plane," he said with a laugh.

She smiled. "Okay, we go," she said and stood up to join him.

Outside the passengers-only section they stood together for their goodbye. He linked his arms around her, she slipped hers around his waist. This was the only time that she would make such a public gesture of affection. They squeezed each other. Then, releasing slowly, they looked into each other's face. Her eyes were moist now, not with a twinkle, but with sadness. She reached up and kissed him.

"Bye."

He resisted moving, not wanting to leave go of her.

"Go on," she said, pushing him away a little.

They let go of each other. "Bye bye Ita, I won't be away too long."

He looked at her face again; a tear trickled from her left eye and ran down her cheek. She laughed a little and pushed the tear away with her hand. A second appeared on the other side, then a third on the left again. She abandoned her attempts to remove them and took his hand instead. She led him towards the automatic doors. "Go on, Stuart, don't miss your flight."

He turned and kissed her one last time, looked at her face with its two small tears and passed through the doors. He waved at her and mouthed a 'bye' to her through the glass.

She waved and stepped back. He walked off, looking back as he went. She stood waving and smiling though the tears until he was out of sight.

Once out of her sight, Stuart's own eyes filled with tears and he pulled out his hanky and dabbed the corners of his eyes. Then he straightened up and made his way to the departure lounge. They were already calling for boarding and he walked straight on. When the aeroplane took off, he looked down at the darkening Jakartan landscape and his eyes moistened again.

Stuart wandered around the efficient marble halls of Changi Airport, buying the cheapest bottle of duty-free gin he could find, buying Catherine her favourite perfume to supplement the presents already purchased. He thought little about what had happened during the trip and what could happen on his return to England. He was distracted by the bright lights and the people milling around the airport. Everything was so fresh, the parting with Ita so recent that somehow it didn't seem real: he was just on another trip upcountry and he would be back in Jakarta soon.

These unrealistic thoughts and visions faded as he boarded the aeroplane for its fourteen hour, one stop, east to west flight back to the UK. He ate, drank, listened to the piped music on his headphones. He watched the film, but sleep and peace of mind would not come. His mind was alternately filled with visions of

Ita, of Indonesia and with glimpses of home, of his family. He remembered visions of Indonesia and of Ita, of massaging her in her room in the heavy heat and humidity with the smell of the oil, the mosquito coil burning in the corner, the sound of the small lizards playing out their lives around the light. He thought of the walks with Anwar through the streets of Yogjakarta, the air filled with the smell of the barbecuing satay, the evening at Borobudur and of the hundred sailing ships in Jakarta, of the intense green of the landscape and of the rice paddies. He cried a few times as these thoughts piled up in his tired, emotional mind.

Then he thought of Britain, of England and the damp greyness of Cheshire in the approaching winter. He tried to find something bright in this, the autumn with its colours, kicking up the leaves on the path on a walk with Colleen, but it was a small token. He pictured his wife while she awaited his arrival, wondering what her reaction would be. His earlier confidence about his ability to lie and deceive her was evaporating as the miles between them decreased. He wondered how to approach her; she would know, she had told him, she would know. He had to be confident, awake and alert to deflect her in the opening encounter for that would be the critical time: the first few minutes.

He stared morosely at the movie screen, not really watching or listening. He willed sleep to come. Eventually it did, but the kindly air hostess awakened him for the landing at the stop-over in Bahrain. On the final leg of the flight to London, he slept only intermittently, getting not much more than three or four hours. It was not enough and he knew it: all his potential for staving off Catherine in the first few moments of meeting her vanished. He realised this as he contemplated the beef breakfast steak sitting in front of him as the journey neared its end. He knew that it had been useless to try to believe that he could have a double life. The only question now was how Catherine would take the situation and whether or not their marriage could survive. In all his twelve years of marriage, he had never had such a thought, never had any worry about the strength of his relationship, but now, as he prodded the beef breakfast steak, he realised that he had to think those thoughts.

# CHAPTER 28

# CATHERINE'S REVENGE

While the Singapore Airlines Boeing 747 Bigtop circled over London in the inevitable, even for a Sunday morning, stacked wait for a landing slot at Heathrow Airport, Stuart considered his method of travelling to Manchester. He considered that the tube and train would be the best method as it was the longest, especially the train on a Sunday, and would, therefore, delay the inevitable confrontation with Catherine as long as possible. Once they had landed, however, he felt different. The fatigue had got to him and the idea of a tube journey and the fight with his baggage upstairs and escalators, especially when he remembered Chan's cardboard box and Ita's carefully packed boat, changed his mind. He settled for the aeroplane super shuttle and a taxi to his home if Catherine was not there at the airport to meet him. She had surprised him at the airport on a number of occasions, even when he had not told her which flight he was on; she had worked out the schedule and guessed on which shuttle flight he would arrive. On balance he felt that she would not be there to meet him from this particular trip.

In the comparative calm of the Sunday morning in the shuttle waiting lounge, Stuart ate a bacon and egg sandwich to fill his stomach, still empty after he had merely toyed with the airline's beef breakfast steak. He had a long wait. There were fewer early morning shuttle flights on a Sunday, and his flight was due to leave at nine-thirty. It left on time, and the flight to Manchester was short and uneventful. Chan's box appeared along with his suitcase and he managed to find a taxi without much trouble. Now that he was on the last leg of his journey, he began to feel nervous and tense. His mouth dried up a little, his stomach tightened and his heart rate went up. He tried to psyche himself up for the coming meeting with Catherine, but in his tired, travel-fatigued condition it was difficult, if not impossible. In the end he gave up and flopped back in his seat.

The taxi arrived and the driver helped Stuart to manhandle Chan's box to the front door. Stuart paid him off with a decent tip. Then he opened the front door and lifted his baggage in piece by piece. He left it all in the hallway and walked straight into the kitchen. Catherine was at the sink preparing food. Stuart wondered why she was always in the kitchen, always preparing food when he came back. It was barely eleven o'clock on a Sunday morning and yet here she was cooking again. Stuart guessed it was the preparations for Sunday lunch. At least that was slightly encouraging: she expected normality – perhaps he could survive. He sat heavily on one of the kitchen chairs, still not having said anything.

"Hello," Catherine said without turning her head to face him.

"Hi," he answered with a sigh.

"You okay? Everything all right?" she continued, still not turning round.

He paused rather too long in answering. "Yeah, I suppose so. Nice to be home," he said, sounding totally unconvincing.

Now she turned to face him. She crossed her legs and leaned against the sink, her hands resting on the edge of the sink. She was not smiling, but nor did her face seem angry or upset.

To Stuart, his wife appeared large and forbidding. He had spent the last three weeks or so in the company of the small, slim Ita and her generally small countrymen. There Stuart was a tall, well-built man. Now that he was faced with the taller, much broader, heavier frame of his wife, he felt daunted by her physical presence.

"Nice to be home, is it?" she asked a little sarcastically.

He looked at her briefly but did not reply, dropping his eyes quickly.

"You couldn't do it, could you?" she said, almost smiling and shaking her head.

He made no move, except to lower his eyes further.

"No, you couldn't. I told you I would know straightaway, Stuart," she continued, her tone curious, not angry, not even upset. She spoke more in the manner of a parent who had found her small child doing something naughty, but not so bad, something that an adult would be able to predict a child doing. She even smiled at him.

He was shocked by her behaviour. He stared at her, his mouth slightly open.

She smiled again, pushed herself off the sink and advanced slowly on Stuart. He looked at her. She seemed to grow larger in his vision, in her right hand a six inch, Sabatier, stainless-steel kitchen knife, an extremely sharp kitchen knife. Both of her hands were clad in rubber gloves which stretched up to her elbows. She wore a full-length apron, a gaudy, PVC plastic one in the colours and print of a bottle of Lea and Perrins' Worcester Sauce.

He focused on the knife. For an awful moment he thought that Catherine was going to stab him, was going to stick him with the knife there in the kitchen; the rubber gloves and apron were to protect her from the blood which would be spilt. He stared at the advancing knife, frozen in terror. He could not move. His life was going to end in their kitchen, his wife the architect of his death, a crime of passion. He would be like the large piece of meat on the sink behind her, dead and trussed up like a Sunday joint. He saw the newspaper headlines flashing though his mind in the short seconds it took his wife to approach him, the seconds which seemed like an age in slow motion replay in his mind. HUSBAND STABBED IN KITCHEN IN CRIME OF PASSION, MANCHESTER HOUSEWIFE IN BLOOD AND GORE SEX KILLING – then his mind went blank.

He looked from the knife to her face, his eyes wide like a rabbit's caught in the headlights of a car.

"Don't look so worried," Catherine said in a reassuring voice, the one she used with the children when they woke from a nightmare.

He looked from her face to the knife and back to her face as she approached closer.

"I'm not going to do anything," she said in the same voice. "Here," she said a little louder, thrusting her right hand out.

Stuart jumped back and let out a small shriek. He looked down to see Catherine thrusting the knife at him, handle first, into Stuart's left hand.

"Now you finish preparing the lunch – beef, vegetables, potatoes. There are some apples for a pie, everything that you need to make a nice Sunday family lunch. You can remember how to do it?" she continued, now in her child instruction voice. "I want it all finished by three, okay?"

He nodded in an automatic response.

She peeled the rubber gloves off one by one, dropping them onto the table in the manner of a stripper, each held between thumb and forefinger in a tantalising gesture. Stuart wondered if she was now going to do a complete strip and rape him in the kitchen. The headlines flashed before him again: MANCHESTER HOUSEWIFE IN BIZARRE KITCHEN SEX ROMP.

She removed the apron and dropped the neck cord over his head. She smiled at him again. "Because I am going out," she said in the same voice.

He looked confused and a little worried.

"Don't worry," she said, pinching his cheek gently and lowering her face towards his. "I'll be back. I'll be back before the lunch is ready."

She stood up straight and left the kitchen without another word to Stuart.

"Ralph, Colleen, are you both coming with Mummy?" she called loudly in the hallway.

"I am," shouted Ralph in reply.

"Is Daddy home?" answered Colleen.

"Yes," Catherine replied.

"Then I want to stay with Daddy," she said.

Ralph came down the stairs to his mother and left without saying a 'hello' or a 'goodbye' to Stuart. He heard the front door close and Colleen's footsteps coming down the stairs.

Stuart remained unmoving as he sat with the apron round his neck and the knife in his hand. Colleen came into the room.

"Hello Daddy," she said in an excited voice, and then, seeing the peculiar attitude of her father, stopped short. "Are you all right, Daddy?" she asked cautiously.

He nodded his head and looked at his daughter, six years old, masses of light brown curly hair and her mother's green eyes. Dressed in a short pinafore dress and woolly tights, she looked like some child in a picture book rather than a real child, his daughter. She was very cute. He smiled at her and she smiled back, still uncertain.

Carefully he placed the knife on the table and then removed the apron.

"Do you want to help Daddy make the dinner?" he asked, knowing what the reply would be.

"Oh yes please," she answered in great excitement.

"Okay, you start setting the table. Daddy wants to go and wash and change." He leant forward as he stood and gave her a little peck on the cheek.

Stuart came downstairs fifteen minutes later, a little more refreshed and still somewhat stunned by his wife's performance. He was confused and concerned by her actions. She must have something up her sleeve, some plan of action which only required his presence and her understanding of his silent admission to put into effect. But he was at a loss as to know what it was.

"Do you know where Mummy has gone?" he asked Colleen as he entered the dining room, where she had almost finished laying the table.

"No." She shook her head vigorously.

"Has Mummy been okay while Daddy has been away?" he asked.

"Mmm, mmm," she said, concentrating on positioning a glass.

He gave up trying to question her and checked her handiwork. She had done a very good job: glasses, sideplates, cutlery, except that the knives and forks were on the wrong sides. She looked so proud that he decided not to tell her, but to secretly change them back himself later. "Okay," he said happily, "very good."

She looked up at him and smiled, shuffling nearer to him and taking his hand.

"Come on," he said, leading her by the hand back to the kitchen. "We have to do the rest of the dinner now."

Once in the kitchen, Stuart's first job was to select and open two bottles of red wine, one good one for the meal, and one cheap one for him to drink while he was preparing. He set Colleen to work peeling potatoes while he prepared the large piece of rib beef on which Catherine had been working when he had arrived. He calculated the times and temperatures and put it in the oven. They worked silently together, each happy in their own way by the closeness and the reunion.

At two-thirty the meat came out and the oven went up in temperature. By two-forty-five, the eight small Yorkshire pudding tins went in and Stuart carved the meat. At three o'clock exactly, he began to put the vegetables into the serving dishes and Colleen carefully carried them into the dining room and set them, steaming, on the table. The meat followed, then the roast potatoes, the gravy and finally the Yorkshire puddings. Stuart was determined not to wait for Catherine and Ralph. If they were late, their dinner would spoil. She had, after all, said three o'clock. At seven minutes past three, just as Stuart was bringing the good bottle of wine through into the dining room in the final act of preparation, he heard a key in the lock and they arrived.

"Oh Stuart!" Catherine exclaimed as she came into the dining room, divesting herself of her coat as she did so. "What a lovely sight – a nice Sunday family lunch!"

She kissed him lightly on the cheek as she passed him to sit down. "Come on, children, sit down and let's eat before this lovely food all gets cold."

Stuart wondered if she had actually lost her marbles, whether she was having a nervous breakdown in front of him. He stared at her in disbelief.

"Come on, Daddy," she said to him. "After all the effort of your cooking it would be a shame to stand there gawping at it and not eating. Sit down," she said, patting his chair, and he obeyed.

"Who did this?" Ralph said loudly and rather boorishly.

"What, dear?" his mother answered in a soothing tone.

"Set the table. It's all wrong, look!" he continued in the same tone, knowing full well that it was Colleen and that his criticism would hurt her very much. "The knives and forks are on the wrong side, you stupid girl." He went on without waiting for the answer to his question.

"Now Ralph," his mother said a little more sternly, "she was trying her best, I'm sure."

Colleen whimpered a little, her eyes filling with tears.

Ralph looked satisfied at that, and Stuart cursed himself for forgetting to change them round and protect Colleen from Ralph's inevitable castigation.

"Let's eat," Stuart said brightly, trying to deflect the nasty turn the conversation was taking.

He succeeded, and they ate. The Sunday lunch was a success. Catherine even complimented Stuart on his change from apple pie to the less labour-intensive and simpler apple crumble, complete with ice cream and fresh whipped cream. Catherine was charming and happy, the children were happy and smiling and Stuart, despite his jet-lag and the situation, became more relaxed as the meal and bottle of wine disappeared. The only note of dissension came at the end of the meal. Colleen had cleared the table with her father's help. Catherine had made the coffee and produced a piece of well-ripened Blue Stilton which she had bought specially for Stuart, knowing that it was his favourite. When they had all sat down at the table again to drink coffee and for Stuart to eat the cheese, Catherine spoke again in her friendly schoolmistress tone. "Now Daddy, are you going to show everyone what presents you've brought back from Indonesia?"

"Mmm?" said Stuart, his mouth half full of cheese and cracker.

"The presents, dear. You always bring something back for us," she prompted.

"Mmmm, yes, of course." He stood and wandered out to the hall where his suitcase and other travel belongings were still residing.

He brought in all the presents and sat down like Father Christmas.

"For Mummy and Daddy," he began in a jolly voice, "a bottle of gin."

Catherine smiled.

"And for Mummy, a bottle of her favourite perfume."

"Oh Daddy, thank you," she said with overemphasised enthusiasm. "And such a big bottle as well."

"For Colleen a tee-shirt and some pretty beads." He handed them over.

"Thank you Daddy," she said a little shyly.

"Oh and I forgot, for Mummy and Colleen some nice cotton, batik-printed cloth for Mummy to make some clothes with next summer." He handed over three lengths of cloth, each in a clear plastic bag.

"And for Ralph?" Catherine prompted.

"And for Ralph," Stuart began, "tee-shirts and shorts for sport and the summer."

"Thanks," Ralph replied gruffly; it was the nearest that he had got to acknowledging his father.

"And what's in those two cardboard boxes in the hall? The big one and the funny-shaped one?" Catherine asked.

"The big one is full of papers for work, that's all."

"And the other one?" she persisted.

Stuart went a little quiet when he thought of the contents: Ita's little boat.

"It's a model boat for Ralph," he said after a few seconds.

Ralph's face lit up. "Radio control?" he said excitedly.

Stuart shook his head and got up to bring the box in. Carefully he unwrapped it on the table and set it before Ralph.

"What that?" Ralph said in a loud disgusted tone. "I told you I wanted a Gameboy or a radio-controlled car or boat or aeroplane or something," he continued, speaking to Stuart but looking at Catherine.

"Well, you can buy those anywhere. This is only from Indonesia – you can't buy them anywhere else," Stuart said quite firmly.

"Well, it's crap, all crap!" Ralph almost shouted in reply.

"Now Ralph," his mother said softly, "don't speak like that."

"But Mummy," he whined, "it's crap! Look at it – it doesn't do anything." He went to sweep it off the table and on to the floor.

Colleen made a grab for it. "I like it, Daddy, I want it in my bedroom." Her little face was looking up at her father.

Stuart smiled. "Okay, you can have it."

He turned to look at the scowling Ralph, "And I'll buy you the biggest bloody Gameboy radio-controlled whatever on Saturday, okay?" his voice displaying a little irritation at his son's rather boorish display.

"Is that okay, Ralph?" his mother asked him, in an apologetic tone.

"Suppose so," he replied grudgingly.

Colleen disappeared upstairs with Ita's little boat and Stuart felt happy that his treasure had found a worthy keeper. With that, the family Sunday lunch ended.

The afternoon and early evening continued pleasantly enough. Stuart retired to bed just after nine, still surprised that the explosion with Catherine had not happened. Maybe it wouldn't, maybe what she had planned was so clever that she didn't need to explode and have the grand row. He contemplated these thoughts as he lay in their bed. Then he slept. Catherine joined him later and was careful not to wake him. He slept until five, was up at six and in the office just after seven, the jet-lag playing its usual tricks.

In the quiet of the almost empty office, Stuart went through his high-piled in-tray and was filling in his expenses sheet when his boss, Frank, strode into the office in his usual high-speed, hunched forward walk.

"Morning Frank," Stuart called, seeing that Frank's head-down attitude would not enable him to see Stuart.

He looked up, a little surprised. "Oh, oh, oh yes, good morning Stuart, nice to have you back." He stopped his walk and looked over the partition towards Stuart. "In a bit early, first day back an' all," he continued jovially.

"Jet-lag," Stuart replied simply.

"My office, ten o'clock. Let me do the mail and then we'll have a talk, okay?" Frank said, resuming his walk.

"Fine."

At ten past ten, Stuart wandered into Frank's office, bringing nothing but a sheaf of expense forms for Frank to sign.

"So how was it?" Frank asked the obvious question.

"Good, spares are coming on well," Stuart began.

"You said that last time you came back, but so far no order," Frank interrupted; it was an annoying habit of his.

"Well, this time we have an order, signed and ready for execution, almost thirty-five thousand in spares," Stuart said with a little note of triumph in his voice.

"Pounds or dollars?" was Frank's only reply.

"Pounds," replied a slightly deflated Stuart.

"Okay, that's good. Now what about the next stages, the new machine supply? That's what's really important," Frank continued.

"Well, yep, I've got a number of tenders to respond to, plus the guy who ordered the spares," Stuart began.

"Tenders?" Frank cut in. "Are you sure that we're not being used just as a check price for the competition, just to bring them under control again?" Frank was always sceptical.

"Maybe yes, maybe no," was Stuart's reply.

"Speak sense."

"Okay, Mr Chan–" Stuart began quietly.

"I thought our agent was someone called Anwar not Chan," Frank interrupted again.

"Mr Chan is the guy who has bought the spares," Stuart explained, a note of exasperation creeping into his voice at the repeated interruptions.

"Oh?" Frank grunted.

"Mr Chan", Stuart began again, "has arranged for us to receive a great deal of information about our competitors." He paused, watching Frank's interest pick up. "The information covers just about everything: technical, price, financing, terms and conditions, everything. So with this we can, or we should be able to, make some very competitive offers on those tenders and some other unsolicited offers which Anwar thinks might be a good idea."

"Could still be an attempt to beat their prices down," Frank said, sticking to his sceptical line.

Stuart shrugged his shoulders. "It's possible," he sighed.

"Okay, listen," Frank said in a more positive tone, swivelling in his chair and facing Stuart. "I want you to do a full report, everything, all the details – people, contacts – and how you see the future, the next steps – you know the type of thing, something more than the average sales and marketing report."

Stuart nodded.

"How long do you need?"

"Give me a week," Stuart said firmly.

"One week, one week and a day, until Tuesday next week then." He paused and looked at Stuart's sheaf of expenses.

"And give me those." He signed them all without so much as a cursory glance and pushed them back at Stuart.

Stuart left his office. A report was not unusual, in fact it was almost obligatory, but one in the amount of detail asked for by Frank was perhaps a little more unusual. Still, Stuart was not worried, because it would give him the opportunity to formulate a strategy for the future and overcome all Frank's doubts. He set to work on it straightaway.

The week passed uneventfully. He worked hard. The jet-lag afflicted him for the first couple of days, but after that it was back to normal. By Friday, however, it was clear to him that he would not be able to finish the report by the required deadline. He composed bits at home over the weekend and used it as an excuse not to visit Catherine's parents with the children. Catherine didn't object to this as strongly as he had expected. After her initial protest, he explained that it was the report on Indonesia and was required by Tuesday. She merely nodded in a knowing way and left him to it.

On the following Tuesday, Stuart was informed by Frank's secretary that he was required to be in Frank's office by eleven o'clock. Stuart tried to get the draft of the report to such a stage that it was at least readable to Frank, to deflect any criticism that he had failed to meet the deadline. He was so concerned about producing the maximum amount of paper for demonstration purposes that he was late for the meeting, waiting for some further printout from the computer.

He wandered into Frank's office almost ten minutes late. John was there as well, sitting half sideways on the window sill, staring out of the window. Frank looked up as Stuart walked in. To Stuart, Frank appeared nervous, his brow furrowed a little, as if he wasn't comfortable with something. John glanced at Stuart and gave a single nod before returning his gaze to the scene beyond the glass. Stuart got a tight, twisted feeling in his stomach. Something was not right, what he could not say, but something was definitely up.

"Report finished?" Frank broke the silence after a few moments.

"Almost," replied Stuart, holding up the unruly sheets of paper that constituted the draft of the report.

"Good. Now what are the prospects, I mean the immediate prospects for new machines, not spares or refurbishment?" Frank started enthusiastically, setting Stuart slightly at his ease.

"Well, the most obvious immediate prospects are for some machines for Mr Chan, the guy that bought the spares," Stuart said.

"Yeah, but they're all small machines if I remember rightly, and there is no profit in them, and, as you know, the board is thinking of getting out of the small end of the market altogether," Frank said in a depressing offhand tone.

"Mmm, but without them, the small machines I mean, it would be so much more difficult to break into this market," Stuart responded, trying to sound hopeful.

"So if we didn't have a small machines section this would jeopardise our future in Indonesia, is that what you're saying?" Frank interrupted.

"Yes, of course, and not just in Indonesia," said Stuart, warming to one of his favourite company hobby horses: the small machine business. "The way we are breaking into Indonesia could and should become the way that we proceed in other markets which have been, well what should I say, closed to us, for whatever reason." He was referring as delicately as possible to the previous arrangements on territory sharing with the other manufacturers.

Frank nodded in carefully considered and limited agreement. "So you believe that the small machines are essential?"

"Yes."

"But unprofitable?" Frank added quickly.

"At the moment, if you believe the figures, then yes," Stuart replied.

"A loss leader then?" Frank was teasing the required answers out of Stuart.

"No, they shouldn't be, they don't need to be," Stuart replied positively, not realising that Frank was leading him.

Frank glanced at the still silent John, and Stuart was sure that a message was flashed between them judging from Frank's eyes and John's slight nod.

"Okay, I've known for a while that you have some ideas and strong feelings about that area," Frank said as he turned to look at Stuart again.

Stuart nodded.

"So what would you say if I offered you the responsibility", Frank paused, "and authority", he continued in a grave serious voice, "to go in and sort out the small machine section, to make a report initially and then implement it, with recommendations for streamlining, rationalisation, job cuts if necessary – to make that section profitable, or at least not so much of a burden on the rest?"

Stuart glanced at John who he knew was looking at him.

John quickly averted his eyes from Stuart.

Stuart shrugged his shoulders and looked at Frank with a confused and slightly smiling face. "You serious? You'd offer me that job, with the authority?"

Frank nodded.

"But with all this work in Indonesia coming up it would be too much to start work until that was all sorted out, say another six or nine months," Stuart started to say, the slight tenseness in his stomach coming back.

"I know," Frank interrupted quickly, "and that's too long away for us – the board wants this problem sorted quickly." He paused and Stuart realised that the reason for the unease was about to be revealed. "So," he continued quickly, "Indonesia would be handed over to John's section, especially as we're so close to orders and we have orders already." Frank waved his hand at John who again averted his eyes when Stuart looked at him. "Once your report is finished, of course," he continued looking directly at Stuart again.

Stuart looked from one to the other a few times. Frank returned his look, John avoided his eyes.

"Is there a choice?" Stuart asked quietly after a long pause.

Frank leaned forward in his chair and looked at Stuart. "It's not good to refuse promotion, is it, lad? Especially when it comes from high up," he said in a quiet but nonetheless firm voice.

"Promotion?" Stuart asked.

"Yes, you'll go up a grade, same as John, and the office at the end is being prepared for you now. We expect the first report in six months for presentation to the board." Frank resumed his normal voice. "You've got a passion for the small machines – as a sales engineer, as a marketing man, you see the need for them. Some others, the bean counters, sorry accountants, can't see the need. You make them profitable, and we can all win," he said brightly, rocking back in his chair. "Any comments?"

"Well, just one," Stuart answered quietly.

"Well?"

"Indonesia is a face to face society, and this applies very much so in business. My relationship with Anwar, and to a lesser extent Chan, is, in my opinion, very important to our future success in that market," Stuart said slowly and deliberately.

"Okay," said Frank, "but at the end of the day both of them are businessmen. I don't believe for one minute that they would throw away a good deal because of personal relationships – doesn't fit. Make that comment in your report, and John," Frank said, swivelling his chair to face him, "you make note of it yourself."

John nodded.

Frank smiled at Stuart.

Stuart didn't agree with Frank's assessment. He was sure that personal relationships were far more important than Frank was giving them credit, but in the face of this *fait accompli*, Stuart didn't have the stomach for an argument.

"Okay, that all?" he said weakly.

Frank nodded and extended his hand. "I think you'll do a good job and it's for the best, for the company and for you," he said as Stuart shook his hand.

John remained unmoving on the window sill and acknowledged Stuart with a curt nod as he left the room.

Stuart was slightly bemused by the meeting and when he left he went straight to the new office that had been allocated to him just to make sure that it was not some sort of dream, or, worse, a joke. Someone had already deposited Chan's cardboard box on the desk. Stuart looked around it. He had always wanted his own office instead of being in the main open-plan area, but he did not really want it in the circumstances in which he had received it. He dropped the draft report on the desk alongside the box. As he did so he became aware of a presence behind him. He turned to see John standing in the doorway.

"Can I come in?" he asked quietly.

"Of course," Stuart replied with no animosity in his voice.

John looked at him and smiled nervously. "I think it's for the best," he began. "For all of us," he added somewhat hastily. "For the company, promotion and your own office for you, and for your family. It's for the best like this," he continued, failing to sound convincing in any way.

"I'm glad that I haven't finished this report," Stuart began, ignoring John's prepared and nervously delivered little speech and pointing at the pile of papers.

"Oh?"

"Yes, because I want to add a few things to it," Stuart continued.

"Like what?" John asked.

"Well you see this box here?" He pointed at Chan's box.

John looked and nodded.

"This contains enough data and information to ensure that we have a very good chance of succeeding in Indonesia: with the right handling it should guarantee success and give our friends a bloody nose in the process in one of their best markets." He paused and looked intently at John. "And if you fuck it up..." He paused again, watching John flinch a little. Stuart rarely swore, so when he did it always had a much greater effect on people. He enjoyed watching John flinch so much that he repeated himself. "If you fuck it up, I will be down on you like a ton of bloody bricks. I intend to make it abundantly clear in the report that that is the situation."

"You sound as if you want me to fail," John replied defensively.

Stuart shook his head. "No, not at all, because if you do fail then the future of this company is a little more uncertain and I want to earn my pension from here; I like this place, the people and the stuff we make. So no, I don't want you to fail, but if you do I will make sure that everybody knows what I think."

"And that's what you will put in the report?" John asked.

"Well, not in so many words, but I will make it clear what I think our chances are and how we should proceed. If there is any failure to achieve what I think we should then I have it written down," Stuart replied.

"Arse-covering, are we?" John said a little caustically.

"No, well a little maybe, but mainly giving you the maximum incentive not to mess it up, that's all."

John turned to leave Stuart's new domain.

"Funny really," Stuart said to his back.

"What?" asked John, stopping and turning.

"Funny that I'm being promoted to the same level as you and yet you are taking over the old job I've been promoted out of. Funny that," Stuart continued with a wry smile.

John looked riled at the comment. Stuart had touched a little raw nerve: John was very position-conscious. "Well, I'm not going to be handling it personally, I'll give it to one of my staff," John replied in a tone of barely disguised anger.

"But you will be going to visit Indonesia?" Stuart queried.

"Maybe, we'll have to wait and see," John replied.

"Okay."

John turned again and left Stuart alone.

Stuart spent the rest of the morning and half the afternoon moving his belongings into his new office. He found a letter from Ita in his in-tray when he moved that into the office. He skipped lunch to read it and wrote a rather depressing reply to Ita, giving her the bare essentials of his job change without mentioning the details. He got stamps from the post room and slipped the envelope in his jacket pocket.

The physical work and effort of moving office kept his mind off the discussion in Frank's office. When he did stop to think about it he was shocked and a little numbed by what had transpired. While he was still in the office he could not put it into perspective or focus his mind on what had happened; he felt confused. By three-thirty in the afternoon he had quite a headache. He excused himself and left the office early. He found a post box and posted the letter to Ita, kissing it once before he slipped it into the slot.

He didn't drive home. Instead he headed east through the start of Manchester's evening rush hour, towards the foothills of the Pennines. He drove out of the city and parked in a small road that ran alongside the banks of the Macclesfield Canal in a spot familiar to him. He had often come here in the past whenever he had problems to resolve or when he wanted some time to think or just to be alone.

For the first half hour or so he just walked without considering the matter at hand. He observed the sky, the landscape, the things around him. The sky was filled with a flat, even-coloured cloud of light grey, high enough to allow a clear view of the hills to the east, but casting a dull, monochromatic greyness over the whole scene. It was not a dark, forbidding grey, the grey that forewarns of impending rain, but rather the greyness of dull, damp days with no wind or rain to freshen and change the air. Beside the canal, at this point below the level of the surrounding land, the dampness was more acute. It seemed to rise from the dark grey, still water, to rise from the verdant vegetation which lined the towpath along which he walked, to ooze from the trees overhead as they dropped their damp, silent multicoloured leaves to the ground in the first flush of autumn. Stuart pushed his hands deep into his pockets and hurried along this section of the canal, anxious to keep the dampness from his bones.

The canal eventually opened out to a section where it was on the same level or higher than the surrounding countryside. The towpath vegetation was less dense, there were no trees overhanging and the air felt fresher. He slowed down and allowed his heart rate to slow after the brisk half hour walk he had so far completed. From here, it was not so far to Bosley Locks, Stuart's destination.

As he walked more quietly along this raised section, he considered what had transpired during the day. He knew, without needing to ask, that Catherine had been behind it. It was not something that she had done quickly or rashly. She had thought about it, talked it over with Ann and then with John. Between the three of them they had devised the plan. He had no doubt that John had been involved. Catherine didn't know the detail of Stuart's ideas for the small machines – only John could have introduced that. How John had sold it to Frank was a mystery to Stuart. Maybe Frank had been told and involved.

Stuart wondered how far up the managerial chain it had gone. He knew that Frank had the authority to do what he had done by himself so Stuart guessed that that was as far as it had gone. He had to give Catherine and her associates credit for coming up with such a plan. By picking an area of work about which Stuart was concerned, an area outside his existing work, they had ensured that he couldn't argue about it. If it was a posting to another country to continue work in sales and marketing, he could have argued very strongly for remaining where he was, but to be given such an opportunity as he had been meant such argument was almost useless.

The promotion to the same grade as John was a final push to make it impossible for Stuart to refuse and retain any credibility within the company. Refusal would have meant a sidelining of Stuart for future career development. He couldn't refuse. They knew it and they had all been very clever. Stuart knew that he had been totally and completely outmanoeuvred. Still, the promotion to the same grade as John pleased him, mainly because he knew how much it would gall John, a couple of years his senior and always regarded as the high flier, to see Stuart at the same level as him. Who had suggested this, Stuart didn't know, but he guessed that it was Catherine, who had always felt that he never got his just rewards in the company. He tried to imagine the scene, with Catherine suggesting it and John trying to argue against it. The fact that the promotion had gone through, probably at Catherine's instigation, made Stuart think about John and his friendship with him. John had sacrificed a lot of pride for Stuart to try to keep Stuart and Catherine together, to keep their marriage intact.

The thought of one of John's contract-oriented people continuing the delicate job developing sales in Indonesia didn't fill Stuart with much confidence. He believed that Frank's assessment of Anwar and Chan was wrong, but how could he explain Borobudur to Frank and retain any form of credibility? Stuart knew that he would have to accept the situation. The only question was how to rationalise it in his mind and reason the plan through with respect to Ita and his feelings for her. He strode on, his mind empty of thoughts, once again looking around him.

A further ten minutes more brought him in sight of the first of the twelve Bosley Locks. He was approaching from the high side and he could only see the black and white balance arms of the top lock. Stuart liked the canals very much. He had been on a student day's 'booze cruise' with his friends. They had all treated it as a nice way to get from pub to pub, but the experience had affected Stuart quite deeply. He read up on canals after that and he had been on a holiday with Catherine and some friends before the children were born, and one other holiday with the children. He had never had the opportunity of passing the Bosley locks or the Macclesfield Canal by boat. He knew the locks and this stretch only from walking. He approached the top lock and sat on the left-hand balance beam of the top gate. Unusually for the seven foot wide narrow canals, the Bosley Locks had double mitred gates at both top and bottom. Most narrow locks had a single gate at the top and double mitred gates at the bottom; some even had single gates both top and bottom. This gave Bosley Locks a pleasingly symmetrical appearance.

He looked down into the empty lock. The water level was about twelve feet below him; the water was dark and still. The sides of the chamber were more or less dry, indicating that it was a long time since the chamber had been full, a long time since any boat had passed through the lock. The upper gates leaked a little water at the sill. He walked on to the bottom gates and sat down again and looked at the remaining eleven locks stretching out in the distance, each with the small pound between.

Now he considered what his response to the situation was to be. Catherine had not mentioned Indonesia or anything to do with it since the first few minutes after his arrival. She had tried, and more or less succeeded, to behave in a completely normal manner, Sunday lunch excepted, since then. In public there was no evidence that anything was wrong. The children didn't seem to suspect anything and even between the two of them there was only a little tension. There was, however, a lot that was not said and she gave him some knowing looks, her eyes saying what she had decided her mouth would not. Knowing now about her plan and its success, Stuart understood her reactions. He also believed that she would carry on in the same way and never mention the subject again, her intention being that the whole thing should be forgotten and healed in the fullness of silent time.

Stuart was the one who had strayed from the marriage, he was the one who had had the affair, but it was Catherine who was doing the rebuilding job, making the effort to save the marriage and not allow his transgression to cause any lasting harm. She and her friends had got together to help him, to help them, through this rocky situation. He knew that he owed it to Catherine to try. He stood up and walked on down the row of locks. He resolved to try, he resolved not to mention Indonesia, to bury himself in his new job and to follow Catherine's carefully laid plan through to its conclusion in the hope that all would be well.

When he reached the bottom lock of the twelve, he sat on the balance beam of one of the bottom gates, looking down the canal. He sighed to himself. He would try, he owed that to Catherine, but what did he owe to Ita? Now that he remembered her again and allowed her to come back into his mind, he knew that to try would not be easy. Here, in the grey, overcast, northern light, away from the heat and humidity, the sunshine, the exotic smells and Ita, he tried to rationalise his feelings. For Stuart, Ita must have only been some passing lust, the last fling before settling down for good with the family. What had Catherine called it: 'the male menopause come early'. Maybe she was right, Stuart reasoned. And yet he knew she wasn't. It was not lust he felt for Ita, it was more, much more. He was in love with her in a more passionate way than he had ever been in love before, even with Catherine when they had first met. It was a love which had grown out of the almost complete satisfaction attained in their sexual relationship, a love built on the most complete and intimate sexual foundations that Stuart could imagine. How could he try for Catherine and still maintain his promise to Ita, his promise not to abandon her? He could not live the double life, now that Catherine knew and his situation had changed so radically. He shook his head to himself and sighed a big sigh.

In the distance a small girl was running down the towpath towards him. Behind her in the distance he could see the flat surface of the water being disturbed as a boat pushed its way forward. It was still too far off to hear the engine, but Stuart decided to wait and watch its progress through the locks.

As he waited, he decided that his first course of action would be to write to Ita, when she replied to the letter he had just posted, and tell her the whole story, the complete details, so that she would understand the situation. He resolved to keep writing to her. He hoped that he could help her in spirit by remembering her, by continuing to communicate with her and to help her in any material way he could, given the eight thousand mile distance between them. He knew that the office situation could change. Once his new job was finished, he would be back in sales and marketing. Maybe something would happen and maybe he could get back to Indonesia. He knew that all these maybes would take at least a year. In that time, Ita could find somebody else and he would be happy.

The little girl was almost up to him. She was breathless and carrying a large metal key for opening the valves or paddles on the lock gates. He stood up and pushed the gate open on his side. He walked round the top of the lock and opened the other for the approaching boat. He could hear the distinctive *tonk-tonk-tonk* of a single cylinder engine. The boat was done out in the traditional style and the engine sounded like an original narrowboat engine rather than a modern four cylinder one.

"Thanks mister," the little girl said cheerfully. "You know 'ow to do vis?" she asked with her small hands resting on her hips.

Stuart nodded.

She smiled back. She was a little older than Colleen; her hair was long, tied back and somewhat dirty. Her clothes too had all seen better days, but she had a bright cheerful smile.

The boat was steered by a bearded man smoking a pipe; Stuart guessed it was her father, there was some resemblance. He slid the boat expertly into the lock and nudged it gently against the closed upper gate. Stuart and the girl closed the lower ones and the girl raced round to open the paddles. The boat rose slowly.

"Thanks to you, sir," the helmsman said, in what sounded like a put-on yokel accent. "My daughter needs a little help and my wife is down below cooking and pregnant," he said by way of explanation. "We want to get to the top tonight, and moor up."

Stuart nodded. The boat rose to the level of the next pound and the man used the boat and engine to nudge the gates open slowly. Stuart closed them behind the boat and then followed up to the next lock.

"You live on the boat?" Stuart asked while the boat was rising in the second lock.

"Yes, we do, sir," the man continued in his yokel accent.

Stuart was convinced that it was put on: everything about the man said that he was trying to create an image.

"We live on the boat and make our living doing things for people along the way," he said with the pipe jammed in his mouth.

"What sort of things?" Stuart asked, curious.

"Well actually," he said quietly in a more normal, slightly refined accent, his real one. "I'm an accountant," he said with a shy laugh. "Most of the time we don't move very far but I do work from the boat and most of my customers are canalside."

Stuart smiled in genuine amusement – a waterborne travelling accountant, that was definitely a first. He helped them through all twelve locks and then resumed his walk through the gathering gloom to his car.

His mind was made up, his course of action clear but his heart was still troubled and life would not be easy.

## CHAPTER 29

## SATURDAY MORNING

In the days, weeks and months that followed Stuart's acquiescence to the situation which Catherine had so skilfully created, the situation did, by degrees, improve. Viewed from the outside, everything looked fine. There were no visual signs, except possibly Stuart's continued weight loss which eventually stabilised at a figure some two stones less than his previous weight, and his propensity to have two or more baths a day. Even their closest friends, Ann and John, appeared to be convinced that all was fine. Surprisingly, even from the inside, Stuart found, things were beginning to look reasonably all right, if not exactly good. There were, however, a number of subtle differences which had grown up, especially the polarisation of family along classical lines: Ralph with his mother and Colleen with Stuart.

Stuart had never been that close to his son; he loved him and had done everything that he considered he should, but the feeling that he was doing what he should do rather than what he wanted or felt in his heart indicated that there was something missing from the relationship. The current situation had served only to increase the gap between them. They rarely spoke except to observe the normal formalities. Ralph's behaviour towards his sister, his intolerance of any mistake or error on her part, further alienated him from Stuart.

This increasing gulf was widened by other changes in their family life brought on as a result of the job change and promotion for Stuart. Stuart had realised very soon that the time scale for the work that Frank had given was tight and the scope of the investigation got bigger as he delved deeper into the problem. This meant that Stuart had to work Saturdays, three a month usually, and Catherine had taken over the job of chauffeuring Ralph around the winter rugby games on a Saturday morning. She joined the band of mothers who, for whatever reason, took their sons to rugby matches rather than the fathers. Stuart suspected that she liked it, huddled against the cold in warm coats and scarves, drinking coffee from thermos flasks and gossiping with the other mothers. Stuart usually found a shopping list waiting for him on Saturday morning which he and Colleen bought in the late afternoon after work was finished.

For every step away from him Ralph went, Colleen came one step nearer. She went to the office with him most Saturdays, sitting quietly playing, reading or drawing in a vacant desk close to Stuart. She never disturbed him and he found her presence on those Saturday mornings pleasing and comforting. Then they went shopping together, pushing the trolley round Sainsbury's stocking up with the necessities.

Just after Stuart had accepted the promotion, Catherine was very nervous around him. She knew, of course, the time when Stuart would be confronted with the plan and he guessed that she was worried his reaction might have been unfavourably expressed within the family. When this did not happen, and as Indonesia was not mentioned by either of them, she settled down a week or so later. For two months she didn't mention his job at all; she accepted the extra work in which he was involved without comment – his Saturday working and the late nights passed with no argument, only understanding smiles and a cup of tea or something stronger for the tired Stuart. Stuart felt that she had made up her mind to save the marriage and she was determined to accept whatever small sacrifices were necessary, that she was trying to achieve a harmonious existence, one which did not evoke or provoke any form of argument which could lead to hard words being said. If she could maintain such a calm and almost happy environment for long enough, Stuart thought that she believed she could have her husband back in the old way.

Even for Stuart, the plan was beginning to work. He accepted her efforts and was careful not to provoke arguments himself. He talked about his work only a little and he helped as much as he could in the house. Whilst things improved, there was still a wall between Stuart and his wife. There was a tense nervousness between them when they were alone together as each skirted round the delicate taboo subjects.

The sexual side of their relationship was non-existent for almost three months. Stuart had lost almost all of his sexual appetite and he made no first moves, although he felt he should. Catherine appeared to be still slightly revolted when he came too close or tried to touch her. She pulled away and avoided physical contact. They had never stopped sleeping in the same bed, but sexual contact or any form of physical contact did not occur for a long time. Eventually, after a long, hard Friday in the office Stuart arrived home late. The children were already in bed and he had gone straight upstairs. Catherine was lying on the bed, half asleep and dressed in her slinkiest silk nightie. He stripped off for a bath and to his surprise found his sexual appetite returning with a vengeance. He slid alongside her and she responded, and they kissed and made love. That first encounter was as passionate as it was surprising for both of them; she had cried a little. After that, they were both, if anything, more rather than less nervous around each other. Stuart had expected that the breaking of the sexual contact taboo would have released feelings for both of them, but it did not. It was more than six weeks before they did it again, and that was a very nervous halting affair, which left both of them unsatisfied. After that they settled down to a series of unsatisfactory encounters with a frequency of slightly less than once every three weeks.

Stuart's acceptance of the situation over time was made easier by the strange absence of letters from Ita. Apart from the first one which he had received and replied to on the day of his job change, he had not received any more, nor had he written any. He reasoned that she had read more into his first letter than he had written, that in her sensitive Javanese way she had understood from the letter that Stuart was really saying everything was finished. He thought that she had found someone else. That thought made him feel a little happier because he knew he could not provide that part of her life in full, but at the same time he felt jealousy at the idea that she was with another man, that she had shared her secret with him, that the special relationship the two of them had enjoyed was not so special after all. With time, Ita faded from Stuart's most immediate thoughts, his memories of her faded into a rose-coloured series of beautiful scenes which flowed into his mind whenever he was relaxed. Sometimes, in the morning, in the half sleep that precedes full wakefulness, Ita's slim brown body, her brown eyes and long black hair came to him. These dreams were of sexual encounters so realistic and fulfilling that he often woke with his heart pounding, his throat dry and the sick feeling of sexual excitement in his stomach. Sometimes there was an embarrassing wet patch in his underpants which required a quick dash to the bathroom. The sexual encounters with his wife were a pale shadow of his dreams about Ita.

Eventually, Ita faded into a memory of a brief passionate affair which he was glad to have experienced but one that would never come again, one that he would never want to come again. He still looked at her photographs, especially the first one he had ever taken with her battered Kodak Instamatic camera, the one of her in profile in the restaurant high above the tea gardens of Puncak Pass. He sometimes got a little lump in his throat when he thought about that camera and how precious it was to her.

By a Saturday morning in the early spring, with the snowdrops and crocuses pushing up, Stuart's workload decreased a little. He had made the presentation to the board, it had been well received and he was now pushing ahead with the implementation of some of the ideas. He didn't really need to work on Saturdays any more, especially if he put in the hours during the week. This had not, however, resulted in a resumption of his fatherly rugby duties with Ralph. Catherine was now so well into the game that she was starting to offer her mother's wisdom to the coach and was keenly following Ralph's particular school team through a cup competition. On this particular Saturday morning they had left early, leaving Stuart in bed and Colleen playing in her room. Stuart lay propped up in bed reading the paper and listening to the *Today* programme on the radio. Catherine had very thoughtfully provided him with a cup of tea which he sipped at intervals, not wishing the luxury of a Saturday morning in bed to be dissipated too quickly.

Ita had not come to him that particular morning, not in his dreams at any rate. But now as he sat in bed fully awake, she came to him: she filled his mind in an entirely unexpected way, with a forcefulness that reduced the radio voice of Brian Redhead to a small distant and indistinct sound. There were no sexual, erotic or exotic images this time, it was not her body that came to him for sexual fulfilment – it was just her face and her eyes in particular. They appeared big and brown, wide and sad, so very sad, more sad than he had ever seen them. He closed his eyes and shook his head to try to clear the vision. It didn't work. He gulped the remaining tea in one swift mouthful and climbed quickly out of bed. He almost ran into the bathroom and began to shower himself with a hot, powerful shower jet, so hot that it almost hurt. Ita went from his mind.

He stood in front of the mirror to brush his teeth and she came again, her eyes so sad and tinged with hopelessness. He looked into them and shivered; he sobbed a little, almost cried as he tried to push the vision from his mind. Eventually she went, her purpose achieved, his spirit shaken and prepared. He didn't bother to shave because his hand was shaking.

He dressed and passed Colleen's room. "You up and dressed, Col?" he shouted to her.

"Yes Daddy," she answered excitedly.

"You want toast?" he asked, knowing what the answer would be.

"Yes please, Daddy."

"Okay, I'll call you when it's ready," he replied from the top of the stairs.

In the hallway was an unusually large pile of letters. Stuart gathered them in his left hand and dropped them on the kitchen table without a second glance. He filled his teacup again from the still warm pot which Catherine had left. Then he cut some bread and prepared to make some toast. As he turned to sit at the table, he saw something in the pile of letters which made him stop in mid-motion. He looked hard, and then, in the manner of someone moving in slow motion as if to avoid a snake, he sat down and placed the teacup on the table. In amongst the junk mail and bills a corner of crumpled light blue coloured airmail letter poked out. It screamed Ita at him. Slowly, with his left hand, he teased the envelope out into the open. It was from Indonesia. He recognised the face of the president on the stamps – it was from Ita, he recognised the handwriting, but it was not like her other letters. They had all been with typed addresses in company envelopes and sent to his office. This one was written in her own hand, but again it was different. It was a faint, weak handwriting performed in a thin, hesitant biro, quite unlike Ita's normally neat and confident style – but it was definitely hers. He turned it over and checked the address. It was unfamiliar to him: it was not her home or office address. He turned it back over and looked at the top left corner. Ita always numbered her letters, starting a new series of numbers with each of Stuart's returns home.

This letter was numbered twelve.

Stuart was stunned by this. It meant that somewhere ten letters had gone missing: he had only number one and now number twelve. He immediately knew that Catherine had arranged for all letters from Indonesia arriving in the office to be intercepted. The thought of what those ten letters had said and the possibility that they had been read by someone else in the office made Stuart angry and upset – that words intended for his eyes alone had been common property. He vowed to try to find the letters or at least determine their fate.

He set down the letter on the table and smoothed the wrinkled envelope a few times. It was the cheapest quality envelope, whereas Ita normally bought nice, good quality stationery for her long missives to Stuart. He was afraid to open it and he smoothed it again before finally picking it up and gently easing the top open. Inside were three crumpled pages of the same thin, cheap-looking blue airmail paper, written in the same hesitant, shaky biro as the address. He laid them out carefully on the table in front of him and started to read, oblivious to the popping toaster behind him.

The letter had the strange address and was dated six days earlier.

*My darling Stuart,* the letter began. He paused for a thought. Despite the fact that she had written eleven previous letters and received only one reply, she still addressed him as *My darling Stuart*: there was no hint of anger or disappointment. He read on.

> *I am so sorry to write to you at your home. I hope that my letter does not cause you a problem in your family. I know you told me only to write to your office address but I am so desperate that I must write to your home. I worried that you have not received my letters in your office. In your letter, my darling, you said that*

> *you had changed your job and maybe you would not be able to come back to Indonesia so quickly. I am not sure but maybe you change office to another address and my letters have not reached you. I know my letters have not reached you because if they had and you knew my situation you would have helped me earlier. I know you will not abandon me. I am now so desperate that I must take the chance of writing to you in your house to tell you of my situation. I know you have not received my letters so I will tell you from the start.*
>
> *When you were in Jakarta last time, I was counting my days so that everything would be safe for us. I counted to the end of the time when you would go back and this was safe. But then when you got delayed and I was so upset I got confused about the days and still thought everything was okay until you went back. The last time we make love in your hotel was not so safe. Maybe you are very strong and I am very fertile because straightaway I miss my period and I am pregnant with our baby.*

Stuart stopped reading and laid the papers down. His stomach had gone tight and he felt sick. He sighed a big sigh. Now he knew why he had had the vision of Ita's sad and hopeless eyes a few minutes earlier. His mind flitted briefly back to the passionate minutes on the floor of his hotel room on that fateful evening. He shook his head to himself and sighed a few times. Then he took up reading again.

> *So after I know, I write to you for your advice. I know I can stop the baby coming, but I want you to help me with the decision. It is very difficult for me because I am Catholic and to stop the baby is a very big sin. I needed your support. You didn't reply so I was afraid to do it alone. Then the time went on and it was too late to stop the baby. At first there was no problem, I not get sick so I carried on working. Our baby also is not too big in my stomach so I could hide it for a long time. Then my boss found out and he*

wasn't happy so I have to leave my job. I save as much money as I could and move out of my room and find the cheap place. I sell everything I don't need to make some more money. Then my mother came to Jakarta to help me in the last months before the baby will come. But even with everything sold my money is almost finished and I am so desperate.

I not ask you to come to Indonesia because I know that it is so difficult for you with your new job, but please can you help me for some money so that I can have our baby with the doctor and get some clothes for our baby. I am so sorry to ask you like this but I have no other way.

Please help me and our baby, my darling Stuart. I know that you not know about this problem because you are good man and you have sent me the advice before now if you knew.

I waiting your reply very soon.

All my love,

Ita

Stuart carefully arranged the leaves of the letter and read it a second time just to make sure of its contents. He did not doubt for a moment that what she was saying was true and not some ruse to extract money from him. She had never asked for any money on any occasion and had even paid for a number of things in the course of their relationship. The tight feeling in his stomach remained, but other than that he did not feel angry or upset. He did not cry at the desperate situation in which Ita had found herself, a situation he had created. Now the mechanical, organised Stuart came to the fore, the one who was so good in a crisis, in the heat of the moment. He folded the letter with great care and put it back into the envelope. His only question was what to do about Ita's situation.

He stood up and buttered the now cold toast, eating it mechanically without tasting it. He finished the rest of the lukewarm tea and cut two further slices of toast for Colleen. He leaned against the sink, waiting and trying to think. The toast popped up, startling Stuart from his reverie. He buttered it while hot and added some jam. The simple basic tasks soothed his mind and emptied it of emotional thoughts.

"Colleen!" he called. "Toast!"

Colleen bounded down the stairs.

"You want to go shopping with Daddy?"

"Mmm, mmm," she said with a mouth full of toast and jam.

"I'm going upstairs for a while, okay?"

"Mmm, mmm."

"When I come down you be ready, clear the plates and everything okay?"

"Mmm, mmm," she said again through another mouthful of toast.

In his mind, which had been clearing while he buttered Colleen's toast, a plan had evolved that, at the very least, helped Ita out of her most immediate crisis: money.

Stuart went upstairs with the letter and into his small office room. He unlocked his briefcase and briefly looked at Ita's picture still secreted inside. Then he drew out five thick airmail envelopes and some airmail paper. He wrote a simple one page letter.

> *Dear Ita*
>
> *I received your letter today, number twelve. You are right. I have not received any other letters from you and I don't know why. You know that I will not abandon you and now that I know what has happened I will try to help you. I will try to come to Indonesia if I can but I don't know how or when. Please tell me if all these letters arrive.*
>
> *All my love,*
> *Stuart*

He wrote four more identical letters and folded each carefully with a sheet of heavy brown paper and pushed them into the five envelopes. He addressed each one carefully and wrote one stroke five in digits in the corner of the first, two stroke five on the second and so on, hoping that Ita would realise there were five such letters, minimising the amount of money which could go astray. Now he had to get the money to put in them. US dollars were the most easily convertible currency so he decided to put a one hundred dollar bill in each of the five letters. He checked his wallet. He had a little over a hundred pounds – not enough. He collected the five letters and Ita's letter and wandered back downstairs.

Colleen had finished her toast, was collecting the plates and beginning to clear away the mess of breakfast. Stuart helped her, anxious not to give any hint of the problem now confronting him.

"Want to come shopping?" he asked as they finished the washing and drying.

"Yes, Daddy, you have already asked me once," she replied in a child's matter-of-fact tone.

He smiled. "Okay, just checking, come on."

They left and got in the car. Stuart drove to the centre of Manchester and parked. His first job was to find a cashpoint machine for the joint building society account. He withdrew the maximum two hundred and fifty pounds. Then they walked to the large Thomas Cook travel agency in the shopping centre.

"You go in there, Col," he said, indicating a large bookshop opposite, "and wait for Daddy. I'll buy you a book if you want."

She nodded in response and trotted happily off.

Inside Thomas Cook's he changed enough of the money to give him five one hundred dollar bills. He then walked quickly to the nearest post office and put a single bill in each of the five letters, sealing each one deliberately and carefully. He then asked for one to be weighed and bought the necessary stamps. He licked them and made sure that each of the five letters was correct in all respects. Then he posted each one individually, giving each a small kiss. Then he left. The immediate crisis was on its way to being solved, he hoped.

The next problem was to get to Indonesia, and the key to that, he knew, was somewhere in the office.

He found Colleen sitting on a small stool in the children's book section of the shop engrossed in a book. "You want that one?" he asked as he approached.

She looked up. "Oh Daddy, where have you been?" she said in a slightly perturbed tone.

"Sorry," he said and took her hand. He paid for the book and they left. "You want to go to Daddy's office for a while?"

"I thought we were going shopping," she replied, whining slightly.

"Yes we will, but I need to check the office first."

"Okay."

Inside the very quiet and still Saturday office, Stuart sat Colleen down at a vacant desk and went directly to John's office. Stuart had not paid any attention to the Indonesian market since he had taken on the new job. He had dismissed John's first enquiry on the subject, a week or so after he had changed jobs, in such a way that John was left in no doubt further questions would not be welcome. Despite this lack of involvement, he knew that things were not good in the progress of obtaining further orders. All orders, even small spares orders such as Stuart's success in Indonesia, were announced in the weekly company newsletter. No further announcements about orders in Indonesia had been made. Stuart knew that that was very bad. He had believed that a few months should see some further success. The fact that not even another spares order had materialised from Mr Chan indicated how desperately bad the situation was. Somewhere in the office would be something that he could use.

In John's office he pulled the file on 'Indonesia General' and took it to his own office. He found the section with correspondence to and from Anwar. It was arranged in chronological order and he soon found the point at which he had stopped working on Indonesia. He found a fax from Frank to Anwar telling him that Stuart was no longer working on the Indonesian market because he had been promoted. The return fax from Anwar expressed great disappointment and regret and demanded that Stuart be reallocated to Indonesia. A second soothing fax from Frank was followed by a resigned one from Anwar who said that he could see why Stuart had been promoted as he had found Stuart to be an excellent and intelligent working partner. Stuart felt a warm glow spread through him at Anwar's praise. At the bottom of this second fax, Frank had scribbled *Told you so, John! He's a businessman.*

Stuart continued to read the correspondence. The first visit of John and one of his junior staff to Indonesia had been arranged. A rather uncomplimentary fax from Anwar to Frank after the visit showed that Anwar was unimpressed with both John and his staff. *I doubt whether either of these people will have the commitment or skill to pursue the orders in the manner that Mr Morgan would have done*, read one line. *The social behaviour displayed is not what is expected in Indonesia*, read another, and *Your offers are worse than the competitors even though you know exactly what they are offering*, said another, referring to Chan's box. *Please investigate the offers further and keep your staff under control*, was scribbled in Frank's handwriting to John on the bottom of the fax. Anwar's complaining faxes followed at a greater frequency, culminating in one some six weeks previous, after another visit by John's junior. *The drunken and disrespectful behaviour, especially to the women, displayed by your representative has, in my estimation, lost a potential order for our two companies and destroyed much of the hard work put in by myself and your company*, read one of the lines. The final line read, *If you do not remedy this situation as soon as possible I will be forced to bring this to the attention of the president director of your company*.

Stuart found a long fax in reply from Frank, written some two weeks after Anwar's. The response would not have satisfied Anwar, of that Stuart was sure, but it was the last piece of correspondence in the file. Stuart could not imagine Anwar waiting four minutes, let alone four weeks to reply. He knew that there must be some further correspondence lying around. First he searched John's desk and in-tray. Then he moved carefully into Frank's office, conscious that he was, in effect, spying on him. He found nothing in either place. He sat back in Frank's chair, slightly exasperated at having found something, but not enough. As he cast his eye over Frank's desk again, he saw a piece of yellow paper, a post-it note. *Deal with Anwar's latest fax*, he had written; the date was a few days before. There was more.

Stuart left Frank's office and went to the postroom. The postroom was run by an elderly bachelor who had spent twenty years in the army in some sort of clerical position. He kept records of military precision for every piece of correspondence that came in or left, be it letter, fax, telex or cable, trivial or important. Against each item was a note of who it was from, who it was to and any other relevant information. Stuart located the shelves on which these records were kept in the neat and orderly postroom. He started at a date a few months before to see if there was any other correspondence that wasn't in the file. As he glanced down the FROM column he noticed an entry stated simply as INDONESIA. He checked the TO column and saw his own initials and the three letter code for 'letter' to distinguish the type of entry. He looked across to the NOTES column. *Personal letter, shredded unopened*, read the simple entry. His assumption had been correct. Catherine had arranged for all letters to him from Indonesia to be stopped and shredded. He was comforted by the fact that the postman appeared to have been responsible for shredding the unopened letters. No one else knew about Ita's current situation.

He continued to search the records. Two days after Frank's attempt at a soothing fax, he found an entry from Anwar's company. The addressee was down as *The President Director*, and the note column said *Refer to F.J.* Anwar's fax was, Stuart guessed, to the managing director, but he had used the Indonesian term of president director. The postman had decided that, as it was from Indonesia and everything else had gone to Frank, he should refer it to him to be on the safe side. Stuart wondered if the managing director had ever received the fax or knew what it had said. Now he had to see the missing fax. As well as the postal clerk's immaculate, detailed and infallible records, Stuart knew that all correspondence would be copied and stored in a central sequence file as well as the subject-specific office files where the originals would be put. These central files were routinely archived to a distant part of the complex and almost never consulted again. The archiving was done monthly. Stuart wondered if the copy of this vital fax had been archived, never to surface again.

He hurried along to central filing and found the appropriate file. It took him some fifteen minutes to locate the copy. His first job was to copy it and then restore the file copy and return to his office to read it.

It was addressed simply to *The President Director, Ormistons*, with no name, rather than *Montague Holding, Managing Director*, whom Anwar was trying to reach.

*Dear Sir,* it began,

> *I am taking the unusual step of writing a personal communication to you to bring to your direct attention the situation in Indonesia. More than one year ago your Mr James visited my offices to arrange an agency agreement between your company and mine for the sale of textile machinery. This visit was followed up by further visits by your Mr Morgan and some good progress was made. A small order was taken and the prospects for further business were very good. Then, about eight months ago, I was informed that Mr Morgan had been promoted and that other staff would be allocated to this market.*
>
> *Since then no further orders have been made and the prospects have all but disappeared.*
>
> *The reason for this sad state of affairs is that the new staff allocated to this market have not lived to the high standards set by Mr Morgan and the behaviour of your representatives has itself caused a great many problems.*
>
> *The current situation is now so desperate that the only solution I can see is for Mr Morgan to be reallocated to this market and for him to visit as soon as possible to save the future of our joint business here. Failure to act now will result in Ormistons being shut out of this market for the next ten years.*
>
> *I am waiting for your earliest reply*

Frank must have been very grateful that the fax had not reached its intended addressee since it was a damning indictment of what had happened since Stuart had been promoted. Stuart also knew with almost absolute certainty that the managing director had not seen the fax, for something would have been done about it if he had. Stuart now had the ammunition he was looking for, and the next question was how to use it.

His first instinct was to simply put a copy of the fax on Holding's desk, but such an action was fraught with the danger of discovery and might not have the desired effect. He wondered if Anwar had actually tried to talk to Holding; to get Anwar to talk to him was probably the most effective way of notifying him of the problem. Stuart needed to talk to Anwar. He picked up the phone and got as far as dialling the international access code before he though better of it. All the calls from each extension were logged on a computerised system and again the records were stored by the diligent postal clerk. His phone at home was out because they too had itemised bills and Stuart didn't relish the idea of calling from a public phone with a handful of coins, bleeps in his ear every five seconds. What he needed was a private phone where the bill wasn't checked and he was in control. The idea dawned.

"Col," he shouted.

"Yes Daddy?" she said back faintly from the other side of the office.

"Want to go to Grandma's?" he shouted again.

"Yes please," she replied excitedly.

Stuart heard her jump off the chair and run towards his office.

Stuart's mother was always Grandma. Catherine's parents were more formally and grandly titled, Grandmother and Grandfather. Now seventy and widowed some three years previously, she had gone a little forgetful and slightly dotty, as Colleen was fond of saying. She had never really come to terms with her husband's untimely death, only a couple of years after retirement following many years of hard work. She had retreated into a semi-dream world a little detached from reality. Stuart visited as often as he could. Catherine had never really got on with her, and, since the death of her husband, Catherine had found her more and more exasperating and visited only once or twice a year. With the current split in the family, Stuart's visits tended to be with Colleen. Stuart also paid some of the bills in the house and helped his mother out with extra money from time to time. Her telephone bill was not itemised and it was one of the ones which Stuart paid almost every time. It was the perfect place from which to phone and visiting his mother gave him a good excuse to explain his withdrawal of the two hundred and fifty pounds from the joint building society account.

They left the office and drove the hour or so's journey to Grandma's house on the outskirts of Macclesfield. It was an oldish semi-detached house, too big for her and slightly rundown, but it had been their family home for so long that she was unwilling to move into something more suitable with all her memories still around her. Stuart had long given up trying to persuade her and he helped as best he could. Colleen bounded up to the door and banged on it loud and long, calling out, "Grandma! Grandma!" as she did so.

"Take it easy, Col," Stuart laughed.

"Well, she may be in the garden and she can't hear very good, you know," she said, hands on hips in a child's effort to give an adult explanation.

Stuart smiled back as she turned round to see the door opening.

"Grandma!" she shrieked with joy, and rushed up to her for a hug and a kiss.

"Well, Colleen my dear, haven't you grown so," Grandma replied. She always said more or less the same thing when they met. "And Stuart – you look tired. Are you working too hard?" she said with a seventy year old mother's concern.

He shook his head and laughed. "When will you stop worrying, Mother?" he said.

She didn't reply and led them both into the kitchen at the back of the house. The kitchen was warm and inviting, and the smell of cooking, cakes and scones, hung in the air.

"I've been baking this morning: cakes," Grandma said slowly to Colleen. "They are for my friend later but you and your dad can have some with a cup of tea if you want."

Colleen nodded.

"Can I use your phone?" Stuart asked, worried about the time difference and seeing his best opportunity when Colleen and Grandma were engrossed in making the tea.

"Yes, of course, my dear," Grandma replied.

Stuart went nervously into the cold hallway to the telephone. He tried to prepare his speech to Anwar, but in the end he just decided to play it as it came. He dialled. There was a long wait for the connection to be made. Then a long ring before it was answered.

"Hello," a small female voice said.

"Can I speak to Mr Anwar?" Stuart said loudly and slowly.

"Who you?" the voice said back.

"Mr Morgan," he said.

He heard the phone clatter down and the footsteps receding into the distance. He had another long wait. Then another set of footsteps came closer and the phone clattered again as it was picked up.

"Hello, is that you, Stuart?" Anwar's voice came down the line.

"Yes it is, how are you?" Stuart replied brightly.

"What the hell is going on with your company?" Anwar said loudly and angrily, launching into a rather surprising attack without exchanging any small talk first. "I've sent faxes and get no reply, I've phoned but I keep getting put off – I want to give up on you. Since you stopped working with me, after all we said" – the last phrase was expressed in a slow deliberate manner – "there has been nothing but trouble, and the situation is now so bad I'm not sure if we can retrieve it."

"I know, I know," Stuart said hastily. "I was taken off without my consent, for reasons which have nothing to do with business – I don't want to talk about it now, but I will tell you later. I just found out by accident what has been happening. I want to know what we can do about the situation. Can it still be recovered? Can we still turn it round and get the business?"

"Maybe you can – you, not anyone else. I don't want to deal with anyone else, not Mr James, not his staff and especially not that young man he sent here three times. You have to tell your company that you must come here if they are serious about this market, if not I will terminate our agreement immediately." Anwar was angry.

"I can't tell them that," Stuart replied strongly. "It's just not possible. It has to come from you."

"But I've tried! I've sent faxes to your president director and my secretary has tried to phone him but she just keeps getting put off. So it is becoming clear to me that he has no interest in Indonesia." Anwar's tone was defeated.

"Look, Anwar," Stuart said with firm determination in his voice, "he has, he just doesn't know what's going on. He hasn't received your fax because you didn't put his name or correct title on it and he has a private line so you can get him direct. You remember I gave you all his details on my last trip?"

"No," Anwar replied, confused.

"Yes you do. I gave you his name: Montague Holding."

"You didn't. If you had I would have remembered," Anwar replied, his voice confused still, but angry now as well.

"And this phone call didn't take place," Stuart said quietly.

"Ahh," Anwar replied, the idea finally having got through to him. "I'll get a pen and paper to write down those details you gave me last time."

Stuart gave him the necessary information.

"What should I say and when should I ring him?" was Anwar's final question.

"Monday morning. He's an early starter. Just tell him the truth and don't forget that this call never took place. Okay?" Stuart replied.

"Yes, okay, Stuart – and thanks. I always knew that we understood each other. Bye."

"Bye."

The phone went dead. Stuart had fired his ammunition, now he had to wait for its impact. There was nothing else to do except drink his mother's tea and eat her cakes so he replaced the receiver, stood up and went into the kitchen.

# CHAPTER 30

# MONDAY

Stuart's weekend of waiting finished when he wandered into the office very early on the Monday morning after his phone call to Anwar. He had not slept very well over the weekend. He had lain awake for many hours thinking of Ita, pregnant and alone in a society which still regarded unmarried mothers as little more than prostitutes, where she would be an outcast from her friends and possibly her family. He had cried to himself earlier in the morning when she came to him again in his half awake dream state, not the erotic images of earlier times, but again the vision of her sad eyes, her beautiful hair lank and unkempt, her stomach fat with child, her face contorted with the pain... of what? Of delivery, of isolation and rejection, he didn't know. His early start at the office was a way of driving the images from his mind.

He sat at his desk, drank his first cup of office coffee and went through his well filled in-tray. Within an hour, Frank wandered in and murmured a greeting to Stuart and hunched past his door. John followed ten minutes after that. After another half hour, Stuart got up and went out for his second cup of coffee. A small conference was going on between John and Frank and Frank's secretary. John broke off and went quickly into his office. Frank's secretary gathered some papers and handed them to Frank. Then John came out, files in hand, and the two of them set off without a glance at Stuart.

"What's up with those two?" he asked Frank's secretary, Harriet, as casually as he could.

"Oh, not sure. Franny telephoned down first thing and asked for me to send the two of them up. Some flap about something. Frank wanted all the files and papers on Indonesia before he went." She shook her head in resignation. "Always some crisis going on somewhere," she continued.

"Crisis?" Stuart said in mock alarm, knowing that Franny was the managing director's secretary, his heart beating a little faster at the news.

"Well, Franny sounded pretty agitated actually, not like her. She said Montague was in a real sweat over something." She shrugged her shoulders once again.

Stuart smiled at her as the conversation ended and went off to fill his coffee cup. Things seemed to be happening.

Frank and John did not appear for the remainder of the morning. Stuart lost himself in his work, the implementation of his board-approved plan for the small machine section of the company. When he looked at his watch it was nearly eleven-thirty. He had had only two cups of coffee so he rose to get a third before lunch. On the way towards the coffee machine he passed Harriet who was on the phone.

"Oh Stuart," she called to him, cupping the mouthpiece, "what are you doing for lunch?"

"Oh, after all these years you wait until now to ask me," he said with a silly grin on his face as he leaned over the low partition above her.

She grimaced. "It's Franny. Are you free for lunch with Mr Holding today, like in ten minutes?"

He shrugged his shoulders. "If the MD calls for lunch who am I to refuse?" It was only Stuart's second invitation to lunch with the managing director since he had joined Ormistons. He was excited and worried at the same time.

"So you're free?" she asked, still a little confused by his reply.

"Yes," he said with a firm, single nod of the head.

She went back to the phone. "Yes, okay." Then she looked at Stuart. "Downstairs in ten minutes," she said, smiling. "And comb your hair, straighten your tie, tuck your shirt in and put your jacket on," she said abruptly.

He smiled back, ignoring her instructions. "Sorry, looks like our lunch date will have to wait – the MD calls." His voice was put-on posh.

She shook her head and waved him away.

Despite his apparent disregard for her instructions, he nonetheless went into the washroom and checked all the items suggested by Harriet. He put on his jacket and wandered downstairs to the main office reception.

Frank and John were already standing in reception, each looking grave, with tight, grim expressions. Stuart smiled and received a curt, single nod from Frank; John simply glanced at him before averting his gaze to stare at his shoes. They stood in silence for two embarrassed minutes before the managing director, Montague Holding, made his entrance. He came from his office, on the same floor as the reception, and from behind them, six foot four of gangling, angular malco-ordination, glasses and expensive, ill-fitting suits.

"Ahh, hello! All here, good, good, come on," he said jovially, waving his right arm around and smiling broadly. His apparent uncontrolled exterior concealed a sharp, decisive mind and ruthless business acumen. "My, er, car should be waiting." He stood in front of the three of them.

No one moved.

"Stuart, come on," he said, gripping Stuart's jacket sleeve and pulling him towards the door. As they began to move, he put his hand on Stuart's shoulder. "You see, my boy, I liked your presentation the other week, and as you, er, know there is a follow on to your work." He paused to open the door for Stuart. "Good, good," he continued, disappearing into a mumble. "Come on you two," he said, turning as Stuart went through the door. "Don't dally." He waved at the hesitant figures of Frank and John, still standing in the lobby.

Obediently they followed.

The MD's car was waiting, a chauffeur-driven Jaguar XJ6 some five years old, but with leather upholstery and a brand-new shine. Mr Holding sat in the front and Stuart got in on the same side in the back seat. Frank and John went to the other side and John shuffled across to the middle, next to Stuart. As the car started on its journey, John swayed around in his slightly precarious position on the hump above the transmission tunnel. He screwed himself up and leaned away from Stuart, preferring to rub against Frank's shoulder than that of his old friend, Stuart. Stuart realised the severity of the position in which John had found himself as a result of his phone call to Anwar and Anwar's phone call to the managing director. Stuart felt a pang of regret at the gap between him and John. They had always been good friends and John had been doing nothing more than following the plan of his wife and Catherine, of that Stuart had no doubt.

But then he remembered Ita and her situation and he felt a little easier. John had largely got himself into this position; he could have made some business but he had failed; even with Chan's box of goodies, things had not worked out. Stuart looked out of the window and leaned hard against the car door to help John in his desire not to touch him.

"We'll go to The Old Coach House," Montague said to his driver as they moved into the traffic.

The driver nodded.

"We've all been there before, haven't we?" Montague asked, twisting himself round in the seat.

John and Frank nodded.

"And you, Stuart, after that presentation on the reorganisation, yes?"

"Yes, that's right," Stuart replied, beginning to realise that he was in the most favourable position for whatever lay ahead.

"How's it going? The reorganisation I mean. Implementation, everything, okay? Or not and problems?" Montague spoke with a uncoordinated flow, much like his movements.

Stuart found it rather disconcerting. "Well, any changes are bound to cause some problems – people don't like to change or adapt, especially if the workforce is being reduced," Stuart replied.

"But so far no problems with the unions?"

"No, not yet."

"Good... good." Montague's voice trailed off as he moved into thought.

The rest of the short journey was conducted in silence.

At The Old Coach House, a small converted manor house, Montague led the way in. Stuart followed in his wake and John and Frank were some way behind, John still clutching his armful of papers and files. Montague smiled and acknowledged the waiters and staff, who knew him well. They sat at a small coffee table in large leather armchairs, very much redolent of a gentlemen's club.

"John," Montague began, seeing John struggling with the files, "give those to the waiter. We'll not be needing them during lunch." He laughed.

John smiled, embarrassed, and handed the files to a waiter.

The menus and wine list arrived. "Drinks anyone?" Montague asked, an unnecessary question. "Gin and tonic for me," he continued. "For you, Stuart?"

"The same."

"And John?"

He nodded.

"Frank?"

"Please," Frank replied, his first word since they had gathered together.

"Okay. Four gin and tonics and, er, make them large ones, you know, no tonics with a waft of gin," Montague continued, addressing the waiter.

Montague handed out the menus, acting as an auxiliary waiter. They examined them in silence until the waiter reappeared with the four drinks.

"Cheers," said Montague good-humouredly.

Frank and Stuart responded in similar vein, but John merely gave a small smile as he raised his glass half-heartedly.

The waiter hovered nearby waiting for their order. Montague waved him back in after a few seconds, almost hitting him in the stomach.

"Ready?" Montague asked, looking around. He found no dissenting voices so he continued, "Chef's pâté and the sole – Dover sole, plain, grilled with no sauce – a few veggies and no potatoes."

He turned to Stuart.

"French onion soup and trout with the prawn and cream stuffing," Stuart replied.

"Would sir like vegetables and potatoes?" the waiter asked in a polite, subservient tone.

Stuart nodded.

"Frank, John, come on, don't dally," Montague said in a loud voice.

"Chef's pâté and a well-done pepper steak," Frank said in his normal voice.

"And you John?" Montague prompted.

"Deep-fried zucchini and a medium-rare pepper steak," he replied in a small weak voice which betrayed the tension he was under.

"So now to the wine," Montague said expansively. "We have fish and steak so one red and one white. Any preferences?" He looked around the table.

No one moved.

"Okay, we'll have a bottle of the '89 Chablis, well chilled for the fish, and for the steak I think a bottle of Australian Hermitage, the Margaret River '91." He snapped the wine list shut. "Okay for you two steak eaters?" he smiled at John and Frank.

"Fine," Frank replied.

Again John just nodded.

Now that the drinks had come and the wine had been ordered there were no more distractions for the four of them. A silence fell on the little gathering. Stuart, Frank and John all knew that it was up to Montague to break the silence: it was his lunch, he was their boss.

"Stuart," he began, tapping Stuart lightly on his right knee, "good to hear that the reorganisation is going well." He paused. "Er," he struggled for the next words, "what are you actually doing at the moment? Really, I mean?"

Stuart waited a while before he replied to make sure that Montague had finished. "Well," he began after a suitable pause, "I'm on with the detailed implementation. It's been gone through with the senior people and now it's down to the detail in the workshop, interviewing all the people, trying to sort out who's to retire early – you know, the nitty-gritty."

"Mmm, yes, yes, yes, I understand," Montague replied, slightly distracted, "but it's all basically routine and detail. The main work's been done?"

"Well, I guess so, but I'd like to see it through in detail just to make sure everything goes well and the best gets done for the future."

Montague didn't reply and the conversation hung in the air. He glanced at John and then Frank. "What do you know about Indonesia?" he asked Stuart slowly and deliberately, having come to the nub of the problem. "Well," he resumed very quickly, "not about Indonesia but about our, well..." He paused and waved his right hand around in a small circle near his head as if trying to start his brain working. "Well, about our, well, the company situation there," he finished fast and slightly comically, not as he had started out, grave and serious.

Stuart waited again to see if there was any more. When he felt that there wasn't he spoke. "All I know is from what I've read, or should I say not read, in the company newsletter." He stopped.

"Meaning?" Montague prompted.

"Meaning that we haven't taken any orders. If we had they would have been announced, even small ones."

"Like the first order we got, well, you got?" Montague said.

"Yes."

"And how does that make you feel, what do you think about it?" Montague continued.

"I'm disappointed. I had high hopes for that market and I believe that we should have made some progress and got some orders before now," Stuart said, choosing his words carefully.

"Why haven't we got any then?" Montague asked Stuart.

"Don't know." was Stuart's simple reply.

"Mmm," was all Montague said as he lolled back in his chair, taking a large pull of his drink.

The conversation paused again. This time it was broken not by any one of the four, but by the waiter telling them that their table was ready. They moved over in silence bringing their drinks with them. The chef's pâté had already arrived and Montague wasted no time in starting. The waiter busied himself with the bread rolls before Stuart's soup and John's zucchini were served. They all started to eat, the topic of conversation temporarily abandoned in the more important business of eating.

Stuart's soup was hot but good. He took a few tentative spoonsful and blew gently to cool it. Montague tucked into the pâté with a vengeance. When he had finished half of it he paused and finished the last of his pre-lunch drink.

"So you don't know why we haven't had any more orders, mmm?" he continued, picking up the thread of the earlier conversation.

"No, I don't," Stuart repeated.

Montague took another bite of pâté, Stuart some more soup and John finished the last of his diminutive portion of deep-fried zucchini.

"What do you think of our agent, Stuart?" Montague resumed once the bit of chef's pâté he had been chewing disappeared.

"Well, I found him to be very good. I think, in my dealings with him at any rate, I think he was reasonably straightforward, even honest."

John snorted. Stuart was not sure whether it was at the last mouthful of drink he took or at what Stuart had said.

"I mean, he appeared so both in my personal relationship with him and in the way he dealt with Ormistons. I think he had some good contacts, that he knew the way the system works. All you really need from an agent," Stuart continued, ignoring John's snort.

"Mmm," was Montague's reply as he considered what Stuart had said.

The starters were all but finished. The waiter cleared the plates and the besuited wine waiter came to their table with a flourish.

"One bottle of '89 Chablis and one bottle of '91 Margaret River Hermitage," he said in an over-posh voice. He showed the labels to Montague and, after his acceptance, opened both with a pomposity Stuart had not seen before in any act, let alone in opening a bottle of wine. Each bottle was offered to Montague to try, even though he was only going to drink from one. The wine waiter knew the pecking order, knew his regular customers and always deferred to them. Once Montague had accepted both bottles, the wine waiter made a dramatic theatrical performance out of pouring two glasses of each for the appropriate people. Then he left. They all tasted a sip of wine and then waited for the main course to arrive.

"Because, you see," Montague restarted the conversation quite unexpectedly, "our agent called me up this morning just after I arrived. He was... er, somewhat, how shall I say... emotional? Yes, that's the right word, emotional, about Ormistons and our business in Indonesia. He was most upset that we hadn't got any further orders and he put the blame well and truly with us, with Ormistons, principally for having taken you, Stuart, off the project." He paused for effect. "So what do you think about that?"

"He's just making excuses for his own failings, trying to set us up for a later sob story when we fail completely," John burst out, his voice quivering ever so slightly, showing the emotion in his voice, displaying the strain he was under. "His commission rates are astronomical and it wouldn't surprise me if he's on the take from our competitors to tie us up and lead us a right old dance," he continued.

Montague watched John, one eyebrow raised, an indulgent smile on his lips. "Yes, thank you, John, you made those feelings abundantly clear earlier this morning."

"Sorry," John said meekly, "but I think it's the truth and I wanted..." He paused, not wanting to say Stuart's name. "...Everyone to understand that," he finished.

Montague nodded. "But," he began, speaking very slowly. "But," he repeated, "of the four of us here, I haven't met our agent. Frank has met him once, you've seen him a couple of times and Stuart has by far the best experience of him and has, from what he said, the best relationship with him. That's the reason I wanted this lunch together, to get Stuart's opinion of him." He stopped as the waiter arrived to serve his main course and other waiters bustled up with the remaining ones.

The conversation again paused while the business of eating took priority.

When they had all made something of a start on their respective dishes, Montague rested his knife and fork and began again. "Knowing that he called me and knowing John's feeling and, I might add, Frank is of a similar opinion, although held with a little less fervour than John's," he waved his right hand in the general direction of Frank and John, "how do you see the situation with him?" Montague took up his knife and fork and started to eat while he waited for Stuart's reply.

Stuart paused in his eating. His reply was carefully measured. "Well," he began slowly, "if our agent" – he, like the others, avoided using Anwar's name – "has said something like that – that it's in some way our fault, that we are to blame for the lack of orders – then I would think that there is some fairly large element of truth in it. That's not to say that he wouldn't stoop to exaggeration to emphasise his point, but there must be some truth in it." Stuart had tried to be as diplomatic as possible in saying that he didn't believe John's interpretation of the situation one bit.

John shook his head; Frank chewed his steak and made no move.

"Mmmm, okay, so you think that there is some truth in it? That he's not just arse-covering in advance?" Montague said.

Stuart nodded in mid-chew.

"Mmmm," Montague said again, contemplating the situation.

He took a sip of wine and invited the rest of them to follow. The wine waiter reappeared to perform another mini-melodrama over refilling the glasses for each of them. Montague smiled politely at the performance and the wine waiter graciously accepted his praise.

"As you said, you are disappointed with our lack of performance. Do you think that if you had remained in control things would have been different?" Montague said after another mouthful of lunch.

"Hindsight is a wonderful thing," Stuart replied, trying desperately not to drop John and Frank further in it than they already were. "I cannot say yes or no to that question. In the report I wrote, I put what I thought was possible at that time on the basis of my experience. Things could have changed. Maybe he is out of favour now, I don't know," Stuart stalled.

John glanced at him with a little more friendliness in his eyes.

"You see, he, our agent, Mr An... er, what's his name?" Montague continued.

"Anwar," Frank said.

"Yes, Mr Anwar specifically asked that you, Stuart, be put back in charge of that market." He paused and looked directly at Stuart. "What do you think about that?"

"It's just another ploy by him to make an excuse for later," John butted in.

"Okay, John, we know your feelings on the matter. What we need now is Stuart's opinion – he probably knows Mr Anwar best." Montague turned to Stuart.

Stuart could only shrug his shoulders and look a little lost for words.

Montague helped him out. "You seem to have struck up quite a relationship with Mr Anwar. He spoke very highly of you, of your abilities and your understanding of the ways of doing business there."

"Yes, I did have a very good relationship with him, both in business and personally. It's very important out there, face to face, knowing people, far more important than it is here in the West." Stuart saw Montague nodding in agreement. "But I cannot say whether or not his demand is reasonable or not – I haven't had any involvement for months and I'm not in a position to judge." He paused and looked at Montague.

Montague nodded sagely again before waving his hand around, encouraging them to finish eating and drinking. He had already finished his meal, the smallest of those delivered, and Stuart had almost concluded too. Frank and John, on the other hand, were struggling with very large steaks. Montague allowed them some time and silence to finish their food.

The wine waiter appeared and performed again. Both bottles were empty and Montague waved him away before he could ask if they wanted any more. The plates were cleared and sweet menus offered. Frank and John both refused the menus, but Stuart took one, as did Montague. The waiter hovered.

"Just coffee for me," Frank said.

"And me," John added.

Montague sighed loudly. "Is anyone going to keep me company?"

"I'd, er, rather like some cheese," Stuart said quietly and hesitantly to the waiter.

Montague beamed. "Two cheeseboards and some..." He looked hard at Stuart, prompting him.

"Port," Stuart answered, much to Montague's delight. "Cockburn's Special Reserve," he added.

The waiter disappeared.

"Okay, can you two" – Montague gestured to Frank and John – "have your coffee over there in the lounge? I want to talk to Stuart alone. We'll join you in a minute."

They nodded without protest at what was quite an extraordinary snub by the managing director and stood to leave the table.

Montague waited until they were gone and the waiter had delivered the cheeseboard, some crackers and the port. Then he settled himself in his chair, smiled at Stuart and helped himself to a number of crackers and some Cheddar.

Stuart followed suit, preferring the Blue Stilton.

Then Montague began to talk. "I don't know why our friend Mr Anwar decided to ring me, on my private line. I don't know how he had the number, and..."

Stuart made to speak but Montague waved his hand for him to be silent.

"I don't want to know, it's not important," he continued, examining Stuart's reaction very hard.

Stuart put on his most innocent look.

After a few seconds Montague appeared satisfied and continued, "But I am very glad he did. The first minute I thought I had some loony on the phone – he was ranting and shouting – but once he calmed down and explained himself, I became worried. If what he said was true then we had a serious internal problem. So I called Frank and John to check everything and sure enough I found some things that I was not, am not, happy about." He waved at the waiter who stood just out of earshot. "Bring me the small blue folder that's with those files behind the reception," he said as the waiter approached.

"You see," he continued to Stuart, "he said he had sent me faxes that hadn't been replied to, that he'd tried to phone but had been put off. And this fax", he said, handing the blue folder the waiter had just delivered over to Stuart, "was the last one he sent, and the most damaging."

Stuart took the fax and read it. It was the same one he had found on Saturday morning. He nodded gravely to Montague and cast a glance at Frank and John sitting at the lounge table in full view but out of earshot. They both knew the contents of the blue folder.

"So you can see that Mr Anwar has quite a belief in you, and no confidence in who is in charge now, and has effectively given up on us. That's not what was supposed to have happened, is it?" It was a rhetorical question, inviting no response. "I've talked to Frank and John about this, about why you were moved off this assignment and how this situation has been allowed to develop to this point. Oh, I know the fax is wrongly titled and doesn't have my name on it but Frank kept it from me for four weeks. That's unacceptable and he has already been, well, bollocked over it, not to put too fine a point on it."

Stuart smiled.

"Now, and this is the delicate bit. Frank said by way of defence that he was protecting you, that something had happened with your personal life and that he felt it was in your best interests and the company's best interests to have you off that market and in head office. He said that he and John were doing the best they could in Indonesia and that the real problem was our agent, Mr Anwar. Now Frank wouldn't tell me what your problem was in detail. He mentioned something about a young family et cetera, but I don't really buy that, and I also don't buy the company interfering in its employees' private lives. We are not a nanny state here. People should be able to sort out their own lives without expecting the company to intervene." He paused for a sip of port. "Were you consulted about the job change? Did you agree with it?"

Stuart shook his head. "I wasn't consulted and I didn't agree with the decision but it was made clear to me that I was being given no choice."

Montague nodded. "Okay. Well, I know what it's like travelling abroad. I did enough of it in my early days and, well," he chuckled a little, "I had quite a reputation until my wife found out." He laughed again, this time out loud. "We came close to divorce but we sorted it out, I carried on travelling and ended up MD. So I do know what it's like and I'm not going to question you about the situation, what happened or tell you to pull yourself together et cetera, et cetera. It's up to you to sort it out in the best way that you feel you can." He signalled the waiter for some more port.

"What are we going to do, about Indonesia and Mr Anwar? Do you think that you can turn the situation round?" Montague continued, changing tack.

"Until I've read the files, talked to John and Anwar, I can't say – I've had no involvement since I changed jobs," Stuart replied.

"How long?"

"Don't know. Three or four days to find out what's happened and make some notes."

"Okay, so if you started straightaway, this afternoon, with that pile of files John brought with him, by Friday we could have your opinion?" Montague asked.

Stuart nodded.

"What we also need in parallel is someone to assess Mr Anwar and his complaints," Montague continued, looking seriously at Stuart. "Who would you suggest for such a duty?"

Stuart was confused. Was he supposed to say himself or nominate someone else? "Well, as I really need to be the one to sort out the story here, it needs to be someone else; and anyway if I do go it could be said that my opinion was somewhat biased." He paused.

"How about if I went?" Montague said quietly.

Stuart hadn't thought of that, but as he did, he realised that it was an ideal solution. He nodded. "Anwar has an ego. If the managing director flies out to see him to solve the problem he would be very happy and it would make him redouble his efforts, I'm sure." He nodded again.

"Right, I'll leave this evening, that's the best flight: the evening one from Heathrow?"

Stuart nodded again, shocked at the swiftness with which Montague intended to react to the situation. He was just beginning to realise how much Anwar's phone call had shaken up Montague.

"And I can give the name of the hotel to your secretary," Stuart added.

"Now if I arrive back on, say, Saturday morning, would you come in for a meeting and if necessary would you be prepared to leave on Monday?" He paused to let Stuart reflect. "I'm asking you in all seriousness now, if you – and I mean you, not anyone else in this company – if you feel that your personal situation would prevent you from going then I will understand."

Stuart shook his head. "I will go. If you believe, after your trip, that I am the best person in this organisation to sort out this mess then I will go."

Montague nodded and smiled, satisfied. "Let's join the others for some coffee and brandy. I think that those two look as if they could do with one." He grinned.

They stood up and walked over to Frank and John. Two more coffees arrived and Montague ordered brandies for all of them. Stuart knew that he would need to take a taxi or the bus home. He guessed the others would be in the same situation, except Montague, who had his chauffeur.

"Now then, you two," Montague began warmly and in a friendly tone, "I'll tell you what has been decided and how we will proceed." He paused for a good look at the two of them. "As of now, Stuart will take hold of all those files over there," he gestured towards the reception desk, "and he will go through them, and all the other relevant documentation, to see what he thinks can be done. I want you both and that young chap you sent out to Indonesia to give Stuart whatever co-operation he needs. Okay?" he said, nodding at John and Frank.

They nodded meekly.

"Good. Frank, you have been working quite closely with Stuart on the small machine section so I think that you can look after the implementation work that Stuart has started, at least in the short term. When we know what is happening we can look again." He paused for another look around them. "Now I am going to Indonesia this evening to see for myself our Mr Anwar and what his problem is. I plan to arrive back on Saturday morning and we will convene a meeting early, say eight o'clock, in the office to discuss our future plans – that's all four of us here." He looked around for affirmation.

Stuart nodded; Frank and John also nodded, but both had a startled look on their faces at the swiftness and seriousness of Montague's response to Anwar's phone call.

"Good. Now Stuart will report what he has found and then we will all discuss our future course with reference to that and what I find. As a precaution, I think you, Stuart, should book yourself out on Monday evening to arrive Tuesday."

Stuart nodded. One week to wait.

"So that is the agenda for this lunch, complete and finished." Montague sat back in his chair and raised his brandy glass for the first time. "Cheers."

The rest followed suit.

"And as we've had a bit to drink this lunchtime I want all of you to take taxis home at company expense." He beamed round them at his own generosity.

They all smiled and nodded and sipped the rather excellent brandy with a little more relish.

"You see," Montague began in an expansive voice from his position of repose, "this market, Indonesia, is very important to me, to Ormistons." He sipped his brandy again. "I started work for Ormistons straight from school. I was an apprentice on the shopfloor, then in the drawing office, then they sent me to the local college and on to university. They gave me everything I had and I worked myself silly for them. I was a designer, a commercial man, a salesman and, by the time I was forty, a director. Then old Watson, God bless his cotton socks, popped off and they gave me the job of MD when I was a few days short of my forty-first birthday. I love this company – it's been bloody good to me and I've given it the best of what I have to offer." He paused for further reflection and to wave an order for some more brandy for them all. "Now I want to step down – many people say I should have stepped down years ago, but we'll ignore them," he said with a laugh. "But I felt that I couldn't do it, not with the current situation. You see," his voice went quiet and conspiratorial, indicating that he was letting them in on some secret, "we had, what shall I say, arrangements with other people for a long time. Now those are breaking up: it's not the same game, not the same world. I don't want to leave the company hidebound by those old systems and to have people point at me and say 'he got out while the going was good'. I want to leave a legacy for this company that's strong and vibrant so that I can look at you all in twenty years and still be proud." His voice became loud and strident again. "And the first part of that is to establish ourselves in the markets previously closed to us by these arrangements. Indonesia is the first one, the first challenge. So if we do this one well then it's a model for the rest; if we mess it up then it's still a model but not really the right one." He looked solemnly at the assembled company. "So that's why I am going this evening, that's why Stuart is going to look at it all and that's why I expect full co-operation from all of you. It's that important." He stopped and took up the newly delivered brandy glass. His speech finished, his dominant personality silent, the conversation stopped: no one else felt able to follow him.

Once the brandies were finished, he signalled for the bill and they all stood to leave. Stuart collected John's files at Montague's direction; then he accompanied Stuart as they left.

"Is there anything else I can do for you?" he asked in a low voice.

Stuart looked at him, a little confused.

"To ease any problems you might have," he continued.

"Well, if you could just tell my wife what you have told us about the importance of this market and my potential future involvement, then that would help."

"No problem. I'll get my secretary to draft up a letter for me to sign. Addressed to your wife directly?" he asked.

Stuart nodded.

Montague held the door and they boarded the waiting Jaguar.

When Stuart finally arrived home, by taxi, it was late, after seven-thirty in the evening. He had spent the remaining portion of the day with John, talking and discussing what had happened in Indonesia over the previous months. John had been quite civil; he had even apologised to Stuart for the situation in Indonesia and had thanked him for the way in which he had responded to Montague's questions over lunch. Montague's secretary had handed Stuart an envelope addressed to his wife and Stuart held it tightly in his hand as he approached the front door of his house. He was nervous but outwardly composed for the coming confrontation with his wife.

He let himself in gently and went straight to the kitchen where he expected to find Catherine at her sink, as he usually did before a confrontation. However, this time she wasn't there; instead she was in the lounge watching television.

"Hi," she said with a warm smile as he came in. "You're late. I've already fed the kids, but there's some left for you. It should still be okay."

He sat down heavily. "It's no problem. I had lunch today."

"Oh, with who?" she said, her head on one side, her face a little confused.

"With John, Frank and the MD," he replied, his face serious.

"Trouble?" she asked, picking up his note.

"Of a sort."

"About your programme for the factory?"

"No, not about that, that's fine – everything is going well with that," he said.

"So about what?" She was becoming irritable at his evasiveness.

"About my previous job, before I started on the factory reorganisation. There are some tremendous problems with that work." He paused and looked at her. "Well, here, I think you should read this, it's addressed to you from the MD." He handed her the letter.

She looked at it gravely and then at him. "Have you been sacked?" she said in a hushed tone.

He smiled broadly and shook his head. "No, I haven't. Read it."

She looked relieved because Stuart had not been sacked, but then her worried look returned as she turned the envelope around in her hands, not wanting to open it. She looked at Stuart again and then decisively ripped it open.

She read it without a change of expression, her lips moving slightly as she read. Then she lowered it and looked at Stuart. "Do you know what this says?" she asked.

He shook his head. "No. I can guess the contents but I haven't read it."

She handed it to him. "You'd better read it then," she said quietly.

*Dear Mrs Morgan,*

*I do not intervene or interfere in the personal lives of the employees of the company except in unusual circumstances, nor do I believe that it is the company's duty to make compromises in its business to alleviate the personal difficulties of employees. I firmly believe that all my employees and their families are sufficiently mature to be able to solve their own problems without* the intervention of people from the company whose own lives may be just as problematical. As you will find as you read this letter, I think that you will understand the nature of the circumstances and why I find it agreeable to write to you personally.

As an employee myself, of Ormistons for almost forty years and the managing director for almost twenty years, I have a deeply held feeling for the company and its employees. I want to leave Ormistons in a condition better than I found it and with prospects for the future which will ensure that I can still visit the place in twenty years time and recognise the company and the spirit.

This is a changing world and a company like Ormistons must change, adapt and regroup constantly to follow those changes, to stay ahead and to keep the financial and technical results good to safeguard our collective employment. Part of the current change has been an erosion of the barriers around the world which simultaneously protected us in and excluded us from the various markets around the world. We must now fight harder in the protected areas and must view the formerly excluded ones as a challenge and opportunity for the future.

Your husband was chosen by the management to spearhead the first challenge in a new market, that of Indonesia. It was and still is very much a test case, a proving ground for the future. During his time in the market he performed some remarkable feats. He brought back orders, he established agencies and put Ormistons in a very strong position. Since his promotion, our performance in that market has left much to be desired to the point that our very involvement in that market is under threat. Stuart has fulfilled the duties in his new job with more than ample success. His programme is already being implemented and the benefits are being felt. However, the fact remains that his time could probably have been spent more usefully for the good of the company in *continuing to deal with the Indonesian market. There are others in the company who could have fulfilled Stuart's role in the office but few if any who could have continued the work he started in Indonesia.*

*I myself am leaving for Indonesia this very evening to assess, at first hand, the condition of the market and the possibilities for recovery. Should my findings show that we can recover, then I must ask your husband to return to Indonesia to bring the work he started with such promise to a successful conclusion. This is by far the most important job that your husband can undertake for the company.*

*He has already been asked if he is willing to return, should it be necessary, and he has been given the time to consider this position. However, I have impressed upon him the severity of the situation in Indonesia and I believe that if the situation warrants it, your husband's presence in Indonesia will be required.*

*Yours sincerely,*
*Montague Holding*

Stuart let the letter drop and looked at Catherine. Her face had hardened, her eyes were cool: she stared back at him.

"So you're going back?" she said finally.

"Not necessarily," he replied truthfully.

"I think so," she said. "I knew this would happen some time, the only question was when."

"Again, not necessarily. If John had done his job properly, as I said in my final report, then no, it wouldn't have occurred," he said.

She stood, walked over to the dresser and rummaged for a packet of cigarettes, which she found. She sat again and lit one, blowing out smoke in a long, satisfied breath. "I suppose you're right about that," she sighed. "But will you go, if he asks you?"

"Yes," he said simply. "I have no choice. If the MD calls, then I must do what he asks."

"I knew this would happen sooner or later, whatever John did or didn't do, and I've tried to ask myself what I would do when it did happen." She pulled on the cigarette again.

Stuart hated the smoke, hated the sight of her smoking.

"If things had been all right between us then I wouldn't mind," she said.

"You don't think things are all right now?" he asked.

"Oh come on, Stuart!" she said angrily. "Of course they're not! God knows I've tried! I've worked at it well, and so have you, I know. But things are not the same as before. I was just beginning to think that they could be given more time and now this." She pointed at the letter. She inhaled deeply again from the cigarette and started to speak, blowing the smoke out at the same time.

Stuart hated it even more.

"I will just say that if you come back with so much as a scent on you of..." She paused. "...Of her," the words were rasped out in the smoke, "then you can find a lawyer. And don't think that you can fool me, that you can have both – you can't fool me and you can't have both. I will know." She pointed her smoking hand with the cigarette at him, her eyes hard and cold, narrowed.

"Don't be so extreme, Catherine," he said, alarmed.

"Extreme!" she snorted. "I'm not the one who's been humping around the world and I'm the one who's been trying desperately to rebuild this marriage so I don't think I'm being extreme. Just remember, I will know, and if I suspect even one per cent, find yourself a lawyer." She pointed the smoking fingers at him again for emphasis.

In that moment, Stuart hated his wife: her cold eyes, the smoking cigarette, the vicious tone in her voice, the finality of what she had said.

"Want some tea?" she asked, still standing.

He nodded.

As Catherine left through one door to the dinning room, Colleen came in through the other from the hall. She came up to her father.

"Daddy, if you and Mummy are going to get a divorce like my friend Amalea, then I want to stay with you. I don't want to go with Mummy and Ralph is horrible to me, always picking on me and making me cry. I like being with you best, with Daddy," she said, her eyes welling up with tears.

He clutched her to him, rubbing his face against her mass of hair. "Don't worry, it won't come to that. Mummy and Daddy will solve the problem," he said in his most reassuring voice.

He may have reassured her for the moment, but he did not reassure himself for one second.

## CHAPTER 31

## "I KNEW YOU'D COME BACK"

Exactly a week after Catherine had read Montague's letter, to the hour and almost to the minute, Stuart was strapping himself into his seat for the short forty-five minute flight from Manchester to London as a preliminary for the thirteen hour flight to Singapore. He had not been on an aeroplane, or any business trip, since he had come back from Indonesia the last time; the old schoolboy rush of excitement at the prospect of travel was coming back.

The week since the lunch with Montague had gone extremely fast in some parts, whilst other parts had dragged interminably. The work part had gone quickly, the home part, especially the weekend after the Saturday morning meeting, very slowly. Stuart had had to work very hard to firstly understand the full situation, to question John and his staff, to talk to Anwar and Montague by phone and then to work out new offers, technical and commercial, with the company and with the banks and government offices. John had been very co-operative. He knew the difficult situation in which he was and he was grateful to Stuart for the way that he was behaving. They all pulled together as Montague had requested. Frank took over Stuart's existing work on the reorganisation and helped with the new offers where he could. About two-thirds had been done and the rest would have to be done on the run during the trip.

Montague had returned on the Saturday morning and the meeting had been held as planned. Montague was extremely positive about the future. He was certain that Ormistons was not yet shut out; he was sure that Anwar was the man and that Stuart needed to return immediately as planned. Anwar had taken Montague down to Surabaya to meet Chan, with the rest of the time being spent in Jakarta, including a round of golf. Montague had evidently got on well with Anwar and Anwar was fired up again. Stuart had realised this from his phone calls with Anwar, especially on the Friday. Stuart presented what he had found, showed the things he wanted to change and revise some of the offers, and described what was still to be done. They were all allocated work by Montague, and the meeting had finished by eleven.

Stuart wound his way home slowly that day. He told Catherine straightaway that he was going on Monday. She said nothing, she just gave her cold, hard stare and lit another cigarette. The rest of Saturday and the following Sunday went so slowly. They barely spoke and the atmosphere was tense and hostile. Both the children recognised it and clung to their respective favoured parent all the more. When it was finally time to leave on Monday afternoon, Stuart had come back to the house especially to say goodbye, to see if there was any relaxation in Catherine.

She had stood at the front door, legs crossed, arms folded, with a cigarette in her mouth, giving him the cold, hard stare: no hint of relaxation, no hint of compromise, the finality of the situation confirmed. Only Colleen came down the path with him, holding his hand. He got into the taxi and she kissed him through the open window.

"I love you, Daddy, please come back for me," she had said with tears in her eyes. A picture of Ita saying, "You will not abandon me," flashed through his mind and he nodded and smiled at Colleen. "Of course I will," he had said.

She had smiled back through the tears.

Now as he sat, readying himself for take-off from Manchester Airport, his thoughts of his life in England faded and his mind turned to the prospects ahead.

An hour and a half later he found himself wandering round in the still incomplete Terminal Three at Heathrow, checked in, security checked, immigration cleared and ready to go. He looked in the duty-free and wondered what to buy for Ita. Then he had the sudden thought: what to buy for the baby? Here he was, thirty-eight years old, married, with two children, wondering what to buy for an unborn baby, his child, by a small woman from a foreign country. He stopped and shuddered, shook his head as the thought became too much for him and then walked out. He bought a couple of magazines and then drank some tea to distract himself.

When boarding time came he moved down the ramp towards the plane door. There, standing in the doorway, as she had been the first time he had ever boarded a Singapore Airlines plane, was another radiantly beautiful Singaporean air hostess welcoming him on board. He had, in the eight months since his last trip, forgotten just how beautiful they were, the women of South-East Asia. Every small woman with black hair had caused him to turn his head in England, but now that he was confronted with the real thing again the surprise he had felt on his first trip was rekindled. She directed him up the stairs to the top deck. For once on a long-haul trip he was travelling in the business class, Raffles Class, because no economy booking could be made for this sector of the outward trip. In the top deck area it was spacious, almost club-like in its atmosphere. The hostesses were much more attentive, if that were possible, and they all used his name from the start. He was able to work, eat in comfort, drink a lot of good wine and watch half a film. Just before he dropped off a stewardess passed him and offered him a 'Do Not Disturb' sticker. She stuck it on the chair behind his head and then he fell asleep. His sleep was so deep that he wasn't woken for the dreaded airline breakfast; instead he was only woken when the same stewardess lifted his chair into the upright position for landing at Singapore.

He was barely awake as he stumbled off the plane to wait for the connecting flight. He wandered aimlessly around, gradually waking up. Then he was on another Singapore Airlines flight, surrounded by a new crew of equally exceptional air hostesses. He never noticed the male flight attendants; he was not even sure if there were any. Then he was passing through Indonesian immigration, queuing for half an hour, and then he was passing straight through customs.

Then he was out in the front of the building with the warm, humid night air wrapped around him like a cloak, the smell of the clove cigarettes hanging in the air like some exotic perfumed incense. Then the sea of brown faces was looking at him over the tall, black, iron fence posts. He turned left and passed out into their midst. The taxi touts approached but he brushed them aside and made for his friendly pink-capped hotel man. He took an ordinary taxi. On the journey to the hotel his eyes became familiar again with so many sights that had slipped from his memory: the roadworks, the traffic, the sheer number of people who crowded and crushed everywhere in the tropical night. It almost felt like the first time again.

Once at the hotel, he insisted on carrying his own small case. He didn't want the customary wait for the bell boy, for speed was now of the essence. The receptionist greeted him like a long-lost friend. She shook his hand and welcomed him back. He completed the formalities quickly and was then upstairs in his room, frantically showering and changing. He carefully wrote Ita's new address on the back of one of the hotel cards.

Then he went downstairs to the front of the hotel.

"Taxi, sir?" the doorman said.

Stuart nodded in response.

A taxi arrived and the doorman held the door open for Stuart. Stuart tipped him two hundred rupiah for his trouble.

The taxi driver looked at Stuart in his mirror.

Stuart handed him the piece of paper.

The driver turned and took it, squinting in the light to read it properly. He looked surprised and read it a second time, turning it over to see if there was anything else. Then he pointed at the card and looked at Stuart.

Stuart nodded.

"Okay, okay," the driver said, lifting both hands in gesture of resignation.

Stuart realised that the area was probably not the most salubrious neighbourhood in Jakarta and the driver was reluctant to go there.

They drove along streets Stuart recognised, down a wide avenue, tree-lined, with fast and slow lanes, then across some traffic lights and down a second wide road, not tree-lined but lined with scruffy buildings, small stalls and vacant patches of ground. The driver turned off and Stuart lost all sense of direction. They crossed a small dark river that flowed between sloping stone walls, past what looked like a market and then they stopped.

"Here?" Stuart said.

The driver nodded.

"You wait?" Stuart asked, gesturing downwards with his hand.

"No!" the driver said loudly, shaking his head, thrusting his hand out for the money and leaving Stuart in no doubt.

Stuart paid him, stepped out into the warm night and felt the sweat begin to trickle almost immediately. Then the smell of the river, of small and dirty drains, hit him in both nostrils. He coughed a little. He looked around and felt a hundred pairs of brown eyes staring at him. Directly in front was a small alleyway between two dilapidated houses. He crossed the road and looked down. A small group of people had stopped and was staring openly at him. He wanted the taxi back, he wanted its air-conditioned comfort, he wanted to run away – anywhere away from this awful scene – but he remembered Ita and stood his ground.

A small boy came up to him, perhaps eight or nine. Stuart showed him the card. The boy appeared to read it carefully and then handed it back to Stuart. Stuart looked at him imploringly and the boy looked back, his head on one side, as if trying to assess something about Stuart. The boy made a signal with his hands over his stomach, to indicate a fat tummy. Stuart nodded and smiled, repeating the gesture himself.

"Ita," he said slowly.

The boy nodded and led the way down the dark alleyway.

Stuart tried to count his steps and watch the turns: one to the left, up two stairs, one to the right, one to the right again, duck for the low roof sticking out. But he was soon lost and he doubted if he could find his way out. Maybe the boy was leading him to his friend for a friendly mugging, Indonesian style. But they pressed on, going deeper into the maze of rundown and dilapidated houses, shops and small businesses: a tailor on one side, a small food shop, a one seat barber, a motorbike repair shop, everything for life in fifty yards of muddy path. And then the boy stopped in front of one door, a small door, not as tall as Stuart. A small step above the path level over a muddy gutter reduced the height further.

"Ita?" Stuart said again.

The boy nodded and knocked on the door for Stuart.

The door was opened by an older woman with a brown, weatherbeaten face, the skin wrinkled round the eyes, but tight and smooth over the forehead. Her hair was black with a few grey lines, pulled tight into a bun on the back of her head. She wore the traditional sarong, waistband and jacket. Stuart examined her face closely: there was something familiar about it, but something he could not place. He looked into the eyes briefly and saw some small part of Ita. It was Ita's mother without a doubt. He smiled at her but got no response.

"Ita?" Stuart said to the woman.

She looked at the boy and then at Stuart. She nodded and opened the door a little further, stepping back to allow Stuart in.

Stuart smiled at the boy and handed him a five hundred rupiah note. He took it and examined it closely. Then he smiled at Stuart and sat down by the door to look over his banknote once again.

Stuart entered the small room. It was dimly lit by a single bulb of perhaps only forty watts. The floor was bare cement, but brushed clean. A small table, broken glass-topped with a rusting metal frame, was surrounded by three chairs with low backs and patched upholstery. The room smelled musty like the entrance hall of Ita's previous house, but here the musty smell was almost overpowering. The whole place reeked of damp and decay, of mildew and rising damp. The woman closed the door and he moved into the centre of the room and looked around again. Three doors led off. One was open to an outside area which Stuart guessed contained the kitchen and bathroom; the other two were closed. The woman pointed at one.

"Ita?" Stuart said again, smiling.

She nodded but gave no acknowledgement of his smile.

Stuart approached the door. Now his heart was beating hard against his ribs, his throat was dry: on the other side of the door was Ita, pregnant and alone. He could still turn, he could still run, he didn't need to be here, he didn't need to come back. But he didn't run or turn or stop. He pushed the door gently and it opened, swinging in to reveal a small room lit by a small table lamp. Beyond the lamp was a low bed, a bit bigger than a single but not much, and in the middle of the bed was a curled-up lump with black hair flowing out.  It was Ita.  He had come back, he had kept his promise by her, he had not abandoned her.

He heard the door close behind him and he took a step forwards towards the bed.  Then he stopped and glanced round the room.  The ceiling was made from woven bamboo, like the ceiling in the main entrance room.  It was painted white and stained brown from leaking rainwater.  The walls were also painted white, a thin, wishy-washy white that gave the room a shabby, uncared-for appearance.  There was an uneven brown tidemark around the walls showing the level to which the rising damp had risen in the past.  A small window was covered by a piece of cloth fixed with drawing pins.  The floor was rough concrete.  Beyond the bed was a small cupboard made from brown-painted wood like the bed.  On it was an electric fan, its flex still coiled neatly in the manufacturer's clip, showing that it was new.  A pile of baby clothes lay next to it, still in their polythene wrappers.  Beyond that a bottle of Johnson's Baby Powder, some baby oil and other baby equipment.  Wedged between the baby oil and baby powder, Stuart could see a number of airmail envelopes, his airmail envelopes – they had arrived.  Under the small window was a new baby crib, a wickerwork basket on a folding wooden stand, lined with a nice patterned cloth with a mosquito net over the top.

Stuart felt a lump coming to his throat as he looked at Ita's preparations for the coming baby.  Then he looked at a second cupboard at the foot of the bed.  On the top was a picture of him mounted in a cheap plastic frame.  Next to that was the little bonsai tree standing on his monogrammed linen handkerchief, the S at the front.  The small boxes which had contained the chocolates and the orchid he had brought from the hotel for her one day lay on the other side of the tree.  Now tears welled in his eyes.  He fought them back and dabbed his eyes with his hanky.

He turned back to the bed and moved closer.  "Ita," he said in a whisper.  No movement.  "Ita," he said a little more loudly.  Still no movement.  Then he sat on the low bed and touched her left arm gently.

She moved a little.

"Ita," he called again.

She half turned over; he could see her face, her eyes still closed.

"Ita," he called again. Then he could see her face fully as the eyelids began to move.

He was shocked. Gone was the bright, healthy, brown complexion, replaced by a grey pale pallor, with heavy bags below the eyes. Her cheekbones appeared to stick out more, her cheeks were hollowed, her lips almost indistinct, so much had they faded in colour. Her hair looked thin and lank and it had no shine. She looked like the vision of her which he had had on the Saturday that the letter had arrived.

The eyes opened. They were still the same, still and deep as he looked into them when they opened. First they registered confusion at the face staring down, then, by degrees, recognition, then disbelief and finally happiness.

"Stuart?" she said quietly. "It's really you? I'm not dreaming?"

He shook his head.

A smile came to her pale lips; they parted to reveal her teeth, still white and still perfect. "You came back"

He nodded again.

She lifted her right arm and put it over his left shoulder, pulled herself up and close to him. He helped her and they wrapped arms around each other in a long and relieving hug. They were back together.

When they broke the embrace, Ita looked better to Stuart's eyes. Her face seemed brighter, the pale look gone. There was a knock at the door and the woman who had let Stuart in came in with two cups of tea on a small tray. She set them down by the lamp and said something to Ita.

"Stuart," Ita said, "this is my mother. You can call her Ibu or Bu for short."

Stuart smiled and extended his hand to take the one she had offered. They shook hands and she touched her right hand to her chest, receiving Stuart to her heart in the traditional Javanese way. Stuart followed suit and Bu looked at him but did not return his smile. Then she left them alone.

Stuart helped Ita to sit up, puffing the thin pillows as best he could and seeing the lump that was their baby for the first time. He laid his hand on it.

"Does the baby kick much?" he asked.

She shook her head. "Sometimes but not much. I got your letters, two yesterday and three the day before. You sent five, right?"

"Yes, each one with a hundred dollars in. You got all the money?"

"Yes, thank you so much. The reason I'm so tired is we went shopping today for all this." She waved her hand at the new baby equipment. "And then to the doctor for an examination. He says our baby is small and that I am a bit low in weight and my blood is low in iron. He gave me tablets and told me to eat more." She smiled at him. "It's so good to see you again, so good. My mother told me you would never come back, but I knew you would. Did you find the house easy? Was there a little boy waiting for you?"

"Yes there was. He came to me and then led me here. I was worried at first but I'm glad of him now."

"He's a bit slow. He doesn't speak much, but he's been my friend ever since I came here. I told him to wait for an *orang bule* to come, a white man. I said he would come one evening. So he's been waiting in the front every night for six weeks. I was so sure you would come."

"If I had known about your situation I would have come before. I'm happy to see you again, Ita. I've missed you a lot, but I'm so sorry for..." He pointed at her stomach. "It's my fault."

She smiled at him. "No, it takes two people to do this. It's my fault as well." She stopped smiling and looked at him seriously. "But, Stuart, what happened? Why you didn't get my letters?"

He looked at her with equal seriousness. "It's a long story. You are not tired?"

She shook her head.

"Okay. Well, before I came here the last time, my er..." He paused, embarrassed. "My wife", he began again with some resolution, "found out about us. It was an accident and she was not happy."

Ita dropped her head and bit her lip. She avoided his eyes as she spoke. "I'm sorry, Stuart, about that – I never wanted to make a problem for you like that. I just wanted you here, I didn't mind in England with your wife. I'm sorry."

"She was very upset, very angry with me. I told her, absolutely truthfully, that I had never been unfaithful to her before. She told me that I had to tell you it must stop when I came back last time."

"So that was what you were talking about when you came back the last time?" she asked, looking at him again.

"Yes."

"In bed after we already make love three times?" she asked, her eyes sparkled a little.

"Yes, correct," he said with raised eyebrows and a smile.

"So why didn't you say those things before we, well, you know, like in the taxi or anywhere but in your hotel room?" she asked.

"Because everything I had thought about since my wife found out went away when I saw you again. I knew that you were more than someone I had just slept with a few times. I knew that I was, *am* in love with you and that I couldn't just stop. I thought that I could carry on like you said, with you here in Indonesia and my life in England. It sounded so easy when I was here."

"So what happened when you got home?" she asked, her voice quiet.

"My wife knows me too well – she knew the moment I walked in the house that I hadn't done what she had told me to do, that I had seen you again and carried on with our relationship."

"Oh," she said. "So is that why you changed your job, so that you wouldn't have to come to Indonesia again?" Ita asked, still in her quiet voice.

"No, that's not what happened," he said, looking at her to show that he was being serious and truthful. "That's not what happened at all." He paused to let the words sink in.

She looked at him for a while and slowly the seriousness on her face relaxed a little, she understood he was telling the truth and her worst fear, that he had deliberately chosen to stay away from Indonesia, was reduced, but not eliminated.

"What actually happened was that while I was here, after my wife found out, she went to her friend, her best friend, who is the wife of a good friend of mine who works in the same office. She told her and my friend what had happened. Between the three of them they made a plan to get me a new job to keep me away from Indonesia. Then my friend went to my boss and asked him if the plan was a good one. They planned to promote me and give me a job that they knew I would be very interested in."

"So you took this new job for the promotion and because it was interesting?" she said, her voice cool and questioning.

Stuart was a little shocked by the attitude she was displaying. She was so happy to see him and he had expected that to override all other considerations. But she had not allowed her joy at his return to stand in the way of her finding out what had happened and resolving the questions which she must have been turning over and over in her mind for the last eight months.

"No," he replied firmly. "I was given no choice. I could not refuse, I had to accept. If I had refused then my future would have been finished. If I left my company then the chances of me being able to come back here were nil. If I stayed then, maybe, I thought, I could find a way to come back. The new job only had a short life, less than a year before I would have been found something else in the company; maybe at that time I could have come back to work in Indonesia. My wife and her friends were very clever in doing it the way they did."

"So what happened to my letters? You really didn't receive them?" she asked, changing her tack a little.

"No, I didn't, and that was my wife's doing as well."

"She read them?" Ita asked, horrified.

He shook his head. "No, they were intercepted when they arrived in the office and were destroyed unopened. I am sure of that."

She nodded, relieved. "So what changed? Why can you come now?"

"Your letter to my house changed everything," he replied.

"Your wife didn't find it?"

"No she didn't. It arrived on a Saturday, she was out – it was luck."

"So she doesn't know about our baby?"

"No, she doesn't. I tried to sort out the most immediate problem, money, and sent the five letters to you. Then the same day I went to the office to see if I could find a way of getting back here as soon as possible. I found that things here for our company were very bad. So I called our agent and he said they were very bad, if we didn't do something very quickly then we could forget Indonesia as a market. I told him to call my big boss, the managing director. He did and our MD came here last week. When he went back we had a meeting and he said that I had to come here straightaway to resolve the situation."

"And your wife and her friends in your company?" she asked.

"Well, my friends in the company got told off by the MD for not telling him what was really happening, and my wife was, is very unhappy," he replied with a big sigh.

"What will you do when you go back? With your wife, I mean?" she asked, her voice quiet.

"Ita," he replied, "my wife is not important here and now. I have to worry about you and the baby, I have to worry about the job, sorting out the mess, winning some orders and making a future for my company here. I have not thought about what will happen when I go back – it's not the time for that," he said, completely truthfully, for he had given the prospects of return no thought, except to understand that it would be traumatic. Beyond that he had not thought, nor did he want to think any further.

She appeared satisfied by his response and settled down, her face more happy, and took up the cup of tea. Stuart did the same.

"You look tired, Stuart," she said, her manner normal, the cross-examination over.

"Yes, I suppose I do. It's past twelve," he said, looking at his watch, "and I've been travelling for twenty-four hours. But you are the one who needs the rest."

"I'm fine, much better now that you are here with me," she said with a smile. "How long will you stay?"

"At least a month, perhaps longer. It depends."

"So you will be here when the baby comes?" she said excitedly.

"When is it due?"

"The doctor said a week, maybe less."

"Well, if I can be here then I will be. Tomorrow I have to go to our agent and find out what the plan is for the next few days," he said, setting the cup of tea down.

"Will you come tomorrow night, to see me?" she asked, looking up at him with her big, brown eyes, the playful Ita coming to the fore.

"Yes, but after that I don't know. It will be all over Java, I think: Surabaya, Yogja, Solo and others. Most of the time we'll be on the road. I'll make sure that you have enough of everything though." He pulled a bundle of notes from his pocket. "Another two hundred thousand for you," he said, passing them over.

She put down the cup and took the money. She opened the drawer in the bedside table, put the money in and took out a bunch of white papers.

"Copies of my letters," she said, handing them over to Stuart. "A copy of each one except the last two. I wrote them after I lost my job."

He took them. "Ita, I will have to go. You need sleep and tomorrow I have to work early."

She nodded. "But first come here." She reached out for him, kissing him on the lips, warm and comforting. They held the embrace for a minute then released each other.

Stuart stood to leave. "Until tomorrow night," he said.

"Bye, bye Stuart. I always knew you'd come back," she said, settling herself lower in the bed. "The little boy will be waiting for you. He will get you a *bajaj*. No taxis in here, but it's late and not so busy or hot so you'll be all right." She smiled and waved a little as he opened the door to leave.

Ita's mother was sitting on one of the patched chairs. She stood as he came out and held the door for him. The little boy was waiting by the door, the precious five hundred rupiah note still clutched in his hand.

"Bye, bye Bu," Stuart said self-consciously.

She almost half smiled at him but didn't, then said something indistinguishable in Indonesian.

He nodded as if he understood and then left. He followed the little boy and looked back once. She was still standing watching him go.

The little boy flagged a *bajaj* and Stuart showed the hotel card to the driver. He gave the little boy another five hundred rupiah note. His eyes lit up and he smiled and nodded his head.

The driver of the absurd, three-wheeled, orange contraption which is a *bajaj* revved the engine and let the clutch out with a jerk and they were on the way.

Stuart abandoned the *bajaj* below the hotel and paid the driver a thousand rupiah: he looked happy. And then he walked the last bit up to the hotel.

He took his key, ordered his morning call and then dropped thankfully into his clean bed in his air-conditioned room. He was back, he was with Ita, and for the moment that was all which was important to him. He smiled to himself as he lay waiting for sleep. He smiled as he remembered her in her little room, the new baby equipment all around her, the bonsai tree still there, his hanky used as a tablecloth. She was so lovely, so adult in some ways and yet childlike in others. He knew that he loved her, he knew that the last eight months had been a long suppression of emotion, hoping in vain that Ita would go away and that Catherine would come back. Catherine had almost come back; perhaps a year more away from Ita and she would have, he didn't know. His only concern now was his responsibility to Ita and to his job. These thoughts wandered around his tired mind as he tried to sleep.

Sleep was long coming. He took out the sheaf of papers which were Ita's copies of her letters to him. The first one he had received and read. The second was written in a worried tone: she was late and unsure. The third: she was sure that she was pregnant and wanted his advice. In the fourth, she asked why he hadn't written back, she asked for his advice again and wanted to know if she should have the pregnancy stopped. She said it was a big sin for a Catholic but if he wanted she would do it. The fifth letter was becoming increasingly desperate in its tone: she pleaded for him to write to her, just to have some news and support. Again she wanted advice on her situation. The next three were of similar tone, becoming increasingly desperate with each letter. Then the ninth: she said it was too late for an abortion and she would have to have the baby and she asked if he help her. In the tenth, the last one of the copies, she said that her job was finishing and that she would be moving to another house. She pleaded with him in desperation, for help, for support, for him not to forget what had been said at the airport when he had left the last time. Number eleven, written from home, had no copy and he had received number twelve.

    He held the sheaf of papers to his chest and closed his eyes. A tear or two squeezed out from each eye. What had he put this poor girl through, how badly had he upset her situation and wronged her? He clasped the letters more tightly and willed sleep to come to release him from his thoughts. Eventually, after another half hour, he slept.

# CHAPTER 32

# A JAVANESE SALES TOUR

The next day, Wednesday, found Stuart walking into the reception area of Anwar's smart Jakarta office block early in the morning. He was nervous. It was some eight months since he had seen Anwar and he knew that he had gone back on his side of the unwritten agreement between them. He didn't know if Anwar would be angry or not. He stood by the receptionist whilst she dialled the number, smiling at her to disguise his nervousness.

"You can go straight through," she said, returning his smile.

He nodded. "Thanks."

He had got part of the way into the main part of the office when Anwar appeared at the door of his office.

"My dear Mr Morgan, Stuart, so nice to see you – welcome back to Jakarta." He gripped Stuart's hand with a firm, long handshake of genuine welcome. "Come into my office." He led Stuart, his right hand resting on Stuart's shoulder. "Tea please, no milk, no sugar, just like Mr Morgan likes it," he said, as they passed his secretary sitting by the door.

Once inside the office, Anwar bid him sit down before he sat himself. He smiled broadly. "Well, it is really good to see you again, Stuart, and looking so refreshed and so healthy and so ready for action."

The tea arrived and was set down on Anwar's table.

"Please," Anwar said.

Stuart took a sip.

"Now, I was very pleased to meet your Mr Holding, Montague. What a man – so knowledgeable, so astute. We had many long discussions, many long talks about the situation." He lowered his voice. "It was bad, Stuart. I was ready to give up. I am not telling lies or exaggerating or covering up for my own failings. Mr Holding asked me if I was, but I told him no, then he convinced me of the need to continue." He resumed his normal voice. "And so I have redoubled my efforts and we have a very busy programme ahead of us in the next two weeks."

"What exactly went wrong, after I left?" Stuart said quietly, wanting to find a little out before they went on to discuss the future.

Anwar shook his head. "Your Mr John wasn't so bad, but he was too inflexible. He thought he knew what the customers wanted better than they did themselves. He offered machines he wanted to offer, what he thought they should have, rather than what they wanted. He disobeyed the first rule of selling: 'The customer is always right'," he said with a flourish. "Then the other man!" Anwar shook his head as he continued, "Now he was a total disaster! A social incompetent, well, at least here. He ran around with the girls all the time in his hotel. He was more interested in talking to them anywhere any time than carrying on with the business. He got hopelessly drunk when we had a dinner, a very important dinner, with Mr Chan and his wife. Well, the wrong man completely." Anwar paused, took a sip of tea and shook his head again, as if still disbelieving his own story.

"Well, I hope that those things are past and now we are back together again that we can pull the situation back," Stuart said brightly, his curiosity satisfied for the moment.

"It is not going to be easy," Anwar said, slowly rocking back in his chair. "It will be almost as difficult as it was breaking in the first time." He paused and considered Stuart for a time, examining his expression and trying to feel him out. "My first question to you, Stuart, is what have you done about the existing offers that your company had made? Improved them, matched them up to the requirements, what?"

Stuart nodded. "Yes and yes. We can go through the detail of it all later. First I want to know, what the programme is for the next few weeks. You said we were going to be busy."

"Yes, first, obviously, we have to go and see Chan – that's tomorrow, so we can go this evening, if that's okay with you?"

Stuart looked a little concerned. He wanted to see Ita again before he started travelling. "First flight tomorrow would suit me better," he said.

"Fine. Well, not the first, eight o'clock is fine."

"And then?" Stuart prompted.

"And then two, maybe three days with Chan, then on to Solo, Yogya on Sunday, for the week. Beyond that we have to play it by ear. It could take over the next weekend as well. I think it's best if we stay down that end of the island and don't try to keep coming back to Jakarta. We can concentrate and really get some work done. Is that okay for you?" Anwar said.

Stuart nodded: he couldn't disagree because he was here to work and sort out the problems. Ita, even in her condition, would understand, he felt sure, especially with her mother in attendance.

"I've cleared my diary for the next two weeks, which wasn't easy," Anwar said in a serious tone. "I promised Mr Montague that I would give it everything, so I expect the same from you."

"You'll get it from me, Anwar, you know that," said Stuart with equal seriousness.

Then they smiled at each other, the rapport between them beginning to fall into place again.

The rest of the day was spent in re-establishing himself in the specially allocated room in Anwar's office building. Stuart went over the details of the revisions that he had managed to make in the previous week with Anwar, explaining the changes and pointing out the benefits. Anwar had many useful comments on the work and he appeared to be moderately satisfied. Stuart did more work on some of the unfinished ones, calling the office in Manchester for more data and prices in the early evening.

Then it was back to the hotel for a wash and change before he left for Ita's place.

He arrived there some time after eight in the evening. The area was much more crowded than it had been the previous evening. Something like a small market had been set up along the sides of the streets, selling second-hand stuff, almost anything, from car and motorbike parts through to children's clothes. In the crowd he felt much more threatened and intimidated than he had the previous night. So many more pairs of eyes stared at him, the white man in this crowded local neighbourhood. A small crowd formed around him, not threatening, just staring. He tried to remember the way: which alleyway was it? He was confused. It looked different with the stalls and people along the main road. Then he felt a tug on his right hand and the small boy from the previous night stood looking up at him, smiling.

Stuart smiled back. "Ita?" he said.

The boy nodded and led the way, still holding Stuart's hand. The crowd parted for the two of them, but the eyes still stared.

At Ita's door the boy knocked again and waited patiently for his five hundred rupiah note, which Stuart gave him as the door opened. The boy settled down to wait, adding the note to the two from the previous evening.

Ita's mother opened the door for him. She regarded him coolly, as she had done on their first meeting. Her eyes were a little softer, perhaps, but her lips did not offer even the hint of a smile to Stuart. He crossed into the small, dingy house and went straight to Ita's room.

She was lying propped up on pillows, listening to a small radio. She looked better than the previous night: her hair was newly washed, her face a little brighter and less pale. But there was still tiredness in her eyes, a general look of exhaustion, of weakness.

"Stuart, you have come again, so last night wasn't a dream," she said in a little voice, quivering slightly.

He walked straight over to her and kissed her on the cheek. "No, it wasn't a dream. I'm here again, it's real." He kissed her again, on the lips, a slow kiss, his eyes closed, a warmth spreading through him at being back with Ita again.

They broke off and he sat on the edge of the bed. They looked at each other in silence for a while, examining, searching each other's face for some information, some news, some evidence of thought.

They were interrupted by Ita's mother bringing in two cups of tea. Stuart sipped his straightaway: he was dry and thirsty and the tea was only lukewarm. He drank it more or less down in one swig.

"What are your plans?" she asked quietly when he had finished. "Do you know yet?"

He nodded and sighed. "I leave tomorrow, for Surabaya, then on to Solo, Yogya. We will be away over this weekend, maybe next as well, it depends on the progress."

"Oh," she said quietly, her eyes looking down.

"The baby is due in how many days, ten maybe?"

She nodded. "Maybe less, the doctor said."

"I could be back. As soon as I come back to Jakarta, I'll be here. If I am in Jakarta, I will be with you."

She nodded again. "I understand."

He smiled. "Don't worry, everything will be all right. You have money – you can get a good doctor, your mother is here. You will see, everything will be fine. You'll soon be a proud mother yourself." He tried to jolly her along.

She looked at him. "I know I have my mother, but now you're here I would like you to be with me." She looked down. "But I understand what you are here for and what is so important to you and your company. I want you to be here again, in the future, so I understand." She looked up at him again, her big, brown eyes expressive as ever. "Do your job, Stuart, for both of us, and for him," she said, stroking her stomach. "Please do it well so that you can come back here many times."

"I will, Ita, for you, and especially for that little one in there," he said, pointing at the lump.

She smiled and rubbed her stomach gently. "I'm afraid," she said quietly.

"Of what?"

"Of having a baby. It's not easy, it's hard and I'm afraid something will go wrong."

"Don't be. So many women have babies. In Indonesia how many mothers, how many children?" he smiled and put his hand under her chin, lifting her face to look into his.

"I know, but for each woman it's different. You are European man, I am Indonesian woman: you are big, I am small. Maybe our baby will be big also, too big for me." She paused and looked up at him.

He smiled as best he could at her natural fear, the fear of a mother-to-be.

Her head dropped again. "I'm afraid Stuart," she whimpered.

He put his arm around her and pulled her close, his physical presence and physical contact so much more reassuring than words alone.

He stayed for two hours. They talked, cuddled together, held each other, kissed a little and then it was time to go. Stuart stood up to leave and pulled another three hundred thousand rupiah from his pocket.

"Make sure you have a good doctor and get the best you can," he said as he laid the money on the table. "You have enough?" he asked, looking down at her.

She nodded. "Plenty of money. Thank you so much. I knew I was right about you: you would come back." She smiled again. "Bye," she said.

He waved a little wave and then found his way out into the dark, dank alleyway. The little boy was still waiting, sitting cross-legged on a piece of cardboard by the door. He led Stuart out of the maze and on to the main road, found the *bajaj* and accepted his payment with a smile.

The next day Stuart was able to leave Jakarta for Surabaya with a reasonably happy heart. Ita was doing reasonably well. Anwar was in a good mood and he was happy to see Stuart back. He was actually beginning to enjoy the prospect of doing some business again after the eight month lay off, but it was going to be a hard few weeks.

The meetings with Chan and his wife took three days and culminated in a dinner for the four of them in Surabaya. The dinner went on very late and Chan insisted on taking them all to a discotheque afterwards. At the very end of the evening, in his typical style, he handed Stuart a large envelope. The contents turned out to be an order for forty-five thousand dollars worth of spares and, much more importantly, a letter of intent to purchase some new machines with a total value of over three million dollars, subject to suitable commercial and payment conditions being agreed. The money was coming from Chan's own resources and some loans.

Stuart was surprised and overjoyed at the two letters. It meant that he had a lot of work to do in Jakarta when he got back from this trip: settling the terms and sorting out the details of the contract with Anwar, Chan and Stuart's company. The visit to Indonesia was getting longer.

They left Surabaya late on the Sunday morning, travelling by car through the heat of the day on the seven hour journey to Solo, or Surakarta, in Central Java. On the Monday, they visited one of the large factories that Stuart had visited on an earlier trip. For the first day and a half, he met no one and sat outside a progression of offices waiting while Anwar ran around. By lunch, in a tiny, non air-conditioned restaurant, on the second day, Stuart was getting fed up.

"What's going on, Anwar?" he asked in an exasperated tone. "We've been here for a day and a half and all I've done is sit outside offices."

"Yes, I know, but you must be patient."

"Why, what's the problem? What's the hidden agenda?" He was slightly irritated by the reply.

Anwar sighed. "There is nothing hidden really. They have already had our offer, and others. They are evaluating those offers, and what I am trying to do is change our offer: post bidding, it's called. That's not really good business practice. They don't want to accept any changes, but I'm working on it."

An embarrassed "Ahh," was all Stuart could muster.

"I think that I have managed to do it and this afternoon, some time, we may get in to put some new figures on the table." Anwar continued, "So just be patient, Stuart. I won't let you down."

Anwar was true to his word. Stuart was called in mid-afternoon. They spent the rest of the day and half the next discussing at great length technical specifications, commercial conditions, prices and financing. Eventually they came away with a whole list of points for clarification and an agreement to meet on the following Monday. Back in the hotel Stuart handwrote a long and detailed fax to his office for information on those bits he couldn't deal with himself.

Later that afternoon they left for Yogjakarta, a two hour drive across Central Java in the shadow of the mystical Gunung Merapi, Yogjakarta's guardian volcano which occasionally expressed its discontent with the people by erupting; or so Anwar told Stuart when they stopped for a cup of coffee in view of the classical volcano silhouette. They arrived late but the rooms were ready and cool. Stuart had a shower, a quick beer with Anwar and then he retired, travel-weary and exhausted.

The next factory took Anwar only a morning to sort out. He and Stuart went in before lunch and then adjourned to a nearby restaurant for a long and convivial lunch. The meeting continued all afternoon and all the next day too. At the end they had a series of objections and questions worked out for Stuart to answer. Meetings for the next week were arranged as the trip stretched out into the end of the following week. Stuart was concerned about Ita, but he knew that he had to swallow and hide his concern: Anwar and the job, at this moment, came first. When the meeting finished on Friday evening, Stuart wondered if they would be able to slip back to Jakarta for the weekend. He decided to broach the subject with Anwar.

"What's on tomorrow?" he asked as they rode home to the hotel in the car.

"Why?"

"Just wondering. We've no meeting planned for tomorrow, next one's on Monday."

"Mmm. When will your office respond on all that stuff you sent them on Wednesday?" Anwar asked, after a moment's consideration of Stuart's motives.

"Should be in your office in Jakarta for us tomorrow morning," Stuart replied, with a little hint.

"Right," said Anwar with a degree of certainty. "I'll have my secretary fax it through to us here and then we can work on it in the hotel and get everything ready for Monday. There's no need to waste time going back to Jakarta."

Stuart nodded. Anwar was right. There would be so much to do to get the messages into a series of reasonable replies by Monday morning. It made sense not to waste half the time going back to Jakarta. He accepted it, but he was still disappointed. He spent the first part of the evening writing another fax of questions for a response on Tuesday or Wednesday of the following week. Then he and Anwar had a long leisurely dinner and a few drinks before Stuart became tired and sleepy.

On the following day, Saturday, they sat and worked from mid-morning until the early evening in Anwar's room. They worked quietly and efficiently, bouncing ideas back and forth, writing and rewriting sections of the replies until each was happy. They had a long night out, eating, walking around the wide, busy

Maliboro Street and the small, intimate lanes beyond before ending up in the hotel disco until after two. This time Anwar did not have a liaison with anyone, secret or otherwise. On the Sunday, the work continued until they departed for Solo once again.

The meeting on Monday stretched, exhaustingly, to Tuesday afternoon so their schedule back in Yogjakarta had to be rearranged. At the end of the meeting they did not have an order or even a letter of intent, but what they did have was the basis on which the company could place the order with Ormistons: the commercial conditions, the price and, most importantly, the financing arrangements. Some of the questions would take time to answer. Stuart would need to talk to the banks in Jakarta and his office to ones in the UK. The embassy and the appropriate government departments in Whitehall would also be involved in sorting out the details of the offer and the export insurance which Ormistons would need. But it was so much more than they had had only two weeks previously.

They left for Yogjakarta again on the Tuesday evening, arriving at almost midnight. Stuart flopped exhausted into bed without so much as a clean of his teeth.

The next day, the Wednesday, was a bit of a let-down: the company which had seemed so positive on their last visit was now pulling back from a deal. They had become evasive and spent much of the time looking at the ground and avoiding eye contact. The meeting was almost over by lunchtime, but Anwar persuaded them to reconvene afterwards.

In the hotel, Anwar was busy on the phone and with the hotel receptionist, examining the guest register. Stuart sat in isolation in the small coffee shop, drinking weak, milkless tea, watching with confusion, but with no desire to ask after his last questioning of Anwar. Eventually Anwar sat down at his table.

"Well?" Stuart asked.

"Well," said Anwar with a sigh, "just as I thought."

"Mmmm?" Stuart prompted.

"Our friends have been here since we were last here. The word is getting round."

"Our friends?"

"Yes, your German friends and their agent, my friend, Mr Sutarno." Anwar stared ahead, pensive.

"That's good," said Stuart brightly.

"Why?" asked Anwar, not looking up.

"Well, if they've been here, we have them worried, we've got them thinking."

"Actually you could be right. My friend doesn't normally set foot outside Jakarta unless he's going abroad. He leaves all the factory and client visits to his staff. It's beneath him, he's got so big and powerful." Anwar nodded to himself, agreeing with his own statement.

"So that gives you an insight into the behaviour of this morning. They looked to me as if they had been frightened. They were afraid to talk to us, and I don't think that it was evasiveness brought on by having a better offer up their sleeves – they'd been bullied," Stuart continued.

Anwar nodded in a sage manner, his hands clasped in front of him as he sat back in his chair.

"Okay," he said loudly after a moment's reflection, "you have work to do here?"

"Yes."

"I'm going back to that factory alone. I'll call you later."

"But I thought we were both supposed to go back," Stuart protested.

"I know, but you said yourself they were afraid. Now we understand why, and to continue in the same way this morning will get us nowhere. It will have to be sorted out from the top down."

Stuart knew that Anwar was right. He nodded and Anwar smiled.

"See you later. Wait here, in the restaurant, and I'll call later," Anwar said as he stood to leave.

In the event Anwar didn't call, coming back to the hotel some time after five. Stuart had spent the afternoon sitting obediently in the restaurant, writing faxes and analysing the data he had already received to prepare for the next round of discussions. He smiled at Anwar as he breezed into the hotel.

"Afternoon, thanks for the call," he said joking.

Anwar gave a little laugh. "Sorry, things didn't work out quite like I planned. However..." he said the last word expansively, drawing it out, holding the promise of good news for Stuart. "Tomorrow, some time, we have a commitment to meet the big boss man." There was a distinct twinkle in Anwar's eyes.

The tomorrow some time turned out to be four in the afternoon. They were ushered into a large office. The president director sat behind a co-ordinated, large desk. He smiled as they entered and set down his pen.

"Gentlemen," he said, extending a hand to Stuart first and then Anwar. "Please sit."

He indicated an uncomfortable-looking, low-seated and low-backed couch which ran round two sides in a corner of the room. A small coffee table stood in front of the couch. After they had all sat down and exchanged cards, a lady arrived with three cups of black, gritty Javanese coffee. Stuart grimaced at the sight: he knew it would be sweet and he would have to drink it and hate it.

The president director smiled around at the two of them.

"Thank you for meeting us at such short notice," Anwar began in a formal tone. "I am happy that you can receive us."

The president director beamed again.

"And we hope that we can show you some information which will be of interest to this company," Anwar continued.

The president director nodded. "I know your company long time," he said, addressing Stuart. "And I am very pleased to receive you here. I know some of your offer for these machines but we have a worry about you." He furrowed his brow for effect.

Stuart looked back, equally concerned.

"My worry is that you will sell us some equipment that will not be the same as our existing ones and then leave us a problem for the spares and maintenance. Maybe you don't have the office here and just want to sell and go."

Stuart smiled. "No," he began in his most reassuring tone, "we at Ormistons don't work like that. We have a long-term commitment to all of our customers. As an example, we have just supplied spares to Indonesia for some machines that are more than fifty years old and which were originally supplied to South

America and have come here through two different factories in two different countries on their way to Indonesia. So we are committed to providing that long-term support." He paused.

The president director looked at Anwar and said something in Indonesian. Anwar replied and the president director nodded and looked impressed.

"Now what is interesting about this project, these particular machines, is that you have a plan to set up a whole new line. The question of compatibility with the existing machines doesn't come into it," Stuart continued.

Again the president director nodded.

Then they began to talk details, the major items dealt with.

The meeting lasted more than an hour. They left well after five, the tropical sun already on its way down.

"Good meeting, Stuart," Anwar said excitedly once they were in the car on the way back to the hotel. "Good, very good. We can get a good shot at them later on. The president director is reasonably new and he isn't so bound up with the Germans. We must give him a very good offer."

"When?"

"Two to three weeks."

Stuart was happy: the trip was lengthening again. "And now?" he asked.

"Back to Jakarta," Anwar said happily. "We've done enough this trip, don't you think?"

"I do, I do," Stuart replied equally happily.

They caught the last flight out of Yogjakarta's small airport. Anwar had booked them into the small business section and so they enjoyed a little more comfort on the short flight to Jakarta. Anwar and Stuart were silent for most of the flight, each engrossed in his own thoughts. Stuart was happy: they had a letter of intent from Chan; a spares order from Chan; an agreement with another company and a way through a previously closed door. The total business potential was in excess of twenty-five million dollars, three and half million at Chan's, some seven million at the factory in Solo and the rest at the factory they had just left. That was the ultimate goal: to get that one would ensure his future in Indonesia and in the company. Everything was going well with the business, if not exactly according to plan.

In the midst of his happy considerations his mind turned to Ita. He remembered her situation and, for a brief moment, he was angry. With no baby, everything would be perfect. He could, he was sure again, work out a way of having his family life in England and his relationship with Ita during his visits to Indonesia. But with the baby it was going to be so difficult. The responsibility, the money he would need to supply – the whole thing disturbed the good feelings he was having after his business success.

He slid into one of his morose moods, helped along by the exhaustion he was feeling from the previous two weeks of non-stop travelling in the heat of Java. He just wanted to get to his hotel room and sleep. The flight neared its end and the plane made the final approach. Stuart looked out at the lights of Jakarta with a heavy heart. He didn't want to go to see Ita, he didn't want to be involved: he wished that he was somewhere else.

## CHAPTER 33

## STUART'S RELIEF?

Once safely ensconced in his hotel room, Stuart flopped on to the bed and fell asleep almost instantly. His sleep didn't last long for the bell boy rang the doorbell to deliver his suitcase. Stuart rose from the bed and stumbled to open the door, cursing himself for not bringing the case up himself. He tipped the bell boy despite the disturbance: it wasn't the poor man's fault. Then Stuart opened the case, pulling out the dirty laundry and dumping it in a pile beside his feet. Then he stopped and pondered for a moment.

It was almost nine o'clock and he was tired and miserable – he did not want to go and visit Ita. He knew that he should go, but he really didn't want to. He sighed as the better side of his nature came to the fore, through the tiredness and miserable feelings, to remind him of his promise to her. He knew that he had to go, he knew he would go, but even so he didn't want to and he sighed a second time, louder than the first.

Carefully, deliberately and slowly, he selected a set of clean clothes from the suitcase and laid them out on the bed. Then, equally slowly, he undressed and had a long shower. He soaped himself liberally, washing all his body with care. Then he shampooed his hair, allowing the foam to run over his body as he rinsed, massaging his tired body as he did so. It felt good and soothing with a slight hint of private sensuality. He was reluctant to leave the shower. When he finally did switch it off and climb out, steam covered the mirror, preventing him from shaving. He filled the time by cleaning his teeth, cutting his finger and toenails and cleaning his ears. Once the mirror cleared, he shaved with exaggerated caution and precision. He went into the bedroom, wrapped in a towel, feeling content and well. Had he lain back on the bed, he would have been asleep in a minute. He was tempted, but resisted.

He sat and watched the television for a while before he dressed slowly. When he was finally ready he watched the television again, delaying the departure, possibly hoping that Ita might be asleep when he arrived and that he could appease his conscience by visiting without meeting her.

Eventually, well after ten o'clock, he stood and left the safety of his hotel room for the uncertainty of the visit to Ita. The taxi driver made the usual complaints about the destination: every one of them he had used had made the same complaint.

He arrived at the entrance to the small alleyway. He stood in the warmth of the tropical night, watched by local people with the same staring curiosity as always. He looked around for his friend, the little boy. After a minute he appeared and Stuart felt relieved. The boy looked up at him, his eyes strangely sad. He took Stuart's hand and guided him into the maze of buildings.

They arrived at Ita's door. Stuart knocked, but the boy shook his head, reached up and opened the door, allowing Stuart to step in. Stuart handed him his customary five hundred rupiah note. The boy took it and added it to the little roll of similar five hundred rupiah notes that he had collected from Stuart. He had stored them in a small plastic envelope.

Stuart stepped inside the house. It appeared to be deserted. Ita's mother was not in attendance, but otherwise the room was the same as he remembered. He looked back at the boy who stood in the doorway . The boy's face was even more sad-looking and Stuart was sure that he could see tears on his cheeks. The boy closed the door and Stuart's stomach tightened. He felt his heart beat faster and a monstrous blackness stole over him: something was wrong, very wrong.

"Ita," he called softly. "Ita," a second time, this time louder. "Ita!" finally in a stronger voice.

"Stuart?" a weak voice came from another room. "Is that you, my darling?" the voice continued.

At least Ita was there. His feelings of dread lessened a little. He stepped forward and opened the door which led into Ita's room. She was lying in bed, on her back, her head tilted towards the door.

"Oh Stuart," she said, her voice small, weak and full of emotion, "you came back again. Oh, it's so good you're here." Her mouth managed a small smile.

He looked at her as she lay in the bed, her stomach strangely flat, her hair lank and untidy, its beautiful sheen lost, her skin grey and pallid, her eyes sunken and red, her face desperately unhappy. He saw the baby supplies, unopened on the small cupboard, the cot still standing in the same place. His stomach tightened again, he felt giddy and sick.

"What happened, Ita?" he said slowly.

"Our baby, Stuart. Our little boy, he died, Stuart, he died," she said, her voice quiet, her emotion just under control, but her eyes were filling with tears.

"What?" he gasped. He felt as though he was going to be sick; his legs wobbled and he stumbled forward and sat on the bed for support.

"He died, Stuart. Our lovely, little baby boy died," she repeated, her voice now quivering with emotion as she remembered, the control of her first statement giving way.

"When?" Stuart whispered, unable to believe what he had heard.

"He didn't live long, Stuart. The doctor and nurse cleaned him up and gave him to me just after he was born. He was so small. His hair was like yours, not black like mine. I held him for a moment and his eyes opened and he looked at me and I thought he smiled, his little mouth opened." She stopped speaking; she smiled a little at the recollection of the baby's beauty. Then she put a tissue to her eyes, the memory of what happened next overcoming her attempt at controlling her emotions. "I have never felt so happy in my life as that moment. The nurse took a picture with my camera." She resumed, her chin crumpled and her voice wobbling. "Our baby in my arms. I wanted to show him to you so you could see how beautiful he was, to share him with you, because he was from our love, from you and me and I was so glad you didn't get my letters and tell me that we had to stop the baby because he was so beautiful."

She stopped again, her eyes fell away from Stuart's. Her tears dripped off her chin. "And then his eyes closed and his mouth closed and he went very still." She continued, her voice very small, "I knew something was wrong so I screamed for the doctor. They tried but he was already gone in my arms."

She tried to dry her eyes with the tissue but there were just too many tears. "So small, so little, so beautiful – our baby, Stuart. We just give him life and then he was gone." The tears came in a stream now as she recounted the story for Stuart, remembering and reliving the happiest moment of her life, followed by the most unimaginably terrible moment.

Stuart stared at her, his eyes glazed and fixed, still unable and unwilling to believe what he had just heard, the unbelievable tragedy of it all. He felt the tears welling up in his eyes. His eyes closed and the tears came, flowing down the side of his nose on to his cheeks, dripping off his chin, running down the sides of his face and off the side of his jaw. He screwed his eyes tightly shut and his shoulders moved up and down a little as he sobbed silently. His hands were clasped tightly together until they almost hurt. He cried as he had never cried before. He cried in a way that he hadn't believed it was possible for him to cry. He felt such total desolation. He had never been this close to death before – even his own father's death, as unexpected as it was, had not affected him like this. His head fell forward, his whole body consumed with the grief. He dropped his head on to Ita's legs and she put her hands on his head, stroking him gently to soothe him.

Then he sobbed out loud. He put his arms to her body and squeezed her, holding on to her for support. When the sobs subsided, he looked up at her and into her face. She appeared a little more composed than before. Her eyes still wore the look of grief but not in the same way as before; now she had someone with whom she could share her grief and she was relieved of some of the burden.

He continued to look at her face. It was strangely contented; the tears had stopped coming. She stroked his hair.

He lay down and held her again for quite a time. They held each other, clinging to each other to draw comfort.

Finally Stuart lifted his head again.

"When?" he said slowly. "When did all this happen?"

"What's today?" she said.

"Thursday."

"The Friday after you left. The pain started and my mother took me to the hospital in a taxi. It was a long time in the hospital. The pain coming all the time until I was screaming. But the baby would not come. For so long he would not come. I was tired, weak and in so much pain. And then he came, on Saturday night at nine-twenty-three in the evening our little boy came." She stopped and the tears came back. "I felt so wonderful when he was out," she continued, sobbing as she did so. "And then they weighed him, cleaned him and gave him to me. He was so small, just one point three four kilograms. He was too small and too weak and my giving birth was too long." Her voice cracked and gave up completely as she cried out loud again, wailing and sobbing.

Stuart's eyes closed and he clung on to her in desperation. She had suffered alone with this for almost two weeks. Stuart could not imagine how she had survived for so long, how she had kept going, unable to reach him and share it with him, even to tell him. He felt the tears running down his cheeks again, into his mouth where he could taste the bitter, salty taste. They held each other in a grip of pain, a grip of shared grief, something so powerful that it engulfed them both. For how long they lay, Stuart could not say. But after a time, a long time, their shared grief subsided from sheer exhaustion.

He sat up and applied his big hanky first to her eyes and then to his own.

She tried to smile through her pain. "Over there, Stuart," she said, pointing at her small chest of drawers.

He turned and saw the bonsai tree, still flourishing, with his hanky as its mat, the small presents he had bought her which were so carefully preserved, and then the lump came to his throat again and he cried a little again. He opened the top drawer and saw her camera and a small cardboard album marked 'Baby'. He lifted it out carefully. He held it up to her and asked the question with his eyes.

She nodded.

He opened the small album and looked at the first picture. Ita and her mother were standing in the entrance to the hospital, Ita with a pained expression on her face, trying to look cheerful. Then Ita was in the bed, smiling, with the doctor and nurses in attendance. Then another with her mother sitting on the bed, and then another of Ita. The next one showed Ita, sitting in bed smiling, triumphant, the small baby in her arms, his little head and his light-coloured hair just visible over the edge of the blanket. Stuart's eyes closed again and he held the photograph to his chest. His head went back and he cried in great shoulder-heaving sobs. After a minute or two, his composure recovered, he looked back at the picture and then he was unable to stop himself crying again. Next was another one of Ita and the baby; this time his face was visible, his eyes open and a baby smile on his small mouth. Stuart looked closely at the picture. Even as the baby was there, just born, Stuart could see himself in some of the features of the little face; he could see Ita's eyes; he could see his own shape in the baby's head. He examined it closely. There was no doubt in his mind that it was his child. Then the next photograph was one of a solemn procession of dignified Javanese people. Ita's mother was supporting Ita and there were a number of other sad-looking people and a tiny coffin.

Stuart cried again, his tears almost dry from the continued crying. He stared at the picture, held it to his chest and then stared at it again. The rest were of the funeral ceremony in the church with the priest and afterwards in the small house in which he now sat.

When he had finished looking at them he carefully replaced the pictures in the drawer and shut it. Then he looked at Ita.

She tried a smile again. "He was beautiful, yes?" she asked him.

"He was the most beautiful baby, Ita. Why did he die, our little boy, why?"

She shook her head. "God is strange sometimes."

He nodded. He was not religious, but in this situation he wanted something to cling on to and the thought that maybe their little boy was in a better place gave him some small comfort.

He had no idea what to do next. He looked at Ita and she looked back. They stared at each other in the hopeless confusion of their grief. In the event they did not have to decide what to do: the next moves were decided for them. Stuart heard the door open in the main room.

Ita looked afraid, her eyes wide like a scared animal. "My mother!" she whispered, her voice tight with fear. "Oh God, my mother," she repeated.

The door to the bedroom opened and Ita's mother stood in the doorway. She looked at Ita and then saw Stuart. She glared at him with ill-disguised hatred. She shouted at him in her own language and pointed at the door.

Stuart looked at her and then at Ita, confused.

"Go Stuart, please go," Ita said, her voice pleading.

Stuart stood up. "Why?"

Her mother set off again, shouting louder, her face stern and taut, the veins in her neck and temples standing out. Ita shouted back at her, and the two of them shouted at each other. Tears came to Ita's eyes, running down her cheeks. She clung on to Stuart's hand.

Her mother took hold of the sleeve of Stuart's other arm and pulled him. She pointed at the still open main door and shouted at him and then at Ita.

"What's happening, Ita?" Stuart said in desperation, his eyes filling with tears again.

"Please go my darling," Ita said through her own tears. "Please go," she said determinedly.

He let go of Ita and acquiesced to the pull of her mother.

Ita shouted long and loud at her mother, but it had no effect, for she continued to pull Stuart to the door. The small boy stood in the doorway looking in. His face was full of tears. He pushed past Stuart and Ita's mother and ran to Ita, jumping on the bed and wrapping his arms around her.

"Ita!" shouted Stuart from the doorway.

"Stuart!" she shouted back. "Please come back tomorrow. I will talk to her. Please come back!" she said, her voice pleadingly desperate.

"I will, I will tomorrow!" he shouted as her mother pushed him bodily over the threshold and into a small group of people who had stopped in the alley to watch the commotion. The door slammed shut behind him to another volley of shouting from Ita's mother.

He was alone in the alley. The smell of the open drains rose to his nostrils: he gagged and felt sick. He retched. The group of people didn't disperse, they just stood and stared.

"What the fuck are you all looking at?" he screamed at their silent, staring faces.

Almost as a single body they recoiled at his anger, moving away from him, but still staring. He had lost his guide, the little boy, but by now he believed that he knew the way. He set off and the people parted to allow him through, still staring. Then he broke into a run down the dark, twisting alleyway. He tripped on a broken tile, sprawling on his hands and knees, cursing again in the darkness. He took a left turn and caught a string that held up a dirty, stained advertising canvas which formed the front of an impromptu, alleyway café. The string didn't snap but stung his cheek, cutting into his face. He ducked down and ran on faster. He bounced off a flaky, white-painted wall, grazing his knuckles, and he ran faster, desperate to get out from that place. And then he was at the main road, panting, dishevelled, his face and hands scratched and bleeding, his eyes red from crying. And again the stares came from the people on the street. He paused to catch his breath, breathing deeply to control his emotions. Once under control, he set off walking in the direction of the hotel and safety.

A three-wheeled, orange *bajaj* cruised past, its driver looking at Stuart, but he shook his head and the driver accelerated away. Stuart wanted to walk. He glanced at his watch. It was after eleven-thirty; he didn't realise that so much time had passed. He walked on, over the black, stinking river which flowed, contained between two sloping stone walls, with the debris of life visible on its oily surface. He walked on to the main four lane road, quiet now in the late evening. He passed a number of groups of people sitting in small roadside cafés, some watching intently down the road. Some smiled at him, some stared, one or two offered the inevitable greeting, "Hello Mister." Stuart didn't feel like responding, but he smiled nonetheless.

Then he heard what they were looking down the road for. Faintly at first he heard a distant whine, the whine of small motorbikes revved up high. He stopped just beyond one group of people and watched. A group of small motorbikes came speeding into view. Seven or eight, they went past too fast for him to count. Each had a helmetless rider who sat as low as possible, each with the throttle opened as wide as possible as they raced a crazy street race along the deserted road. Stuart wondered how fast they were going; sixty or seventy miles an hour on the small

100 or 125cc motorbikes. No protection, no chance of survival if anything went wrong, a race of dare and death for the thrill.

He sat down, tired from the walk and emotion, and wondered how long it would be before the next racers came past. A woman from the nearby group came over and offered him a bottle of water. He thanked her and drank heavily from it. He handed it back and smiled. She smiled back and offered him a seat with the group. Politely he declined. The noise came again. This time they sped past in the opposite direction on the far side of the road. A few moments later a single rider appeared and shouted at the group. Money changed hands. The result had been announced and the bets paid.

Stuart stood and left, waving at the group who smiled back. He pressed on along the wide road. A second set of motorbikes came past ten minutes later, equally fast, equally crazy, the tee-shirt-clad riders with expressions of grim determination as they pushed their small machines to speeds for which they were never really intended. Stuart smiled at the thirst of youth for adventure and thrills.

He came to a wide junction and turned left. He soon realised that he had made a wrong turn, but he pressed on, since it was as far to go back as it was to continue. Eventually he came to the main thoroughfare, Jenderal Sudirman, a street he recognised well. The junction with the road he was on was under construction, a bridge and clover leaf were almost completed. He managed to find his way to the road and walked along, confident that he knew where he was going. After half an hour of walking, he came to a river crossing. On the right, beyond the river, were a series of nightclubs and bars, ones that he had seen from the taxis and cars as he had been driven past. He was thirsty and the desire for a cold beer suddenly became overwhelming.

He went into one club, looked and came out. Then he went into a second and found the bar. The waiter looked at him strangely when he ordered the beer. Stuart caught a glance of himself in the mirror behind the bar and was shocked at his own appearance. He quickly ducked into the toilet and cleaned himself up as best he could. When he returned to the bar and his drink, a long-legged girl with wavy hair was sitting on the next stool. She smiled at him and took a drag from the cigarette she was holding most sexily. If Catherine had smoked like her, Stuart thought, he would have encouraged her to smoke. He sat down and drank the beer in two gulps and asked for a second.

"Thirsty?" she said huskily.

He nodded.

"Me too," she said with a wink.

He nodded to the barman and the barman produced a drink for the girl.

"Thanks," she said, easing closer and touching his thigh with hers. She took a mouthful of drink and then put her hand on his thigh, high up. Then she ran it down his leg and then up and round to the inside of his leg, creeping up higher. She smiled sexily at him. She was very good at her game.

Stuart, in spite of himself, felt attracted to her for a brief, fleeting moment.

"Only one hundred," she said. "US dollar," she continued. "Which hotel you stay in?"

Stuart shook his head. He finished his beer quickly and asked for the bill. He paid and smiled at her.

"Thanks for the company," he said, in all seriousness.

"Thanks for the drink. See you next time, lover," she pouted back, picking the drink up, swivelling the stool round and moving off to look for pastures new.

Outside again and refreshed, Stuart set off down the small road, fronted by these bars and nightclubs. At the bottom he turned left and followed the familiar route taken on some taxi journeys. On the right-hand side was a railway line, beyond that an earth embankment containing the wide, sluggish river he had crossed on the main road. A little further along the right-hand side was full of open-fronted restaurants which were right on the road. Cars were parked in front of a few. They all seemed to advertise the same food, 'Sop Kaki Kambing', although Stuart had no idea what it was. They were all run by people with the same name: 'Pak Kumis', 'Pak Haji Kumis', 'Pak Abdul Kumis' and more, maybe fifteen or twenty of them. He walked past them all, ignoring the pleas of the waiters for him to try. "Very good, mister!" they shouted. "Sheep foot soup," they said by way of explanation. He shook his head, revolted at the idea.

He went under a road bridge and turned left at a set of traffic lights as he had seen the taxi drivers do. As he rounded the corner he could see a great deal of activity up the street. Many people lingered on the pavements, and cars cruised slowly along, stopping occasionally. He continued to walk. A girl moved out of the shadow of a tree towards him. "Hello mister," she said, almost inevitably. She was tall and wearing a short tight skirt. She was not particularly attractive. He carried on.

More girls approached him, of different shapes and sizes and different levels of beauty or otherwise. They all had the same question and he had the same reply for all of them. At the junction of the road with a smaller one, where he turned left. Another girl approached him wearing a long dress. She stood before him and opened the dress. Underneath she wore nothing: he saw a pair of large breasts and a mound of hair. He was shocked to the point of stopping walking. He looked again and saw, as well as the feminine features of the breasts and the hair, masculine features, the muscular calves, the veined hands and the lack of waist. He looked at the face. Whilst it was beautiful, it was not quite right for a woman. Stuart realised that it was a man, at least some form of transsexual or transvestite. He hurried on. Another approached, this time with only breasts bare, but he looked hard and was convinced it was another man. Maybe they were all men. Suddenly Stuart got the feeling that this was not a good place to be, that it was not good to be wandering the streets of Jakarta at two o'clock in the morning along streets lined with prostitutes, homosexuals, transvestites and transsexuals. He felt worried and his heart beat faster. He walked with greater determination and avoided the eyes of the people on the street.

He came out on to a main street again, lined with shops and restaurants, all, at this late hour, closed. He knew that he did not have far to go. He made his way at a slower pace past the shops and restaurants and along tree-lined avenues towards the hotel. He reached it with relief just before three in the morning. He was utterly exhausted and had no energy left for any further grief.

The receptionist looked at Stuart. "Are you all right, Mr Morgan?" he asked with genuine concern as Stuart stood there waiting for his key. Stuart nodded and avoided the man's eyes.

Then he was in his room, flopped on the bed, only pausing to remove his shoes before he fell into a deep and dreamless sleep.

## CHAPTER 34

## ANWAR'S HELP

Stuart's deep and dreamless sleep was rudely disturbed by the room boy opening the door to make up the room. When the room boy realised that there was someone still sleeping, he backed out apologetically, bowing his head. "Sorry, sir, sorry, so sorry" he said, backing away from Stuart with exaggerated humility.

Stuart groaned and sat up. He felt terrible. He had had barely four hours sleep on top of two weeks travelling; the loss of his baby son – he could now think of the little boy as 'his' – whom he had never seen; the angry confrontation with Ita's mother. Everything came back to him with a fierce reality from which the short sleep had allowed him only a brief respite. He looked at his watch. It was after nine-thirty.

"Shit!" he exclaimed loudly, and then, "Shit!" again, a little less loudly but through gritted teeth. He was late, not for a meeting, but to get through the amount of work he needed to do. He rushed a shower with no shave or shampoo. He bundled his laundry into a bag but didn't fill in the form. Then he grabbed the remaining clean clothes from his suitcase and put them on, unpressed and creased. Then he rushed out of the room and to reception.

"My key!" he said to the girl. "And please can you send laundry to my room – I've not had time to fill the form in. I trust you." He managed a smile.

"Yes, sir, fine Mr Morgan," she replied, with a bright smile hiding her concern at Stuart's appearance and manner.

He left by taxi as usual.

Once in Anwar's office, Stuart settled himself down in the Ormistons room. The secretary brought him a cup of tea. He set about the draft contract with Chan, his immediate concern.

After forty-five minutes or so, Anwar walked past the office door. He paused and looked in on Stuart. Stuart sensed his presence but did not react.

"Ahh," Anwar said to attract his attention, "good morning Stuart, you okay?"

"Yes fine," said Stuart without looking up. "I'm busy on Chan's draft contract," he said, the words correct, but the manner of his words gave all the meaning, said, as they were, in the tone that only the English could master and which meant 'leave me alone' very clearly.

"Okay good," Anwar said, the meaning clear to him immediately. He moved away from Stuart's door.

Stuart was instantly sorry for his words. Whilst on the one hand he could tell himself that he told Anwar the truth, the manner of his telling indicated a lot more and he knew that his message had got through to Anwar. Anwar didn't deserve that from him. Stuart thought about chasing Anwar, but he left it alone and went back to his work.

Stuart was conscious of Anwar passing his door on a number of occasions. He seemed to pause at the door each time and look in, checking on Stuart and trying to see what was the matter. Stuart didn't look up.

Eventually Anwar braved Stuart's caustic tongue again. This time Stuart looked up and smiled at Anwar.

Anwar was surprised at Stuart's appearance now that he could see his face – the scratch on Stuart's cheek, the grazed knuckles on his left hand, the unshaven face and uncombed hair.

"Are you all right, Stuart?" he asked with genuine concern.

Stuart nodded.

"Well, it's Friday and it's almost lunchtime. What do you say if we have a nice lunch together?" Anwar continued brightly, trying to hide his concern for Stuart.

Gratefully, Stuart nodded. "Yes, I would like that very much. What time?"

"Half an hour?"

"Fine." Stuart settled back down to work and Anwar wandered off, a little more happy that Stuart was talking, but, if anything, more concerned about Stuart's condition.

They left more or less at the time they had agreed. Anwar took Stuart to the same Japanese restaurant they had been to on their first evening together. They sat at a smaller, ordinary table, one without the large cooking surface as the centrepiece.

The waiter hovered nearby. "Drink, sir?" he asked, looking at Stuart.

"Beer."

"Same for me," Anwar added quickly.

They sat in silence, each unsure how to begin the conversation. The drinks arrived and provided the starting point. Stuart started to drink, finishing the whole glass in two gulps. He realised just how thirsty he was. He waved at the waiter for a refill.

"Thirsty?" asked Anwar, smiling.

"Yes, I am, didn't realise it."

"I would have thought that you had had enough of that," Anwar said, pointing at the beer glass.

"Why do you say that?" Stuart asked, slightly puzzled.

"Well, you look so tired, washed out, as if you had drunk too much last night," Anwar continued, probing.

Stuart let out a big sigh as the waiter appeared with another glass of beer for him. He drank the first half before replying. He sat back in his chair.

"I wish that I had. My only problem would be a headache, perhaps a stomach ache and the knowledge that by this evening I would be starting again." He paused for a further, smaller sip of beer. "But the problems this time are not so easily dismissed or solved." He stopped, reluctant to continue. He finished the drink as an evasion tactic.

Anwar regarded him steadily from his position, sat back in his chair. Then he leaned forward, linked his fingers together and rested with both elbows on the table, his thumbs touching his chest. "So you have a problem?" he said quietly.

Stuart made no move to confirm or deny.

"So you do have a problem," Anwar continued, taking Stuart's silence as an admission, "with – let me guess – a girl. Yes?"

Stuart allowed a flicker of acknowledgement to show, but he didn't offer any comment; he wanted to see where Anwar's train of thought would go.

The flicker was enough for Anwar to press on. "I knew that you were heading for this sooner or later. What do you English say, er, 'riding for a fall', yes?" Anwar looked at Stuart for approval of his English.

Stuart smiled and nodded. "Riding for a fall," he repeated quietly to himself.

"I have had the idea that you would since we were in Surabaya."

"Surabaya?" Stuart questioned, puzzled.

"Mmm, you remember: 'the wider cultural sense'?"

"Oh yes," Stuart answered, smiling.

Anwar smiled as well. "Yes, the wider cultural sense, good words. But I knew what you meant straightaway then. You'd met someone and you were testing the ground, feeling your way forward."

Stuart shrugged his shoulders and finished his glass of beer.

"Now, you met her in a bar somewhere in Jakarta," Anwar began, but he was distracted by the waiter standing by.

"Your order?" he said.

Anwar was temporarily flustered, as neither of them had looked at the menu. "You Stuart?" he said, looking hopefully at Stuart.

Stuart shook his head. "No idea."

"How about a set lunch?"

"Fine."

Anwar spoke to the waiter and he turned away.

"And one more of these," Stuart called after him, waving his glass.

"Where was I?" Anwar asked.

"In a bar in Jakarta."

"Oh yes, in a bar in Jakarta and you became, well, what's the word in English – not in love but almost, erm, infatuated? That's the right word, isn't it, infatuated?" he repeated himself, happy again at his command of English.

Stuart had settled back in his chair and went back to small silent signs of acknowledgement.

"The old mysterious East meets West again," Anwar continued. "You are not the first European man to do this and you most certainly will not be the last," Anwar said with a knowing, sage smile. "And no doubt she had..." He paused for effect. "...a sad story to tell you," he continued. "As I said in Surabaya last time: a sad story."

Stuart acknowledged the remark.

"Which one was it?" Anwar asked.

Stuart made no move.

"Was it the 'I had a husband who left me with a child' or 'I am waiting for the nice foreigner man to come back like he said he would' or 'I wanted to marry someone my parents didn't agree with' or some other variation on the same. And there's usually a child involved in a sad story," Anwar said.

"No, no child," Stuart replied almost truthfully. He didn't add 'not any more' or words to that effect, but they ran through his mind.

"So which one was it, which sad story did she tell you to get you infatuated?"

"None of those really. Well, the last one I suppose. She wanted to marry someone from a different religion. It didn't work out for her," Stuart replied quietly, not wanting to reveal too much of the secret Ita had given him.

"Is that all?" Anwar asked. "It doesn't seem to be much of a sad story."

"Well, he convinced her that because they were already engaged that they should, well, consummate their relationship before they got married."

"I see."

"And as you said, also in Surabaya, in the wider cultural sense, that to be a virgin was very important. So that was her sad story: she lost her virginity to a man she thought she was going to marry and since then she feels that she cannot get married, to an Indonesian man at any rate." Stuart felt as though he had to say something of her story, not all, but something to make Anwar understand that Ita was not some bar girl who had hoodwinked him, tricked him into the current situation.

"Oh I see," said Anwar slowly. "So what happened this time, now? Why the tired and emotional face?" Anwar was being unusually direct.

Stuart offered no response at all this time.

"Did she leave you for another – or is she married? Has she asked you for a lot of money, or borrowed some from you and can't repay? And you have finally discovered what she wanted all the time: your money?" His tone was that of the parent with an unruly child.

Stuart allowed himself a little shake of the head.

"Mmm," was all Anwar could muster at first. "So she wasn't into you for a lot of money then?" he asked after a while.

Stuart shook his head. "No, in fact until recently she didn't ask me for anything. She even paid when we went out sometimes. She had a job, a secretary – she speaks English very well – she used computers; she seemed to be well paid."

Anwar looked a little surprised. "So she had an ordinary job?" he said in a tone which implied that any girl met in a bar in Jakarta, not married and not a virgin would be little more that a prostitute: the word 'ordinary' was said with raised eyebrows. "Mmm," he said again and went silent, his initial idea that Stuart had met some bar girl who had taken him for a lot of money defeated.

They stared at each other for a minute, not sure which way to take the conversation, then the first course arrived to distract them. It consisted of some small rice snacks and a bowl of clear, hot soup with bits in. Stuart picked up his wooden chopsticks and began to demolish the rice snacks, realising as he did so that he was very hungry.

"Is she anything to do with why you didn't come back?" Anwar said, after Stuart had finished the snacks and was picking up the soup bowl for a drink.

Stuart looked over his bowl at Anwar and gave a slight nod. Stuart wanted to be honest with Anwar and there was no point in trying to cover up this part.

"So our business, my company's and yours, was endangered by this girl," Anwar said, his voice a little hard and angry.

Stuart sipped the soup and didn't respond.

"Is that so? Is that what happened?" Anwar pressed again.

Stuart put his bowl down. "Partly, that's partly true."

"Well, it's not what I wanted to hear. You must always separate business from your private life, Stuart – the first rule of doing business: never let your private life affect your work." Anwar was lecturing Stuart in a schoolmasterly tone he found irritating.

"Do you feel that I ever allowed anything to affect my work? Haven't I always worked hard and dedicated myself to the work here?" Stuart asked, his voice a little raised.

"Well yes, you have always worked very hard and very effectively, and no, I don't think it directly affected your work here," Anwar replied, on the defensive at Stuart's raised tone and anxious to keep the lunch and their relationship friendly. "*But*," he emphasised the word, "it obviously affected us indirectly, because you were not able to come back to finish it and some idiot was sent in your place."

"Fair point, but I have always separated the two, work and pleasure," Stuart began. He paused while the waiter cleared the plates, using the opportunity to order another drink. "And I think that is just as true of Indonesia as it is of any other place I have worked," he continued. "But here, some other people felt that I couldn't or wasn't separating the two and they felt that they had to intervene."

"Who?"

"Well, my wife for one. She was behind the job change and getting me out of this country. She hoped that if I stayed away then everything would be all right."

"And you agreed with her?" Anwar asked.

"No, I didn't, but she had been to one of my bosses, her best friend's husband, and they made up a scheme, gave me an offer I couldn't refuse: promotion, an area I was interested in and the knowledge that if I refused I was finished in the company."

Anwar sat back and looked pensive. The waiter arrived with the main course, a small tray of food items and a small bowl of boiled rice. Stuart looked at the meal. He had no idea what each bit was, but he was so hungry that he moved straight in and ate with greedy speed.

When he had finished all the food, Anwar had barely started. Stuart waved for yet another beer and looked closely at Anwar, waiting for him to resume.

"So how or why did you want to come back now?" he asked finally, putting down his chopsticks.

"When did I last come here?" Stuart asked.

"Well, September I think. Yes, it was September – the rainy season was just beginning," Anwar answered, confused at the line of Stuart's reply.

"Correct, it was September. And where are we now?"

"May, of course."

Stuart smiled at Anwar and waited for the light to dawn.

Anwar struggled to see the connection and then he counted slowly, his lips moving as he repeated the months. Then he spoke, "Nine months between, yes?"

Stuart nodded. "Nine months, correct."

"She is pregnant," Anwar said quietly, slowly drawing the words out. "That's the problem, that's why you phoned me, that's why you took an interest again, isn't it, mmm?" he said, rocking back in his chair, a veil lifted from his mind.

Stuart nodded.

"It's all becoming clear now. Not the reason I would have wanted for you to come back, but I'm glad you did." He stopped again to eat a little more. "But one thing puzzles me," he began again. "If you knew she was pregnant, why didn't you come back before? Perhaps you're just the scapegoat for someone else's baby?" he said, his head on one side, his eyes slightly closed.

Stuart shook his head again. "I didn't know until a week or so before I came," his voice was quiet and strained.

"So when is the baby due? Or is it here already and last night you were becoming a father again, walking around the hospital until very late, waiting?" Anwar said, leaning forward, his voice quiet initially, but rising with a note of happiness as he thought of a small, newly arrived baby, even hard-nosed businessmen in Indonesia being just as susceptible to the charms of a new baby as any other Indonesian.

"No, that is not what happened. It, or should I say he, arrived a week last Saturday, while we were away. She had him by herself, well, with her mother in a hospital." He paused, his voice quivering, barely under control, his chin crumpling.

Anwar looked at Stuart and then leaned back in his chair. "So now you have a big problem." Then Anwar noticed the expression on Stuart's face, close to tears. "What, what's the matter? What else is there?" he asked, leaning forward again and coming closer to Stuart.

"The baby died, Anwar, he died. He only lived a few minutes, long enough for her to hold him, to think that he was alive and that she had had a baby boy and then he died in her arms. I never saw him. I only saw his photograph – two little snapshots of his short life is all that I have. He was my child, of that I am certain." He stopped, unable to continue without breaking down.

"Well, in some ways your problem's solved itself," Anwar said rather callously, without thought for Stuart's obvious emotion. "I mean you can walk away from the situation now – you have no reason to..." His voice trailed off getting slower and quieter as he saw Stuart's face, the eyes filled with tears. Anwar knew that he had said the wrong thing and began to finish his meal to cover his embarrassment.

When he looked up again, Stuart had recovered his composure. He had half drunk another glass of beer and was smiling a little at Anwar.

"Yes, I suppose my problems have been solved – I could walk away. But I don't know. I mean how are Indonesian women in this situation? Babies are so precious here. She has no support apart from her mother, who is very angry; she has lost her job; she has lost any self-respect for herself that she had built up since she wanted to get married the first time – all that I have destroyed. I'm worried that she may do something, well, extreme. I couldn't have that on my conscience, I couldn't live with that."

"I would not worry too much about her from that point of view. This is Indonesia. Things are not the same here as they are in Europe. She will survive, get by, make things better. She will sit in bars again and tell her sad story like so many others. Don't worry about her. She will survive. They all do," Anwar said, his voice matter-of-fact in tone.

"But I can't accept that, Anwar, I can't. This may be Indonesia and things may be different here, there may be different ideas of what is right and wrong, but I'm not Indonesian, I'm European, more particularly English. One thing the English are very good at is guilt. We really are into guilt and doing the right thing." He paused to finish the beer. He was still hungry. "Is there any other food here, any desserts?" he asked.

"I'll get the menu," said Anwar.

"I can't help what happened before to her, but she rebuilt her life and didn't use her sad story, she didn't tell anyone about it but me, so please don't ever tell anyone else about that, not ever, even though you don't know her and have never met her. Don't say anything to anyone," Stuart pleaded.

"All right, you have my word," Anwar said seriously. "Not even to my wife," he continued.

"Whatever life she rebuilt, I destroyed: her job's gone; her friends gone; her mother's very angry; and now, on top of all that, the baby's gone. At least with the baby she would have had something to cling on to, something to live for. I could have helped her, given her support when I'm here. She would have been happy, but even that chance of happiness for her has gone. She's a Catholic, and if we English as a breed are into guilt in a big way, then the Catholic Church is into guilt ten times more. She must be in hell now, she must think that this is some form of punishment delivered from God for her sins. My conscience will not let me disregard her and walk away," Stuart said finally to Anwar, his voice firm and slightly raised.

He turned to the waiter. "Flambéed bananas please," he said politely, with a smile as if he had just been discussing the weather rather than something so terribly sad.

Anwar sat quietly back in his chair, his hands clasped in front of his face. He sat like that until the waiter delivered Stuart's flaming bananas.

"What are the worst, likely and best scenarios for your work, our work, here in Indonesia?" he asked.

Stuart looked dumbfounded at the question. After telling Anwar all of that, he now asked about work.

"The worst is to be like now – Chan's spares order, his letter of intent and nothing more. The likely is his spares, turning his letter of intent into an order and getting another letter of intent. I would be very satisfied with that."

"And the best?" Anwar prompted as Stuart took a mouthful of banana.

"The best would be to convert all of them into orders, but that's not going to happen, I don't think," Stuart replied after he finished his mouthful of banana.

"No, maybe not, but I am sure that we can get somewhere between the likely and the best. Maybe two letters of intent, or, more likely, a second major order," Anwar said in all seriousness.

"You think so?"

Anwar nodded with a knowing look on his face. "How long for you to sort out the work that you need to do?" he asked after Stuart had taken in his expression.

"A day to sort out Chan's draft order, then he'll need a week or two to check it. We need to see the banks about the others and maybe the embassy, plus some work back home which I could set up in the next couple of days." Stuart answered the question, still unsure of where it was leading.

"Good, I'll set up meetings with the banks for tomorrow morning. You work hard on Chan's draft order and the information that you want from your head office and by Saturday evening, tomorrow, we could have a lot of this set up."

Stuart nodded, still confused.

"You have your passport with you?" Anwar now asked, again confusing Stuart.

"Yes, well, in the office."

"And some photographs, passport photographs?"

"Yes." Stuart was still confused.

"That's good." Anwar paused and leant forward on the table, coming close to Stuart. "Stuart, I know you, I've known you for a while, more than a year. We've travelled together and we've done business together. I have always liked you, the way you worked, your character. I don't know what your situation is like in England – your factory, your office, your family. I know you have a family, you have children. My advice would be to forget this girl in Indonesia, to go back to your family after you have sorted out the business in Indonesia and then for you to choose the right man to send here to carry on where you left off."

Stuart began to open his mouth to protest, but Anwar waved his hand to suppress his words.

"But, because you are my friend and I can see that you are determined to do something for this girl... What's her name by the way?"

"Ita."

"For Ita, I will help you. First, if she can speak English as good as you say that she can and she has some knowledge of working with computers, then, when she has recovered, I will give her an interview for a job. I can't promise to give her a job, but I will try."

Stuart smiled.

"What else do you need?"

"Time, the time to be with her, to see how well she is, to help her through this difficult time – that's what I need, just to be with her and make sure that she is well enough," Stuart answered.

"Time for just the two of you, not here in Jakarta with work on your mind," Anwar continued.

Stuart nodded.

"Okay, this", Anwar reached into his jacket pocket, "is the address of my villa on Bali."

"Villa?" Stuart said, unable to hide a note of astonishment in his voice.

"Well, it's not what the French would call a villa. We call any sort of holiday home a villa. No, it's really quite small. We bought a piece of land in Bali twenty years ago. Since then we have built a small, two-storey villa bit by bit over the years. First a living room, then a bedroom, then a bathroom and so on – all very basic facilities. We only got electricity two years ago and there's no air-con, but it's comfortable, with its own small beach. It's a good place to relax."

Stuart took the card.

"When you have finished on Saturday, you go there for ten days, two weeks even. My secretary will arrange the tickets for Sunday morning. I'll get a message to the housemaid and gardener there and they will pick you up. We have a small Suzuki jeep as well so you can get around the island. There's no phone but there is a hotel quite close by. You can call me and receive and send faxes from there. I will need to go into Java again, around the other factories to see what can be done. You said yourself that Chan will need a week or so and we will need to see the embassy – two weeks will disappear easily. You talk to your office today and explain the situation." He nodded in a final manner, the problem resolved.

Stuart smiled and accepted Anwar's gift graciously.

Anwar paid and they left.

That afternoon Stuart worked very hard. Chan's draft order went out by fax just after four and he spent an hour on the phone to the head office, devoting some time to Frank, but more to Montague. He got full backing to continue in whatever way he thought best to bring in the maximum amount of work possible. Then he phoned his wife to explain the work situation to her, which she accepted without any comment. Then he began to work on a long fax to head office.

Anwar set up three meetings for Saturday morning together with a lunch appointment.

Anwar's secretary produced two business class round trip tickets to Bali at five o'clock, outwards on Sunday morning, return open.

Stuart finally left well after eight, with some work still to do on the fax to the UK, but tiredness was creeping up on him and he wanted to get to Ita before it was too late.

He dropped his bag off at the hotel and left without the customary shower and change. He arrived in Ita's street and looked for the little boy, his friend. He was there, waiting at the entrance to the small alleyway. Stuart smiled at him and he smiled back, appearing happier than the previous evening. Stuart gave him two five hundred rupiah notes, one extra to compensate for the missed one last night.

He took Stuart's hand and led him into the now familiar maze of small passageways and houses. He knocked on Ita's door.

Her mother opened it and saw Stuart. She tried to close the door, but Stuart had his foot in and his hand on the door. She shouted loudly at him and threw her shoulder against the door.

Almost immediately Stuart felt people stopping behind him in the narrow alleyway. He looked down at his friend, the little boy. His face was confused.

Ita's mother shouted loudly again and pushed the door harder. Stuart was shocked and confused.

The crowd behind him grew, the people coming from nowhere to see what the cause of the noise was.

"Ita!" Stuart shouted at the top of his voice, then "Ita!" again.

"Stuart?" she said in response to his call.

He saw her standing in the doorway of her bedroom, dressed in a long, grubby and creased dressing gown. Her shoulders were hunched and she held on to the door for support.

She shouted at her mother. Then she talked to her mother in a quiet but nonetheless stern and determined voice.

Her mother looked from Stuart to Ita and back to Stuart.

Ita repeated whatever she had said and her mother slowly relaxed the grip on the door. Her face softened a little and Stuart pushed against the door. It still resisted.

Ita said something again and her mother stepped back, allowing Stuart in.

He glanced behind him at the fifteen or so people who were standing in the yard, looking in watching. He came into the room and gratefully listened while Ita's mother closed out the audience and shut the door. Stuart walked over to Ita and she took his hand and led him into her room.

She closed the door and offered Stuart a seat on the bed. They say down beside each other.

Stuart and Ita looked at each other, staring into each other's eyes, looking, searching. They smiled, then kissed a gentle touch, a kiss of rejoined bonding, not a kiss of sexuality.

"Stuart, you look so tired," she said. "What happened to you?"

"I walked home last night, all the way from here."

"You walked home, to your hotel!" she said incredulously. "In the dark, at night?"

"Yep, I did. I got back at three o'clock and I worked all day today, so I guess I probably do look tired," he said.

"You crazy to walk home in Jakarta like that, crazy." She shook her head in disbelief at him. She linked her left arm through his right and leaned her head against his shoulder, both to comfort herself and sympathise with his tired condition. "I'm so glad you came back. I was worried after last night with my mother. I thought you would never come back. But you're here." She squeezed his arm.

"What was that about, just now when I came in with your mother? I thought after last night you were going to talk to her," Stuart said, responding to her squeeze with one of his own.

"I did. I told her about you, about how you were so good to me, but she believes that you have brought shame on the family and that our sin made the baby die. It is hard for her – she is so traditional. To her babies only happen outside marriage to..." She paused, not wanting to say it. "To... well, call-girls." She paused again. "So I had to tell her everything, about last time when I was young, to make her believe that you were not the cause of my problem, that it was a long time ago, and that you were the best man that I had ever met, the most kind, the most understanding."

"So now three of us know about last time," Stuart said, trying to forget and regretting that he had told Anwar something of her story at lunch. "So why was she still so hostile, so angry tonight?" Stuart asked.

"Please try to understand how difficult it is for her. Even though I told her, she cannot be changed overnight. Please understand her."

"I do, I can understand something of what she feels," he said.

There was a knock on the door interrupting his chain of thought and Stuart tensed as it opened. He was expecting another barrage of abuse from Ita's mother.

Instead, she came into the room with a tray and two cups of tea. She set it down on the small table at the side of the bed, looked at Ita and then at Stuart and then backed out of the room.

Stuart was sure that she almost smiled at him.

"I have something for you," Stuart said after she had closed the door.

"What?" she said eagerly, a little of her childlike side coming out after a long hibernation.

Stuart handed her the envelope with the tickets.

She took it and pulled the two tickets out. "What is it?"

"Two tickets."

"What sort of tickets?"

"There are two plane tickets, one for you and one for me," Stuart said in the sort of voice he used to address Colleen.

"Plane tickets? For an aeroplane, you mean?" Ita said slowly, her eyes filling with wonder as she looked at the small paper in her hand. "I've never been on an aeroplane before!" Her wonderment was now tinged with apprehension. "Will it be all right?"

"Of course it will." Stuart almost laughed at her worried tone.

"Are you sure?"

"Of course I'm sure. I go on aeroplanes all the time. It's good, you'll enjoy it," he said, trying to reassure her. "Don't you want to know where we are going?"

"Where?"

"To Bali."

"Bali?" she said, her voice excited. "I've been there once when I was small, by bus, a long time ago. It's very beautiful in Bali."

"My agent has a small villa there; he has lent it to us for two weeks so we can go and relax together."

"Oh, a villa, that's wonderful! Er... fantastic," she said, finding it hard to find the English words to express her feelings. "When are we going?"

"Sunday morning. I have to work all day tomorrow. I'll come here in the evening and then we can stay in my hotel on Saturday night and then go early on Sunday morning from there. Is that okay with you?"

She nodded enthusiastically.

"Do you have a bag or a suitcase?" he asked.

She shook her head in the childlike manner that made her so irresistible.

"Okay, well you get everything ready for tomorrow evening and I'll bring a bag."

She nodded in the same manner.

Stuart spent the rest of the evening going through what she should take, what she should wear on the aeroplane, all the details of the new experience to come. After an hour or so Stuart felt tiredness overwhelming him as the time passed beyond ten-thirty.

"I have to go, I've got meetings tomorrow, all morning, starting at eight."

"I understand," she said. "What time will you come tomorrow?"

"I don't know. Late afternoon, early evening. It will be okay with your mother?"

She nodded. "Don't worry, it will be fine with her," she said.

Stuart stood up and opened the bedroom door. "One last thing," he said.

"Yes?"

"Who was the doctor?"

"For our baby?"

"Yes."

She moved over to the bedside table. "Here is his card." She handed him a business card.

Stuart took it and slipped it in his pocket. "Thanks."

She stood and came over to him in small, halting steps, her shoulders stooped again. She wrapped her arms around him and hugged him. He cuddled her back.

"Can I have my ticket?" she asked in a small, little girl voice.

"Yes sure," he said, reaching into his pocket for the envelope. "Don't lose it."

"I won't. I just want to look at it," she said.

He leaned down and kissed her. They squeezed each other and then Stuart left.

He felt happier now than he had felt at any time since Ita's letter had arrived. The little boy seemed to sense his happiness as he walked alongside him; he looked up at Stuart and smiled, squeezing his hand and giving little murmurs of happiness, the nearest he could get to speaking. He found Stuart a *bajaj* and waved to him as the *bajaj* drove away, another five hundred rupiah note clutched in his hand.

## CHAPTER 35

## BALI

Saturday, for Stuart, was rather hard work. He had still not recovered fully from his travelling or the traumatic return to Jakarta. He and Anwar started with a meeting at eight followed by one at nine-thirty. The third one was cancelled at the last minute and Stuart used the time to write reports and requests for more information to fax back to head office. Then they had a two hour lunch appointment from twelve onwards which went very well. Stuart then finished off writing his reports, because he wanted to send them by fax before he left for Bali. Anwar and the rest of the office staff, with the exception of the office boy and security guard, had already left when Stuart was ready to send the fax. Anwar had confirmed that everything had been arranged in Bali and that they would be met at the airport when he left some time after three in the afternoon. He said goodbye, wished him and Ita all the best for their time in Bali, gave Stuart a long, firm handshake and a pat on the back. Stuart was finally ready to leave once the fax had been sent and confirmed.

In the entrance to the office, he was surprised to see Anwar's driver sitting reading a newspaper.

"Mr Anwar still here?" Stuart asked.

"No, Mr Anwar go home already. I stay for you, Mr Stuart. Mr Anwar say he want me to drive for you today," the driver replied.

"Okay, fine, good," Stuart replied, rather surprised by Anwar's generosity. He knew that this driver was the only one who drove Anwar's new green Mercedes, which was less than three months old. "Which car?" he asked.

"The Mercee," the driver replied with a smile. He stood up and led Stuart out of the building to the waiting car.

"Where to, hotel?" the driver asked as he held the back door open for Stuart.

"No, first I want to go shopping, to Pasar thingy. What is the name of that big shop in Blok M?"

"Pasar Raya in Blok M, yes?"

"Yes," and with that, Stuart settled down in silent, air-conditioned comfort and was whisked down Jenderal Sudirman, past the office blocks, past the row of bars where he had staggered a few nights before, and on to the tree-lined streets which led to Blok M. The driver entered the shop compound and was allowed to park right by the door of the shop, a privilege afforded only to Mercedes and larger BMW cars. Stuart felt like royalty as the door was opened for him to step out.

Once inside, Stuart went immediately to the luggage section and chose a substantial holdall for Ita, one with a heavy zip and locks. He also bought a small leather wallet and asked the cashier for ten brand-new one thousand rupiah notes. He carefully filled the wallet with the new notes. Then he went to the art and craft section and bought a piece of expensive, hand-painted batik cloth to form a sarong for Ita's mother.

The driver was waiting beside the car, leaning on the rear wing. As Stuart approached, he stood up and straightened himself. He held the door for Stuart. "Where now, Mr Stuart?" he asked again.

"Here," Stuart replied, holding the doctor's card that Ita had given him the night before.

The driver nodded and then drove off.

It was quite a drive to the hospital where Ita had had the baby. It was a large place situated on a road junction between two major roads. It looked clean from the outside, but, as usual with most places in Indonesia, it was thronged with people, with cars trying to get in, to leave, to pick people up or just to park. Stuart was grateful for the driver who left him at the main entrance and then went off to park by himself. Stuart went to the main reception desk.

"Can I see this doctor?" he said slowly, holding the card.

The girl scrutinised the card and then him. "He woman doctor, special for woman," she replied in rough English.

"I know," said Stuart. "I don't want consultation, I just want to talk to him."

She shrugged her shoulders and telephoned. After a few conversations she handed him the phone. "Doctor."

"Hello, is this Doctor Raharjo?" Stuart asked.

"Yes, speaking." The voice was deep and rounded.
"My name is Morgan from England," Stuart replied.
"What can I do for you?"
"I would like to ask about a patient of yours who had a baby here two weeks ago, on Saturday two weeks ago, a girl called Ita." He paused, waiting for a reply. When none came he added, "The baby died."
"You have some involvement?" the doctor asked.
"Yes."
"Okay, let me speak to the receptionist again."
Stuart handed the phone back and he waited apprehensively until she put the phone down and looked up.
"Up the stairs, on the left," she said.
Stuart followed the directions and after a few wrong doors found the door of Doctor Raharjo's office. He knocked and waited for the response.
The doctor was standing by a filing cabinet, leafing through the hanging files inside. He stood up and faced Stuart as he came in, inviting him to sit down. He was a shortish man, quite well-built for an Indonesian man, with broad shoulders and a little bit of an expanding waistline. His wide, square face was very brown; he wore steel-rimmed glasses and had a small, straggly moustache. To Stuart he didn't look like the sort of slim, thin Javanese men to whom he had grown accustomed: he was altogether bigger. He had an air of arrogance about him which Stuart disliked immediately. It was the sort of attitude in a doctor for which Stuart would change doctors.
"I don't normally discuss patients with anyone unless they have a close relationship. What is your involvement in this?" the doctor said after he had settled himself down in a high-backed swivel chair behind his desk. "Are you the father of the child?"
"Yes, I am," Stuart said.
"What do you want to know?" the doctor asked.
"What happened first of all? Why did the baby die?" Stuart replied.
"Well, she was weak, she didn't look as if she had had enough nourishment during the pregnancy. She obviously had something on her mind that was worrying her – she looked sad all the time. It was a long labour, very long, she was exhausted,

and the baby was very small and weak. I was very surprised when he was born alive." He shrugged his shoulders in a dismissive gesture that Stuart found rather callous.

"You did all you could for both of them?" he asked.

"Yes of course," he replied, somewhat disgusted by the insinuation. "This isn't Europe – we don't have all the equipment that you have, we don't even have enough access to the operating theatre in case an emergency comes up. But with what we had, we did all we could," the doctor replied, glaring at Stuart.

Stuart nodded, his opinion of the doctor confirmed. "And how do you view her chances of having another child in the future?"

"No problem. She would need to rest a lot, eat well," he replied half-heartedly.

"Is there anything else?" Stuart asked.

"Well, while she was in labour she kept asking her mother for someone called 'Stuart'. That is you, I take it?" he asked.

"Yes, I wanted to be here, but I was on business, travelling, so I couldn't be. It's a long story, but I couldn't," Stuart replied.

"It's always a long story," the doctor said in a bored, knowing manner.

"What about her condition now?" Stuart asked.

"She should be all right. She needs rest, gentle exercise and the right food. She needs someone to be around her, preferably you, I suppose," the doctor replied, now completely bored with the conversation.

"And her mental condition – is she likely to do anything extreme?" Stuart continued.

"Difficult to say. I doubt it, not if you are around and can take the time to look after her," he said, looking at his watch conspicuously.

"Well, we have a couple of weeks together starting tonight, maybe that will be a start," Stuart said.

"It will be a start, but the effects of a baby's death can linger for years, usually until the next baby is born successfully." He smiled at Stuart for the first time. "I have to go – another baby to deliver."

He stood and Stuart followed him as he opened the door to leave. The doctor led the way out and walked the same way as Stuart.

"Even though I've been delivering babies for many years", he began, his tone quiet and almost apologetic, "every one that dies upsets me. That's the truth." The doctor stopped and looked at Stuart. "Nice to meet you and thank you for coming. Most absent fathers of this type never show their face at all."

He offered his hand to Stuart. Stuart took it and they shook hands.

Stuart was now confused about his initial opinion after this little outburst of compassion. Perhaps he wasn't the cold-hearted doctor after all.

From the hospital it was on to Ita's house, a fairly short drive away. The driver looked a little apprehensive as he parked in the small, shabby street with its dirty drains and poor-looking inhabitants. Stuart's friend, the little boy, came running over and grabbed Stuart's hand, smiling widely.

"Don't worry," Stuart said to the driver. "He's my friend. He will look after the car, just tell him."

But the boy needed no telling: he shooed away the other small children who had gathered and stood resolutely by the driver.

Stuart handed him his present.

His eyes filled with wonder as he opened the wallet and saw the crisp new notes inside. He took out his plastic bag and carefully removed the notes Stuart had already given him and then secreted them in the wallet with the new ones. Then he pushed the wallet deep into his pocket and gave a triumphant smile.

Stuart disappeared into the maze of alleyways. It was the first time that he had been there in daylight. The place appeared much worse in the daylight because there was no darkness to hide the filthy, cluttered drains, the rubbish piled high at the sides of the path, the dirty, shabby buildings and the people, poorly dressed and staring. The smell seemed more acute in the heat of the day, the pungent stink of dirty drains, and probably human excreta, rose around him in an almost tangible way. He was grateful to reach Ita's door and knock. He pushed it open just as Ita's mother stepped up to open it.

For the first time she gave him a genuine smile. She extended her hand to him.

Stuart smiled back and shook her hand gently. She touched her chest, receiving him into her heart, after shaking his hand. He followed her gesture and she bowed her head.

Ita was up and dressed, the first time that he had seen her in anything but the bed or the grubby dressing gown. She wore her Levi jeans, now more loose-fitting than before, and one of her large, baggy tee-shirts. She walked with her head a little bowed, her shoulders stooped as if she were weak, ill or exhausted. As it was some two weeks now since she had given birth, Stuart guessed that the posture owed more to her mental condition than to her physical condition. She was bowed down by the weight of her tragedy.

"Hello Ita, my darling," he said warmly without a trace of sentimentality, going over to her, trying to reassure her that he was still here, that nothing had changed, that everything would work out for the best.

"Hello Stuart, it's good to see you again," she said, slipping her arms around him and giving him a feeble squeeze. They kissed once, lightly on the lips.

"Here," he said, offering her the bag. "For your clothes."

She took the bag and admired it, opening the main part and then the side pockets, examining all its features.

"And this is for your mother," he continued, holding out the small package.

"Give it to her," Ita said, not taking her eyes off the bag.

Stuart turned and handed it to Ita's mother with a smile.

She graciously accepted it and sat down with the package on her knee, unopened.

Ita looked up and said something to her mother, who then opened the package. She smiled when she saw the contents and ran her hands through the folds of cloth. She said something to Ita.

"She says that it is very nice, very good quality and that it is too good for an old woman like her. She says thank you very much and she will only wear it on special occasions because it's so good," Ita translated.

"Tank wery much," her mother said slowly and haltingly.

Stuart smiled. "My pleasure." He turned to Ita. "Tell her that she is a good mother and that she deserves the best in her old age."

Ita translated and her mother smiled at Stuart.

"And also that I do not think that she is an old woman, I think that she is still very beautiful."

Ita glanced at Stuart.

"Go on, tell her," he urged.

She translated again and her mother laughed and shook her head. Stuart was now on the way to being a friend with Ita's mother.

In Ita's bedroom, Ita had already laid out all the clothes that she wanted to take on her bed. It was a quick and easy job to pack for her. When they had finished, she handed Stuart a small photograph album.

"For you, Stuart, our baby picture," she said, her big, brown eyes moist, her voice a little shaky.

"Thanks," he said, looking down into those eyes again and seeing all that he used to see – the deep sensuality, the tinge of sadness – and he found them as irresistible as before. He leaned down and kissed her on the cheek. They intertwined arms and held each other for a while, reaffirming human contact.

With the bag packed, they prepared to leave.

"Does your mother have enough money?" Stuart asked as he shouldered the bag.

"Yes, don't worry, I have enough money left from you," Ita replied. "She will be fine."

Ita kissed her mother and Stuart shook her hand and then they set off down the alleyway once again. Ita's mother accompanied them to the main road, where the large green Mercedes stood in isolation, the driver leaning against it, the little boy standing guard, the other children at a respectable distance, and the adults mostly dispersed, bored with staring at the strange car in their midst.

"This car?" Ita said in amazement.

"Yes, special for you – you deserve the best."

"From who?" she asked.

"It belongs to my agent, he lent it to us."

More kisses and handshakes and then Stuart and Ita left Ita's mother and the little boy standing waving in the street and drove off.

They went straight to the hotel. Stuart dismissed the driver who said he would be outside the hotel at eight the following morning. Stuart and Ita walked into the reception area, arm in arm, with a bell boy following with Ita's bag and Stuart's briefcase. Stuart collected the key and they continued on their way. Ita continued her hunched shoulder, weak-looking, small-stepped shuffle. Stuart found this a little melodramatic, but he humoured her, holding her arm and supporting her as she walked. They went up in the lift with the bell boy and into the room, all three. Ita showed no signs of her earlier embarrassment or caution at entering the hotel. Gone were the secret dashes, the hiding in the bathroom when the bell boy or room service arrived. She even tipped the bell boy before Stuart could get his wallet out.

"I need a shower," Stuart said when the bell boy had finally left.

She nodded. "Okay, I want to watch some television." She picked up the remote control and Stuart went off for his shower.

When he came back, fully dressed except for his shoes and socks, Ita was engrossed in a film.

"You want a shower?" Stuart asked.

"Mmmm, later," she said, not turning her attention from the screen.

"You want to eat out, downstairs maybe?"

She looked at him now, her attention diverted for a moment. "No, I just want to stay here with you, watch television and eat something in the room. When the film finished I have a shower, order some food. Okay?"

Stuart glanced at his watch; there was less than half an hour to go on the film at the outside. He decided to wait.

When the film was over Ita asked for some food and went into the bathroom. The food arrived at the same time as she finished her shower. She came out of the bathroom dressed in a hotel towelling robe, towelling her hair. She talked to the room service man, indicating where she wanted the food.

Stuart was amazed at her complete turnaround; maybe she was now past caring. He didn't ask.

After the food was finished, Stuart undressed and climbed into bed. Ita took off the towelling robe and climbed into bed dressed in a big tee-shirt. They cuddled up together, his arm around her shoulders, her head resting on his chest. They watched another film to the finish and then fell asleep.

The following morning they were both awake before seven and packed and checked out by eight. Anwar's green Mercedes was parked in the position reserved for such cars, right by the entrance. They rode to the airport in style and at speed, the Sunday morning traffic being light. The driver helped them into the terminal building with the bags and bid them goodbye.

"I never been on the inside before," Ita said, looking round as they queued to pass the customary security check. "What's this for?" she said as Stuart loaded the cases on the conveyor belt.

"Security, X-ray, looking for guns or bombs."

"Oh, is it dangerous then? Many people carry guns?" she asked with genuine concern.

Stuart laughed. "No, they don't fortunately. That's what the X-ray is for."

"Oh."

"Now, come on, we have to check in," Stuart said, looking for a monitor. He found one and checked the flight number and check-in desk. "Over there, the far counter." He led the way, carrying all the bags, with Ita following quietly in his wake, still amazed by all the new sights around her.

"Here," he said, dropping the bags by the side of the Garuda Indonesia Club Class check-in. He handed his ticket over. "Ticket, Ita, please."

She looked surprised. "Oh, oh yes."

She struggled to find it in her small handbag, and handed the ticket over to the woman behind the counter. Ita looked over the counter, watching the proceedings with avid curiosity.

"Seats 1A and 1B for you, is that okay?" the woman asked.

"Fine, so long as they are non-smoking seats."

"Yes, any baggage?"

"Yes," Stuart replied, lifting the bags on to the conveyor. "Two pieces."

The woman checked them in, attaching the tags. She pushed the button and the bags moved off.

"Where are they going?" Ita asked, a little panic creeping into her voice.

"Don't worry, they'll be there at the other end. Well, hopefully they will." Stuart smiled at her.

She nodded but looked unconvinced.

From the check-in, it was up the stairs to the departure area, under the brown steel columns which supported the wide, steeply-pitched roofs, the sides wide open with a gentle breeze blowing across. After a slow walk around the main open area, and with still an hour to go, Stuart led her into the executive lounge.

"This is nice," she said. "Does everyone get this when they fly?"

"No, this is only for Business Class. Usually I'm out there flying on economy," he said with a longing tone. "Want a drink, snack? Over there it's all free," Stuart said.

Ita ate sparingly and drank some tea. They waited in silence, eating and drinking to fill the time. Ita was becoming nervous while they waited, glancing at the clock, her watch, sipping tea in small nervous pecks. Then the tannoy announced that their flight was boarding. She jumped up.

"Stuart, we have to go," she said excitedly.

"It's okay, don't worry. We have plenty of time."

"But she said we have to go," Ita insisted.

"All right," Stuart said with a laugh, "we have to go."

They moved into the much less comfortable departure lounge, sitting on hard, plastic chairs with low backs, with the air-conditioning less than effective. They waited for a further fifteen minutes before another announcement invited them to board.

Ita jumped up again. "Come on, we can go now?" she said, her voice even more excited than before.

Stuart followed without protest this time, allowing her to enjoy the delights of her first flight to the full, not marring it by any harsh or foolish words. He led her down the gangway, turning left at the first junction towards the front of the aeroplane.

They entered at the forward-most door, Stuart handed the boarding passed over and they sat in the front row, Ita on the window side, Stuart on the aisle.

Ita investigated her new surroundings: the wide seat, the overhead panel, the lights, the air control, the seat recline, the air hostesses and the bustle of people moving.

"It's very big, this aeroplane," she said quietly. "It will be all right to fly?"

"Yes of course. It's an A300, not the biggest, but maybe holding three hundred people if it's full."

"Three hundred!" she said, her eyes opening wide in wonder again.

The pre-take-off bustle and hustle continued until the doors were shut and they began to shunt back from the stand. The customary safety demonstration started.

Stuart ignored it, preferring the in-flight magazine.

"Stuart," Ita said with an air of exasperation, grabbing his arm. "This is important, we must watch, please," she pleaded.

"I've seen it so many times, every flight."

"But she said it was important," Ita insisted.

Stuart put the magazine down and watched.

Ita followed her every word, looked under her seat for the life vest, checked her seatbelt, and rehearsed the drill to put on the oxygen mask, her face an earnest study in concentration.

With the demonstration finished, and the taxiing well in progress, Ita looked out of the window. At the end of the runway, the engine note began to rise. Ita looked at Stuart, her face worried.

He shook his head and smiled.

She looked out of the window again.

Then the brakes came off, the plane rolled forward, gathering speed. The engines came up to their final setting.

The plane bumped down the runway, Ita looking at Stuart for reassurance. Then the rotation came and she grabbed his arm.

He patted her hand.

"Oh look," she said as Jakarta fell away. "Oh... Oh!" was all she could manage.

The rest of the flight passed quickly. It was only an hour and a half and they managed to serve a pre-breakfast drink, breakfast and a round of tea and coffee. Ita was fascinated with the little china salt and pepper cellars and put hers in her handbag along with a teaspoon. She glanced furtively around as she did so to make sure that she was not observed.

Stuart looked on with a smile.

As they commenced their descent, Ita looked around in surprise at the sudden change in engine note and the sinking feeling that followed. Stuart reassured her.

The approach to Bali's main airport, Nusa Raja, can be either across land or over the sea, close to the island's main beach, Kuta. They approached over the sea.

Ita looked out of the window with growing concern as the sea came closer and closer. She gripped Stuart's arm again. "Where do we go down?" she said. "All I can see is water."

"Don't worry, the land will come."

She looked out of the window again. She was visibly relieved when the ground suddenly appeared and the plane touched down with a bump.

The plane came to a stop and they were led down the steps towards the terminal. To Ita's relief the bags duly appeared and they wandered out into the arrivals area. Stuart looked around for their lift. Eventually he spotted a small, slightly chubby man with thinning grey hair dressed in a shapeless, red tee-shirt, grubby, white pants and flip-flops. He held up a sign that said 'Mr Stuart Mbak Ita'.

"Over there," Stuart said, pointing and hurrying over.

The man smiled an almost toothless grin – one or two black teeth were all that remained – when he saw Stuart and Ita come over.

"Mr Stuart, yes, and Mbak Ita?" he said.

They both nodded.

"Okay, okay, me Pak Oka," he said, and then added a few words of Indonesian to Ita before he turned and disappeared.

"He's gone to get the car," Ita explained.

The car was a small Suzuki jeep-type vehicle, white in colour and a little battered. Stuart gave Ita the front seat in deference to her condition and he crushed himself on one of the two side bench seats in the back together with all the luggage. The roof was a little low and he was forced to bend his head a little to avoid constantly bumping it. The seat back was low and the sideways orientation of the seat made for an uncomfortable ride. To fight any chance of car sickness he bent further forward to see out of the front window.

"How long will it be?" Stuart said.

Ita asked the Pak Oka. "He says about an hour and a half. Why?"

"It's not very comfortable in the back, but I'll survive," Stuart replied as his head came into contact with the roof again.

From the airport they moved swiftly on to the main road. They skirted around the main city of Denpasar and moved out into open country, travelling west. Pak Oka drove with the usual gusto of Indonesian drivers, honking and flashing his lights, trying to overtake, swerving left and right, looking for that small advantage that never gave any advantage in reality but which made him feel better. Stuart was thrown around in the back and he clung on to the back of Ita's seat for support.

Ita rode it all out with the graceful ease of one used to it.

In the countryside, Bali was like Java only more so. The paddy fields were even more beautiful, terraced into fantastic layers of glinting, sparkling water that ran around the sides of hills, down into river valleys and to the foot of the steepest rocky outcrops. Clumps of palm trees, banana trees and large rocks were blended into the vast array of fields in a smooth continuous sweep which seemed to flow over the landscape without jarring the eye with the transitions.

Then the road turned down the side of steep gorge, too steep even for Balinese paddy fields, then turned into a vicious switchback over a bridge before beginning a long climb up again beneath a roof of heavy, green, shady trees, a steep bank of red tropical soil on one side, a rocky drop to the river below on the other.

Then they ran through villages, similar in many ways to those on Java, but with subtle differences. There were no mosques, but Hindu temples instead, each with their carved statues with little black and white chequered sarongs, each with a pile of smoking incense in front. Eventually, the villages became less frequent and the road was right out in the countryside. It was a wide road, the main road from the capital of Bali, Denpasar, to the ferry terminal at Gillimanuk for boats to Java and beyond, Pak Oka explained through Ita's interpreting. Sometimes on the left side, they could catch glimpses of the sea but not yet any beaches, while on the right they could see the vast areas of paddy fields punctuated only by land still forested or too inaccessible for the rice farmers to use.

After more like two hours of driving, Pak Oka turned left off the main road, down a small road, more or less metalled, but with a poor bumpy surface and many potholes. Stuart had to cling on for dear life as Pak Oka showed little willingness to slow down. They entered a small village and Pak Oka waved at the people as he went along, shouting greetings to some, slapping a quick handshake to others as he guided the jeep slowly through the crush of people.

He turned right off the road, between two shops and came to a set of white metal gates some six feet high and fairly ornate. There was a postbox on the left and above it the name of the house, 'Villa Patra'. They had arrived.

Pak Oka opened the gates, drove through and closed them again, locking the substantial padlock as he did so. Beyond the gate, the road was a dirt-surfaced track which was nonetheless well kept and quite smooth to drive on. It bent almost immediately to the left, dropping quite steeply. First it passed between high grass-covered banks with stone drainage channels on both sides and small flowering shrubs set at regular intervals into them. Then the road passed through a small embankment, the sides of which were held in place by substantial trees, giving the road a green canopy of shade. Then it turned right over a small stone bridge and, still running downhill, clung to the side of the hill. The right side, the hill side, had a small stone retaining wall before the grass banks and flowering shrubs began, on the left a stone kerb before the large trees which reinforced that side of the road. After a few hundred yards, the road levelled off and Stuart could see Anwar's Villa Patra for the first time. The road went to the side of it and there was a small lean-to garage for the jeep. The building was two-storey in white with a tiled roof. The ground floor seemed to be half buried in the hillside at the back with a stone wall running across the back of the building before a grassy bank sloped away and up higher than the roof level of the villa.

They stopped before the garage and Pak Oka helped Stuart out of the back and collected the luggage. Stuart opened the door for Ita and held her hand to help her out. They walked, hand in hand, to the front of the villa. There was a low, curving stone wall on the left which started a yard or so from the corner of the villa and ran across the front. In the centre was a gap which allowed access to the garden sloping away down the hill. Big windows with natural wood frames and many small rectangular panes of glass opened out on to the small terrace enclosed by the villa and the stone wall. They passed two such windows before arriving at the main door, which was opposite the gap in the wall. The door would be centrally disposed when the villa was complete, but the far side was still a building site of piles of bricks and iron bars, bags of cement and heaps of the black volcanic sand.

Inside the door stood a small rotund lady wearing a sarong and blouse. She had grey hair and a lined, wizened face. She introduced herself as Ibu Oka, Pak Oka's wife, the cook, cleaner and everything else in the house.

She led them upstairs to the first floor bedroom that they were to use. This room had the same big windows, set back from those on the ground floor, making a small balcony that ran across the front of the villa. The roof continued out beyond the front of the villa, giving some protection from the rain to the balcony. Split-rolled bamboo blinds hung under the eaves to allow protection from the sun. The bedroom was simply furnished with a big bed, a table and a wardrobe. The floor was tiled and had one small carpet. A ceiling fan turned slowly to give some relief from the heat.

Ibu Oka showed them the bathroom: white tiled floor and walls with an Indonesian-style bath and toilet. The whole house was spotlessly clean and neat.

Ita immediately sat on the bed and said she wanted to rest. Ibu Oka disappeared and returned with some tea and bowls of soup for Ita and Stuart. After they had finished the soup and Stuart the unpacking, Ita changed into some light clothes and lay down to sleep. Stuart was much too awake for sleep, so he changed into his shorts and tee-shirt and went out to explore the surroundings.

There was another smaller bedroom on the first floor, furnished with two single beds and a wardrobe. It had a single window looking out to the side. He went down the wide wooden staircase, which, like the front door, would be central when the villa was finished, and looked into the single main room on the ground floor. It was a living room and dining room all in one. It was furnished in the same simple style as the rooms upstairs. At the front were some low rattan chairs, good quality ones with colourful cloth cushions. A large rug filled the space between the chairs and this was the only adornment to the white tiled floor. Beyond the rattan furniture was a large wooden table and eight chairs, a dresser and what looked like a drinks cupboard. The walls had a number of well-chosen pictures, some paintings, some photographs, together with a number of small pieces of carving. A ceiling fan turned lazily over the rattan chairs at the front of the room and a gentle breeze slid in through the two wide-open windows, pushing the white net curtains into gentle waves. The whole villa was so well done, with not a hint of the ostentation or showiness which was visible to some extent in Anwar's house and very visible in many other houses in Jakarta, especially those owned by the Chinese business community. Stuart was very impressed and liked the place immediately: it felt quiet and restful. He wondered just how much Anwar was really worth.

At the back of the room was an open door. He walked over and pushed his head round. It was the kitchen and Ibu Oka was busying herself washing up. She smiled at him. She had almost as few teeth as her husband, but her face was friendly and genuine. The kitchen was open to the sides and the rear was formed by the wall that ran behind the house. It was roofed over, tiled and very clean. It was well equipped with a modern cooker, two fridges and a sink. He smiled again at Ibu Oka and went back into the hall and out of the front door to explore the wider surroundings.

The front terrace was partly paved and partly loose pebbles. There were two circles of paving on either side of the central path which led from the doorway to the gap in the terrace wall.

Stuart walked forward to the wall and looked over. The ground on the other side of the wall was a good yard lower than the level of the terrace. It finished in a broad border filled with shrubs, small trees and flowers. Beyond the border was a fan-shaped lawn which ran downhill away from Stuart towards the line of trees and jungle-like scrub. Over the top of the trees Stuart could see the sea. The view was beautiful.

He spent ten minutes simply surveying the scene laid out before him, resting his hands on the edge of the wall as he did so. When his contemplation was finished, he moved over to the gap in the wall and began to descend the set of steps to the lawn. The lawn was well kept, although the variety of grass was somewhat coarse by English lawn standards. As well as being bordered by the well-kept bed at the foot of the terrace wall, it was bordered on the two sides, left and right, by equally beautiful borders. The garden was an absolute credit to whoever kept it up and to whoever had laid it out.

As he strolled down the lawn, he became aware of a presence behind him. It was Pak Oka. Pak Oka gestured to Stuart and Stuart followed him to the left, over towards the edge of the lawn and down a little path he had not seen before. The path led down beneath the trees at the edge of the lawn. They passed into the shade of the trees and walked along an earthen path to a small clearing in the trees. Here the sunlight streamed in again to reveal a series of benches and pots all laden with plants, shrubs and trees in various stages of development from a tiny twig up to small trees ready for planting out. Some of the cuttings were in nice red-brown clay pots, but the vast majority was in old paint tins, old food containers or anything else that could be pressed into service to grow plants in. There was a small wooden shed which held all of Pak Oka's tools, and a rickety old chair stood beside the door along with his equally rickety bike. He pulled Stuart's arm and led him around to the back of the shed. Here, on another series of wooden stands, was an array of small clay pots, like those Stuart was used to in England, but with holes around the sides. Each sported a fine bamboo rig up which the plants in the pots climbed. The plants were all orchids, mostly in flower, with vivid white and purple colours.

Stuart had never seen so many in one place before; he had only seen the odd ones on the hotel trays when they brought room service. Here he was confronted with dozens, maybe even hundreds of orchids in a vast array of exotic, tropical beauty.

Pak Oka smiled his toothless smile and pointed to himself and then the plants and gabbled away in his own language.

Stuart nodded enthusiastically and smiled back. Pak Oka was obviously the architect of the gardens and the grower of the many plants that graced the gardens of Villa Patra. He was very proud of his achievements. Now that Stuart had shown an interest, Pak Oka took him round the rest of the garden, showing him the unusual plants and flowers which inhabited the borders.

When he finished showing Stuart the garden, he led him to the bottom of the garden where the grass lawn ended. Down there, under the trees, was another path. This time it was a paved path with stone-lined drainage ditches on either side. It led downwards and into the jungle-like forest that lay between the garden and the sea. In the areas not tended as garden by Pak Oka, the jungle was very much untouched. It looked reasonably tidy and Stuart suspected that Pak Oka collected much of the fallen debris to avoid the danger of fire. As they walked down the path small animals and birds flitted around causing little noises that surprised Stuart. He looked around and tried to see the source of the rustles and whispers, but they were always too quick for him. The path turned a sharp left with a stone wall on the corner protecting walkers from the steep drop that opened up in front of them. The path was now descending steeply on stone steps across the face of the slope. It was still surrounded by trees which gave shade as they walked down the path as it clung to the side of the hill.

Suddenly the path levelled out, turned right and they were standing under trees on the edge of a white, sandy beach with the blue-green tropical sea before them. Stuart stood still and took in the sight slowly. The beach was not very deep from front to back and it would not have been much to get excited about if it were a holiday destination. But as it was not a mass holiday destination and it was, in fact, their own private beach, uncrowded and completely clean, it was close to being perfect in Stuart's eyes.

Pak Oka nudged Stuart and pointed at a small hut on their right in the shade of the trees. He opened the padlock and door and let Stuart inside.

Stuart saw that it was an Indonesian beach hut, complete with a changing room, a set of chairs and a table.

"Mr Anwar's?" Stuart asked.

Pak Oka nodded with another toothless smile.

Stuart walked out into the sunshine and along the beach. "Mr Anwar," he said, pointing at the sand.

Pak Oka nodded. He walked away from Stuart and drew a line in the sand. Then he walked back past him and drew a second.

"Pak Anwar," he said, pointing at each line in turn.

Anwar, it seemed, owned a couple of hundred yards of beach. Beyond Anwar's territory, Stuart could see no other evidence of habitation or human activity. The beach ran into a rock headland to the left a few hundred yards beyond the line in the sand and to the right it continued to a jungle-covered spit of land a considerable distance from the boundary of Anwar's patch. Pak Oka retired into the shade and lit a cigarette, leaving Stuart to walk along the beach by himself.

Stuart took his shoes off and walked into the warm sea up to his knees. Then he took his shirt off and walked further, up to his chest. He swam a little, riding the small waves. He could see much bigger waves further out which seemed to be breaking away from the land. Stuart guessed that there was a reef which protected the shore from the big waves.

He strolled along the beach a few hundred yards in either direction, as far as the rocky headland in one and halfway to the jungle-covered headland in the other. Then he returned to Pak Oka, collected his shoes and tee-shirt, and they walked slowly back up the house. Anwar had made a shrewd investment in paradise when he had bought this land twenty years ago. This place certainly was as near to paradise as Stuart had ever been.

Stuart found Ita awake in the bedroom. He told her about the place, the gardens, the orchids and the beach.

She listened to his glowing description and followed his hand as he pointed out the highlights from the balcony. She said that she wanted to see it all but not for a few days, since she had to rest and drink her *jamu*, traditional medicine. In the mid-afternoon an old woman dressed in a sarong and traditional blouse arrived, carrying a big wicker basket filled with bottles.

The woman, Ibu Oka and Ita spent a long time discussing and then the old woman mixed an awful-looking potion in a glass. Ita drank it down in one, retched a couple of times and then pronounced it very good. The old woman looked at Stuart, who had been a curious observer of the whole thing. She made a very crude gesture with her forearm and fist and then she and Ibu Oka grinned and laughed wildly. Even Ita chuckled a little, the first time she had laughed since Stuart had come back.

"She wants to know if you need any help," Ita explained.

"Help?" Stuart asked, confused.

"Yes, help with your love life," Ita said, smiling again.

The old woman repeated the gesture and said something which brought a fresh round of raucous laugher, Ita joining in fully this time.

"She says that because of what has happened you don't need anything at all and maybe you should visit her later tonight because her husband is not strong any more," Ita said, looking at Stuart, a mischievous glint in her eye.

Stuart gave an embarrassed smile back and looked at the floor.

That afternoon Stuart had almost two hours' sleep alongside Ita on the big double bed beneath the ceiling fan. When he woke, Ita was still sleeping. Stuart went down to the terrace again. Pak Oka was working on the border below him.

"*Mau jalan jalan?*" he asked Stuart.

Stuart looked confused.

Oka indicated a walking motion with two figures of his right hand.

Stuart understood and nodded.

Pak Oka came up to the terrace and led Stuart past the unfinished part of the villa and along a path which cut diagonally across the slope above the villa. The path led into the natural jungle outside the cultivated area, but, like the jungle around the lawn, it had been cleared of major fallen debris. After a couple of hundred yards they came to a gate which Pak Oka opened. Initially they then walked along a narrow earthen path between the trees before coming to an open area made up of small scruffy fields with pineapple bushes and banana and papaya trees in a disorganised mess of cultivation. Pak Oka led Stuart across the main road and up a wide track which had two ruts for vehicle wheels and a central grassy mound. On either side, stretching up and away into the distance were nothing but rice paddies, beautifully arranged in the curving terraces around the hills and valleys.

They continued to walk for about half a mile before Stuart turned left down a small footpath. He stopped at a large outcrop of rock, to which the paddies came right up. He was able to climb up the rock from the path and sit on top. In front of him was a wide view of the paddies below, the road and the trees and jungle which led to the sea beyond. The sun was just beginning its descent over to the right over the sea and Stuart settled down to watch the coming sunset. Pak Oka took up a seat below Stuart and got out a cigarette, one of the foul-smelling, clove-impregnated ones. The pungent smell wafted up to Stuart and brought back his first arrival in Indonesia with vivid clarity.

The two men watched in silence while the sun went down in a blaze of orange and red. Then they slowly made their way back to the villa for the evening meal.

The first four days at the villa followed a similar pattern. Ita slept a lot both at night and during the day. The old *Jamu* woman came twice a day and fed Ita with a variety of evil-looking potions. Ibu Oka bound Ita's stomach up in a tight, white cotton band at night. Ita explained that all of this was to help her stomach recover its normal shape. As the days progressed she seemed less frail; she stood up fully as before, her shoulders erect and not bowed. Her voice became stronger. Her hair began to recover its shine and sheen and she began to look like the old Ita whom Stuart had first met.

Stuart recovered his sleep very quickly. After the first day in fact, he took to having an early morning swim and walk along the beach. In the afternoons he walked up to the big rock, sat, looked and contemplated. Pak Oka was his silent companion on these walks and contemplations.

At first everything in Stuart's mind was a confused jumble of thoughts – his wife, his children, Ita, Frances, Anwar, John,

Frank and Montague – they all spun round in a confusing dance. But slowly, as he continued to allow his mind the freedom to roam, they formed into a regularised pattern and he was able to complete the story of what had happened, the first step in analysing the problem of what to do next.

The whole thing from the start had been a series of coincidences and had one of them been different, then nothing would have happened. The coincidences seemed too bizarre and way out to be just coincidences: maybe this was meant to happen, maybe it was his fate, her fate, but then he rationalised his thoughts. Life was a series of bizarre coincidences and anyone who thought that they could plan and go against this was usually wrong. Had he not met Frances in the bar of The Inne, then he would never have met Ita. More importantly, had he not upset Frances when he did, then his fantasy with her may have happened and again he would not have met Ita. Had he been more, or for that matter, less, involved with Frances, she would probably not have asked him to dance the lambada on stage, which brought him centre stage and let Ita see him for the first time. Then when he returned to Indonesia a second time and Frances was still there but ready to leave, he was given a glimpse of her again and he was left feeling empty and hurt, and there was Ita to fill the gap. Ita's initial behaviour – her coolness, the lack of contact – served to entice him more. He had wondered if she had done it all as part of a plan, but he now realised that she was not so devious. Then there was the night when he had been late – her drunkenness, her night in his bed with a hangover and the Saturday in Jakarta and her forgotten handbag in his room. Had he not been late who knows what would have happened. Had she not forgotten her bag would they ever have made love? Again, a linkage of chances and happenings which was tenuous in the extreme.

After Stuart's return home, his excitement at the cricket, rushing out and leaving his briefcase open and Catherine's discovery of Ita. The long time it gave her to plan for Stuart's inevitable return to Indonesia. When he did return, there was Ita's cool reaction at the airport, his failed mission to tell her that it had to stop and the present and the reaction it had brought. He thought long and hard about that night: the most incredible night in his life when it comes to pure, sexual pleasure, the first sight of her naked body, then in the shower. Everything came back to him as he sat on the rock, with a clarity that was sometimes painful and embarrassing. Then there was the missed flight back, his anger and Ita's confusion over the dates that had resulted in her becoming pregnant. Had Catherine not found out, then Stuart could probably have carried on with Ita without problems. Maybe he would have been under less pressure when it was time to go home and perhaps he would not have become angry and confused Ita so much. Certainly Catherine's discovery and her long gestated plan had made the rest inevitable. In trying to snuff out the relationship, Catherine had chosen the strategy that was guaranteed to have completely the opposite effect. Had Stuart been able to go back or receive a letter then the baby could have been stopped without much problem, but the news blackout imposed by Catherine through his office and the forced job change had sealed their fate.

So now they were here, in Bali, in paradise, recovering from a pregnancy and the death of an infant child, their baby, a child Stuart had never seen except in a few grainy, slightly fuzzy photographs. So many things could have prevented the situation from developing the way it did, so many things could have been different, but they weren't. The exact set of circumstances needed to get them to where they were now had occurred and here they were.

The present was easily categorised: they were here for two weeks, Stuart had another two weeks or so of work beyond that and then they would see how Ita was and what he would do. Although Stuart did not usually allow his mind to roam about the possibilities for the future because, as had been the case when he had let his mind fantasise about Frances, almost inevitably things turned out different than he had thought and planned. In this case, however, the situation was such that he had to. He had to consider all the possible options for his future, for Ita's future and for the future of his family back in England. It was not an easy series of thoughts, but he knew that here, in Bali, he had to think it through, make a decision and stick to it through thick and thin both here in Indonesia and at home in England.

The base option, he supposed, was to do pretty much as Anwar had said as an introduction to his offer of help: to go back to England and forget about Ita. Stuart's conscience would not allow that. The minimum it would allow was to make sure that Ita's physical condition was restored, that she was healthy and had a job again. Then he would go back with the orders he had from this trip and, using the power that gave him, select the right individual with whom to come back to train for future work here, allowing Stuart to go on to higher things at home. He would try to cool the relationship over the next four weeks or so and again during the next one or two trips that he would have to make with the new man, and encourage Ita to go out on her own and find somebody new. But this option assumed that he wanted to cool and eventually reduce the relationship with Ita to something around or more probably below the level of friend, that he wanted to go back to Catherine and rebuild the relationship with her and that he wanted to give up the travelling life and become more or less completely desk-bound. The hardest part would be rebuilding the relationship with Catherine and he would have to give it his full commitment from the second he stepped off the plane, with no wavering. He thought about Catherine: her hard stare as he had left; the cigarettes that she smoked; the English middle-class provincial attitudes that she displayed and her slide into becoming an archetypal Englishwoman in figure and hairstyle. The base option was definitely a hard one.

But beyond it, what was there? Anything less than total commitment from him would inevitably result in what Catherine had said before he had left – lawyers and divorce. Was he ready for that? Was he ready to throw away almost thirteen years of marriage and watch the break-up of his family like so many others, to follow a path which he vowed he would never follow when he got married? That too was a hard option. Once the word 'divorce' had come into his mind, it raised a whole series of new options and questions.

The first was about the children. What about Ralph and Colleen, what would happen to them? They were always the first victims of divorce. Stuart could not face the idea of leaving Colleen alone with Catherine and Ralph. He wanted to get custody of her in any settlement, but would Catherine agree?

Would a judge agree and allow Colleen to become a lonely child living with a father who travelled a great deal? Stuart didn't consider it likely.

Then there was the financial settlement. Catherine would undoubtedly want and get the house. That wasn't too much of a problem – it was the only one they had ever bought and the mortgage repayments were small. Stuart could afford them and still buy somewhere else providing that Catherine and the judge were not too heavy in their demands for maintenance. What about the rest of the furniture and stuff? These thoughts became too detailed for him to handle in the face of the overriding concern that he could not get custody of Colleen, not if he was living alone in England. What was the alternative? To take Ita back so that he would not be alone?

He didn't really want to subject her to the British climate and the possibility of a sarcastic, cutting backlash from Catherine and her friends which would make life a misery for the newly emigrated Ita. No, that wasn't really an option to consider except as a last resort. That left one other way: here, Indonesia. He believed that if Anwar could work his magic and conjure up one or, better still, two orders, then Stuart could virtually write his own ticket for his future in the company. If the sales potential here and in other countries in South-East Asia was good enough, then Stuart could make a case for establishing a regional sales office, like the one in Delhi in India, with himself as the manager. That would allow him enough money to pay everything associated with the divorce settlement, to have Colleen with him and to have Ita. It was another option, possibly the best, but one that would take a great deal of hard work over the next year.

His thoughts were almost completed: he had considered the past, how he had arrived where he was, the present and the possible future options. Now was the time he had to decide, here in Bali. Before they returned to Jakarta the decision had to be made.

He was, however, interrupted in his contemplation on the rock on the morning of the fifth day. Ita announced that she felt much better and Pak Oka said that he had to go to town so they went with him. Stuart called the office from the nearest hotel, but Anwar was out in Java and there were no fax messages from England.

They shopped for a swimming costume for Ita. Stuart wanted a bright purple one with very high cut legs and a side made up of criss-cross lacing with a two or three inch gap between the front and back portions. Ita refused to try it on, picking a more sober, plain black one, but Stuart bought both anyway. The three of them had an *al fresco* lunch at a small push-along stall before they returned to Villa Patra in the afternoon.

Stuart took Ita down to the beach and she changed into her black costume. Stuart persuaded her to try the purple one as well and then wouldn't let her have the black one back. It was, after all, a private beach with no one to see except him. They walked in the sea. Ita wouldn't swim properly at first, but she splashed in the water at waist height. She tried to hide under the trees and in the hut out of the sun, but Stuart dragged her out for a walk along the beach.

Ita's recovery marked the end of his contemplation. Ita became stronger by the day and the holiday proper began. Despite Ita's trying to hide under the trees, a remarkable thing happened to her skin. Very quickly she became much darker than before and she acquired lines where the costume ended. The effect was to instantly improve the way she looked, to make her look healthy and fit. The short swims and walks along the beach toned up the muscles of her legs and arms and helped to pull her stomach in, although the *jamu* and white cotton band had had a considerable impact on that already. Her breasts were still a little larger than before, but even they were recovering and the sag was slowly disappearing. Her physical recovery from the pregnancy was spectacularly good. Stuart remembered how long it had taken Catherine, especially after the second, to get back into anything like her previous shape, and here was Ita, barely three weeks after, with her body almost back to its original shape.

She took to wearing only the purple swimming costume and looking very good in it too. And, once she had started, she positively revelled in getting brown, unlike her earlier protestations that pale whiteness was a much better colour.

After a few days of this, Pak Oka let Stuart drive by himself and gave him Anwar's map of Bali. They went off alone to Kuta Beach, to Sannur Beach and Nusa Dua, to see the sights, to swim in the sea and eat. They stayed out late and visited pubs and discos and danced into the early hours one night. Then they climbed into the mountains to Kintamani, a town that overlooked a great volcanic crater lake. They descended to the lake shore along the precipitous, twisting road and Ita negotiated a rate for a boat for themselves and ten other tourists. They visited small hamlets on the other side of the lake where the side of the crater was even more precipitous than the one they had just descended, access to which was only by boat. They looked at the bodies of the villagers, 'buried', as they were, under coffins of bamboo beneath the trees in a particular location. They crossed to the other side were there was a hot spring and a curative bath.

In the evening they found a small guest house which had a number of cottages spread out over the hillside. Each had a small fireplace which Ita found fascinating. Stuart told her that every house in England used to have one, and, despite the heat, Stuart lit a fire and they sat and cuddled in its unnecessary warmth.

When they went back down the mountain they called at the hotel and Stuart called Anwar's office. There was a fax from England which they faxed to the hotel while they waited. Anwar was still out, but the reports for Stuart were encouraging. It looked as though Stuart's best business scenario was going to be the likely result.

During all this time they didn't speak about the past or the future, there was only the now. Eventually it would end, of course, and it did when they had been there for almost two full weeks. Stuart and Ita called at the hotel to telephone Anwar's office. Anwar was in and he asked Stuart to come back the following day, by whatever flight he could get, though Ita could stay if she wanted. The reason for the urgency was the imminent signing of Chan's order, the necessity of preparing for one more order and the attempt to negotiate for a third. Anwar estimated that three weeks would be necessary to finish it all.

"What?" asked Ita as Stuart put down the phone, his face a little disturbed.

"We, well, *I* have to go back tomorrow."

"To England?" she asked, her voice shocked.

He smiled. "No, only to Jakarta. Maybe three weeks more in Indonesia to sort out one or maybe even two more orders, big ones," he said. "And Mr Anwar, my agent, said that he wanted to interview you for a job in his office, if you agree."

"Really?" she said, her voice surprised and delighted.

Stuart nodded. "Come on, we have to see if we can get a flight tomorrow. Do you want to stay here, in Bali? You can if you want to."

She shook her head. "No, I want go with you, find a job and get out of that small room and get my mother back to her home."

Stuart managed to find two seats on the midday flight. He called Anwar again and told him. Anwar said that the car would be waiting for them.

They went back to the house and went down to the beach for a last swim. Stuart watched Ita with growing admiration: her body was now fully back in shape, her emotions somewhat repaired. Her whole person was looking as attractive and desirable as it had ever been: the slim legs, now firm, tanned and brown; the hair, jet-black and shiny once again in the Bali sun; the purple swimming costume emphasising everything that was good about Ita's physique. He was very proud of her. He knew that he loved her, he knew that the minimum that his conscience would allow would never satisfy his emotions. He knew that he had to make the decision today, before they left.

They wandered back up to the villa in the late afternoon. Ibu Oka was preparing satay for the evening meal and Pak Oka was setting up a small satay barbecue on the terrace. Ita and Stuart went upstairs to wash. In the bathroom, Ita stripped off her beach robe and slipped gracefully out of her swimsuit. Stuart dropped his trunks and they helped each other to wash in the cold water from the tiled bath. Stuart finished first and went back into the bathroom still naked. He spread a dry towel on the bed and lay down.

Ita came out with her hair wet, her body wrapped in a towel. She used a second towel to vigorously dry her hair, flicking her hair to remove moisture. Then she pushed it back and looked at Stuart. He smiled up at her.

Slowly she undid the towel and lowered it to the ground.

For the first time since he had been back he felt the tingle of sexual anticipation rising within him as he took in the sight of the naked Ita before him.

She smiled down at him again, but this time her eyes were a little misty, a little far off. He knew what was coming, it was only a question of how.

She lay down beside him on the bed, on her back and not touching him. They lay silent except for the sound of their own breathing and the slow beat of the ceiling fan. Time seemed to be suspended.

Then their hands touched. They both rolled at the same time to lie facing each other, eyes open and looking deeply into each other's face.

Stuart saw the dark pools of sensuality opening before him again and he abandoned himself to them once more. They leaned forward into an embrace, arms sliding over the other's body, hunching closer, kissing, moving to get bodily contact from the head downwards, legs sliding in between legs, melding, joining again for the first time in more than nine months. They kissed with a passion, with a determination, with a greed to be kissing again. Her body felt as it had before, smooth and sleek, her skin warm from the sun, smooth like silk, and the smell – he had forgotten the smell of her. It rose through his nostrils and into his brain like the strongest perfume, intoxicating him. As they kissed and stroked with their respective free hands, Stuart felt Ita sink back, rolling slowly on to her back, he following her. He lay, half over her, his leg between hers, nuzzling her, feeling her move against his thigh. Her breath was becoming short, her eyes were tightly closed, her kissing rising in passion. He moved slowly and deliberately over her.

She moved her legs wider to accommodate him, moving her hips in anticipation of the motions to come.

He held back from her, not wanting to be too quick, knowing that she might still be sore, that gentleness was required. He pushed himself closer to her and she snorted as she kissed him. He entered her a little; she broke off the kiss and gasped out loud. He saw that there was no pain, only pleasure. He eased himself in deeper until there was no more left.

She was pushing up to meet him, not gyrating wildly, just pushing and moving very slightly. Her head rolled from side to side, her eyes screwed shut. She bit her lip and then opened her mouth in a wide gasp, her head arching backwards. She let out a long moan. Her hands flew to his bottom and she bucked once, pulling him in. Her head rose up, her chin to her chest. She moaned again and her hips twitched and her legs went rigid.

Stuart felt a sudden tightening feeling in his groin. Her hand dug into his buttock and he shuddered and groaned as he felt the contractions coming with little or no movement. He strained, his breath held, as he tried to force the sensation to come, for the longer they delayed the greater the effect when they came, and, finally, while she bucked against him, they came.

The two of them held themselves stiffly in post-orgasmic tension. Then the relaxation began and they sank down on to each other, the flush of sexual pleasure wilting slowly away. Then he rolled off and they lay side by side, only touching with hands.

After a while, during which Stuart dozed, they got up and washed and dressed without a word. Only smiles and knowing looks into eyes were necessary. They stood on the balcony and watched the sun going down and smelt the sweet smell of barbecuing satay coming from the terrace below.

Later in the evening, after they had eaten the satay, Stuart sat on a high-backed wicker chair on the terrace. The sun had gone down and some small light came from behind him from the windows of the living room. Over the sea in the distance the moon was rising and casting a silvery sheen over the tropical ocean. It was a beautiful sight. Stuart had a can of beer in his right hand and he was drinking it slowly. His decision had yet to be made.

Ita came out after she had finished helping Ibu Oka with the plates. She carried a cushion and she set this on the floor between Stuart's legs. She sat on it and rested her left arm over his left leg, leaning her head on her arm and allowing her hair to flow over his leg. Her right hand rested on his knee. She was silent. The only noises came from the small lizards that scampered about, the occasional rustle in the trees some way off and the soft clink of plates from the kitchen as Ibu Oka washed up.

Stuart looked down at Ita, at the hair which flowed over his legs. Then he looked at the sea before him with the moonlight casting its unearthly glow. He sniffed the air and caught the remnants of the smell of cooking satay mingled with Pak Oka's clove cigarettes.

He looked up at the dark sky with its unfamiliar stars and then down to Ita again. He smiled at her and stroked her hair.

She responded by nuzzling closer into his leg, kissing it lightly.

He sighed a big sigh, finished the can of beer and let it down silently on to the ground. He took one more look at Ita and made his decision, finally, irrevocably and, in the end, very quickly.

Ita stirred and turned her head up to look at him. She looked up at him with her head on one side, her eyes searching his face for evidence. She knew what had just happened, and now she wanted the result. She looked at him and then her questioning eyes softened, becoming those deep pools again and then she smiled at him. She turned back to her former position and squeezed his leg. Without being told, she knew.

Stuart looked at her again and stroked her hair with his right hand. He looked out to sea and knew that, whatever happened henceforth as a result of what he had just decided, nothing could ever be the same again.